THE STERKARM HANDSHAKE

SUSAN PRICE

An Imprint of HarperCollinsPublishers

Eos is an imprint of
HarperCollins Publishers.

Library of Congress Cataloging-in-Publication Data
Price, Susan.
    The Sterkarm handshake / Susan Price. — 1st U.S. ed.
        p.   cm.
    Summary: Having traveled to a sixteenth century border clan
in England through a tunnel created by a twenty-first century
company, Andrea must decide in which era she will live.
    ISBN 0-06-028959-7. — 0-06-029392-6 (lib. bdg.)
    ISBN 0-06-447236-1 (pbk.)
    [1. Time travel — Fiction.   2. Science fiction.]   I. Title.
PZ7.P9317 Sp   2000   99-54844
[Fic] — dc21

                    Typography by Larissa Lawrynenko
                                    ❖
                        First Eos Edition, 2003
            Published in the United Kingdom in 1998
                        by Scholastic Press
                        www.harperteen.com

CONTENTS

THE
STERKARM
HANDSHAKE

16th Side: A Robbery

FROM OUT OF THE surrounding hills came a ringing silence that was only deepened by the plodding of the pack ponies' hooves on the turf and
the flirting of their tails against their sides. Above, the
sky was a clear pale blue, but the breeze was strong.

There were four members of the Geological Survey
Team: Malc, Tim, Dave and Caro. They'd left the 21st
that morning at eight, coming through the Tube to the
16th, where the plan was to spend four days. None of
them had ever been so far from home before, and they
often looked back at the Tube. It was their only way
back.

It was when they lost sight of the Tube among the
folds of the hills that trouble arrived.

Three horses, with riders, picked their way down the
hillside toward them. The horses were all black and
thickset and shaggy, with manes and tails hanging almost
to the ground. The riders' helmets had been blackened
with soot and grease, to keep them from rust, or covered
with sheepskin so they looked like hats. Their other
clothes were all buffs and browns, blending into the
buffs, browns and greens all around them. Their long

leather riding boots rose over the knee. On they came with a clumping of hooves and a jangling of harness, carrying eight-foot-long lances with ease.

"It's all right," Malc said. "Don't worry. They're just coming to check us out."

"There's others," Caro said. There were men on foot, about eight of them, running behind the riders.

The riders reached them first, and circled them, making the geologists crowd closer together, while still clinging to the halters of the pack ponies. The riders' lances remained in the upright, carrying position, but this wasn't reassuring.

Up came the men on foot, and the riders reined in to let them through. The footmen were all bearded and longhaired, and had long knives and clubs in their hands. A couple had pikes. Without any preamble, they laid hands on the ponies' halters and tugged them out of the geologists' hands.

"Don't argue," Malc said. "Dave, let it go. Let them have whatever they want."

Two of the riders dismounted, handing their reins to the third—a boy of about fourteen—who remained on his horse. They had a look of each other, the riders, like brothers. The first to dismount, his lance still in his hand, was probably the eldest. He was bearded, but no older than about twenty. He went straight up to Malc and began to pull the backpack from his shoulders.

"I thought they'd agreed not to rob us anymore," Caro said, taking off her own backpack as the other dismounted rider came toward her.

"Just don't annoy them," Malc said.

As Dave and Tim shrugged out of their backpacks,

one of the bearded footmen called out something—in a speech that sounded like coughing and snarling. His companions all laughed.

The geologists looked anxiously at each other. They didn't understand the joke, and were afraid of how far it might be taken.

The second dismounted rider suddenly caught Tim's hand and pulled his arm out straight. For a moment Tim looked into an almost beardless and strikingly pretty face—and then the young man was dragging at his wrist-watch, pulling the expandable bracelet off over his hand. He stared Tim in the face for a moment, and then snatched off the geologist's spectacles before moving on to Dave and grabbing at his hands too. Dave took his wristwatch off and gave it to him.

Malc and Caro, catching on, quickly took off their wristwatches and handed them over.

The first rider—the bearded one handling an eight-foot lance as if it were a pencil—seemed not to like the pretty one having all the watches, and a coughing, snarling argument started between them. While it went on, Malc caught sight of Caro's face, set in a grimace of fright. The other two looked much the same, and he supposed that his own face also reflected his painful uncertainty and fear.

The argument ended with the pretty thief handing two of the wristwatches to the one with the lance—who immediately turned to Malc, grabbed his waterproof and pulled at it, snarling something.

Malc pulled his waterproof off over his head. The others hurried to do the same.

The pretty rider gestured at their other clothes. Take

them all off, he seemed to mean. Certainly, when they hesitated, there were more peremptory gestures and snarled words.

Caro saw the way the footmen gathered closer as she pulled off her sweater, and she stopped, only to be shoved, and staggered on her feet, by the horseman with the lance. When she still hesitated, he grabbed at her shirt, pulling the buttons undone and exposing her bra.

"Caro, do as they want," Tim said. "It'll be all right. We're here."

Malc, Tim and Dave all edged closer to her, trying to shield her, but she knew perfectly well that there was nothing they could do to protect her, outnumbered and unarmed as they were. She took off her shirt, shaking with fear. There was nothing remotely exhilarating about the feeling. She felt sick and desperate, and wished she'd never left the humdrum safety of the 21st side.

They took off all their upper clothing, but still weren't undressing quickly enough for the liking of their attackers, who dragged at their arms, and pushed them, to hurry them up. One of the footmen, by pointing, made it clear that he wanted their boots—and then, when they were seen to be wearing thick socks, the socks were pulled off their feet and their trousers tugged at.

They stripped down to their underpants, which caused hilarity, and the pointing and jeering was as threatening as the shoves.

Despite being so funny, their underpants were taken too, leaving the survey team standing naked in the breeze. Their skin roughened with goose pimples.

Their attackers walked around them, examining them from all sides, pointing, making remarks and laughing.

Caro closed her eyes and held her breath, feeling her heart thumping heavily under her breastbone.

But then the riders mounted again, and the whole party left with their loot, the footmen leading the pack ponies.

The survey team were left, shaking but still alive, to walk over rough country, naked and barefoot, all the way back to the Tube and the 21st.

2

21st Side: The Other End of the Tube

BRYCE WAS TRYING to make his budget work, and thinking of opening up a game of X-Fighters instead, when his phone rang. He reached for it with relief.

"Mr. Bryce? Alex here." The head of the guards at the Tube. "I think we need you. The Sterkarms are playing games again."

"Be right there."

Dilsmead Hall was a large and beautiful mansion built by a nineteenth-century manufacturer, and Bryce's office was on its upper floor. FUP had taken it over, to house their northern enterprise, but had taken a much-publicized pride in preserving as much of the house as possible. Bryce hurried along a wide landing of golden, polished wood. Framed portraits hung on the walls, and a large arrangement of silk flowers stood in a copper vase on a small table. A sweet smell of polish hung in the air.

Bryce didn't bother waiting for an elevator but ran down the polished wooden stairs. A big window on the half landing gave him a view over the Hall's grounds: green lawns, bright flower beds and big, spreading trees.

On the ground floor he followed what had once been

a service corridor—narrow and dark, with plastered, painted walls—toward the rear of the house. He emerged onto the wide graveled drive that ran all around the Hall. On the other side of the drive, on the grass of the lawn, were the buildings that housed the most expensive, secret and technologically advanced of all FUP's projects: the Time Tube.

Nearest to him was a small shed, painted a drab olive green. A notice on its door said, "Danger! No unauthorized entry." Inside was what made the whole project possible: a cold-fusion reactor, no bigger than a small family car. Until it had been developed, the Tube itself had been merely theoretical.

Beside the generator was a small prefabricated office, one of those raised above the ground on stilts, with steps leading up to its door. It had the flimsy, temporary appearance of all such buildings, and looked shoddy beside the solid redbrick of the Hall. Its paintwork, a bright, pale yellow, had rapidly become grubby and grayed as the rain had layered it with dirt. The office held the control room for the Tube. Technicians seated at computer consoles monitored the power output from the generator, the degree of torque on the Tube, the electromagnetic field, and many other things that Bryce, as head of security, didn't pretend to understand.

The Tube itself ran along the side of the office, from front to back. Bryce noted that its whole length was visible—that was, its whole length was here in the twenty-first century. Which meant that it had been closed down. Which meant trouble. Which usually meant the Sterkarms.

The Tube was housed in a piece of huge industrial

concrete piping, raised about six feet off the ground, and supported by a framework of steel girders painted a harsh, flat blue. It was open at either end, and in front of each huge round mouth was a platform, big enough for a truck to drive onto and park when it emerged from the Tube. The platform nearest Bryce was aligned with the control room, and a door opened onto it from the office. The platform at the other end projected well beyond the office and was supported in the air, aligned with nothing. The mouths of the Tube, at both ends, were masked by hanging fringes of plastic strips.

From each platform a ramp with a surface of textured rubber sloped down to the ground. The one nearer Bryce touched the gravel drive. The one that sloped down from the rear platform didn't quite touch the grass of the lawn, and concrete blocks had been placed to support it, when it was present. That ramp hadn't been built for Dilsmead Hall in the twenty-first century. That end of the Tube spent a lot of time in the sixteenth century. It was easy to tell which end was which, because the end that spent all its time in the 21st was dirty. The concrete was gray, and streaked and stained where it touched its supporting girders. The concrete of the half that spent much of its time in the 16th was still white and unstained. The rain of the sixteenth century wasn't full of dirt, and it wasn't acid.

Bryce, like almost everyone else involved in the project, had made the experiment of climbing the cleaner ramp, while it was "home" in the 21st, and lifting the plastic strips so that he could look through it. Usually there would be some colleague standing at the other end, on the platform outside the control room, waving and smiling.

When the Tube was operational, the cleaner end of the Tube disappeared. Bryce had stood on the graveled drive and watched. You heard the noise of the Tube spinning—some part of it, hidden inside the concrete pipe, spun, so he was told. A roar, increasing in pitch to a whine, and then passing almost out of hearing. And then one end of the Tube vanished. It didn't fade, as he'd imagined it might when first told about it. As fast as a light switching off, it blinked out of sight. The Tube then appeared to end in midair, halfway along its length. The girders seemed to end—you could see their squared ends, apparently cut through.

He'd stood and watched as people walked through. From the platform you simply saw them walk through a tunnel, quite straightforwardly, to the other end. If you were outside, standing on the gravel path, it was much stranger. Only half the pipe was visible. You might know that someone was walking through it, but no one fell out of the apparently open end of the pipe. Whoever was in the Tube vanished halfway along, just as the pipe itself did.

Neither the pipe nor the girders were broken off, the control room's supervisor assured him—a pretty woman far too young, in Bryce's opinion, to understand such things, and with a head far too small to contain such knowledge. The cars didn't vanish either. The whole Tube still existed, but one half had passed through to another dimension. It was as if the Tube had been pushed halfway through a hole in a wall. It was still whole and complete. You just couldn't see half of it.

But in that case, Bryce had said, he would be able to see the wall, and he wouldn't be able to see the ends of the girders, looking as if they'd been cut through.

Ah, well, said the supervisor. The analogy didn't follow through in every detail. She'd tried to explain about dimensions, drawing diagrams on her notepad, but Bryce had to admit he couldn't follow a word of it. There were dozens of these dimensions, it seemed. What he had always thought of—and still liked to think of—as the "real world" was just one of them. The idea worried him.

The Tube was enough to give anyone the heebie-jeebies. While the business end was "traveling"—that is, was away in the 16th—you could look through the Tube from the platform outside the control room, and look into the sixteenth century. You couldn't see much except the hanging plastic strips masking the Tube's other end, but you were looking down a tunnel five hundred years long.

But if the people in the 21st looked through from the other end of the Tube while it was "traveling"? This was difficult, because the "broken end" of the Tube was raised off the ground, but some had managed it by sitting on the shoulders of others. They reported that it was just as the physicists had said—you simply looked through to the platform outside the 21st control room. Yet colleagues standing on that platform were simultaneously looking through to the 16th.

Thinking about the Tube too much made his head spin. There was some talk among the physicists, for instance, of people leaving the 21st, spending a day in the 16th, and then being fetched back to the 21st only a minute after they'd left. So they'd have gained a day, except for that minute.

Bryce was grateful that, early on, it had been decided not to attempt anything like this. The two time streams were to be kept compatible, simply to reduce the stress on the human operatives. No one wanted to spend a difficult day in the 16th and then, on returning to the 21st, find another full day of work stretching before them. Time-Tube lag, it was agreed, would be even worse than jet lag.

For himself, Bryce tried to think about the Time Tube as he did about his fridge, and his multimedia console. He wasn't sure how any of them worked. He just expected that they would, was glad when they did and got on with his life.

He ran up the outside steps of the control room and went in, pushing past some people who were standing in the doorway.

The control room was usually a pleasant, well-ordered place, the loudest sound the hum of the air-conditioning and the occasional beep from a computer, the light dimmed by blinds over the windows. But at the moment almost everyone was standing and everyone was chattering and exclaiming.

Bryce was allowed through to the center of the room, where four people were sitting on chairs pulled away from the desks. All of them had on white lab coats, but their legs and feet were bare. All of them were drinking from plastic cups.

"I thought they were going to kill us!" the woman said. "I was so scared! I thought they'd kill us!"

Bryce recognized the Geological Survey Team that had been scheduled to go through to the 16th that morning, taking pack ponies loaded with all the equipment they would need to spend four days over there. "Anyone hurt?" he said.

One of the men—longhaired and bearded, as all male geologists seemed to be—got to his feet. "This isn't good enough! I want to see Windsor! We all want to see Windsor!" His colleagues nodded. "We could have been killed!"

"Have you phoned through to the med room?" Bryce asked the supervisor. She nodded. "I think we should get you to med, don't you?" All of the geologists' bare feet were cut, bleeding and bruised. "They can't walk over gravel in that state. I want some volunteers. You, you, you and you." Bryce had held a command in the army. "Make chairs with your arms—you know how to do that?" A couple of the men he'd chosen clasped their hands together and made a chair for the young woman. "Yes, like that. You, you, you and you. Come on, move."

The geologists were lifted and carried away. One, over his shoulder, said, "We want to see Windsor!"

Bryce took his mobile phone from his pocket and showed it to him. "I'm calling him." But before he did, he turned and looked up at the overhead monitors. "Damn!" The monitors were connected to security cameras on the other end of the Tube, 16th side. One of the screens still showed a distant corner of the chain-link fence around the compound, and the other a beautiful view of the sky. "Haven't they fixed them *yet*?"

The supervisor came to stand beside him. "They sent someone to look at them."

The motor that swiveled one of the cameras had failed, and before maintenance had got around to fixing it, a bad storm 16th side had damaged the other. "It'd be quicker to fix 'em meself," Bryce said. "But no, can't do that. That's maintenance's job. God, I thought it was hard getting things done in the army."

"Well, I suppose it's not urgent," the supervisor said, and Bryce sighed but turned away. He hadn't time to explain—he had to get after the geologists and call Windsor. But that was the problem: No one thought these two little security cameras were important, and they thought he was making a fuss about nothing. So maintenance played a game of Keep the New Security Boss in His Place. What did those two little cameras matter, when there was a big steel fence round the compound and all those security guards on patrol? (Security guards with guns they didn't know how to use anyway, was Bryce's thought.) It worried Bryce that people consistently underestimated the Sterkarms.

* * *

Windsor leaned on one side of the medical room door, while Bryce leaned on the other. The geologists, wrapped in silver-foil blankets, sat on the couch, or chairs, on the room's other side.

"We're taking our lives in our hands, going back there!"

Was there a gene that compelled hairy people to become geologists, Windsor wondered, or was there something about the practice of geology that enforced hairiness?

"We thought it was all sorted out! You gave us *assurances*!"

The eyes of the man speaking could hardly be seen for hair, but his rabbity teeth flashed through his beard and threw spit about as he ranted. The man beside him

13

squinted all the time because his spectacles had been stolen.

"They shoved us about—really roughly. I really thought they were going to kill us."

Even the young woman was hairy, though in a much prettier way. Her mustache was quite faint, and rather fetching, and her long, straight hair was as tangled and untidy as that of the male of her species. Windsor wondered what she looked like under her foil blanket. It made a distraction from her monotonous repetition of the same few words: "Everything, they took everything! *Everything!* I thought they were going to kill us."

"We want to know what you're going to do about it!" Rabbit sprayed spit. "We won't be going back— *nobody* will be going back—until we have guarantees. Guarantees! That the situation is under control."

Windsor leaned against the wall behind him, making himself comfortable and folding his arms. He didn't like being yelled at by employees, and for God's sake, what did they expect him to do about it? "I shall talk to them again, naturally. There must have been a misunderstand—"

"That isn't good enough!"

"No, not good enough!"

"You're expecting us to go back there, to put ourselves at risk, and saying you'll talk to them again just isn't good enough! We thought you *had* talked to them!" The others chorused and nodded agreement, hair flying, beards bobbing.

"We need guards," Malc said. "It's mad, sending the teams out alone."

Dave was nodding. "Armed guards. Just a couple of

men with guns, that's all it would need."

Bryce said, "Not a good idea."

That annoyed them, Windsor saw with amusement, and turned their hostility onto Bryce rather than him. "What you really mean," Malc said, "is it's an expensive idea."

"It wouldn't cost much," Bryce said. "And cost isn't my first concern. What worries me is that it wouldn't stop the Sterkarms from attacking the teams—you'd just be adding guns to the loot. It'd make you a bigger prize. And if a Sterkarm got hurt or killed . . ." He looked across at Windsor. "Well, then you'd have a blood feud on your hands. They're big on blood feuds."

"Makes sense to me," Windsor said. Cost *was* one of his first concerns.

"If they'd been at feud with us when you met them," Bryce added, "they wouldn't just have robbed you—they'd have killed you all."

"Oh, so they can rob us with impunity!" Malc shouted. "But we mustn't do anything to annoy them, even though they broke an agreement!"

"What do you want us to do?" Bryce asked. "Kill them for stealing your lunch?"

"I don't think armed guards are a good idea," Caroline said, pushing hair off her face. "I mean, they only have spears. It wouldn't be very fair."

Windsor smiled again. You had to laugh at these liberal types. It was a pity the Sterkarms didn't have such high-minded standards of fairness. It would make life a bit easier if the Sterkarms had any idea of fairness at all.

"I think I know who the men were who robbed you," Bryce said. "Going on your description, I'd say it was the May and his cousins."

Windsor looked across at him and raised his brows. "Who?"

"One of the horsemen was 'pretty,' you said. I think that was probably Per Toorkildsson Sterkarm, known as 'the May'—it means 'the Girl.' The other two with horses would be two of his cousins, the Gobbyssons. There are three of them, but I only know the name of the eldest—he's called Little Toorkild, to tell him from his uncle. He might have been the one with the beard."

"You've lost me completely," Windsor said.

"Well, put it this way," Bryce said. "You made an agreement with Old Toorkild Sterkarm that, if you kept him supplied with aspirin, he wouldn't rob our survey teams." He nodded toward the Geological Survey Team, wrapped in foil. "His son and nephews have just robbed one of our survey teams."

"Are they still raiding as well?" Windsor asked.

"What do you think?"

"In other words," Malc broke in, "they haven't taken a blind bit of notice of anything you've said, and all the assurances you gave us about our safety after the last robberies were worthless. You let us go through there—"

"We didn't know that," Windsor said. "When we gave you those assurances, we were acting in good faith. We'd kept our end of the bargain, and we had no reason to think that the Sterkarms wouldn't keep theirs. We shook hands on it."

Bryce gave his slow smile and said, "It was a Sterkarm handshake." The geologists and Windsor all looked at him blankly. "You know," he said. "The Sterkarm badge."

Everyone there knew the Sterkarms' badge. Few of

16

the Sterkarms could write, and the badge was their signature. It showed, in red on a black ground, an upraised arm, bent at the elbow and holding in its clenched fist a dagger.

"Well," Bryce said, "there's a story to it. Ever noticed that the arm's a left arm? Look at the hand holding the dagger and you'll see it's a left hand. And most of the Sterkarms are left-handed, right? They even build the stairs in the towers to go around the other way from other people—y'know, the stairs in most towers are built to go around clockwise, so they can be defended by a right-handed swordsman, but that's no use to the Sterkarms. So *their* stairs go around the other way, counterclockwise, to give a left-handed swordsman the advantage. That's how you can tell a Sterkarm tower."

Windsor, still leaning against the wall, said, "Wouldn't a better guide be the fact that you'd be knee-deep in Sterkarms?" He was glad to see Bryce's face redden a little as his lumpen calm cracked.

"Anyway," Bryce said, determined to have his say, now he'd started, "when men meet, they shake hands. With their right hands. That is, they give each other their weapon hand to hold, to show they don't mean any harm. But the Sterkarms are left-handed. So a Sterkarm can give you his right hand to hold and still draw his dagger with his left. So if somebody makes a bargain with a Sterkarm handshake, it means that they never had any intention of keeping their word. I think when Old Toorkild took those aspirins and shook hands on the deal, it was a Sterkarm handshake."

"Thank you, Mr. Bryce!" Windsor said. "Both entertaining and informative!"

"Just doing my job," Bryce said.

Malc stood, his foil blanket rattling as he drew it round him. "We're not going back, none of us, not until you take this situation seriously—"

"I take it seriously!" Windsor said. "Do you think I enjoy equipping survey teams and then seeing them ripped off by a lot of hairy bog trotters? I've got money of my own invested in this project, I might remind you, and I personally resent—" He broke off as a pager beeped in his pocket. Taking it out, he read the message that ran across its little screen. "The ambulance I called has arrived to take you all to the hospital to be checked over, at FUP's expense. We treat you so badly." He opened the door of the medical room and looked out into the corridor. There were some men in dark uniforms, looking around as if they didn't know where to go. "Are you the ambulance crew? In here." He stepped aside to let them go into the med room. To Bryce he said, "Come with me."

As Windsor and Bryce walked quickly through the corridors of Dilsmead Hall toward Windsor's office, Windsor said, "Couldn't you have dealt with that yourself?"

"I could have," Bryce said. "But they were making a fuss about seeing you. And I thought you'd want to know. Be kept informed."

"I could have been kept informed without being dragged down here to listen to a lot of whingeing from beards—and since you're such an expert on the Sterkarms, can you explain to me why they aren't in awe and trembling of our magical powers? I thought they were supposed to think we're Elves?"

"They do think we're Elves—"

"They seem less than terror stricken to me."

"James, probably the only reason that girl wasn't raped and those men killed is that the Sterkarms thought they were Elves." They reached the elevators and, naturally, had to wait for one. Bryce would have preferred to climb the stairs. He folded his arms. "I wouldn't rely too much on them being scared of us. They might be, but—it's like hoping a ferret won't bite you because it's scared, when truth is, the more scared a ferret is, the more *likely* it is to bite you."

"Ferrets?" Windsor said. "Did I ask you about ferrets?"

"I'd say the Sterkarms have a certain respect for us because we're Elves—they're not sure what we might be able to do if they make us really mad, so they're a bit wary. Probably more important, they're not sure what goodies they might be able to get out of us, if they string us along a bit. They really like the aspirin."

"Yeah!" Windsor was diverted. "Five pence a truckload for generic aspirin, and the Sterkarms think we're giving them some sort of miraculous magical potion. You have to laugh."

Bryce nodded. As head of security, he had to oversee the distribution of aspirin. Whole packs were never given to the Sterkarms. The twenty-first-century packs were opened, and the paper strips containing four tablets were handed out. This ensured that the Sterkarms ran out of them quickly, and valued them even more highly.

It also ensured that a black market sprang up in the tablets, as his own security men traded with the Sterkarms for women and mementos such as lance heads and helmets. It was impossible to restrict such trading altogether, but Bryce tried to suppress it as much as possible. The sheer orneriness and treachery of the Sterkarms themselves was a great help to him. Stories had already reached him of Sterkarms wheedling aspirin out of his security guards and, once they had the tablets in their hands, immediately abandoning whatever deal had been agreed. They knew they could still get aspirin through the official FUP channels. They knew, too, that no matter how many times the security guards were cheated, they would still try again. The Sterkarms were not only treacherous—they were smart.

"If they go on the way they're going," Windsor said, "they can kiss their whole supply of aspirin good-bye; I promise them that."

The elevator came and they stepped inside. "You haven't been through there as often as I have," Bryce said. "You have to see it before you can believe how poor the poorest Sterkarms are. They build their houses in a morning. They're brushwood lean-tos. They have nothing. No furniture, no more clothing than they stand up in. When you send a survey team through, with pack ponies, warm clothes, metal tools—I mean, Christ, one of our packed lunches is a feast to them. It's a bit like waving a big juicy steak in front of a hungry dog and expecting it not to make a grab for it. After all, I doubt if the poorest of the poor beggars get to see many of your aspirin."

"My heart bleeds," Windsor said. "You're just through telling me that it was Old Sterkarm's son and nephews who robbed the team. They're not poor."

They'd reached Windsor's outer office. "Hello,

Sexy," Windsor said to his secretary, who was fifty years old, fat and gray, and made no attempt to look anything except clean and neat. She looked up. "I don't want to be disturbed until further notice, okay?"

Bryce, following Windsor into his private office, said, "Not poor by their standards, no. Poor by ours. But you're right—my best guess would be that the May and the Gobbyssons were having a bit of fun—and helping out some of their poor relations. They like to keep family ties strong."

Windsor went behind his desk and sat in his big black chair, leaving Bryce to choose one of the low soft chairs in front of the desk. Windsor had a coffee corner where people could loll in comfortable chairs and talk things over on equal terms, but he wasn't in the mood to use it. "I'll put a stop to their fun. Why do they all have such stupid names? Gobbysson! And they all seem to have half a dozen names each. I can't keep track of them."

"They're all named Sterkarm," Bryce said. "And then they're all named after each other. Toorkild's named after his father, and he names his son after his brother; and his brother names his eldest son after Toorkild, and Toorkild's a common name anyway. So you've got dozens of Toorkild Sterkarms, and they all have to have nicknames to tell 'em apart."

"Bloody stupid people," Windsor said. "How many of our lot are over there right now?"

"No teams," Bryce said. "We've only been sending one team at a time through since the last time the Sterkarms got outrageous. But there's young Andrea, of course."

"Andrea?"

"Andrea Mitchell. But she's safe."

Windsor squinted as he thought. "Isn't she that big fat girl we've got living with them? And you say she's safe?"

Bryce, who rather liked Andrea, was slightly offended on her behalf. "James, remember, the Sterkarms haven't actually hurt anyone with their fun and games. They've ripped us off, they've shaken people up—and I agree it'd be good to put a stop to it—but they haven't hurt anyone. They could have done that if they'd wanted to. And Andrea is their guest. They won't hurt a guest. Anyway, they like her. She's very good at her job. Most of what I've learned about 'em comes through her. Do you read her reports?"

"I have a hell of a lot to do."

"She walks down from the tower to hand them in at the Tube regularly. Handwritten. I get a secretary to run up a few copies, and send one back for Andrea. She's planning to write a book, y'know. Bright girl."

"Fascinating!" Windsor said.

"What I'm saying is, Andrea isn't at risk, and we've pulled everybody else out for the moment."

"God," said Windsor. "Everything at a standstill again." No teams going through, no mapping, no surveying being done. A billion pounds, and then some, of technology standing idle because some pig-thick sixteenth-century yobs made an agreement and wouldn't stick to it.

Bryce said, "We'd be better off going back further. I mean way back, to when there weren't any people. No problems then, and the coal and oil and gold would still be there, wouldn't it?"

"To the best of my belief," Windsor said, "at the time when there weren't any people, Britain was under the sea."

"Oh. Well. Build platforms. Anyway, we could still go back to a time before the Sterkarms. If we could just get rid of them, we'd have fewer problems."

"Feel free to go and tell the physicists their jobs, anytime," Windsor said. "I bet they'll be thrilled to have your input. They've already pushed the temporal span to the limit, while keeping dimensional penetration as slim as possible—and that's what's giving us the spatial shortfall."

Bryce shook his head. "Now you've lost me."

Windsor didn't bother to hide his contemptuous expression. "A few more years of research might iron out all the bugs, but what's going to pay for the research? The company's put the GNP of about fifty countries into it already, to bring it this far. It's come down from above that they want to see some money back. If we can demonstrate that the thing can actually come up with a few barrels of oil, a few ingots of gold, we might be able to generate some more investment."

"So we're stuck with the Sterkarms," Bryce said.

"Until we can make the accountants' eyes shine. Maybe then we can push the Tube through to a time or dimension where the Sterkarms don't exist. Please God."

Bryce pulled a wry face, nodding. He looked over at a big framed photograph that hung on the office wall. It showed, against a stormy, indigo sky, the Sterkarms' tower, standing high on its hill. "We can try embarrassing Old Toorkild. Tell him we know it was his son and nephews who robbed us—but he's embarrassment-proof, I think. There's only one real way to stop them."

"And that is?" Windsor said.

"Give them the things they want."

"What, waterproofs and plastic lunch boxes? We're supposed to be preserving their way of life. Punters aren't going to pay good money to travel back five hundred years to see the Sterkarms wearing baseball caps and drinking Coke. No, I'll tell him: One more step out of line, and no more aspirin. See if I care if your rheumatics play up."

"You can try that." Bryce let the pause go on awhile. "If we can't keep the Sterkarms quiet, we're going to have Scotland and England on our backs as well."

"I don't need reminding of that," Windsor said.

Long before FUP had come along, the Scotland and England of the sixteenth century had been perpetually annoyed by the Sterkarms and the other families of feuding raiders who lived along the border.

The Scottish-English border had never been clearly drawn, and the result had been a long strip of "debatable land" over which neither country could enforce law. The wardens, officers of the English and Scottish crowns, had struggled, with too little money and too few men, to capture raiders, retrieve stolen goods, keep up with constantly changing feuds and alliances, and bring to trial offenders who laughed at them. Being granted the post of warden was a punishment. The best prospect a warden had was to come to terms with the most powerful family in his district, accept their bribes and place himself under their protection. An honest warden died young, of exhaustion or violence.

Both Scotland and England would have been glad to have the borders settled and quiet, but neither could agree on the exact line of the border. Scotland claimed Northumberland and Cumberland as rightfully belonging to the Scottish crown, while England insisted that the border should be set even farther north than it already was. FUP offered a solution.

It had taken a great deal of expensive consultation with experts on sixteenth-century life, language and costume, and the forging, in the twenty-first century, of a great many gold coins that would be acceptable to the English and Scottish courts, 16th side. And then FUP had sent representatives to the two kings, to propose, in Latin, that the governance of the difficult border lands be privatized. Let the Elves take it on, at their own expense. No longer would England or Scotland have to find the money to keep castles garrisoned and in repair, or to compensate citizens deprived of their goods, or to imprison, try and execute captured raiders. The Elves would undertake all that. The Elves also pledged to keep the debatable lands quiet, preventing the former evil predations and disturbances. There would be peace on the borders.

What would the Elves get out of it? Well, if the two great sovereignties would grant them the right to raise taxes, and the right to the produce of the borders . . . They were also willing to pay tribute to the two crowns and, in token of this, please accept this gold . . .

It took long and complex negotiations, and payment of a great deal more gold, before the suspicions of Scotland and England were overcome, and the Great Seals of both countries fastened to the contract. But it had been managed.

The Scots and English wardens, relieved of their duties, had departed with a mixture of relief and sorrow that Bryce understood. It's often the hardest, most unforgiving posts that create the greatest commitment in the unfortunates who have to fill them.

"Border men!" said the Scot. "They rob and thieve and murder but have a hundred smiles and a thousand honeyed words to save their necks when caught. Remember that. And never shake hands with a Sterkarm."

The English warden, who had been owned for almost the whole of his service by the Grannam family, had said, "They're ill to tame, the border men. May Christ preserve your soul! And beware of shaking hands with a Sterkarm."

But it seemed that all the research, all the planning, all the painstaking negotiation and diplomacy needed to persuade England and Scotland to FUP's way of thinking was as nothing compared to dealing with the Sterkarms.

"Can I leave it to you to arrange our visit 16th side?" Windsor said. "Make it soon. The Sterkarms have got to learn that we Elves control the borders now."

3

16th Side: At Home with the Sterkarms

I'M SO LUCKY, Andrea thought.

The hall occupied almost the whole second floor of the tower, and in the early evening, as the night meal was ending, it was noisily crowded with men, women and children. Some were still gathered around the two long trestle tables that ran the room's length, standing as they ate. Others, after a day spent out on windy hillsides, were pressing around the fire, bringing bread and beer with them. The sound of laughter and chatter resounded from the plastered stone of the walls.

The light came from a few candles placed on the tables—they smoked and stank of mutton fat as they burned; and from the large fire of peat and dung built in the stone fireplace. The red-and-gold firelight constantly faded and brightened as the flames rose and fell or were swayed by drafts. It seemed to provide as much darkness as illumination. Someone leaning over a table to reach for a piece of bread threw a big, dark shadow over half the room; and darkness jumped and shifted among the rafters. In the farthest corners, and in the doorway leading to the stairs, the darkness was deep.

The peat smoke from the fire smelled of leaves and earth, though with a harsh catch that bit at the lining of the nose and throat. The smoke hung in the air, thick, gray and drifting, often obscuring the rafters and sometimes even the faces of people standing. It reddened eyes and set people coughing, though the Sterkarms were so used to it, they hardly noticed that they coughed.

Andrea could have filled a page with notes about the various whiffs and stinks that drifted about: the fruity tang of beer, a gust of stale old sweat every time someone passed or moved, and someone nearby had very cheesy feet. Other people smelled of sheep and of horses. It wasn't that the Sterkarms themselves were especially dirty—it was early in the autumn, the weather was mild, and many of them still swam in the river every day. But their clothes, being mostly of wool, were difficult to wash without spoiling and harder still to dry, so they tended to stink from weeks of wear.

I am lucky, Andrea thought. Her feet rustled in the thick strewing of straw and herbs that covered the hall's stone flags. Overhead, the whitewash on the beams and planking of the ceiling was almost hidden under layer after layer of soot deposited by the smoke. From the rafters hung many, many rounds of flatbread, all strung through the hole in the center of each piece on the same length of twine. So lucky to have the chance to see this and, yes, even to smell it. So lucky to be able to listen to the stories.

The family table, the only one provided with chairs and stools for the diners, was set across the hall at right angles to the others. Andrea sat there, alone. Her hostess, Isobel, had harried her son and husband off on some errand as soon as they'd swallowed their last mouthful, and then had disappeared herself. Ever since Andrea had brought them the news that "Elf-Windsor" was coming to visit the next day, Isobel had been in a fret.

Sweet Milk had kept Andrea company at first, but then he'd gone away too. At least that had given her a few minutes to write down what he'd told her, in the notebook taken from her pocket. She'd had to hold it awkwardly in one hand while writing with the other, because the boards of the trestle table were too greasy to rest the book on. The Sterkarms used thick squares of stale bread for plates, and the gravy soaked through.

Sweet Milk's story was exactly the sort of firsthand account she needed for the book she planned to write when she went home: an account of the Sterkarms' way of life. Even if she never got it published, it ought to help her get a post in some university's anthropology department.

The chance to live with the Sterkarms had been one she'd just had to grab. The job had seemed fated to be hers. She'd only heard about the job by chance, and then had almost not bothered to apply. But she'd been almost at the end of her studies and beginning to look around for work. She thought her Danish had swung it for her—her mother was Danish, and she could speak a reasonable Danish herself. She never would have been able to pick up the Sterkarms' thick dialect so quickly otherwise.

Of course, she was a dimension removed from her own world, so this wasn't the sixteenth century of her own timeline—if she'd understood the scientific explanations at all correctly. But, she'd been assured, the two dimensions were so close, there was no essential difference. "The dimensions diverge inasmuch as Anne Boleyn wore a red dress to her execution in one, and a pink dress in the other" had been one rather distasteful explanation. The scientists had been more interested in whether oil, gas and gold had exactly the same properties in both dimensions.

But to be *in* the sixteenth century, even if a dimension removed from her own. To be talking with sixteenth-century people, seeing how they lived at first hand, experiencing it herself! She could never think about it for more than a couple of seconds at a time because it made her dizzy. If she ever let herself truly feel how incredible, how miraculous—the technology! The implications!—then she was sure her mind would fly to bits.

She wished she could think as the Sterkarms did: that all she had done was to step over the magical boundary between Elf-Land and Man's-Home. In an odd way they feared the Time Tube as magical and supernatural while, at the same time, regarding it as entirely natural. But then, so much of their world was inexplicable to them. They didn't understand why the sun and moon rose and set or moved across the sky, or what dreams were, or why people fell sick. The arrival of the Elves was just one more inexplicable thing that they had no choice but to accept as true. She made a note.

She read again through the notes she'd just made.

Sweet Milk told me when he was about ten, reivers came and burned down his family's home. He thinks they were Grannams, probably on way home from reiving Sterkarms. They came on SM's little holding and took the chance to reive a few more goats and sheep. Sweet Milk, his mother & siblings ran away, watched riders by light of burning house. Sweet Milk's father stayed behind, very foolish if brave. When family went back next day, father was dead. Sweet Milk says his body torn all to pieces, so many lances had been driven through him. Tears ran down into his beard as he told me this. The Sterkarms aren't at all ashamed to show their feelings.

Andrea's own eyes had filled as she'd listened, and she'd found it hard to swallow, but she was always embarrassed by tears and tried hard not to show them. "No use crying over spilt milk," her father had always said. Besides, researchers were supposed to keep a distance between themselves and their work. She tried. It wasn't easy.

Sweet Milk said he held one of his small sisters in his arms and watched his mother crouch by his father's body and howl like a dog. His mother, and six children, had been left with nothing but the clothes on their backs and what little grain they could rescue from the burning house.

She read it over and over, shaking her head. It seemed extreme to her—the robbery, the burning, the murder, the destitution, all piling one on another—but it helped her understand the world she was in. No one among the Sterkarms thought Sweet Milk's story strange. Such things happened commonly. That was why the towers were built, with their fifteen-foot walls; why the out-buildings had no entrances on the ground floor; why

31

every man went armed and no one ever left the tower alone.

Something banged on the table, surprising her and making her look up. It was Sweet Milk come back, and setting down a fresh jug of beer. He seated himself heavily on a stool and grinned at her through his beard.

He was a big man, probably in his thirties, with long dark hair and a dark beard. His hands were big and thick fingered with scarred knuckles, his face usually grim, and he rarely spoke. He'd made Andrea nervous when she'd first met him. He'd seemed as threatening as any twenty-first-century biker. Then she'd got to know him, through Per, who treated him with familiar, affectionate contempt, and she'd found that Sweet Milk was good-natured, shrewd and funny. She valued his friendship a great deal. It had been Sweet Milk who'd told her about "the Sterkarm handshake," and he was an influential man at the tower—Toorkild's foreman when farming, and his second in command when fighting. Toorkild thought so highly of him that he'd given him the responsibility and great honor of being Per's foster father. And yet Sweet Milk wasn't a Sterkarm. He was a Beal.

"I've written down all tha told me," she said, "so I can remember it all." She held the notebook up for him to see, and he peered at it. To him it must seem nothing but wriggling lines and scribble. He couldn't read or write even his own name.

"Elf-Work," he said, grinning. He had big, square teeth. When Andrea had first come among the Sterkarms, she'd expected to find a lot of stunted, puny creatures with rotten teeth, and had been surprised, even

32

faintly disappointed, to find how wrong she was. The grit that got into the bread from the grindstones did wear down their back teeth, but since none of them had ever tasted sugar, and they drank a great deal of milk, the rest of their teeth were good and strong. Some even whitened them by chewing on hazel twigs.

"Canst spell me with that?" He nodded at the writing.

"No. And I wouldn't spell thee, Sweet Milk, even if I could."

"Ah, thou needst no Elf-Work to spell me, Honey."

Andrea looked down at her notebook, pretending that she hadn't heard and hoping that, in the red light, the flush on her cheeks wouldn't be seen. She couldn't get used to being admired and complimented. Back in the 21st she was "Big Fat Andy," and had learned to expect that men would look straight past her. But what the 21st called "big and fat," the Sterkarms called "bonny." Tall as she was, full fleshed, broad beamed, bosomy, thunder thighed—the eyes of the Sterkarm men lit up. They noticed her all the time, and it was disconcerting. Would a looker like Per have given her even one glance if he'd been born and raised in the 21st?

"Wouldst tell me what happened after thy father was killed?"

He seemed disappointed that she wasn't going to flirt, but took up his story again. His family being Beals, in a part of the country where Beals were few, there had been no one who would, or could, give them aid. Sweet Milk and the other children had helped his mother build another house—like the one burned down, it had been nothing but a flimsy shelter made of branches and mud and thatched with heather. The widow had labored on,

33

trying to make a living with nothing, from nothing. Her younger children had sickened and died, and after a couple of years, Sweet Milk had wandered away, to try and find some less hungry life for himself.

Had Sweet Milk been a Sterkarm, his life would have been easier. Sterkarms were as thick as grass in that country, and also as thick as thieves. A Sterkarm widow and her children would have been helped by someone, and the dead man would have been avenged. But the Sterkarms felt no obligation to help a Beal.

"So I was a loose man in the moss," Sweet Milk said—that was, a man without family to help or protect him, living rough in the hills, marshes and moors. This wild, sodden, mountainous country made such a life hard, and if you killed game or sheep, or even gathered berries, on land claimed by the Sterkarms, you were likely to end up hanged—or, if there was no handy tree, held down in a stream and drowned. Sweet Milk had thought about going to some other part of the country, but where would have been the gain? The Beals weren't a strong family anywhere. Walking would bring him into Grannam country, or Allyot country, where he would be no better off.

In the end he'd walked up to a Sterkarm tower and asked for work, shelter and food. "If they'd killed me, I should have been out of the rain."

If they'd ever caught him butchering their sheep—and he could admit now that he had done that—the Sterkarms would certainly have killed him, but it was all but impossible for them to kill someone who asked for their hospitality. If even a Grannam, one of their worst enemies, had come to their gates asking for food and shelter, he would have been given it and treated with courtesy. Whether, having left their gates again, a Grannam would have got very far on his road was another matter.

Sweet Milk, once through the Sterkarm gates, had set about making himself indispensable, setting out to win praise for every task he was given, looking for jobs and doing them before he was asked, determined to become so valued a servant that he would never again be loose in the moss.

"Tha've done very well," Andrea said, her head leaning on her hand. She'd been listening, fascinated, trying hard to remember every word, since she didn't want to distract him by writing while he talked. "Sweet Milk—why art called 'Sweet Milk'?" It was typical that as almost the only man at the tower who wasn't named Sterkarm, and so didn't need a nickname, he was always, but always, known by the most baffling she'd heard yet.

"Dost not know?" He grinned.

She shook her head. Most nicknames were obvious: "Nebless" or "Noseless" meant a man whose nose had been cut off, or who had a big nose; "Half-lugs" was someone who was deaf, or who'd had one ear cut off, and "Gob" or "Gobby" meant "mouthy" or "big mouth." But "Sweet Milk"? It meant "fresh milk," as "sweet water" meant fresh, drinkable water, and it was true that the Sterkarms drank a lot of milk, in all its forms, and valued fresh, whole milk highly, but Andrea still couldn't quite see the connection. You'd be looking at Sweet Milk a long time before he reminded you of anything either sweet or milky.

"I'll no tell thee, then," he said.

He wanted her to wheedle it out of him, and she would have done, except that Isobel came bustling up and set her hands on the table. Sweet Milk sat back and fell silent. Every man in the tower was afraid of Isobel.

Leaning across the table, Isobel held Andrea's attention with her amazing eyes, which were huge, round, so pale a blue they were almost silver, and just like Per's. "Entraya! Have you any of the wee white pills?"

"Oh! I don't—" Andrea began searching through the pockets in her skirt, shirt and jacket.

"But one of my mays has her cramps, and she's too shy to ask thee, the sheep-head. Oh good!"

Andrea had produced, from her jacket, a paper of aspirins, and had torn two off. Isobel didn't ask for any more. The Sterkarms, almost always tactful and well-mannered on their own ground, understood that the Elf-May would not want to give out her wee white pills by the handful. She was always quick to give them to anyone who asked while she had them.

"The poor may will be grateful," Isobel said. "And Entraya, will I make up a bed for the Elf-Man?"

"There's no need, Isobel. Elf-Windsor won't stay the night."

That was plainly not what Isobel wanted to hear. She had obviously decided to make up a bed, to show that she had a spare bed and the linen to furnish it. She'd come to ask Andrea's advice only as a ploy to stir up and involve as many in her plans as possible, from her husband, Toorkild, to the skivvies in the kitchen, and the very hens and goats in the yard.

"I'd better make up a bed," she said. "Then he can stay if he should choose. Or if something should happen.

I'd die if I hadn't a bed to offer him. I'll put my mother's wolfskin cover on it." She looked at Andrea again and poked her in the arm. "The same one I shall spread on thy bed."

Sweet Milk grinned. Andrea affected to look coolly around the hall, pretending that she hadn't even noticed he was amused, though she knew as well as he did that Isobel was referring to her and Per's wedding bed. Isobel was looking forward to inviting many guests to the wedding feast, and bossing people about for weeks beforehand. Even more eagerly she was looking forward to the fun of being a mother-in-law and granny, because, of course, Per and Andrea would continue to live at the tower. It would have been cruel to spoil her anticipation by telling her none of it was going to happen. She wouldn't have listened anyway.

One of Andrea's cool glances fell on Isobel's hand where it rested on the boards. There on Isobel's wrist was a watch, with an expandable bracelet. Twenty-first-century machine work, there was no mistaking it. On a sixteenth-century wrist.

Before Andrea could ask where the watch had come from, Isobel had turned away and, calling to some of her women, hurried off. Probably to set scores of people hunting through the storehouses for the pieces of a particular bed, and then to set others to putting it together, and still others to finding out linen and blankets and sweet herbs to strew it, all in honor of "Elf-Windsor," who would never see it.

Andrea stood. "Dost know where Per is?" she asked Sweet Milk.

"Which one?" It was the answer you invariably got if

you were stupid enough to ask for someone by their name instead of their nickname. Even more stupidly, she said, "My Per."

Sweet Milk laughed. "Which is *your* Per? Dog's-Breath? Wanton?"

Answering "The May" would just have given him more material to work with. "Oh, never mind!" Leaving the shelter of the high table, she pushed her way through the crowd of people beyond, craning her neck to see over shoulders, or ducking to peer between bodies. It would be easy to miss Per in the crush.

Isobel's watch had to have come from the wrist of some twenty-first-century incomer—it didn't take a lot of thought to work that out. She would have suspected the security guards of trading with the Sterkarms, except that it had been a woman's watch. That suggested another, more immediate source. There were several women geologists and mapmakers among the researchers sent out from the Tube. They've robbed another survey team, Andrea thought. And they *promised* they wouldn't!

What made her feel worse was the suspicion that Per could, if he chose, give a very full account of how the watch had come to be on his mother's wrist. She doubted if he would so choose, but she was interested to hear what he would say.

Through the shifting gaps in the crowd she caught a glimpse of a big hound's flank silhouetted against the fire and knew she'd found Per. The hound was Cuddy, and unless dragged away from him by force and locked up, she was always close by Per.

The firelight became more brilliant and golden as

Andrea pushed her way closer to the hearth. Showers of red sparks and black smut flew from the crackling, spitting fire. Her heart beat faster, with odd little skips and jumps, because she was going to be with Per again, even though she'd been separated from him less than an hour. They were possibly going to quarrel, too, and that brought up the frightening prospect that they might fall out forever, and the pleasing one of making up.

> Oh, see you my tall love, with his cheeks like roses?
> Why will he break my heart, gathering him posies?

The Sterkarms had taught her scores of songs. No matter what you wanted to say, the Sterkarms knew a song that said it.

> Oh, his hair it shines like gold,
> And his eyes like crystal stones—

She reached the front of the crowd and had to raise her hand to shield her face from the full force of its heat and brilliance. The harsh reek of a gust of smoke almost choked her. From the smoke emerged the fireplace's wide stone hood, with its carved and painted badge: a black shield displaying, in red, an upraised arm holding a dagger. The badge showed its full colors and then sank into darkness as the light of the fire washed over it and then faded. It was the family name in picture form—"Sterkarm" meant "strong arm." Not being noble, the Sterkarms had no more right to the badge than they had to keep hunting hounds like Cuddy, but much they cared. Who was going to come into their country and tell them their rights?

To the left of the fire was a settle—a bench with a tall back and sides and a top. A sort of box with a seat in it, designed to keep away the drafts that blew in at the hall door and through the narrow, unglazed windows. Cuddy now lay before the settle, at Per's feet. Per was with his father. The Sterkarms, father and son, made—for Andrea—a rather startling picture that she paused to memorize for her notes.

Despite being known as "Old Toorkild," Per's father wasn't much more than forty. He was bothered by aching joints and rheumatic pains but was still a strong, active man, his hair and beard only just beginning to turn gray. He was darker than his wife and son, but the big, pretty, pale-blue eyes that looked out from his thickets of hair and beard were exactly like theirs. If his beard had ever been shaved, perhaps the likeness would have been stronger still, since Toorkild and Isobel were cousins.

Toorkild sat nearest the fire, baking his aches and pains. Per was pressed so close against him that, to be comfortable, he'd slung one leg over his father's lap. His head rested on Toorkild's shoulder, his face turned up to watch Toorkild as he spoke. Toorkild looked down at him, and they gazed steadily into each other's eyes. They were holding hands. Of all the people crowding around them to share the fire's heat, only Andrea thought this at all odd.

After all, Andrea thought, wrenching her prejudices out of their frame, what *was* odd about it? Everyone knew that Isobel and Toorkild doted on their only son. To raise a laugh at the tower, you only had to imitate

Isobel by saying, "Where's Per? When will he be back? Has he had something to eat? Has he a cloak? Who's with him?" And, it was said, if you wanted the eyes out of Toorkild's head, your only difficulty was in persuading Per to ask him for them.

Nobody had told the Sterkarms that, when a child was six, they were "too big" to be kissed and cuddled anymore. The Sterkarms blithely went on kissing and cuddling their children even when they were forty-six—and older. Nobody had ever even hinted to Per that it was unmanly to hold his father's hand or to kiss him, because no one at the tower thought it was. So Per went on doing it, as unself-consciously as when he'd been three. Toorkild didn't have to struggle to show his affection for his son by coughing and shaking his hand at the full stretch of their arms. Andrea realized that she was really quite jealous. How long was it since she'd leaned her head on her father's shoulder like that?

"It isn't for one year, or for two," Toorkild was saying, wagging his finger. "Mind, when a man weds, he gives to his wife the keeping of his home, of all he owns, his good name, even his life. And the making of thy bairns. Now, wouldst give all that to a careless woman?"

Per had never taken his eyes from his father's. His head moved against Toorkild's shoulder as he shook it slightly.

"A woman o' good family, who's been well raised and who'll breed true, that's what's wanted. Tha want her strong and clever—"

"Like Mammy," Per said with a sigh, nodding.

"Aye, aye, like tha mammy. I'm glad thee mind it! Dost think running the household tha mammy does is easy? Honest and trustworthy, that's how tha want a wife. And when tha's found her, and wed her, never forget what thee owe her, and never grudge her what's her due. The mays, the women . . ." Toorkild waved his hand. "Tha'll fancy this one, tha'll fancy that one, they'll come, they'll go, but thy *wife* . . ." Toorkild tapped Per on the nose, making him smile and draw back his head. "Choose one like tha mammy. There's not a man alive can say he's got a better wife than me." Toorkild patted Per's cheek. "Look what a son she made me."

And there on Toorkild's wrist, as he raised it to touch Per's face, was a big wristwatch. Andrea forgot that Toorkild, it seemed, didn't think her a suitable wife for his son, but only one of the mays—even though an Elf-May—who came and went. She stepped forward and said, "Master Toorkild—"

"Entraya!" Toorkild said. "Me little Elf! Give me a kiss!" It was always hard to embarrass Toorkild.

Per kicked his leg from his father's lap and jumped up, as tall as Toorkild, if half his girth. In the bright red-gold light of the fire he looked extraordinarily handsome, so handsome that Andrea was almost ready to forget about the wristwatches—was the quarrel worth it?

He wore a tight-fitting and rather showy jacket of green suede, the sleeves cut into ribbons to show the loose sleeves of the linen shirt he wore underneath. The front of the jacket was decorated with scarlet embroidery and large silver buttons. The Sumptuary Laws of England—if you considered the Sterkarms to be English—made it illegal for the likes of Per to wear such expensive buttons, but then, the jacket probably hadn't been acquired legally either.

On his legs Per wore close-fitting breeches and, instead of his usual long riding boots, buckled shoes and black woolen stockings pulled over his breeches and fastened above his knee with red garters. They made his legs look very long and helped Andrea understand why men in her own world had always been so keen on black stockings and garters. The firelight made his roughly cut mop of fair hair shine copper and gold, lit his eyes like silver and burnished the pretty face that gave him his nickname.

He pressed close to her, embracing her and enveloping her in his blunt, musky smell, as undeniably intriguing as it was unpleasant. She pushed against his chest before he could kiss her, holding him off.

"One eye's blink!" she said. "Master Toorkild— may I ask, what's that on your wrist?"

"Entraya, Sweeting, we're 'thou' to each other." Toorkild came to stand at her other side, making her feel, as she stood between the two men, that she was at the bottom of a deep well. Stooping, Toorkild pressed his springy, prickly mass of beard against her face in a kiss. His smell, a mixture of sweat, sheep, horse, dog and the fur of his robe, was even thicker than Per's. It would be easy to feel overwhelmed by them, but Andrea refused to be.

"What is this on thy wrist?" Though speaking to Toorkild, she looked at Per.

Per stared right back at her, smiling, amused but not even slightly abashed. As his father was stuck for an answer, he said, "I gave it Daddy."

"And the one thy mammy's wearing? Was that from thee an' all?"

He grinned, slipped his arm closer around her, and tried to kiss her again.

"Per! They're Elf-Work! How didst come by 'em?"

"I found 'em," he said, so seriously, and opening his beautiful eyes wide in such a parody of innocence, that she knew he was both lying and laughing at her. "Beside a trail. The Elves must have dropped 'em as they went by." He smiled, plainly not caring whether she believed him or not.

It made her angry, but at the same time she wanted to laugh. And he knew it. "Per! Wristwatches don't fall off like that."

"Maybe they put 'em there for me to find." His smile reminded her that, when FUP had first come into the Sterkarms' country, they had deliberately left out small gifts of forged gold coin, bolts of cloth and food, as a way of making friends. Prove me wrong! his smile said.

"Per, tell me the truth. Didst rob the Elves?"

"Nay!" he said, with a shocked indignation that again bordered on parody. "I should not rob the Elves! They've been so good to us!"

Andrea folded her arms and studied the two of them, the father and son, and she swung between belief and disbelief and half laughed. Was that remark about the goodness of the Elves ironical? Did the Sterkarms understand, and resent, why the Elves handed out their magical pills so grudgingly?

She looked at Toorkild, who at once turned from her to kiss his son's head. He ran his hand over Per's hair, neck and shoulders with exactly the same air—though with more smugness—that he used when stroking his horses or cattle. Careful breeding, good feeding and good care had produced an animal of whose health, strength and beauty he had every reason to be proud. He turned to look at Andrea again, and she was faced with the almost identical pairs of eyes: Per's daring her to disbelieve him, and Toorkild's asking, Would such a good boy lie?

She said, "Oh!" and turned her back on them.

Per at once put his arms around her from behind and began rocking her and nuzzling her neck. "Ah, be kind, Sweet! Be not angry!"

She felt herself becoming all giggly and gooey and fond—proof that all those silly songs she'd always despised had more than a grain of truth in them—and she was furious with herself for feeling ridiculously swoony and such a pushover. She tried to unclasp his hands, which were joined in front of her, but his grip was so strong, she hadn't a hope. She said sharply, "Art lying to me?"

He licked the tip of his tongue up her neck, making her shudder, and pulled her tight against him. "I lie about all but this." His nose and his breath stirred her hair and the down on her skin, like a shock of static electricity. Kissing her ear, Per whispered, "Will I hunt tonight, if moon be bright? Will I shoot at the bonny black hare?"

Another song came to her mind:

> The higher on the wing it climbs,
> The sweeter sings the lark:
> The sweeter that a young man speaks,
> The falser is his heart.
> He'll kiss thee and embrace thee,

> Until he has thee won:
> Then he'll turn him round and leave thee,
> All for some other one.

She turned to face him. "I don't believe thee." Then she put her arms around his neck and they kissed. He's too beautiful for me, she thought, and he's already got two children running around the tower yard, and FUP are going to sack me if they ever find out I'm fraternizing with the natives, and it's all just—

> Come all you pretty young maids,
> A warning take from me,
> Never try to build your nests
> At the top of a tall tree:
> For the green leaves they will wither
> And the branches all decay,
> And the beauty of your young man
> It soon will fade away.

But while it lasts, she thought, I'm so lucky.

And later, sitting on the settle beside Isobel and Toorkild, with Per sitting on the floor beside her with his head leaning against her thigh, she was still feeling lucky. Per's head was heavy and hot where it lay against her leg, but his hair was cool, smooth and soft as she moved her fingers through it. She was doing what Isobel said every girl should do for her young man—searching his hair for lice, though she hoped that she wouldn't find any. But this was sixteenth-century *life*! She had to learn to be less squeamish. Every now and again Per would tilt up his face, smiling, asking for a kiss, and she would bend down and oblige him. So lucky.

And one of the tower women was telling a story. She was really listening to people making their own entertainment, in the days before television and radio. She wondered when she would find time to write down an account of it—Isobel didn't like anyone wasting more candles than necessary, and Per hated her writing even more than her reading, because she was so much harder to distract from it—"Let me just finish this sentence." He didn't know what a sentence was. . . .

So she'd have to remember until she got a chance to write it down. Somebody had said, "How about a story?" and enough others had agreed for Isobel to be asked to tell one. But she'd said no, she had too much on her mind. Then, by general agreement, another woman had been named, and pressed until she asked, "What story?"

Several voices had called out the story they wanted, disagreeing and trying to shout each other down. Some had ignored the whole business and carried on their own talk as well as they could under the noise.

The shouting had become a contest between those who wanted the story of Guthrun and those who didn't. Per didn't, and had stood, the better to make himself heard. Guthrun, in the story, was a woman whose lover had been murdered by her brothers, who then married her to another man, by whom she had two sons. To be revenged on her brothers, she murdered these children herself and had them casseroled and served to her husband. She laid the blame for this meal on her brothers, and rejoiced as they were executed by her husband. The twenty-first century had nothing to teach the Sterkarms about soap opera or melodrama.

It was a well-known story, and the name "Guthrun" was, to the Sterkarms, a byword for a treacherous, faithless woman. Her great crime, to their way of thinking, was to betray her own blood. Her brothers had merely been doing their duty, saving their family honor by killing her lover, who was of little consequence. But she had, unthinkably, killed her own blood.

The tale was told too often, Per said; he was sick of it. Bread and straw were thrown at him. Cuddy leaped up to his defense, and Swart, his other hound, woke and yapped. Then someone suggested the story of Vaylan, and there was laughter, and everyone changed their mind and began shouting for the story of Vaylan instead.

"No, no, not Vaylan!" Per said. "Guthrun sooner than Vaylan!"

It was no use. The agreement of everyone else was too complete and determined. Andrea was puzzled. She didn't understand why Per was so fiercely against the story of Vaylan being told, or why everyone else insisted on it with such malicious glee. It seemed to be considered a just punishment for Per's disagreeing about "Guthrun."

Per sat down at her feet again, though he hugged his own knees rather than lean against her. He was in something of a bad temper. The chatter and laughter went on for a while, until people began to call for quiet so the storyteller could begin. Even then the quiet wasn't complete. People didn't listen in meek silence, as Andrea had always imagined they would. There were people ignoring the story altogether and carrying on their own conversations, and people arguing over the telling, and asking others what had just been said, and getting up and climbing over others to get more beer, or to be closer to the fire, and then coming back again, and all the arguments these comings and goings provoked.

But the story was begun, there, in the half circle of flaring, dancing golden light that played over the gathered people—the men, the women and the children—with the peat smoke hanging overhead. The storyteller raised her voice and said, "Once upon a time, and then it was a good time, though not your time, nor my time, nor nobody else's time, but once upon that time . . ."

Andrea felt the thrill go to her toes.

The story was of Vaylan, a smith and a hunter, who had been hunting with his bow one evening when he saw three great swans fly in over the sea. They landed on the strand, threw off their feather coats and turned into three beautiful women, who began to dance in the moonlight. Vaylan hid and watched them. . . .

The listeners called out ribald comments, but when it seemed one man was going to begin an anecdote of his own, he was cuffed and silenced, and the storyteller was begged to go on. She let them beg awhile before allowing herself to be persuaded.

"Vaylan thought he couldn't bear to live unless he had one of these beautiful mays for his wife. . . ." So, creeping from his hiding place, he had stolen one of the feather coats so that only two of the women were able to change themselves back into swans. The third begged him to return her coat, but he steadfastly refused, promising instead to be a good husband to her. And, after her sisters had flown away, the Swan-May became Vaylan's wife.

Now Andrea realized why Per had not wanted this story told, and why the tower people had so gleefully insisted on it. Swan-Mays were Elves too. The story was about a mortal man who married an Elf-May and, as far as Andrea could remember, there wasn't a single story of the kind that ended happily.

But all the chatter had died. People who had not wanted to hear a story had started to listen, and the burning of the fire could be clearly heard. Even Per had propped his chin on her knee and was listening.

"Vaylan locked the feather coat in a big chest, and made sure he kept the key on him, night and day. But he kept his word to the Swan-May, and dressed her in silk and gold, and never she went a day hungry or cold. Never one blow did he strike her, meant or unmeant, and never an angry word did he speak to her . . ."

Andrea felt Per stir against her and, glancing down, saw him looking up at her.

"And little by little she stopped her grieving for her sisters and her own land, since Vaylan loved her every night . . ."

There was an uproar of laughter, and comment, and Per pulled at Andrea's hand, grinning brightly, until she tweaked his nose and made him duck his head.

"And a child every year she had!"

There was more mocking, admiring, laughing comment that set the hounds to yelping and pacing restlessly about. "Canst match Vaylan, Per?"

"Match him and pass him!"

There was more laughter and scoffing.

"Oh, poor Entraya!"

"Tha'll be worn to a thread, may!"

The storyteller waited until they were silent before going on. Seven years passed, and then the Swan-May's eldest son brought her the key to the big chest—it had fallen from his daddy's belt. Straight to the chest went the Swan-May, unlocked it, took out her feather coat, put it on and flew away. The storyteller's gaze, and that of many of the audience, followed the Swan-May's flight up into the smoke, and beyond the rafters, into the sky. "And two other swans came and flew with her, and away they all flew, across the western sea."

Andrea looked down at Per and saw that there were tears on his cheek, and he swallowed hard. She looked away, embarrassed, finding it hard to accept, as she always did, how easily the Sterkarms cried.

Vaylan was sore, sore grieved, but had the hope that the Swan-May would return, and swore his oath he would wait for her, if need be, until the world ended. . . .

Per snuffled and nodded in firm agreement.

He spent the years while he waited working in his smithy, and became so skillful a smith that when he made a flower of gold, the bees came to it. The king of England heard of his skill and sent for him to be his smith. But Vaylan wouldn't leave the spot where his Swan-May might return. The king was so angry that he sent soldiers to take Vaylan—

Per raised his head from Andrea's lap and said loudly, "Mammy, tell the proper ending, tell thy ending!"

The storyteller broke off, and people turned to glare at Per. Several voices cried out for the storyteller to go on, and Isobel said, "Per, ssh! Lisa began it, Lisa must end it."

"But she'll tell the wrong ending! I don't like her

ending." The people standing and sitting around the fire responded with a wave of angry sound, telling him to shut up and to go away if he didn't like it.

"I'd like to hear the ending, Per," Andrea said.

"But her ending's no good! Tell it Mammy's way."

The protests rose again, but the argument was never to be settled. From above, from outside the tower, came an untuneful clanging of metal on metal. Everyone stopped shouting and looked upward. In the silence the sound grew louder, falling down from the roof of the tower and coming in through the windows in the thick stone walls. It sounded like someone banging hard on the side of big metal cauldron. Andrea stared about at the firelit, startled faces before she realized what the sound was.

The alarm bell. On top of the tower, on its stone roof, was a large beacon, always stocked with fuel, ready to be lit as a signal to the other Sterkarm strongholds nearby. Beside it was a metal bell, to be rung vigorously, to rouse the tower.

From the stairs of the tower came a man's shout: "Sterkarm!" The alarm and rallying cry of the Sterkarm family.

Andrea's heart seemed to jump up into her throat, where it hammered wildly. An attack! Fighting. Sharp cutting edges, sharp points. Bleeding, injury, death. Reaching out with both hands, she took a tight hold on Per's arm.

4

16th Side: The Alarm

INTO THE HALL FROM THE dark stairwell came two men, one a man of the watch and the other a stranger to Andrea. The tower's people scattered back from the fire, clearing the hearth, so that the newcomers could walk into the warmth and light.

The stranger was wet, his hair and beard hanging in thin, dripping strands. He walked hunched over, gasping for breath. Isobel and Toorkild rose from the settle and ushered the exhausted man to it, making him sit close by the fire. Isobel sent a woman running for towels, and herself ran to the high table to fetch a cup of beer and a plate of bread.

Toorkild sat beside the man, and Per crouched in front of him, calming Cuddy with one hand, to hear what the man had to say. He spoke breathlessly, in a hoarse, low voice, so that even Toorkild and Per had to lean close to catch his words. Sweet Milk came from somewhere to stand behind Per, leaning down to hear and resting his hand on Per's shoulder.

Andrea stood back a little with the other tower people, not wishing to be in the way. She started when Per jumped to his feet, pushing Sweet Milk aside, and said, "Grannams!" A grumbling ran through the crowd. The name "Grannam" always meant trouble for the Sterkarms.

Per stepped up on a stool someone had set by the hearth and, with the fire flickering behind him, raised one arm high. "Beacon! Bell! Ride!" Jumping down, he yelled, "*Sterk*arm!"

With an outbreak of shouting, and a scuffling and running of feet on the stone floor, the crowd broke and scattered. Everyone in the hall knew what to do. Some simply got out of the way. A couple of men grabbed the excited Cuddy and Swart by their collars and dragged them off to be locked up. Many ran for the stairs, Isobel among them, to run either up to the rooms above or down to the byre below. The stairs were narrow, but the people were orderly and quiet. Their feet clattered on the steps, but there wasn't much shouting or any pushing. Soon, from below, came the noise and vibration of the tower door being heaved open, and horses being led into the yard.

Andrea stood frozen, looking around. The quiet, purposeful action all around her was unnerving. They're going to ride! she thought, realizing what it meant. They *promised* they wouldn't . . . Just as they promised not to rob the survey teams.

The hall was half empty now, and a strong draft blew in from the stairs. It had blown out some of the candles, and the room was darker, the light from the fire redder as it leaped over the upper walls and rafters. Andrea moved closer to the group about the settle and looked down at the seated man. He had run to the tower over rough country in the dark, bashing himself on rocks and wading through streams, and now it was almost all he could do to keep awake. Per was kneeling in front of him, looking into his face and holding a cup of beer for him, as the man tried to chew on a lump of bread. Toorkild, standing over him with folded arms, said, "How many?"

"Gigot," the man whispered. That was as high as anyone present—except Andrea—could count, but there must have been about twenty Grannam riders, or the man would have said "gigot and dick" or "gigot and gigot."

Per looked up at his father. "Gigot!" Andrea couldn't tell whether he was outraged that the Grannams had dared to come into their country with so many riders, or so few.

A bellow came from the door—a man pausing to tell them that the beacon had been lit before running on down the stairs. Isobel came running in, together with another woman, carrying between them Toorkild's jakke, helmet, sword and riding boots. Panting, Isobel dumped them all with a clatter and clash on the bench nearest to their owner, and then came to listen, hands on hips, to the talk.

The riders were Grannams, the exhausted man was saying. He'd known some of them from market days in Carloel. They'd run off every one of his sheep, aye, and his horses and his one cow.

Toorkild was pulling on his jakke—a sleeveless, quilted jerkin that fastened high about his neck and came down to just below his waist. Between its layers of cloth and leather were stitched squares of iron, each drilled through so it could be fastened firmly in place.

The whole made a light, flexible protection against weapons. "Which way did they go, man?"

Per's jakke, helmet and boots were brought into the hall by another man. Sitting on the stool, Per kicked off his shoes and pulled on the long boots that would protect his legs when he rode through scrub and might also—with luck—save him from a sword cut.

Watching, Andrea thought: Per's going to ride! No one even mentioned the promises they'd made to FUP. And Per could get hurt. Killed. She felt quite sick, as if she'd been punched in the belly.

The farmer was detailing the most likely way for the Grannams to have gone, naming small streams and hills—things that meant far more to the Sterkarms than they did to Andrea. She sometimes thought they had a name for every bush, every stone and every large clump of flowers in their country.

I ought to say something, she thought. I ought to stop them. But she couldn't think of anything she could say that they might listen to.

Men wearing boots and jakkes and helmets were looking in at the hall door, as if to say, What's taking so long? Per was fastening his jakke over the embroidered green jacket. Andrea, seeing him, felt a familiar, dizzying sense of dislocation. To her, thigh-high boots like those he was wearing were firmly associated with pantomime princes and nightclub drag. She could never quite rid herself of the notion that the swords were toys, the helmets props, and the long boots only intended to look playfully butch and sexy. To be reminded that they had far more mundane purposes made her feel even sicker.

Toorkild was seated on the stool, dragging on his

boots, when Isobel grabbed at his arm and cried, "You can't go!"

Andrea was as astonished as Toorkild. Was Isobel reminding him of the promises he'd made to FUP? It would be unlike her.

"Away, woman."

"The Elf-Man is coming tomorrow!" Isobel was holding his shoulders. "I forgot! But you have to be here!"

Toorkild stopped in the middle of pulling on his second boot and looked at her, caught between the duty of hospitality and his duty to pursue the Grannams.

Per came and crouched behind his father, resting his chin on Toorkild's shoulder and linking his arms around his neck. "Stay thou, Daddy. I'll go."

Andrea saw, with fear, that he was delighted by the idea of leading the ride himself.

Another glance told her that neither Isobel nor Toorkild was happy about it, though it wouldn't be the first time Per had led at least a division of a ride. "Folk'll say I'm too old!" Toorkild fretted. "The lad can stay and greet the Elf."

There was an outcry from both Per and Isobel. Per had no intention of being left behind, while Isobel said, "It must be the master to greet the guest! Though Sweet Milk can very well lead the ride," she added, reaching for Per's arm.

A ringing clang broke into the steady rhythm of the bell. Per had struck his helmet on the table beside him. "Sweet Milk!" He broke off, speechless at Sweet Milk being placed above him.

"Maybe . . ." Andrea stepped among them, spreading

her hands peaceably. She had to try and say something. "Maybe the answer is not to ride? Master Toorkild, thou madest an agreement with the Elves. Thou promised thou wouldst not ride more and thou wouldst let the Elves settle thy quarrels. Stay at home. Tell Elf-Windsor about it tomorrow, and let him deal with the Grannams."

They heard her out in silence, staring at her with a patient, disbelieving curiosity. What a strange may she was, and what strange ideas she had. But then, she was an Elf. As soon as she stopped speaking, they turned away from her.

"While you bicker," the farmer said, "the Grannams ride with my sheep."

Toorkild pulled on his second boot, got up and took charge. Pushing Per before him, he made for the stairs. Everyone followed, pouring out of the hall and into the narrow stairwell, rattling around and around, heel to toe, pushing at each other's shoulders, down to the dark ground floor of the tower, and ducking out through its small door into the damp, chill night.

There was a small space before the tower, and it was crowded with horses and men—thickset, shaggy little horses, and men wearing homemade tin-pot helmets, and jakkes and long boots. Some carried longbows and quivers. The iron heads of long lances stuck into the air. Beyond the men and horses, pushed into the narrow ways between the crowded outbuildings, were the women and children of the tower, and the old men who no longer rode.

A shifting yellow firelight fell over it all from above, making deep shadows under jaws and brows, shining on helmets and glinting lance heads. The light came from the beacon high above on the tower roof—the beacon that would soon bring riders from other Sterkarm towers. Toorkild's people would send them after their own riders.

Sweet Milk was crouching, rubbing the chest of a middling-size dog and playing with its long ears. It was the only dog that would be going with the ride—Toorkild's sleuthhound, a most valuable animal.

Toorkild seized Sweet Milk by the arm, and the man stood and listened while Toorkild spoke to him urgently. Per, turning back, found Andrea and Isobel close behind him in the doorway of the tower. He touched his mother's breast, put his arm around her and kissed her cheek—but then leaned past her to touch Andrea. "Give me a kiss for luck!"

Isobel pulled down his head and gave him several kisses haphazardly, wherever she could reach. "You must—" she said, between kisses, "bring every kiss—back to me."

"I will, I will." He was still looking at Andrea.

She came forward and wrapped her arms tightly around him, feeling the hard iron plates in his jakke shift and scrape. He was thinner than her, and younger, and holding him made her feel, suddenly, desperately protective; she wanted to hang on to him with all her strength, so he couldn't go anywhere. Stupid, since he was far stronger than she was and certainly wouldn't thank her for trying to shield him. But what did he know, silly kid, being brave and showing off? "Don't go, Per, don't go! Tha'll be hurt!"

He laughed as he broke her grip on him, delighted to

be worrying her. From the yard, his father was shouting for him. "Don't go!" he said, as if it was a good joke. He gave her a quick kiss that landed on the side of her nose, and ran to his father.

"Good luck!" Andrea shouted, waving wildly, feeling guilty because she hadn't given him the lucky kiss he'd asked for. "Good luck, good luck!"

Toorkild, his hands cupped for his son's foot, was waiting beside Fowl, Per's horse. Per could jump into the saddle without using the stirrups, but that night his father wanted to be his stirrup, and Per obliged. Straightening, Toorkild threw him up easily, then stood by as Per tightened Fowl's girth. Setting his hand on Per's knee, Toorkild said, "Harken to Sweet Milk."

For answer, Per stooped down and kissed his father's head, then urged his horse forward. The whole firelit yard was full of movement as horses shifted and men mounted and then reached to take their lances from the women or children who had been holding them. Over it all, the bell rang, giving warning.

As Sweet Milk's mount followed Per's, and passed Toorkild, Andrea saw Toorkild look up at his foreman. Sweet Milk nodded, as if in answer, though nothing was spoken. It hadn't needed to be: She knew what favor Toorkild had silently asked, and Sweet Milk had silently promised. *Look out for Per; bring him back whole.*

The riders followed the main path to the gate, which was a little wider than the other tower ways. Their followers filtered by narrower alleys between the tower's many outbuildings. Some crowded through the gate behind the riders, others climbed to the walkways on the wall.

Andrea wouldn't have believed, before she'd seen it, that horses could be ridden over such country in the dark, but the Sterkarms thought a reiver's moon light enough. The horses clopped down the steep path descending the little crag and, with waves and cries of "Sterkarm!" went away down the gentler slope into the valley and the dark.

From the tower came answering calls of "The May! The May!" They sounded thin and forlorn in the dark.

Andrea's throat was tight and her heart felt swollen as she watched the horsemen fade into the darkness. How long had passed since the farmer had come to raise the alarm? She guessed at something like half an hour. In half an hour they were armed, on horseback, and away, riding out to defend their neighbors.

She had to remind herself that this petty, bickering warfare was anything but noble. People were maimed and killed over a few sheep. And the Sterkarms, often enough, rode out to steal sheep, not to rescue them. FUP was right to want to stop it. Per would be safer if FUP somehow managed to do what neither Scotland nor England had ever been able to do, and enforced a peace.

She walked back to the tower beside Isobel, who was holding Toorkild by the arm. All three of them were silent; all three of them thinking of Per.

At the tower, Toorkild stayed in the ground-floor byre to unharness his horse himself. Andrea climbed the stairs behind Isobel, back to the hall on the second floor. Without the men who had left, it seemed empty and achingly quiet—colder, too.

Together, Andrea and Isobel sat on the settle by the

fire. Isobel hadn't a word to say. Her hands were clenched in her lap, her mouth hard shut.

The people remaining at the tower—old men and servingmen, and women and children—came and settled about the hearth. They, too, were silent. But slowly, grudgingly, talk was taken up again, though quietly. Someone remembered the story and Lisa was urged to finish it.

"Where had we got to? Oh, Vaylan being fetched by the soldiers. . . . Well, they dragged him away and took him to this little island off the shore, and so he shouldn't get away, they hamstrung him so he could only crawl. . . ." Lisa's voice trailed away. "I don't want to finish it," she said. "It's too cruel."

Her words were received in silence. The people knew how the story went. Vaylan, a crippled prisoner on his island, was visited by the curious young son of the king. Vaylan murdered him and made bright brooches from his eyes, which he sent as gifts to the boy's mother and sister. From the boy's head he made a drinking cup and sent it to the king.

The princess was so pleased with her brooch that she, too, came to see Vaylan, and Vaylan raped her and sent her back to her father in disgrace, carrying Vaylan's child. On his island, working his smithy while leaning on his crutches, still mourning for his lost Swan-May, Vaylan waited for the king's vengeance, knowing that he had already taken his own.

No good ever comes of consorting with Elf-Mays, Andrea thought, and remembered how she'd failed to give Per his lucky kiss.

Toorkild came back and seated himself between

Andrea and Isobel, who began to talk.

"Vaylan was hamstrung," Isobel said. "And he was put on an island and set to work in a smithy, where the king wanted him to make rings and brooches and chains. But never another thing of that sort did Vaylan make. Instead he crawled all about the island, dragging his crippled legs and gathering up every feather he could find—gulls' feathers, swans' feathers, osprey feathers, hawk feathers. And all the feathers he found he made up, with lashing and glue, into a great pair of beautiful wings. He strapped them to his arms, because even if he was crippled, he still had a smith's strong back and arms. Away he flew, over the heads of the king and his soldiers, away from the island, over the western sea. Away Vaylan flew to the land of his Swan-May and her sisters, and he's there with them still."

The silence of the listeners was appreciative, even grateful. Toorkild put his arm around Isobel and kissed her cheek.

"That's how my mammy always told it," Isobel said. "That's how the Allyots tell it." And she smiled at Andrea, the Elf-May.

5

16th Side: The Ride

A REIVER'S MOON, full and bright, hung low over the hills and washed the sky gray with moonlight. It showed the ground in grays that imperceptibly shifted one into another, a hillock lighter here, a hollow darker there, deeper shadows all black. But men and horses knew the track to the ford well, having crossed and recrossed the ground a thousand times, and they went at a fast trot.

Fowl's jolting strength threw Per up out of the saddle to briefly grip the horse's shoulders with his knees, and as he touched the saddle, the power of Fowl's hindquarters threw him up again. At each rising, the shaft of the lance in his left hand slid in his grip and its butt pressed a little harder against the toe of his boot where it rested. "On!" Fowl's onward lunge strengthened and quickened. He needed no kick, only Per's voice.

Fowl's hooves thumped in the thick turf. Grass and scrub, barely seen in the dusk, skimmed past them. Around and behind them, the hooves of the other horses fell and fell with a thick drumming. There was the creaking of saddles and boots, the rattling of bits, the breathing of men and animals. Per was grinning, his heart and breathing fast, his attention on the shadow-tricked ground ahead.

The ground sloped to the water and the ford, becoming more broken with river stone. Fowl chose his own time to slow to a walk, and Per let him, loosing the reins so the horse could pick his own way, while his shoulders swayed and he swiveled at the waist with Fowl's movements. Patting the horse's neck, he told him he was good, good.

Fowl gave a long, shuddering snort and shook his head, jangling his bit and flurrying his long mane. Another horse and rider, black in the dusk, came close at his side and a second nudged at his tail. The running of the water rose to them, suddenly loud, and they smelled the river and felt its coolness in the air.

Per sang out:

> "My hob is swift-footed and sure,
> My sword hangs down at my knee;
> I never held back from a fight:
> Come, who dares meddle with me!"

From the dusk around him, from the black shapes of horses and riders, came quiet laughter. The horses, splashing, walked into the river.

"Eh, Per, dost reckon that lass—which one do I mean now?" That was Sim's voice.

"Janna!"

"Big Anna!"

"Wee Anna!" Other voices called out, as if to help Sim remember, the names of girls Per had courted in the past.

From behind Per, on his other side, came Ecky's

voice, underlaid by the rippling of water around rocks and the splashing of horses' legs. "Tha means the Elf-May, Sim!"

"Do I? Well, well. Dost think her might be glad to see thee back after this?"

"Her'll be so gladdened, I shouldn't wonder but her'll drag him off that hoss straight into bed."

Quiet laughter was all around Per now, letting him know how well they knew him and all his doings, even thoughts he imagined he had kept to himself. He tipped back his head, his face taking on a pained grin, and then looked to the side to see Sweet Milk laughing at him from within his helmet's shadows.

Sim, whose horse was already climbing the bank, looked over his shoulder and, making his voice lighter than usual, called, "Put tha feet up, Daddy. *I'll* lead the ride!"

More sniggers acknowledged the best joke of all. Per had long ago learned better than to show pique, but as the laughter died, he cupped his hand to his ear. "I hear the Grannams laughing!" Fowl reached the water's edge on the other side and bucked up onto dry land.

Sweet Milk brought his horse close to Fowl as they walked up the bank, reached out a long arm and slapped Per on the shoulder. It was only in the way of things, Sweet Milk thought, that the lad should want to impress the Elf-May and show he was as good as his daddy. Nobody ought to laugh too long at him for that.

Per kicked Fowl to the trot, and Sweet Milk kicked his horse to keep pace. Behind them, to a rolling thump of hooves on turf, the others came, following the track to the reived farm.

They saw the smoke and glare from the burning first. A golden light flowed over the hillsides ahead, lighting the underside of the hanging smoke, then dying to a sullen, red ember's glow before flaring again. Rounding a hill spur, they came in sight of the flames, a red-and-gold shining in the dark. They kicked the horses to a fresh trot.

The farm was surrounded by a bank and ditch, meant to discourage attack. They reined in close by the ditch, and the light of the burning house flicked over them and then withdrew. The heat tightened their skin. Outside the circle of firelight, the darkness was black.

It hadn't been a strong house: just one belonging to a poor crofter, the kind built in a morning. High, yellow flames burned on the collapsed mass of heather thatch, gnawing and crackling on the walls of brushwood, mud and turf. Ash and soot smut whirled down on them in showers of red sparks. Smoke fetched tears from their eyes, and the stink of burning wood and damp heather was thick and choking. The horses shied and fidgeted a little, but it wasn't the first burning they'd seen.

No one came to greet them. "Cast about," Per said to the man with the sleuthhound, and then kicked Fowl on around the edge of the ditch. Sweet Milk rode after him. They peered into the jumping shadows about the edge of the firelight, looking for any sign of the goodwife and bairns of the farm.

The crackling and brilliance of the flames, and the deep silence and darkness that underlay them, brought Per's spirits down. He looked at Sweet Milk, whose face was lit by the fire, and wondered what he was remembering. Per had always lived behind the stone walls of the tower, under the protection of his father's reputation and armed men. His home had never been burned down.

On the other side of the ditch they were clear of the smoke, and Per stood in his stirrups and raised a trumpet yell to echo from the hills: "Sterkarm!" Sweet Milk added his deeper bellow.

They waited while the echoes died, and the crackling and huffing of the fire became again the only sound. They yelled again, twice more, and echoes came back, thinly, from hills hidden in the darkness. But from the women and bairns of the farm nothing. Per's eyes smarted with tears, both of pity and anger. The Grannams had done this. . . .

"They've gone away to friends?" Per said, hoping Sweet Milk would agree. Sweet Milk kept silence and his usual grim expression.

A yelping and a shout came from the other side of the farm, and they kicked on their horses, riding back into the smoke. A flimsy wall fell, sending up a shower of red sparks and making Fowl spring sideways, stiff-legged. Per fought with him as he backed and shied, and he thought: They *dare* do this; the Grannams dare do this, so close to the tower! They think so little of us, they dare— The exhilaration he'd felt earlier was turning to rage. Every Grannam ought to be dug out and killed like a nest of rats except that, like rats, there were too many of them.

The sleuthhound was yelping and whining, running to and fro, its tail up. It had found the trail and was eager to follow. So was Per. Walking and trotting, the ride moved on behind the intent dog.

They half expected the trail to lead to the water's

edge, but instead it veered away from the river and was plainly making for one of the side valleys. Per reined in, standing in his stirrups as he looked up at the overhanging black mass of the hills. The dark sky above them was barely lighter. It could be that the Grannams wanted to lead them into that dark and narrow valley because they had laid an ambush there.

Per's mouth was clamped hard shut, his eyes wide as he stared into the dark. He breathed deep and felt close to trembling. Keen as he was to ride on, if he guessed wrongly here, he could get himself and every man with him killed. Or—nearly as bad—they could lose the Grannams and let them get away to boast that Sterkarm farms were easy targets.

He glanced around at the dim, dark shapes near him: the men, sitting their horses, waiting—impatiently, scornfully, he thought—for his decision.

Follow the Grannams into the valley, hoping that they were too intent on making their best speed to bother with an ambush? No. Even if he were killed, he couldn't bear the thought that Andrea and his mother and father might learn that he'd been so stupid.

Sending scouts to climb the slopes above the valley, to check for any sign of ambush, would mean waiting for the men to scramble up the steep slopes in the dark—and while they waited, the Grannams would be going on their way.

He sat back in his saddle, rose again in impatience, sat again. Fowl turned restively. Quicker for the whole party to climb to the moors above the valley, since that was where the Grannams were headed, but they'd lose the trail in the valley. The sleuthhound might be able to cast about and pick it up again, but they'd be lucky to find it once they'd left it.

No, better to follow the trail in the valley as far as they could. Even if they had to wait for the scouts, they could still travel faster than the Grannams, who were hampered with sheep. "Ecky! Sim!"

The men urged their horses close to Fowl. The animals tossed their heads and long manes a little, but they were herd mates, and soon calmed. Briefly, Per explained what he wanted the men to do, but was disconcerted and irritated by the way they grinned through their beards and glanced at each other while he talked.

Sweet Milk, watching and grinning himself, could see it was Per's new, wide-eyed earnestness that amused them—and all the others. Some long-lived jokes were being prepared, at Per's expense, for when they got back from the ride.

Sim and Ecky gathered up their reins. Ecky reached out and flicked his fingers against Per's chin, making him snatch back his head. Grinning, looking back over his shoulder, Ecky rode away after Sim.

Sweet Milk brought his horse close to Fowl and, when Per looked around, gave a barely noticeable nod. Sweet Milk looked forward, when this miserable business was over, to telling Toorkild that the lad could spot an ambush before he fell into it, and pick the right men for the job. Toorkild would fly up into the rafters with pride.

Per slipped down from Fowl's back, to spare the horse his weight for a little while. He peered into the darkness, searching for any sign of his scouts' movement. Around him other men dismounted. Some led their horses up and down. The cold became more noticeable as the waiting drew out.

Per fidgeted, poking bushes and tussocks with his lance, drawing his sword half from its scabbard and sliding it back again. In his mind he was with the scouts he'd sent forward, trying to gauge how far they'd traveled—and then with the Grannams, going forward at the slower pace of the stolen sheep. Had they reached the end of the valley yet? Had they climbed to the moors above? He wanted to bring back the farmer's sheep, and at least a few of the men who'd stolen them and burned his farm.

Fowl had been amusing himself by giving Per great buffets with his head, almost knocking him from his feet, but now he lifted his head, his ears up, and tugged at the reins about Per's arm. Somewhere behind them the sleuthhound growled. Some sound that the men couldn't yet hear had disturbed them.

Per swung back up into the saddle and leaned over Fowl's neck, patting the horse while he concentrated, listening. The slight shifting of horses around him, saddles creaking, the wind—and there! Horse hooves, coming on at a trot, with a jinking of bits and iron plates in jakkes. Riders.

"Behind us?" Per said, and looked wildly at Sweet Milk. He couldn't understand how Grannams could be behind them—unless they were a few lost stragglers. They would soon be prisoners then. He rose in his stirrups and looked around at the men. They needed no more instruction than that—all of them were riders. In an eye's blink, and with hardly a sound, every horse and man had moved close to trees and bushes, into hollows or close to rocks, which, in the confusing half darkness, would be enough to hide them.

They waited. Per's heart, at the thought that they might soon be fighting, was pumping harder, and his breath was coming fast, with an exhilarating mixture of dread and eagerness.

The louder sound of hooves on the soft ground—riders coming openly. And then the whimpering and snuffling of a hound. Per caught his breath, and then began to laugh in a series of gasps—the party behind them had a sleuthhound and was following a trail. They weren't Grannams then. Reivers had no use for hounds.

The dark shapes of horses and riders were glimpsed, some silhouetted against the light of Bedes Water. Per lifted his head and sang out:

"My hob is swift-footed and sure,
My sword hangs down at my knee—"

From the approaching riders came a laugh and the second half of the verse:

"I never held back from a fight:
Come, who dares meddle with me!"

It was Young Toorkild's voice, and Per's band rode out of hiding to join their friends, the horses snorting and kicking as they were brought together. "Whose men?"

"Gobby Per's. Whose men?"

"The May's, we."

Gobby's men greeted Per as he managed Fowl among the restless horses, searching for his uncle: "Has

Mammy let thee out, then?"

"Art keeping warm enough, May?"

"Nunkie's over here!"

Per was grinning under his helmet as he brought his horse alongside his uncle's, anxious to tell him everything he'd done because, he knew—little though it had been—that he'd done it well. "Daddy's-brother—"

Gobby reached out and patted his nephew's cheek, in place of the usual greeting kiss. Looking past Per, he called out, "Sweet Milk, what dost know?"

Per, startled, glanced toward Sweet Milk and then turned back to his uncle. "Daddy's-brother, I—"

Without looking at him, Gobby raised a gloved hand and gestured for him to be quiet. At Sweet Milk he nodded, waiting for an answer.

There was enough moonlight for Sweet Milk to see the snubbed and angry look on Per's face. He guided his horse toward Gobby through the press of other horses, trying to think of some way of telling Gobby that he was mistaken and Per was leading Toorkild's men. But Sweet Milk was better at knowing when to keep silent than at finding such clever words, and when Gobby asked, he had to answer. As briefly as he could, he told Gobby all they'd found and done. "It was Per's thinking—"

"Have scouts had time enough to get up there?" Gobby asked.

Sweet Milk considered, nodded. "Time enough."

Gobby lifted his arm high, signaled forward. "Then, on."

The ride followed Gobby on into the valley. Sweet Milk brought his horse alongside Per's. Per looked the other way. He was stinging and smarting from the

73

setdown his uncle had given him. In front of men who'd been following his orders, he'd been silenced like a boy who'd spoken out of turn. And Sweet Milk had gone along with it—so did Sweet Milk think he *had* been doing badly? Worse, Andrea would come to hear of it.

Their entrance into the valley was greeted by a gleam of moonlight and the waving of a longbow from high above on the hillside. No immediate danger of ambush then: a warning would have been yelled. They made their best speed up the valley, but it was a steep and narrow trail, winding among tumbled rocks, and often the best pace they could manage was a walk. They would do better when they reached the moors.

No ambush had been laid—perhaps the Grannams couldn't spare the men. As they reached the head of the steep valley, they disturbed a couple of sheep that went bounding away, black shapes in the darkness. They might be a couple the Grannams had lost during their climb. The Sterkarms scrambled, by the same steep sheep paths, up to the moor above. Per dismounted and led Fowl up, and reached the top panting and laughing.

Up there, in the moor wind, they were met by the scouts, and had to wait while the sleuthhounds cast about for the trail. The Grannams must have paused there too, to round up the sheep again after the climb.

"We'll catch them!" Per said to Sweet Milk, as he jumped up onto Fowl, lance in hand. Sweet Milk nodded and grinned. Per had already forgotten to sulk.

Sheep roamed the moor constantly, which confused the scent trail. The hounds cast about, rose on their hind legs to sniff the air, and then led off through scrub and heather until they struck one of the wide tracks that ran across the moor. They sniffed the ground and air again, and ran fast along the tracks. It seemed the Grannams were driving the sheep along the track as openly as if they'd been their own.

The track, a broad strip of grassy turf running through darker heather, shone white in the moonlight, and they pounded along it at a fast trot, the riders rising and falling, even urging the mounts to a canter when the moonlight was strong and the path showed smooth. The wind fluted against their helmets and chilled their hands and faces. Rolled blankets and wrapped longbows thumped against their backs.

Per kicked Fowl on and on, intent on staying near the head of the ride, where he could be into the fight before his uncle or cousins. He scanned the black and silvered land ahead, knowing that Fowl's every stride must be carrying them nearer to the Grannam ride. If they'd come this way, there must be sight of them soon.

Ahead the track split, the main branch going on across the moor but a right-hand branch, little wider than a sheep track, making off through the heather. The dogs were casting wide about the place where the tracks met, sniffing the air, sniffing the ground, running a little way along the main path but then coming back.

The leading riders reined in, waiting for the others to come up, waiting for the dogs to find the scent. Fowl was breathing hard, snorting and shaking his mane. Per patted him as he backed and stamped and, breathing deep himself, looked down and saw how pounded and trodden was the turf of the narrow track, and the scrub on either side of it.

That was the way they'd gone! The track led down

into a valley, where it would be easier to drive the sheep, and where they'd be hidden. What was more, the slant of the valley led toward the Grannam land. That was the way they'd gone! Waving his arm to call the others on, Per set Fowl at the narrow, right-hand track.

"Per! May!" It was a bellow that reached him above the noise of Fowl's hooves, of the lance slithering in his hand, of the creaking of his saddle, the metallic scratching of the overlapped plates sewn into his jakke. He reined in and turned Fowl, to see the dark mass of horsemen that had come up to the place where the tracks divided. Waving arms called him back.

He pointed on along the path, but saw the two horsemen who had begun to follow him walking away from him, returning to the ride.

"Per!" That was his uncle's voice. Gobby was standing in his stirrups, beckoning him with an angry sweep of his whole arm.

Remembering how Gobby had silenced him earlier, Per kicked Fowl on along the path—but Gobby was his uncle. Disobeying him meant disobeying his father too. The ramifications of the quarrel would go on and on. "God's shit!" Per reined in and swung Fowl around in a circle, and had to spend a few moments fighting with Fowl, who disliked such indecisiveness.

"Where wert going?" Gobby demanded, when he trotted back to the main party.

"After the—"

"Quiet!" Gobby had not wanted or expected an answer. His own sons would have known that. He kicked his horse forward, to lead the ride down the broader track.

"The Grannams went that way!" Per pointed down the narrow path with his lance. A rider near him—his cousin Wat—murmured his name warningly.

Gobby turned in his saddle. "Tha've a better nose than the hounds, hast tha?"

"My eyes tell me! That way's all trodden down. That's where they went!"

Young Toorkild, the eldest of Gobby's sons, pointed to the main track and said, "That's the best trodden. Odds on they went that way."

Young Toorkild was almost three years older than Per, and since infancy had tormented his younger cousin by claiming always to be right because he was older, and he often *wasn't*. To see Gobby nod solemnly at Young Toorkild's words was infuriating.

"That track's *always* worn," Per said. "It's used all the time. This one isn't. *Look* at it, Clod-head! It's—"

"God's arse!" Gobby said, astonished. He swung his lance around in his hand so it came butt upward. "Will I shut tha mouth for thee?" He glared at Per, expecting the boy to look away.

Per held his uncle's stare, trying to think of something that would convince him, but Gobby's face grew angrier, and the lance was still raised in threat. Gobby would do no more than tap him with it, but it would be shaming in front of everyone. Per looked aside.

Gobby lowered his lance and said, "Tha'rt nesh. Nesh! Like any son of Bella Hob's-daughter."

Per's head came up again, his eyes wide and his mouth opening. Nesh!—soft, like overripe fruit. Someone would tell Andrea about that.

From Gobby's other side, Sweet Milk's voice came

through the dark. "Forgive me, Master Sterkarm, but lad's right. About path."

There was a low grumble of agreement from all the tower men that took Per by surprise and soothed him a little.

Gobby was ill pleased. "Two men," he said, "to take the little path."

Per walked Fowl onto the narrow, right-hand path, silently offering to be one of the men who rode that way. He wondered if he dared call his own men, the tower men, after him. Would they obey him if he did? He couldn't believe that Sweet Milk would disobey Gobby and follow him, and if Sweet Milk wouldn't, none of the others would.

Gobby saw that Per was again on the narrow path and called out, "By God, that boy is trying my patience! Per! Get back here."

"Why?" Per said.

Gobby rose in his stirrups. "Bring thine 'oss here by me." As Per's mouth opened, he said, "*Don't argue!*" Sitting in his saddle again, he glowered as Per walked Fowl back to his uncle. Others pulled their horses aside to make way for him. As Per reined in, his face furious, Gobby said, "This is no child's game."

"Nay," Per said. "But that's—" Gobby raised his gloved hand, threatening a cuff. Per broke off and sat his horse with lowered head. Not sulking, Sweet Milk guessed, but seething.

Gobby, grinning through his beard with irritation, called out the names of the men who were to ride along the narrower path and return to the main party if they saw the Grannams.

Per watched the two horsemen trot away into the dark and again looked around for his own men—but he didn't dare, he didn't dare! If he called his men to follow him, and they didn't, he could never lead them again.

Gobby motioned the ride forward along the main path, glancing aside to make sure Per was staying with him. Sweet Milk, following, wondered if Gobby had noticed that his ride was dividing into two. The men of the tower were all behind or beside Per. He was himself riding close beside the lad.

The horses trotted, walked, trotted again. Per loved the rise and fall of the trot but now resented every stride that carried them farther along the track and farther from the Grannams. Every time they reined in for a breather, he stood in his stirrups, peering into the dark, trying to see if the two scouts were returning.

The Grannams hadn't been so far ahead, and they'd been driving slow sheep. The Sterkarms had been riding fast. It was getting on for the middle of the night. Per wanted to ask his uncle: So where are the Grannams? He kept quiet, not wanting to sound like a whining child, but he struck his clenched fist on his own thigh, thinking: They'll get away, they'll get *away*!

From the dark mass of riders behind them, a voice called out, "Which road was it they went again?" There was laughter, mainly from Toorkild's men. Per knew the voice for Davy's. Gobby pretended not to have heard.

The ride was moving forward at a fast walk when a cry came carrying across the moor: "*Sterk*arm!" The soft, rhythmic thump of hooves followed, and Per caught sight of movement in the dark.

Their two scouts were returning to them with

enough urgency to risk crossing the rough, open moor instead of keeping to the safer tracks. Per rose in his stirrups and sat, rose and sat, grinning without knowing he was. Fowl, thinking that Per had something interesting in mind, paced with his front feet and skittered half in a circle, crowding other horses. That drew a glare from Gobby, and Per reined Fowl in, patting his neck.

Gobby rode forward to meet the scouts, and Per kicked Fowl after him, needing no prompting now to stay at his uncle's side. Pointing behind him, the first rider called out, "Grannams!" The sheep had, indeed, been driven along the narrower path, and the path led down into another valley, and there were the Grannams with the reived flock, getting farther away all the time.

Gobby turned and saw that it was Per beside him. Per stared into his uncle's eyes, refusing to look away.

Gobby stood in his stirrups and waved, signaling the whole ride to follow him, and then he struck across the moor, leaving the track behind. He set a dangerous pace too, a trot over rough and ill-lit ground, thickly grown with heather and bilberry that concealed holes and dips, but it was either risk the horses' legs and the men's necks, or lose the Grannams.

All around was the rolling thud and thump of the hooves, the clattering of the jakkes, the grunting of the men, the whisk of the brush as the horses moved through it. Per's knees jolted into Fowl's hard shoulders every time Fowl's haunches threw him up, his own breathing was loud to his ears, and he was dizzy with squinting into the blurred and moving dark. And then they were on the heights above the valley. The wind, moaning past them, blew down the slope. The moonlight silvered the hills opposite, touching rock faces and falling streams.

From below came the din of the driven sheep: a harsh, frantic baaing, never stopping. It came from a little behind them. Gobby signaled the ride to halt, beckoned to Sweet Milk, and dismounted.

Per slid down from Fowl and gave the reins to Ecky, who said, "Thou'll catch it." Per followed his uncle—he had, after all, been ordered to stay at Gobby's side. Gobby swung around and saw him, and Per stood still, waiting to be told to go back. But Gobby ignored him, and went on edging his way forward over the awkward ground.

A face of broken rock leaned out over the valley. They went out onto it, careful of where they put their feet in the tricky black-and-gray light, and crouched among the corners of rock, the ferns and rock-rooted bushes, peering down into the valley.

There was little to see except darkness and shadows. Even where the moonlight fell, it showed nothing of which they could be certain. The helmets of the Grannams, like their own, had been darkened with sheep's fat and soot and gave hardly a gleam. Their horses were mostly black, and so were the sheep, all disappearing into the dark.

But the sheep could be heard, as could the occasional shout. The Grannams were down there, sauntering coolly through Sterkarm country, driving Sterkarm sheep. Per, lying flat on his belly and peering down, caught sight of movement and clenched his fists.

Gobby slapped a hand on Per's shoulder. "Thou wert right all along."

Per was startled by the apology. Immediately, he loved Gobby again.

"No easy to get down there," Sweet Milk said. He was looking up and down the valley, at the way the hills folded. "But can be done."

"Take thine and get down behind 'em," Gobby said. The din of the sheep, filling the Grannams' ears, should cover the noise of their approach, and if the darkness wasn't enough cover, then the folds in the hills would hide them. "We'll get down in front of 'em."

They talked of signals. A man of Sweet Milk's party was to sit his horse where he could see both bands. When both were in position to start descending the slopes, he would raise his lance and then ride to join Sweet Milk again. On reaching the valley floor, the first party to find itself ready to attack would do so, raising the cry of "Sterkarm!" The other party would attack as soon after that as it could, in silence.

Sweet Milk turned, half crouching, to go back to the ride and call together the men of his party. Per, thinking all forgiven, made to follow. Gobby stopped him. "Stay with me."

"Why?" Per said.

Gobby gritted his teeth. "Let that be the last time tha says 'why?' to me. When I tell thee summat, do it!"

Sweet Milk had gone into the dark. Per followed his uncle back to the ride, jittery with anger. He should be with his own people, not trailing along behind Gobby, and he suspected that his uncle meant to order him to stay on the hillside, taking no part in the fight, like a boy making his first ride.

For a heart's beat the idea appealed. It would be no

fault of his and, up on the height, no sword could slice off half his face or axe chop through his arm and break its bone. But that feeling passed with the heartbeat. If others fought, he had to fight. He wanted to get a swipe at the Grannams for the farm they'd burned. And the story taken back to the tower had to be that the May had fought, and fought well.

Gobby swung up onto his horse. Instead of going to Fowl, Per went to stand at his knee, looking up at him. "Father's-brother?"

Gobby looked down. "What now?"

"I'm sad for what I said, Father's-brother." Even though he'd been right. But Gobby deserved an apology for having admitted that Per had been right.

"So tha shouldst be," Gobby said. "Mount up."

"Father's-brother?"

"*What?*"

"Will you be so kind, may I go with Sweet Milk?"

Gobby leaned down from his saddle, making the leather creak. "Nay. I'm no thy father. Tha don't get all thee ask from me. Now mount up!"

Per laid hold of his uncle's knee, looking up at him. "You'll let me fight! Be so kind!"

Gobby knocked his hand away. "Thine 'oss!" His exasperation betrayed that, much as he would like to thwart Per, he was not going to.

Per ran to Fowl and mounted, as scared of the coming fight as he was relieved that he was to be part of it. As he settled into the saddle, the horseman higher up the trail, dimly seen against the sky, lifted his lance and rode away. Gobby kicked his horse on, leading his band along the narrow sheep path and down into the valley.

The grass was short and slick under the horses' hooves, and the slope quickly became steeper. Per was among the first to drop down from his horse's back. Keeping hold of his lance, he clung to Fowl's neck and mane and let his feet slither as the horse picked the way down. Fowl brought them both safely to the valley floor.

Even down there, the ground was broken and rough. Gobby's men were assembling in the shelter of a hill spur. Per jumped up onto Fowl's back again and stroked and patted his neck, leaning forward to whisper reassurances and kiss the rough, dusty coat. He took long, deep breaths to steady the beating of his own heart. In the dark were the blurred masses of boulders fallen from the hillside. The valley floor was thick with them. Not a good place for a charge. The fighting was going to be close.

The constant braying of the reived sheep was louder as the first of them rounded the hill spur. Fowl stamped and shifted, lifting Per up and down like a boat on swelling water. Per, hauling at breath, passed his lance to his right hand and wiped the palm of his left on the top of his leather boot. He drew his sword half from its scabbard, making sure it drew easily, before taking a fresh grip on his lance with his left hand.

Through the dark he glimpsed the bobbing shapes of the sheep and, behind them, the first dark mass of a horse and rider.

"*Sterk*arm!" The yell echoed from the hills. A horse in front of Per sprang forward, and Per felt Fowl's strength gather and rise under him as Fowl, without waiting for Per's order, followed. Per leaned forward and swung down his lance to the ready.

At the noise and onward rush of the Sterkarms, the sheep broke and bounded wildly every way, bleating ever more frantically. The Grannams yelled and swung their horses around, or swung their lances down. There was trampling and horses' squeals, cries of warning and surprise, smacks and crashes of blows.

Per, seeing a broad Grannam back turned to him, drove his lance head squarely at its center. The jar knocked him back in his saddle, knocked breath from him, and sent Fowl to his haunches. Per's feet were braced against the stirrups, the lance shaft and the iron plates of his jakke bruising his arm and side.

The lance head clanged against the metal plates in the Grannam's jakke, shoving him forward onto his horse's neck, but didn't unseat him. Reeling, he struggled to get upright in his saddle again, trying, at the same time, to turn his horse, to use his own lance against Per.

Per drew back his lance and took aim, driving the point down at the man's hip, where the jakke ended, more with the intent of toppling him from his horse than injuring him. The lance head entered the man's thigh—Per knew it by the resistance and then the yielding of the flesh as the point entered, and by the wild yell torn from the man. Per kicked at Fowl: "On!" Arms waving, the Grannam fell from his saddle.

Per twisted his lance as the man's weight dragged it through his gloved hand, and it came free. His own hair moved under his helmet in fear of the unseen blow he felt coming at him from behind, but he reversed his lance and whacked the Grannam's horse on the rump with the butt end. The horse bounded away, the wounded Grannam yelling and dangling from the saddle.

Per wrenched Fowl around, pressing himself low against the horse's neck, but no one was threatening him. As he rose in the saddle again, he was gasping for breath and sweat was running down his face from under his helmet. The darkness of the narrow valley was an uproar of bleating and shouting, a stink of sheep and blood, a thumping and panting, a din of iron, all echoing dismally between the hills.

The fight was already ending, the din dying away, the press of horses slackening. A brightening of the moon showed Grannams surrounded, threatened by lances. They were throwing down their weapons and calling out their ransom prices, hoping to save their lives. Per threw back his head and filled his lungs. He'd come through unscathed. A few bruises, nothing more.

Reining in Fowl, he rose in his stirrups, peering about for any of his own tower men. And then he thought of how the story would be told back at the tower and realized that he hadn't done enough. One man toppled from his saddle wasn't much to set against the burning farm— or the dressing-down Gobby had given him. Would Andrea be impressed with one man downed? Kicking Fowl, he guided him around the knot of horsemen and prisoners, hoping for some unfinished skirmish.

His eye was caught by movement farther down the valley. Horsemen, flitting through the shifting moonlight, going recklessly fast over the rough ground, two of them. Grannams for sure—escaping! He raised his bloody lance, yelled, "Sterkarm!" and kicked Fowl after them.

Most Sterkarms were busy with the prisoners. If they heard the call, they left it to others to answer. It was

Sweet Milk, riding down from his end of the valley, where his share of the skirmish was finished, who saw the chase of riders. Rising in his stirrups, he recognized the pursuing rider by his movements, by the lance in his left hand.

Sweet Milk cursed, broke off, yelled, "The tower!" Looking around, and seeing few taking any interest, he changed the shout to "The May!" A couple of horses were kicked toward him. He pointed down the valley with his lance, kicking on his horse. After him came Sim, Davy, Ecky and Hob.

As his body was jarred by the hard ride, Sweet Milk tried to watch the rough and rock-strewn ground ahead of his horse, and watch the chase too. Somewhere at the back of his mind was a grudge that he had to stir himself to this when he'd thought the worst of it was over.

The Grannams were still ahead, but Per was catching them. Both would turn on him. Sweet Milk felt a desperation, a sense of reaching to catch something he knew was going to fall through his fingers and smash. Filling his lungs, he yelled, "Per!" He wasn't heard.

The leading Grannam set his horse at the steep hillside; if there was a track there, Sweet Milk couldn't see it. The second tried to follow, but his horse balked, slipped back, fell and rolled.

Sweet Milk saw Per set Fowl at the slope, intent on chasing the escaping Grannam whose horse was, with difficulty, scrambling toward the hilltop. One Grannam wasn't worth the risk. Sweet Milk filled his lungs to call Per back again, but before he had the breath, he glimpsed a man on foot running nimbly up the slope toward Per: the Grannam from the fallen horse, unhurt but with sword upraised.

A horse passed Sweet Milk, racing. Ecky, with lance leveled. Sweet Milk yelled, *"Per!"*

Per heard only the rattle of stones dislodged by the Grannam above him, saw only the frightened backward glances of the man, which urged him on. The unhorsed man he'd forgotten. He kicked Fowl again, who disliked being alone, without other familiar horses around him, and was unwilling to climb the difficult slope. He kept turning his head back to the valley floor, and Per pulled his head around, kicked him, urged him on, whacked his rump with the butt of his lance, set on taking his own prisoner, a man Gobby would have let escape.

He didn't hear Sweet Milk yelling, and only saw the swoop of the sword blow from the corner of his eye when it was too late to avoid it. Down the blade came, hard as a cudgel blow but with a cutting edge—and it felt like a cudgel blow, hot and bruising, when it hit his thigh above the top of his boot. He yelled out in sheer surprise, though a sharper cry was pulled from him when the sword blade was dragged free of his flesh.

Sweet Milk heard the cries, saw the sword dragged back and raised for another blow. Then Ecky's lance skewered the Grannam low in the back, below his jakke's edge, and took him to the ground. Shouting approval, coming up hard and turning his horse aside from the slope only at the last moment, Sweet Milk drove his own lance home, the blow jarring through him.

The dizziness of fright and pain cleared from Per's head, and he realized that he was still alive and still in the saddle, and so couldn't be badly hurt, despite the blood. The slightest cuts bled most anyway. Looking up, he saw the Grannam above him, struggling on the slope. He could still be captured. Per's own heart was racing, pounding, urging him on. He whacked Fowl's rump and kicked him. The kick hurt his leg, but not much. "On!"

Sweet Milk left his lance in the Grannam and jumped from his horse to run up the slope toward Per, scrambling with his hands where it was steep. He knew from his own experience that deep wounds often felt like nothing more than a hard blow, especially if taken in hot blood. The lad might hardly know he'd been hurt yet. Reaching the narrow path where Fowl was shaking his head and refusing to move, Sweet Milk caught at the bridle.

Fowl had seen Sweet Milk coming, and smelled him, and knew him. Of the two, Per was the more startled by Sweet Milk's sudden springing up, and raised his lance.

"Sterkarm! Sweet Milk!"

The lance was lowered. "Out the way!" Per kicked Fowl again, ignoring the pain in his leg. Fowl jumped on the path, rattling his bit. Sweet Milk, buffeted by Fowl's head, staggered and almost fell down the slope. He clambered onto the path above the horse, shouting, "Thou'rt hurt!"

Per's own yells deafened him to Sweet Milk. He knew only that Sweet Milk was in his way. He swung his lance around and threatened Sweet Milk with the butt end.

From up the valley came an echoing shout of "Sterkarm!" as Gobby called them back. Hearing it, Per gave Fowl another kick. It was Ecky, scrambling up the slope, who got Per's attention by slapping at his wounded leg and then holding up his hand, black with blood. Per looked down and saw the leg of his breeches, wet and black, and the moonlight catching the lips of the wide wound. He looked up and saw the Grannam disappearing over the slope above, and tried yet again to urge Fowl on, but now he knew the pain in his leg was from something more than a slight cut. Sweet Milk grasped Fowl's bridle and firmly turned the horse off the path and down the slope. Fowl nimbly and gratefully found his own way down.

Per wiped tears from his eyes, pushing up his helmet and smearing blood across his face. The tears weren't of pain—he felt little—but of anger. He'd been bested, cut, and he'd lost his prisoner. Sweet Milk's fault! Sweet Milk and Ecky, getting in his way . . . He knew, though anger wouldn't yet allow him to admit it, that his own carelessness had been the fault. He'd assumed the unhorsed man was no further danger and hadn't been enough on guard. The other riders came circling closer and their anxious faces, peering at him, made him wish them all a hundred miles away and himself alone. But he was glad they were there.

Gobby yelled again. Sweet Milk, down at Fowl's side, said, "Shut tha gob, Gobby."

Per surprised himself by laughing, and Sweet Milk looked up, grinning. "Let's look at this." He shoved Fowl around until Per's wounded leg was in the best of the moonlight. Even so, it was hard to see—and Fowl kept turning his head, nudging at Per's foot and Sweet Milk's arms. Fowl knew something was wrong. Ecky came and held the horse's head.

Sweet Milk squinted and felt around the wound, making Per gasp and shift in the saddle. "God's teeth! It didn't hurt—"

"It'll hurt plenty," Sweet Milk said. Even in the poor light he could tell it was the worst he'd feared when he'd seen the blow go home. Not a sidelong slash that would have lifted a flap of flesh, but a straight-on, downward cut that, like as not, had gone to the bone. "It's deep," he said, while thinking: There'll be no stitching that. It'll fester. Jesus, it'll cripple him. The bleeding was slow— that was something to be thankful for. Black blood dripped to the ground and down Fowl's flank. Sweet Milk thought of all the miles they had to go before reaching home. The leg would be working all the way.

Sweet Milk unslung his bedroll from his back and crouched beside Fowl to open it. Inside he had some old rags, for bandages.

Sim and Hob came up on Fowl's other side, on horse-back. "Here, lad," Hob said. "That's who tha've to thank." He held up, by the hair, the head of the man who'd made the wound. Sim was wagging the hand that had struck the blow.

Per looked at the head. He knew its face, and his shoulders flinched in a shudder. "Jem," he said. If it hadn't been for Sweet Milk and Ecky, his own head, hacked from his body, could easily have been dangling from someone's hand.

"We've got the sword—for tha mammy," Hob said.

Sweet Milk, as he folded cloth into a pad, shook his head. Like many others, Hob believed that if Isobel washed the sword blade that had cut Per's leg, and rubbed it with ointment, it would heal the wound. But Hob hadn't seen how deep the slash was. Sweet Milk pressed the pad against the wound and held it in place. Fowl stood like a rock. "Hold it," he said to Per, and bound the pad in place with a second strip of cloth, slipping it between Per's leg and Fowl's side.

"If tha'd hit me with that butt end," he said, looking up at Per, "I'd have had thee off there and knocked seven colors out o' thee. Tha knows that, don't tha?"

Per laughed. Laughter came easily; he felt dizzy and lightheaded, as if drunk.

"Try to keep it still," Sweet Milk said, and remounted his own horse, which Davy had caught for him. His own bruises were beginning to burn and ache. The metal plates of his jakke had been driven into him in several places. He thought longingly of his safe bed.

They rode gently back along the valley to rejoin Gobby. Sweet Milk watched Per as they went. There seemed nothing wrong with the boy—except, maybe, he was a bit quiet. Fowl, stepping gently, obediently followed the other horses, so that Per had no need even to kick him on. But the wound was a bad one.

The other end of the valley was full of the harsh baaing of sheep as Gobby's men tried to gather them in the dark. Gobby himself came riding to meet them. Before he reached them, Ecky and Sim had called out, angrily, that the May was hurt.

Per turned his face aside, looking down, as Gobby nudged his horse close to see the bandage on Per's thigh. The white linen showed, a blur in the dark, but was already blackening. "Badly?" Gobby asked.

Per said, "Nay." He wouldn't have told his uncle of the wound, and wished the others hadn't.

Sweet Milk said, "It's deep."

Gobby said nothing. Per, whose temper had already been rising in expectation of his uncle's anger, was puzzled by his silence and said to Fowl, "Walk on." Fowl, on his best behavior, walked forward without a kick.

"Where art going now?" Gobby demanded.

"To help with sheep."

"To help with—!" Gobby said. "Stay there and don't move! I wish tha'd half as much sense as a bloody sheep."

Per reined in, feeling mutinous and comforted. The cut to his leg couldn't be that bad, if Gobby was still yelling at him. He would be able to ride back to the tower, and have something to boast about. Something to worry Andrea with.

Gobby was silent, drawing his thumb along his lower lip again and again as he stared at Per. Sweet Milk, guessing his thoughts, said, "There's Davy Gibb's place." It was a small farm, little more than a hut, but it was within an hour's ride. Per could be left there while his blood settled. A litter could be rigged at the tower and sent out to fetch him the next day.

Gobby's eyes flicked to Sweet Milk's, showing that he'd been thinking the same thing. He went on stroking his lower lip.

"I can ride," Per said. The cut muscles were starting to smart, but he could stand it. He wanted to ride through the tower's gate, not be carried through it.

Gobby ignored him but shook his head at Sweet Milk, who nodded in agreement. It was autumn. Reivers were riding every night. Huts and shepherds offered no protection against them. Any Grannam ride would know Big Toorkild's Per May. They'd probably take him for ransom, but there was always the chance they'd kill him, in revenge for the Grannams killed on this ride. Or sell him to the citizens of Carloel, who'd hang him.

Sweet Milk thought of offering to escort Per ahead of the sheep, at a faster pace—but it would be no use. A fast pace, over the rough, broken ground that would take them directly to the tower, would put an even greater strain on the wounded leg. And there was no knowing whether other Grannam rides were out. Two men, one wounded, would be easily taken.

Gobby dragged his thumb along his lip again. He had three sons of his own—two to spare, he joked—but he wouldn't have given up any one of them. He could not, and would not, take the smallest risk with his brother's one tup lamb. The ride, with its armed men and its slow-moving sheep, was the safest place for Per to be.

Sighing, Gobby looked at Sweet Milk, and gave the slightest of nods toward Per. Sweet Milk needed no such order.

Gobby turned his horse, said to his nephew, "Stay!" and rode away to check on the gathering of the sheep.

Per sat his horse. The helmet on his head felt heavy, and the lance awkward in his hand. His thoughts kept circling around the man he'd stuck in the thigh, and the head that had been held up to him, with Jem Grannam's face. He neither thought nor felt anything very clearly, except a fuddled desire to laugh.

Sweet Milk, sitting his horse a little behind Per, watched him while, in his head, he rode every stride of the long ride home.

6

16th Side: Lunch with the Sterkarms

WINDSOR DROVE HIS scarlet Range Rover up the ramp and onto the platform before the Tube. Bryce, who had been waiting for him, opened the passenger door and got in. "All set?" Windsor said. "Let's give 'em hell!"

The green light beside the Tube lit up, and Windsor drove forward into the hanging screen of plastic strips, which rattled against the car and slithered over its windshield. Then they were into the Tube, its white tiling vaguely reminding Bryce of a urinal. In addition to the light filtering through the screens at either end, there were cat's-eyes in the road and lights set into the roof overhead.

Going through the Tube was bizarrely mundane, Bryce always found. Your brain told you that you were doing something impossible, exciting, strange, wonderful—but your eyes and ears told you that you were only driving through an old road tunnel. There was a fixed, tarmacked road under the wheels, and the curved walls were covered with tiles, pierced with maintenance panels. There was no sensation of it spinning. Crossing from one dimension to another, and going back five hundred years in time, took roughly a minute or less. Though he supposed that minute actually lasted five hundred years.

The Dow-Jones Index was being read on the radio, and Windsor was humming some unrecognizable tune to show how unimpressed he was. Bryce made a guess at where the center of the Tube was, the point at which they would vanish from the twenty-first century, and gripped the edges of his seat, bracing himself in case something went wrong and his atoms were disassembled. In fact, they left the 21st a little later than he guessed—the transition was marked by the buzzing of static as the radio cut out. There were no other strange noises, no bump, no eerie sensation. The roadway and the tunnel simply continued smoothly on, until the car was brushing through the hanging strips on the other side.

Windsor braked the car on the platform just outside the Tube. Bryce looked through the windshield at the rutted mud of the compound below, surrounded by its high chain-link fence and, beyond that, the moorland hills of the Sterkarms' country. Five hundred years had just been sidestepped. They were also about twenty miles farther north than the spot they'd left in the 21st—Bryce wasn't exactly sure why. There'd been talk of wishing to avoid the small sixteenth-century city of Carloel, where everyone's business was too readily known to everyone else, but also technical talk of a "temporal-spatial dislocation."

What was truly hard to grasp was that the hills before him, though solid and in every way real, were not in the same world as the one he'd just left.

A security guard stepped out of the office alongside the platform and stooped to look at them. Recognizing his immediate boss, Bryce, and Bryce's superior, Mr. Windsor, he smiled and waved them on down the ramp.

Windsor drove down the ramp and across the small compound to the gate. A guard opened it for them, dividing the big FUP logo, and then joining it again as he closed and locked the gate behind them.

Windsor stopped the car, a great shiny, metallic scarlet box on the green hillside. "How long are we going to have to sit here?"

Bryce smiled. "The Sterkarms don't have watches."

"They have the ones they stole from our geologists," Windsor said.

"Yeah, well . . . I told young Andrea nine thirty—"

"Which it is now, and there's not a sign of them."

"We'll just have to be patient," Bryce said.

Windsor tutted and got out of the car, slamming the door. The metallic sound echoed back from the hills. As Bryce got out of the car into the wind, he had a feeling of immense space opening around him. He joined Windsor in leaning against the car's hood. "What a view," Windsor said.

Before he admired the view, Bryce took his pistol from its shoulder holster and checked it over. It was his own and, unlike those carried by the security guards, it was loaded. He didn't think there was any chance he would need it—if he had seriously thought that he might, neither he nor Windsor would be here—but if anything did go wrong, he was prepared. He noticed Windsor smirking at him and waited for some crack about playing soldiers. Windsor was one of those who thought that, because they weren't like him, the Sterkarms were nothing more than overgrown, rather dim and naughty children.

But it was a wonderful view. The FUP compound was built about halfway up a hillside above Bedesdale, a long, wide valley cut deeply through the moors. Long hill spurs, now from this side, now that, sloped down from the hills toward the river of Bedes Water. Between the spurs were narrower side valleys, making the shape of Bedesdale a long, intricate zigzag. It was impossible to see very far up or down the valley, because the long hill spurs blocked the view.

But from where they stood, just outside the gates of the FUP compound, it was possible to catch a glimpse of Toorkild's tower. Look across the width of the valley to the hills on the other side—and look high up, high on the shoulder of the nearest hill spur. There, just poking above the ridge of the spur, was the top of the tower. It was actually built on the slope of another hill, farther away than the one that blocked most of it from view, but it stood tall enough to give the Sterkarms' watchman a clear view up and down the valley. The Sterkarms had a better view of the FUP compound than FUP had of them. As the bird flew, the distance between them probably wasn't much more than a mile, but by the time you'd climbed down the hillside and over the rough valley floor and forded the river, and climbed up the opposite hill, you'd have been walking for a good hour and a half. And then you had to walk back. Andrea said she'd never been fitter.

It was rough country, but fresh and beautiful. Above them, the sky was thick with clouds moving so fast before the wind that patches of clear blue were torn open, letting through the sun. The sunlight shone in patches on the hillside around them, and on the slopes across the valley, gleaming on red bracken, lighting green and tawny grass—and then vanished as the break in the clouds closed, leaving the hillsides shadowed, grayed. But somewhere else other patches of sunlight were dancing briefly before closing.

Scores of little streams were falling down from the hills in silver streaks, to join the silver of Bedes Water as it ran down the valley. Here and there were stands of trees, pretty birches mostly. Some of them, the ones highest on the hills, where the wind blew coldest, were beginning to turn yellow.

Bryce was never sure if he imagined it, but the details of everything, even outcrops of rock and bushes on the opposite hillside, seemed pin sharp, as if there were a lens in front of his eyes, magnifying things and intensifying colors. There seemed to be more tints to the colors here than there were at home in the 21st. More greens, subtle but distinct: rich greens, luminous pale greens, golden greens, tawny greens. In the stone, the bracken, the trees, there were tawnies, russets, grays, ochers, purples—and all the colors seemed to softly vibrate somehow, to shimmer.

It was the air. It was so clean, so clear. His eyes were no longer looking through a filter of smog and dust. Behind them, the bright-yellow paint of the office was as bright and fresh as when new, and the concrete of the Tube was pure white.

Windsor let out a long sigh. "People are going to pay big money for this. Just listen to that silence!"

The silence was, indeed, more a presence than an absence. It made you realize that what passed for silence in the twenty-first century was more often a din of disregarded sound: of traffic, and people talking nearby, of radios and televisions, of piped music, of machinery running. The silence of the 16th's hills seemed to travel to them from miles away, to coddle their ears in fold upon fold of silence. When there was a sound—when a sudden gust of wind flapped their coats, or a sheep bleated miles away—it was startling. Then they realized how much the silence had calmed them, without their being aware of it, how it had slowed their hearts and made them draw their breath more deeply.

"Yes," Windsor said, sighing again. "How can you beat this for a get-away-from-the-rat-race vacation? We'll be able to ask any price."

"Not if the Sterkarms are going to keep up their little games."

"Oh, I can deal with the Sterkarms," Windsor said. "God, they can't even write their names. And it's early days. By the time we get vacations here under way, the Sterkarms will be walking to heel and fetching sticks, don't worry."

They're ill to tame, the border men. . . . Bryce, who'd seen more of the Sterkarms than Windsor, tried to picture this. He said, "It's a shame we'll spoil it all."

"We're not going to spoil anything," Windsor said. "We'll improve it. Improve it and preserve it, not spoil it."

"But coal mining," Bryce said. "And drilling for oil. And tourists are going to want electricity—it all adds up to pollution, doesn't it?"

"You're still in the past!" Windsor said. "Catch up! Cold fusion! Clean, cheap power!"

"But isn't there a—"

"It's perfectly safe," Windsor said. "One hundred percent. And the pollution at home was built up over two hundred years. Way back then, they didn't care how much mess they made—but we've learned a lot. We know about filters and safeguards—and we've got a big incentive to keep this place clean! Money! All this . . ." He waved a hand at the landscape spread before and below them. "It's all money in the bank. Are those sheep or goats?"

A little troop of animals had appeared from a fold of the hillside below them and went trotting past, following a narrow track down into the valley. They had long, shaggy coats of wiry hair rather than fleece, black with the odd rusty brown streak. All of them had at least two horns—several had four, in a sort of star burst.

"They're sheep," Bryce said. "They do keep goats, though—for their milk."

"Free-range, organically bred meat on the hoof," Windsor said. "Unpolluted by insecticides, antibiotics or radioactive fallout. That's why they're so tiny and skinny, of course, but the health-food mob won't mind that. The health-food nutters are just going to eat this place up. See that river down there?"

"Water," Bryce murmured. The Sterkarms called it "a water," not a river, and he liked the phrase.

"Fresh trout, fresh salmon, freshwater mussels—and oysters! All plentiful, unpolluted and cheap. Freshwater pearls! Vast shoals of fish in the sea, not just oil!" He spread his arms wide. "Their fishing grounds haven't been vacuumed clean of fish by factory ships until there's nothing left but sardines—there're still whales out there! Do you know how much ambergris is worth an ounce? No heavy-metal pollution in these seas. No mad cow disease in the food chain. Fruit, grain, vegetables, all organically grown."

"There'll be a big demand," Bryce said, and watched Windsor nod. He was wondering himself how long it would be before FUP quietly introduced growth hormones and insecticides and artificial fertilizers into the 16th, to maximize production. How long before they imported big fat modern sheep to replace the hardy but small and skinny Sterkarm sheep. The Sterkarms themselves would probably welcome every innovation once they saw that they would gain from it, so how could you say it was wrong? There was no way he could stop it from happening anyway.

"Whiskey!" Windsor said. "Can you imagine the ad campaign for a whiskey made here? All you'd have to do is list all the pollutants in every make of whiskey made 21st side, just because it's made in the 21st, never mind how special their 'pure, natural spring water' is. And forget 'twelve years old' and 'twenty-five years old'—ours'd be five hundred years old! You wouldn't be able to keep the shelves stocked. I tell you, this place is a gold mine. But here comes the grit in our Vaseline."

Bryce had already spotted the approaching party of horses and people. They were on the near side of Bedes Water, having crossed the ford out of sight, and were just rounding the corner of the nearest hill spur.

"We'll go and meet them," Windsor said, and got

back into the Range Rover. Bryce climbed in beside him. The Range Rover was going to be a shock to the Sterkarms, but it wouldn't do any harm to impress them with the power of the Elves. Slowly, in four-wheel drive and first gear, they lurched down the rough slope.

Andrea was plodding along on foot, having walked all the way from the tower, as she always did. The Sterkarms had offered her a horse many times, but she didn't like horses much, and liked the idea of falling off them even less. Toorkild, from good manners, had dismounted and walked beside her, leading his horse, though walking was normally beneath him. His men either dismounted too or curbed their horses into walking behind and beside them, though occasionally one of the party would canter off to stretch his horse's legs before returning to them.

The Range Rover had been glaringly visible from the moment they'd rounded the hill spur and started climbing toward it: the brightest color in the landscape, a scarlet dot against the green hillside, flashing light from its windshield and mirrors. The men around Andrea exclaimed and pointed. "It's an Elf-Cart," she'd said. "You've seen them before." But the Range Rover was very different from the drab trucks that had been brought through the Tube when the office and compound fence had been set up.

Then it started down the hill toward them, which the trucks had never done. The noise of its engine reverberated across the valley. The horses shied and bucked. The men themselves, as they struggled with the animals, sent white-eyed glances at the thing jolting down the hill. The nearer it came, the stranger it looked. Even Andrea thought so, after spending so long in the 16th. The chrome and glass and metallic finish sending out blinding flashes of light; the great, four square, machine-tooled frame; its coughing, snarling, growling; its strange smell. It was utterly alien.

"Take the horses back," she said. "I'll go and ask Elf-Windsor to stop."

The men were glad of the excuse to fall back from the thing, but after Andrea had gone on a pace or two, she found Toorkild at her side, though he'd left his horse behind in someone else's care. She could feel his apprehension about the big, noisy steel box, but he would never allow himself to appear afraid in front of his men, even less in front of a woman, even an Elf-Woman. And he had to greet Elf-Windsor personally because anything else would be, in his own eyes, insufferably rude.

When they neared the car, Windsor halted it and got out. He remembered Andrea, now he saw her. A big lumpy girl. Her round face was all red from the cold, and her hair was pulled back and pinned in prim plaits around her head. She wore a thick, mannish jacket and a long skirt, with solid boots appearing at the hem. Her choice of dress was obviously practical, and possibly in deference to local custom, but Windsor suspected it was what she would wear to a garden party or on the beach. Big lumpy girls were always prudish, because nobody wanted them to be anything else.

Standing beside Andrea was Old Toorkild Sterkarm, who was the kind of man it took to make Andrea look dainty. He had a big head of thick, shaggy long hair hanging to his shoulders and becoming an equally shaggy beard. He was tall too, every bit as tall as

Windsor himself, and wore an odd kind of cross between a cloak and a coat with a big cape of fur across the shoulders, making him look enormously broad. He was grinning through his beard, showing big, square, slightly yellowed teeth. Luckily for FUP, however impressive Old Sterkarm might look, he was as ignorant and dim as he was wide. He thought France was a town in England.

Toorkild came at Windsor, arms spread, and enveloped him in a powerful, furry embrace and a strong stink of musk, old wet fur and rank, masculine sweat. Before Windsor had time to react, the harsh mass of beard was shoved into his face and a kiss planted on his cheek. He couldn't stop himself trying to pull away but remembered in time that this was the Sterkarms' way. They hugged and kissed everyone, regardless of age or sex. Nerving himself, Windsor grasped the big man's shoulders and gave him a smacking kiss on the cheek in return. Hey, whatever it took.

Old Sterkarm was speaking—that is, he was making a snarling, coughing noise that was incomprehensible to Windsor, even though it was supposed to be some peculiar kind of English. Andrea translated, as Toorkild beamed at Windsor. "It's his pleasure to welcome you again, and he thinks it's been too long. He's brought a horse for you to ride to the tower, and he and his wife will be unhappy if you don't eat with them. They have gifts for you, as they're eager for the friendship of the Elves."

"Tell him it's my great pleasure to be here and that I'm looking forward to meeting his wife again." If Windsor remembered correctly, Mrs. Sterkarm was rather a fetching little piece, if no easier on the nose than her husband. "I'll be delighted to eat with them, but I'll pass on the horse if he doesn't mind. Not dressed for it."

Indeed, Toorkild was staring at the cloth of Windsor's dark suit, which had a smoothness and tightness of weave that couldn't be found in even the best cloth the Sterkarms could steal. "Ask him," Windsor said, "if he'd like a ride in the car."

But Toorkild, asked if he would like to ride in the Elf-Cart, politely declined, saying that perhaps at some other time he would, but that day, he was sad for it but he had to get back to his men and the horses. He would ride ahead to the tower, so that everything would be ready for them when they arrived. In the middle of saying this, he turned to Bryce, opening his arms, hugging and kissing the security man even more enthusiastically than he had Windsor, since he knew him a little better.

"Vordan staw day?" Bryce said, as Andrea had taught him— How stands it? or How are you?

Toorkild laughed and thumped him on the back and said something. Bryce didn't understand a word but smiled and nodded throughout. He gathered that Toorkild was amused by his attempt to speak like a Sterkarm, and was generally being pleasant.

While Toorkild was talking to Bryce, Windsor smirked at Andrea and said, "Well, hello there, Sexy." She looked startled, which was what he wanted. "Who else will call you 'Sexy' if I don't? I see they're not starving you."

Andrea had been thinking that she ought to tell Windsor about the ride the Sterkarms had sent out.

Now she changed her mind.

"Join us in the car," Windsor said. "We can have a few words before the meeting."

Andrea had to translate again, as Toorkild made another attempt to persuade his guests to ride the horses he'd brought for them and then apologized for having to go back to his men. As Toorkild went away down the hill, Windsor opened the door of the Range Rover.

"Get in the back, Andrea. Sit in the middle—then maybe you won't roll us over on these slopes."

Andrea climbed into the car, feeling elephantine and clumsy, and wishing she could suck the blood back out of her face and not give Windsor the satisfaction of seeing that he'd made her blush. She could feel Bryce's embarrassment on her behalf, and that embarrassed her still further. Neither of them was really in a position to fall out with Windsor, however rude he chose to be—which, of course, was exactly why he enjoyed being rude. She couldn't imagine anyone among the Sterkarms ever being so casually offensive. In fact, when Toorkild and Per were with people subordinate to them, they were generally more polite, not less. At least, they were if the subordinates were Sterkarms.

Unpleasant as Windsor was, it had to be said he drove the Range Rover well, taking it down the steep, uneven slope and then over some very rough ground on the valley floor, alongside the river. They rounded the hill spur and came in sight of another part of the valley, a bowl surrounded by cloud-shadowed hills against a gray sky.

They crossed Bedes Water at the ford, driving very slowly through the brown water and over the loose pebbles, and then followed the riverbank again, rounding another hill spur and coming into still another part of the valley. Andrea pointed out the tower on its hill above them. Its full thirty-foot height could be seen now, surrounded by a wall half as high, and all built of the local grayish-reddish gritstone.

Windsor ducked his head to see it and said, "Amazing." The car jolted on toward the steep path that climbed to the tower. "What I wanted to say was, I'm going to have to be pretty blunt with your friends, and I don't want you softening what I say. They've got to start leaving the survey teams alone."

"Okay." She felt a great deal of sympathy for the geologists who'd been waylaid, and had wanted to get Per and Toorkild to feel sorry for them too. Toorkild had been unable to understand what she'd been getting at. The Elves hadn't been hurt, had they? Well, then, what was their complaint? Per had, eventually, expressed some remorse, but she knew that it had been intended purely to please her and that, given another opportunity to rob a survey team, he would almost certainly do it again—just because it teased. She knew this ought to make her angry, but, instead, if she was honest, she had to admit it made her want to share the joke. I shall finish up, she thought, writing to some agony aunt.

Just at that moment, though, she was much more concerned with the steepening ground ahead of them and her memory of the hard climb up to the tower. The path wasn't wide enough for even a cart. "Do you think we'd better leave the car here and go up on foot?"

"I could drive this car up the side of a skyscraper," Windsor said.

Andrea sat back nervously as the car rocked and

swayed and bounced, and fervently wished she and Bryce were walking with the Sterkarms. She'd be glad to see Windsor turn his car over then.

The ground became steeper until the car seemed to be clinging to the slope like a fly. The track was so narrow that Windsor often had to drive on the grass beside it, and would then find a boulder in his way, or a sudden hollow or hummock. Several times Andrea thought—with some satisfaction—that Windsor was going to have to abandon the car, but he coaxed it right up to the ridge of the hillside above the valley, where the wind thumped against the windows and thrummed the aerial.

Even Windsor had to to admit that he couldn't get the car through the tower's gate. The tower itself was built on top of a crag, a large heap of rocks dumped by a glacier, that rose abruptly from the hillside. The path that led up the crag to the gatehouse was for feet and hooves only, and Windsor had to be satisfied with halting the car on the most level spot he could find near the crag. Even there it was tilted at an acute angle.

A crowd of people had come out from the tower to meet them, murmuring with curiosity at the sight of the big, gleaming Elf-Cart. Windsor, Bryce and Andrea climbed out of the car into the hilltop wind that buffeted their ears, tugged at their clothes and pulled their hair.

Toorkild came pushing through the crowd to greet Windsor all over again, with another hug and another kiss, which Windsor thought was doing him too much honor. Mrs. Sterkarm was with him, her fair hair all tucked away under a rather stylish little cap, her cheeks and nose very red from the wind, but her wonderful big blue eyes and smile as pretty as he remembered. She chattered away at Windsor in "English" and offered him pattens for his shoes—wooden soles, each raised on two wooden blocks, that you fastened under your shoes with straps, to raise you out of the mud. There was always plenty of mud in the alleys of the tower, well mixed with dung, clumps of dirty old straw, and vegetable matter too rotted to be identifiable.

While the Elves fastened on their pattens, Toorkild and his wife gabbled. Andrea translated.

"They say, Come in at once, dinner's ready to be served." Rising, she added, "We'll be eating in their private rooms—and they'll be serving you big helpings of the very best they have." She was anxious for her friends, afraid that Windsor wouldn't appreciate their effort.

Toorkild and Isobel led the way up the steep, rocky path that climbed the little crag to the tower's gatehouse, with Windsor, Bryce and Andrea following slowly. It wasn't easy to walk over such rocky ground in the inflexible pattens. Behind them came the general crowd of Sterkarms—every inhabitant of the tower who could get away from their work for long enough to gawp at the Elves.

The gatehouse's big wooden gate, with its massive iron hinges, stood open, and they passed quickly through the short, dark tunnel with its green smell of long-standing water and mud. Then they were through into the tower's yard, which disappointed Windsor all over again. This was perhaps his third visit to the tower, and during the long periods between visits, he began believing his own promotional talk of "authenticity" and "tremendous possibilities for development." It created a picture of the tower in his own head that the real tower could never match. The real tower was cramped, ugly and dirty.

The space enclosed by the wall wasn't large, and it was crammed with many buildings used as storehouses and dormitories. Between them wound narrow, muddy alleys. The buildings weren't picturesque, just inconvenient. They were all rough plastered in a mud color, and had thick, dark thatches that raggedly overhung the lanes and dripped. None of the buildings had doors or windows at ground level. The doors were all in the upper stories and were reached by ladders, many of which leaned against the walls, partly blocking the ways, so they had to be moved or scrambled over. The people who often had the most money to spend on expensive vacations were the elderly, and would they want to climb ladders all the time, or keep moving them out of their way?

The place was no pensioner's dream of half-timbered thatched cottages with gardens of old roses and pinks. It stank. It reeked of sewage and garbage and smoke and old food. And it was noisy. Children screamed, dogs barked, someone was hammering and clanging away at iron with a hammer. Crashes, bangs, yells and gusts of heat and shouting came from another building as they passed—the only building with a door at ground level. The kitchen, Andrea yelled to him, and Windsor had a sudden qualm about eating anything that came out of it. Chickens scattered from under their feet, and a pig ran away from them into a dark alley, screeching with a noise like iron rubbed on iron. You had to wonder about people who were happy to live in such filth. It was all a damned sight too authentic, and would need a hell of a lot of development and improvement before anyone could be expected to pay to stay there. The essential flavor of sixteenth-century life would be preserved, of course, and the improvements could only make things better for the Sterkarms too, so how could anyone object?

Even the tower itself was lacking. Surrounded as it was by a clutter of outbuildings, it lacked dignity while still managing to look as grim as a prison. There were no windows in the ground floor at all, and the only door was tiny, barely wide enough to admit Windsor's shoulders, and so low he had to duck.

Inside was a dark place with a barreled ceiling, lit only by whatever light managed to get in at the door. It stank like a stable. Tangles of dirty straw and dung covered the floor. They stopped in this unpleasant place to take off their pattens, and then the Sterkarms, having first pulled back a heavy gate of iron gridwork, led the way up a dark, narrow and frankly sinister staircase. The first stretch was entirely dark, and Windsor had to grope for each step with his feet. Behind him, Bryce and Andrea were boring on about whether the stairs were really easier for a left-handed swordsman to defend than a right-handed one. The climb, in that dark, confined space, with smelly people ahead of him and behind him, seemed endless. Then a slit of a window admitted a smear of light, but they were so close packed on the steps that all he could see was the place between Mrs. Sterkarm's shoulder blades.

They came to a landing but passed by the door that opened from it, and climbed a second flight of winding stairs, though these were slightly better lit. Eventually, to Windsor's relief, Toorkild opened a door and there was a flood of light.

Windsor followed the Sterkarms into a small room and glimpsed something big as it reared up, blocking the light and seeming to attack Toorkild, who bellowed so loudly that Windsor jumped. The thing dropped to the floor again. It was a dog—a very big dog, a sort of Irish wolfhound thing. It had been taller than Toorkild when it had rested its front paws on his shoulders. Cowed by his yell, it slunk under the table.

The table took up most of the room. There was no cloth, and plates were set directly on the wood. At either end was a large, high-backed chair, and a bench was placed along the side farthest from the hearth.

The fire was made of peat, and a great deal of gray smoke was coiling into the room despite the chimney's stone hood. A painted carving of the Sterkarm handshake decorated the hood, and Windsor, eyeing it and remembering the reason for this visit, thought of the warnings about shaking hands with Sterkarms.

As for the rest of the room, the walls were plastered but otherwise plain. A short flight of steps rose from a spot near the door to another door near the ceiling, which led out onto the tower's roof. The wooden floor was covered everywhere with straw and bits of dried twig and leaf, which made Windsor think of dirt and bugs—and that big flea farm had come prowling out from under the table again! Apart from the table, chairs and bench, the only other furnishings were a cupboard and three wooden chests along one wall.

Bryce started making a fuss of the dog, rubbing its

ears and patting its back. It was one of those long, dangerous-looking dogs whose deep rib cages slope up steeply to high, narrow hips. Its shoulder blades and hipbones rose higher than its spine, and its tail lolloped noisily against its shaggy sides as it nuzzled Bryce's hand, and then reared up to put its paws on his shoulders and look down at him, its tongue hanging out between its teeth.

"Oh, don't encourage it, Bob," Windsor said. He thought such a large dog in such a small room was going to be a nuisance while they were trying to talk—and besides, he could already feel his ankles itching.

Isobel, who was trying to usher Windsor to the guest chair, said, "Entraya, will I have Cuddy taken out? I can have her locked up somewhere."

But when Andrea passed this on to Windsor, he patted Cuddy perfunctorily, saying, "No, no, let her stay." He went to the chair Isobel was offering him and sat, putting his briefcase on the floor beside him. Isobel fetched cushions from a chest against the wall and packed them behind him. Windsor thought it rather pleasant to have her fussing around him, but the cushions only added lumps to what was already a fiercely hard and uncomfortable chair.

Toorkild had taken the chair at the other end of the table, and Bryce a seat on the bench. Isobel offered him a cushion, which he accepted.

"It's good to eat with friends," Toorkild said, "and we'll eat well today! It's sad our bonny lad can't be here. He'd eat twice what any of us can eat and never notice it touching the sides." He laughed and thumped his belly. "And I'm stuff enough to make three of him!"

"Let him come home safe," Isobel said, touching the wood of the table.

Andrea quickly translated for Bryce and Windsor, who were looking slightly puzzled. She added that Toorkild and Isobel were talking about their son who, sadly, couldn't be with them today.

Windsor and Bryce glanced at each other. They had something to tell Toorkild about his precious son. Windsor tried to remember if he'd ever met Sterkarm Junior, but couldn't call him to mind.

Isobel poured ale from an earthenware jug into Windsor's cup, which was a beautiful little thing made of silver. Toorkild and Bryce had cups of pewter at their places, while Isobel and Andrea had cups of wood. The way the Sterkarms acquired things meant that they tended not to match.

As soon as his own cup was filled, Toorkild lifted it and said, "Long life and good health to you, a child every year to you, and may you never drink from a dry cup!"

Andrea hastened to translate the toast, and Bryce and Windsor laughed and agreed to it. They tasted their ale as Toorkild was urging them to do.

"Good stuff," Windsor said. He thought it awful: thick, sticky and sweet. But he knew from his previous visits, when the Sterkarms had pressed snacks of ale and bread on him, he had to be careful with it. The "first-brew" ale they served to guests was far stronger than twenty-first-century beer.

Isobel was stooping over the fire, preparing to serve the food. Toorkild sat in his chair, grinning at his guests. Windsor, struggling to make conversation, said, "Is their son away on business?" He was surprised when Andrea threw him a startled, even alarmed, glance.

Andrea's next glances were to Isobel and Toorkild, to make sure they weren't wearing the wristwatches Per had given them. She'd had to be quite blunt, telling them that she knew perfectly well the watches had been stolen, and would only cause awkward questions to be asked if Elf-Windsor saw them. It had been difficult, even so, to get Isobel to leave off the watch, because it was such a pretty thing and Per had given it to her. Andrea had reminded her that only the Elves could provide them with aspirins. At that moment, the watches were wrapped in a towel in one of the chests on the other side of the room.

Toorkild was waiting to hear what Windsor had said. "Ah—Elf-Windsor wants to know—has Per gone away to work?" Isobel looked around from the fire, and Toorkild was momentarily startled by the notion that his son would perform menial tasks for pay, but then good manners made him smile again.

"Nay!" he said. "Killing Grannams is pleasure and sport!" It was a joke rather effortfully made, but he laughed at it himself, and Isobel did too, though she turned and gave Andrea a stricken look even as she laughed. "Keep him safe," she said.

Windsor and Bryce were raising their brows, curious to know what the joke was. "He says, yes, Per's been called away," Andrea told them. They looked baffled and glanced at each other again. Andrea could see them thinking that the joke must have lost a lot in translation, but couldn't imagine that they would be much amused by Toorkild's little quip either. I'm getting into boggy ground here, she thought. FUP paid her to report on the Sterkarms for them—but she was lying for the Sterkarms because—well, because she loved them. Should a personal loyalty be greater than a loyalty bought and paid for? Per wouldn't have had the slightest doubt. No payment, however high, could buy his loyalty, which was why you should never shake hands with a Sterkarm.

Isobel took the little silver-gilt bowl from in front of Windsor to fill it from the iron pot she'd been stirring over the fire. Andrea was glad to have an excuse for thinking of something else, and went around the table to the fire, where she passed the empty bowls to Isobel and set the filled bowls before the diners.

Windsor looked into his bowl with interest. Having been promised the very best of what the Sterkarms had, he was hoping for fresh oysters, salmon so recently caught it was still swimming, roast haunch of venison, wild strawberries with fresh cream straight from the dairy. The little bowl before him was filled with a smooth, thick paste. Pools and rivulets of a yellow liquid ran through it. He looked up at Andrea as she was setting another bowl before Bryce.

"Groats," she said quietly. It meant nothing to him. "Oats ground very very fine—a lot of work—and cooked for hours, very slowly, with cream and butter. That's the butter, melting out of it."

Isobel, smiling, passed an earthenware platter of pale, reddish-brown slices of meat to Windsor.

"You eat the meat with the groats," Andrea explained. "It's smoked mutton and smoked sheep's tongue—I think there might be some goat too. Raw, just smoked.

Use your fingers to dip it in the groats."

Windsor's expression was one of carefully controlled horror, but Bryce helped himself to a slice of meat, dipped it in his bowl, and said, "It's good!"

Toorkild and Isobel smiled widely. Windsor thought the goo looked repulsive, but he dipped a slice of tongue into it, wondering exactly how the meat had been smoked. With peat, or dung? But his hosts were watching him. He would have to trust twenty-first-century medicine to put him right.

Bryce hadn't been telling polite lies. The tang of the meat and the butteriness of the groats were tasty together, if rather rich for a starter. Still, the notion that he was swallowing aggressive sixteenth-century microbes wouldn't leave him.

A rather awkward silence fell while they were eating the groats. Making light conversation was difficult when everything had to be translated. Windsor wondered how quickly they could get on to the real business.

Toorkild and Isobel emptied their bowls first, and Toorkild held Cuddy back by her collar while his wife escaped the room to order the next course. She didn't go far; they heard her yelling down the stairs to someone, and then she came back, smiling. She opened one of the big chests, and Toorkild helped her bring to the table some objects wrapped in cloth, one of which was very long.

Toorkild took this long thing to Windsor, pulling the wrappings away to reveal a sword with a graceful basket hilt to protect the hand. Toorkild cleared his throat and said, "This we give you in gratitude for your friendship, which we hope will long be ours. May it serve you well and protect you for many years."

As Andrea translated, she watched Windsor's face. He took the sword awkwardly—it was a little long for him to handle easily as he sat in his chair. He drew the bright, sharp blade partly from the scabbard and seemed startled by the harsh scraping sound it made. His expression was slightly stunned, as if Toorkild had hit him.

Andrea thought she knew how he felt. The Sterkarms had been shocked to discover that she had no weapon of her own, and had given her a dagger. She'd felt very odd about it, touched by their concern that she should be able to protect herself, but at the same time the heaviness, sharpness and obvious *practicality* of the weapon had dismayed her. She felt the gift was making a demand she couldn't meet. Of course, she'd known that the Sterkarms' way of life was often violent, but her own life had always been safe and peaceful, and however hard she tried to come to terms with the feuding and riding, the brute reality of it always came as a shock.

She saw the same shock in Windsor's face. The sword he'd been given was in no way symbolic or ceremonial. It wasn't a theatrical prop, or a quaint antique, but an everyday tool for killing people. It had come to vicious life in his hand, and had thrown him a little.

Isobel was giving Bryce a dagger with an elaborate hilt that suggested it had been made to match the sword given to Windsor. Expensive and generous gifts. Andrea wondered who had owned them before they'd come into the Sterkarms' possession.

"Thank you!" Windsor said. "I'm sure I speak both for myself and Mr. Bryce when I say I'm delighted to do business with people so charming and hospitable, and we look forward to a long continuing connection in the future. We shall treasure these gifts."

Bryce was nodding emphatically as he admired his dagger.

To Andrea, Windsor went on, "Can you add anything that's proper?" He wondered how much the sword would be worth 21st side. Once FUP's project really got moving, the bottom was going to fall right out of the market for sixteenth-century antiques, so if he was going to sell, he'd better sell quick.

Andrea translated his speech. She added, "Elf-Windsor says that this beautiful sword will always remind him of the Sterkarms' friendship and generosity. He feels himself honored to be trading with a family as renowned for their courage and pride, for their weapon skill and vindictiveness as the Sterkarms."

Toorkild and Isobel beamed, and Andrea felt quite proud of herself. The Sterkarms loved to be called proud and vindictive. It was nothing more than the truth: They did value themselves highly, above others, and they were prone and quick to seek revenge. They considered both to be excellent qualities.

Toorkild was so pleased by what he believed Windsor to have said that he pulled Windsor up from his chair to hug and kiss him again, and then, while Isobel was kissing Windsor, he pulled Bryce up from the bench to embrace him. Both 21st men were startled but carried it off. Cuddy became excited and jumped about, flailing them with her tail, and making the strangled whining noise that was the closest she could get to a bark. Toorkild gave a shattering roar of "Down, Cuddy!"

"I have presents too!" Windsor said, and stooped for

his briefcase. He took from it two whole packs of aspirin, each containing twenty-four tablets, one for Toorkild and one for Isobel. As an afterthought, he tossed another pack onto the table. "And one for their son."

The Sterkarms had never seen so many aspirins before. Isobel cooed over the pretty neatness and bright, clear colors of the little cardboard boxes, and held one up for Toorkild to admire. "The Elves are the greatest of our friends!" Toorkild said, as someone knocked at the door. "My brother will envy me—he has a wife and three sons and a daughter too."

Isobel had gone to open the door, while struggling to hold Cuddy. Two kitchen girls came in, carrying a pot between them on a wooden bar. As Andrea was translating, Isobel caught her eye. She never liked to hear talk of her brother-in-law's bevy of children, especially not when her only living child was out of her sight.

Windsor, taking the hint, found two more packs of aspirin in his briefcase and dropped them on the table. "I don't have any more with me, but perhaps I could get some more." He met Toorkild's eye as Andrea translated this and thought they understood each other.

Isobel had shooed away the kitchen girls and was now serving up the main part of the meal: a sort of meat pudding. Andrea went to help her. In honor of the guests they were using plates instead of trenchers, silver gilt for Windsor and Bryce, pewter for Toorkild and Andrea, wood for Isobel. They slopped lumps of the meat pudding onto the plates, together with its gravy, while Andrea translated Windsor's remarks about how good it smelled and how hungry he was.

"Good appetite!" she said, as she passed him his plate.

Both Bryce and Windsor found the venison sausage hard work but tried not to show it. The meat was gamy and had some rather unusual textures, and they were expected to eat it with a knife and spoon, and the help of lumps of heavy bread, full of seeds and grit. Meat kept falling off the spoons and splashing in the gravy, and Windsor got some drops on his sleeve. Looking up, he saw Toorkild and Isobel eating with gusto and licking their fingers clean.

"This is wonderful," Windsor said bravely. "Can you ask Mrs. Sterkarm how she made it?"

Isobel fixed him with her round blue eyes and smiled. "I sent our Per to fetch a deer. He brought home a beauty—I've set it to hang. Then I took its heart, its lungs, its liver and its kidneys, and I chopped them all small and mixed them with oats and thyme and sage, and then I cleaned out the stomach and stuffed it with the mix and boiled it."

Windsor looked at his plate, nerving himself to take another bite. Bryce seemed unconcerned.

"Our Per will be sad he missed it," Toorkild said.

"He would eat the whole pudding himself if I let him," said Isobel. "I saved some for him." She gave a firm little nod. "Saved him a big slice."

"Don't worry," Andrea whispered to her, knowing that Isobel had put the slice of pudding aside in the manner of a spell—it was being saved for Per, therefore he must come home safely to eat it. Isobel glanced at her and patted her knee.

The venison pudding eaten, Isobel fetched from the cupboard a bowl of water and towels, for them to wash their hands. She also brought over little wooden bowls, one full of honey, the other of a thick mess of stewed fruit: bilberries, raspberries and blackberries, gathered from the moors. The last course was another bowl of groats, this time served with the honey and fruit.

"A wonderful meal!" Windsor said, when his bowl was empty. "I want to thank my host and my delightful hostess for providing us with such wonderful food—the best possible precursor to business." He hoped the slight churning in his guts was only his imagination.

Andrea passed this on, except that she left out the mention of Isobel being delightful. She was fairly sure Toorkild wouldn't appreciate it.

At the mention of business, Isobel rose. "You must excuse me, I have many things to look into—but you are always welcome, and you must come again soon. Are you sure there's nothing more you want? More food? There is plenty more groats and fruit . . ."

Bryce and Windsor protested that they'd eaten more than enough and it had all been delicious. Isobel listened, and then filled their bowls with what was left of the groats, honey and fruit. "It will only go to waste if you don't eat it. . . ." Which was a plain lie. There were plenty in the tower who would be glad to eat it. "Will I pour you more ale?" She filled their cups without waiting for an answer. "Would you like the fire built up? Entraya, tha'll keep the fire in, good lass. Will either of you have another cushion?"

No, no, Bryce and Windsor assured her. They were warm enough, quite comfortable, well fed. There was nothing they needed.

"There are beds made up," Isobel said, "if you would

stay the night. You are more than welcome."

Toorkild was standing, holding Cuddy by the collar so she shouldn't escape when Isobel finally left the room. "If there's *anything* you'd like?" she said pleadingly.

"Woman," Toorkild said, "away wi' thee." He said it quite pleasantly, and Andrea didn't bother to translate. Isobel went to her husband, clutched his arm and kissed the cheek he stooped toward her before she left. It wasn't so much a show of affection as a reminder that Isobel expected to be told everything that was said while she was out of the room. If she disagreed with anything Toorkild decided, she would express her views forcibly—Andrea had heard her do so on other occasions. Indeed, when Toorkild asked for time to consider any deal, what he usually meant was a chance to ask his wife's advice. All the men of the extended Sterkarm family knew that he was going to ask Isobel's advice—just as they asked their wives—but everyone politely maintained the fiction that men's business was nothing to do with women.

"Now we can talk," Toorkild said, settling himself into his chair. He smiled but, behind the smile, was wary. Though he pretended to believe that the Elves had come on a friendly visit, bringing gifts to bind friend to friend, he knew there was something more to it.

"Yes," Windsor said, nodding to Andrea to translate. "I'm glad to have a chance to talk, because we're a team." He smiled. "We're a team, Toorkild, you and I."

Andrea had to expand a little in translating this. Toorkild knew what teams were, but thought of them in a purely frivolous sense, as people banded together on holidays, to win tugs-of-war, to race horses, or play wild, murderous, day-long games of football. It wouldn't do to use the word "family" instead since, no matter how honored a guest Windsor was, Toorkild would strongly resent the suggestion that he was family. She said, "Mr. Windsor says, 'We deal well together.' You and he."

Toorkild nodded and smiled. His beard hid much of his face, and his smile was so genial that even Andrea, who knew him well, found it hard to see any trace of his skepticism.

Encouraged, Windsor said, "We have the same long-term objective." Andrea groaned inwardly. "We both want to see the Sterkarms prosper," Windsor went on, which was at least easier to translate.

"It's difficult," Windsor went on, "when some members of the team aren't playing with the others. There has to be full cooperation on both sides."

"We have to help each other as much as we can," Andrea said to Toorkild, who beamed and nodded.

"We at FUP have all the skills to score the goals," Windsor said, "but some members of the team seem to be playing for the other side."

"His son," Bryce put in. "And his nephews."

Andrea hesitated about passing that on to Toorkild.

"We have to work together, Toorkild," Windsor said. "We have to play on the same side, for the same team, to score the goals for *us*!"

Well, Toorkild did understand the concept of a football game, even if his idea of a good, fair game was Windsor's idea of a riot between football hooligans. Andrea translated closely. Toorkild sat back in his chair, his face carefully blank.

"We at FUP are sending out survey teams," Windsor

said, "and they are being robbed."

Andrea passed this on.

Toorkild sat straight in his chair and slapped the palms of both hands on the table. "Reiving? Who has been reived? Who is reiving anyone?" Toorkild knew that the best way to silence an accusation was to respond fiercely, with injured innocence, to speak of your slighted honor and threaten to revenge it. "There has been no reiving."

Andrea couldn't meet Windsor's eye as she translated this for him. She didn't know herself how far to believe Toorkild—he had to know how Per had acquired the wristwatch he'd given him, but was Toorkild only lying to protect his son after the event, or had he known about the robbery of the survey team all along? The Sterkarms always did seem to have difficulty in grasping the meaning of the word "robbery." If someone took Toorkild's cattle, he would agree that was robbery. That was an insult to his honor, an unforgivable slight, demanding instant and full revenge. But if he rode and took someone else's cattle, well, that was only natural, and repayment for some time in the past when they'd taken his. Besides, he *needed* the cattle. Riding was what the Sterkarms did. They were good at it. It was only right they should go on doing it.

"I'm afraid another of our survey teams has been robbed," Windsor said. "Their clothes, boots, tools, ponies and food were all taken. Now, I have a problem with this, Toorkild."

Bryce waited for Andrea to translate that, and then said, "We have good reason to think that the robbery was led by Per May and the Gobbyssons."

Toorkild recognized his son's name, and his eyes darted to Bryce's face. He scowled. "We're always blamed! If anyone's reived in the whole country round, we're blamed! If we reived all the people we're said to have reived, we'd have no rest by day or night! Is this why they came to share our salt? To call me a reiver to my face? To call my sweet lad a reiver? If there's been any reiving done round here, it was done by the Grannams! Tell him"—one thick forefinger jabbed toward Windsor—"that my Per is a good lad and wouldn't hurt a midge, and he'd be safe home with his daddy and his mammy easy in her mind if it wasn't for the thieving Grannams. Let him go and talk to the Grannams if he wants to talk about reiving. Down, Cuddy!" The dog, excited by her master's shouting and the mention of Per's name, had jumped up and was pacing to and fro.

Andrea relayed the gist of this to Windsor and Bryce, who both seemed taken aback by the energy of Toorkild's response.

"We are holding talks with the Grannams too," Windsor said, "as he very well knows."

"And our people gave us a description of the band who robbed them," Bryce said. "Tall, fair-haired, blue-eyed, led by two young men and a boy, with horses. The boy was about fourteen. One of the others had what they called a 'girlish' face. Ask him if his son isn't known as 'Per the Girl.' The other two sound to me like Little Toorkild Gobbysson and Ingram Gobbysson." Bryce had been checking in his files. He nodded to Andrea. "Ask him what he thinks."

Windsor and Bryce watched Toorkild steadily as Andrea translated.

Toorkild made a contemptuous sound with his lips and waved one hand. "That could be anyone," he said.

Even as Andrea put this into modern English, the stolen watches were in the chest a few feet from her, and Per was away on a ride.

Windsor pushed together the packs of aspirins, and then shoved them down the table toward Toorkild. Their eyes met. "I hear you get a touch of arthritis when the weather's damp. I hope the aspirins help."

Toorkild leaned forward. "Before the Elves came into our country, we did without the wee white pills. When the Elves have gone away from us, we shall do without the wee white pills. Away into the pit with your wee white pills!"

Toorkild spoke with obvious displeasure, but neither Windsor nor Bryce understood, as yet, exactly what he'd said. Andrea couldn't see any point in translating words which could only make the whole situation worse.

"Hang on a moment," she said to Windsor and Bryce. "I must make sure of this. I just have to check . . ." Turning to Toorkild, she slid her hand across the table to his, beside which it looked small, plump and pale. "Master Toorkild, sir. There are gifts between us, between you and the Elves."

He smiled and took her hand. "We are 'thou' to each other, Dearling. And thou'rt no one of them. Thou'rt one of us, all but one of us."

"It gladdens me to hear that. But I am an Elf, and I'm bound by my word to them. And it hurts us, Master Toorkild, that when we've bought friendship between us, with good gifts, that thy people reive our people. I know, I know tha can't watch all of thy people all of the time, but I thought thy word was more feared than this."

Toorkild looked furious at the suggestion that his people had disobeyed him. He was both pricked in his honor and set on his mettle to prove that he could govern them.

"I didn't tell the Elves," Andrea told him, "what tha said about the wee white pills. Why fall out with them? Thou'rt better off staying friends." She didn't know if she was right to try and patch up the quarrel like this, when it would almost certainly break out again in a little while. But it seemed to her that playing for time would give the Sterkarms and FUP a better chance to settle down into some kind of working relationship.

She could see Toorkild thinking it over. Then he said, impressively, "If my people have taken anything from your people, they shall bring it here, you shall have it back. Every last horse, every last boot. You shall have it!"

Andrea wondered if that included watches, but she passed what Toorkild had said on to Windsor, who was leaning back in his chair with a wary expression she didn't like.

Windsor had been watching Toorkild and Andrea carefully as they spoke together. He couldn't understand what they said, but he was suspicious of Toorkild's sudden capitulation. Of course, louts like Old Sterkarm, who threw their weight about, beat their chests and frightened a lot of small people might well cave in when they met someone who wasn't intimidated by their bluster, but . . . "What exactly did you say to him?" Windsor asked Andrea.

"I wasn't sure," she said. "I mean, I wanted to make sure that he understood. I was just going over what you'd said before and making sure everything was absolutely clear."

"If you'd done that in the first place . . ." Windsor said.

Andrea let it pass. It was more important to have helped Toorkild keep his supply of wee white pills than to defend her own linguistic skills.

"Tell him I'll have an inventory drawn up of everything that was stolen," Windsor said.

Andrea thought she'd better not interfere anymore, or she'd have suggested granting an amnesty, allowing the Sterkarms to keep what they'd already stolen in exchange for agreeing not to steal anymore. But it was like Windsor to insist on everything being returned. He liked to be strict. "Playing tough" he called it. Perhaps he was right. The Sterkarms certainly had no respect for anything that seemed weak. But they didn't respect strength either. If they met strength, they fought harder or, if beaten, became resentful and bided their time for revenge. It was hard to know how best to deal with them.

"I certainly hope we'll have less trouble from the—the *Grannams* in the future," Windsor said, nodding to Andrea to translate. "Because there is talk of sending armed guards out with the teams. He might like to let 'the Grannams' know. We'd hate anyone to get hurt." Bryce was quiet and kept his face noncommittal.

Toorkild showed no concern at the possibility of armed guards. He was probably surprised to learn that the teams his people had robbed *hadn't* been armed.

"I'm glad we've been able to settle this amicably," Windsor said. He looked down into his briefcase. "Oh look. Here's another pack of aspirins I hadn't noticed." He tossed them onto the table with the others.

As far as any expression at all could be read on Toorkild's bearded face, he looked sulky—but he straightened himself in his chair, as if about to say something. Before he could, from outside came a long, soaring shout.

Toorkild's heavy chair skidded back, so forcefully did he rise. He stood still, listening. Through the tower's narrow windows came shouts from the yard, more and more voices joining in. They were yelling, "The May! The May!"

Toorkild went straight to the door, threw it open, and dashed down the stairs, leaving Windsor and Bryce staring.

7

16th Side: Per Bairt Hyemma

UP ON THE TOP FLOOR of the tower, the windows had tiny panes of thick, puddled glass set in black iron frames. Andrea struggled with the catch of one and forced it open, letting in damp, chill air. She could see nothing of the yard except the thatched roofs of the outbuildings, but the sounds doubled in volume: feet running in mud, alarmed clucking of chickens, shutters being thrown open and buckets being thrown down. People yelled as they passed, and what they yelled was "The May! The May!"

Andrea made for the door.

"Would you mind telling me what's going on?" Windsor was annoyed. Toorkild had dashed out the door and away down the stairs without even giving him a look, and now Andrea was following.

"The May!" she said. She clung to the stone jamb of the door, as if holding herself back from running down the stairs. *"Han venda tilbacka!"* They stared at her. "I mean—Per Sterkarm. He's come back."

Bryce got to his feet and seemed ready to go with her, but Windsor still sat in his chair.

"We ought to go out too," she said. Windsor still

132

didn't move. Oh, stay there if you want to, she thought, and ran down the stairs. She could hear Bryce coming after her.

There was no sound in the tower except the thump and scuffle of their feet on the steps, and the drag of their hands on the plastered wall. The hall, when they passed its door, was empty. Through the windows came fainter and fainter sounds of shouting.

At the bottom of the stairs Andrea pushed aside the heavy gate of iron gridwork. The tower door stood open to the yard, letting in light. Pattens were scattered on the floor among the dirty straw. The people had rushed out into the mud without a thought for their shoes or clothes. Andrea would have done the same, but Bryce stopped and began hunting for a pair of pattens that would fit him.

Andrea fidgeted, waiting for him, wanting to say, Oh, come on—but Bryce was wearing a smart suit and highly polished shoes, so she couldn't blame him for delaying. More echoing steps within the wall of the tower told her that Windsor was coming down the stairs after them. From outside came the distant shouting greeting the ride's return. Per would be looking for her and wondering where she was. Bryce was just beginning to strap one patten to his foot. "Oh—catch up to me!" Andrea said, and ran out the door.

The yard, and the alleys between the outbuildings, were all empty and silent, except for a cat and a few chickens. She ran toward the gate, trying to miss the worst of the mud, jumping a puddle, all the time hearing whistles and calls from beyond the walls. Her footsteps and her panting breath echoed as she went through the narrow stone tunnel of the gatehouse, and then she had a view, from the tower's rocky crag, of the tower's people gathered together just below. They were waving, jumping, calling, shrieking, so happy to see their own coming home that they ignored the big, scarlet, shining Elf-Cart parked near them.

Andrea could see the first of the ride climbing the path, some men riding and some leading their horses—and there were Cuddy and Swart, swiftly moving long shapes, coursing around the horses as if herding them home. It was a beautiful scene. The clear, clean air sharpened every detail: the opposite slopes of the valley bright with bronze bracken, purple heather and dark bilberries; the scores of white streams jumping down the hillside to join Bedes Water. The day was fine, if chilly, and the sky above was a clear harebell blue. A small, damp breeze touched her face, and catching the mood of the cheering people, she felt exhilarated. Shielding her eyes and squinting, she tried to pick out Per among the horsemen but couldn't. Which was odd, because he would be in the lead, for sure, and she had come to know his every movement so well, his every tilt of the head and shift of the shoulders.

She began looking for anyone she knew—for Sweet Milk, for Sim or Ecky. Sim was one of the horsemen. He kept turning in his saddle and looking back.

Some men were climbing the path on foot. Sweet Milk was one of them. The man walking in step with him was Gobby Per, Toorkild's brother. With a shock, she realized they were supporting stretcher poles on their shoulders. As the path twisted, she caught sight of the men walking behind, carrying the other end of the poles. The nearer man was familiar. Her hands went to her mouth as she realized it was one of Per's cousins. There was a likeness . . .

The people of the tower started forward, their line bulging like a swelling wave and then breaking. Isobel and Toorkild, she saw, were among the leaders. She heard Windsor and Bryce behind her, coming to join her, clumping along in their pattens, but she didn't turn.

The people surrounded the riders and passed by them, gathering in a crowd about the stretcher bearers. The stretcher was brought on some way closer to the tower, with many hands helping to support it, and then it vanished in the crowd as it was lowered to the grass.

Cuddy and Swart were casting backward and forward, up and down the slope, trying to push through the people. They were whining, the sound rising at times almost to a howl.

Andrea ran. She heard Bryce call out behind her, asking her to wait, but she wouldn't have stopped for anyone. She had to find out who had been brought back on the stretcher—although the tight, clutched feeling at her heart told her that she already knew.

She was met by a solid wall of backs. Somewhere near the front, a woman's voice rose in a wail. As the cry sank in a sob, other voices rose: an eerie, hopeless sound that seemed to quiver through her. It was so frail and lonely on the open hillside. Keening. Keening was for a death.

It made Andrea angry. Such a fuss to make before she even knew what was going on! She ran around the crowd, looking for a way through, and found Cuddy running with her. No use being polite, obviously. Andrea took a man by the arm and hauled him aside. She wormed into the crowd, pushing, saying, "Shift!" Cuddy's weight pressed against her legs, and then, with a strong shove, Cuddy was past her and clearing the way, thrusting people aside with her big head and powerful shoulders.

Stumbling to the front of the crowd, Andrea saw blood. Per and blood. Per lay on the ground, between the lances that were the stretcher poles. All the brightness had gone out of his face. It was clay white, clay damp, streaked and smeared with blood, fresh red blood and darkening, drying blood. Even his lips were white, and the blue shadows under his eyes might have been daubed on with ink, they were so prominent. His head was raised a little on a bundle, and turned from side to side as he muttered and licked his lips. Andrea could hear his noisy breathing, a sound like tearing or rasping.

The right thigh of his breeches was black with blood. His long boot, his jakke and the clothes that made the stretcher beneath him were all stained with blood. All that blood, so much blood, smeared everywhere, spread everywhere. He couldn't have any left in him.

Cuddy went nosing at the wound and Toorkild slapped her away. Toorkild was kneeling at Per's side. He looked up at Andrea, his face wild and marked with Per's blood.

At Per's other side, Sweet Milk was kneeling, holding one of Per's hands—and Sweet Milk's hands, and face, and jakke were all streaked, spattered, marked with Per's blood.

At Per's head knelt Isobel, her hand inside his jakke. Her face and hands and dress were stained with Per's blood, but she was intent and silent. It was the women behind her, bending over her, who keened for a death.

With the chill wind about her ears, and those eerie, despairing wails, Andrea was overwhelmed for a moment by helplessness and panic. Then she thought: No! and was filled with angry energy. She pushed Cuddy out of her way and stepped over Per's legs. Inside her head she was screaming at herself: Do something!

She put her hands over her ears, trying to shut out the keening and give herself a few moments in which to think. Come on, remember. Basic first aid. She'd learned it at college, not that long ago. Dark blood, not spurting . . . Venous bleeding then, not arterial. Thank God for that! *Apply local pressure to stop bleeding* . . . Toorkild was doing that, tears running down his face.

What else, what else? *With any major wound or blood loss, expect to find shock and treat accordingly.* What did that mean? Slowly, infuriatingly slowly, her memory told her. Keep the patient warm. Give reassurance. If conscious, give a hot, sweet drink.

But it was hard even to get close to Per. Isobel was at his head, Sweet Milk and Toorkild kneeling on either side of him, and none of them would move. Cuddy stood astride him, licking his face and neck with a long red tongue, and many other people were crowding around. Gobby was stooping over Toorkild, saying, "We did all we could . . . I drowned the prisoners, had 'em trodden down in Bedes Water . . . He's a brave lad, a brave lad. . . . If he was one of my own . . ."

Another man was brandishing a sword over Isobel's

shoulder. "This is what did it. Salve it good."

"Toorkild—" Andrea began, and then someone else was shouting her name above the heads of the crowd. An English voice, not a Sterkarm. Some sort of scuffle seemed to be going on in the crowd.

"Toorkild—" Andrea said again. She reached over Per, almost overbalancing, snatching at the thick, fur-lined robe Toorkild wore, and which she wanted to wrap Per in.

"Andrea!" It was Bryce's voice. "They won't let me through!"

She could glimpse Bryce's balding head now, his pink face even more flushed than usual as he struggled with several of the Sterkarm men, who were blocking his way and shoving him back.

Andrea jumped back over Per's legs. "Let him through, let him through!" She grabbed at the collar of Toorkild's robe and began dragging it down his arms. To Bryce she called, "Do you know more first aid than I do? He's an Elf!" she yelled at the Sterkarms. "He knows things! He'll help! Let him through! I want the robe for Per, Toorkild! Give it me! Tell them to let the Elf-Man through—please! He might know things that could help!"

Toorkild shrugged out of the robe, stripping himself to his shirt and leggings. He looked over his shoulder and yelled at the men struggling behind him, and Bryce came plunging through the crowd.

"Christ on a bike!" he said, when he saw the blood. He elbowed Toorkild out of the way and knelt beside Per. Isobel looked at him in alarm and raised a hand as if to fend him off, but then made no further protest as

Bryce shoved his hand into Per's jakke and felt for the pulse in his throat. Per tried to push him away, and Cuddy growled at him, but Sweet Milk held the hound by the collar, and Isobel caught Per's hands and murmured to him.

Andrea threw Toorkild's heavy robe over Per. It fell over Cuddy too, where she had pressed her whole length against his side. Well, the big hound's body heat would help to keep him warm. To Bryce she said, "Shock?"

Bryce nodded, keeping his face controlled in a way she didn't like. "And a half! His heart's dingdonging away like the clappers."

Andrea crouched beside Sweet Milk, staring at Bryce across Per's body. "Is there anything we can do?"

Bryce obviously didn't want to answer. Isobel looked from Andrea to him and back again, her expression intense.

Bryce put his hand under Per's head and gently eased the rolled blanket from under him, supporting his head until he could lower it to the stretcher. The roll of blanket Bryce tossed to Andrea. "Prop his feet up. Keep him warm, get him inside." Bryce lifted his brows a little, and moved his head slightly to the side, in what was almost a shake of the head. "Make him comfortable."

Isobel couldn't understand what they said, but she understood the expressions on their faces. For the first time she let loose a long, rising wail that set other women keening again.

As Andrea lifted the robe and pushed the blanket roll under Per's feet, she felt a cry rising in her own throat, and tears springing in her eyes. She held both wail and tears back. Neither would do any good. "Stay there!"

She got to her feet and looked around. "Don't move him, not yet! Stay! Wait!" She pushed aside a man wearing jakke and helmet and ran off.

* * *

Windsor had descended the rocky path from the tower's gatehouse, but he kept well clear of the excited crowd, going instead to stand by his car. He was a little curious about what was going on, but not eager to be caught up in that jostling, stinking mob. Someone would tell him what all the noise was about sooner or later. In the meantime, he was glad to see that he still had his hubcaps.

Becoming bored, he left his car and skirted the edge of the crowd, picking his way around the horses and the youngsters who held them. Glancing at one horse as he passed, he saw something hanging from the saddlebow. He stopped, stared.

Two objects. One round and furry, the other . . .

Both things were bloody, covered with lumps of clotting and blackening blood. He went on staring in a strange calm, long after he had recognized what they were, as if he didn't have to react until he admitted to himself what he was seeing.

A kind of toy, surely? A sort of joke? But what were they made of? In his own time they would have been plastic, but . . .

He couldn't keep up the pretense. The texture and substance of the things had no similarity to plastic. They were flesh, hair, real blood.

He was looking at a man's severed head tied to the saddlebow. Beside it, lashed to the bow with twine, was a severed hand. He swallowed and went on staring as his heart thumped somewhere in his throat. It was hard to believe that the things could look so much like—well, what they were. So complete. Undamaged. So hand-shaped, with thumb and fingers and nails. So normal a head, apart from the blood and the fact that it ended at the neck. The eyes were still there, behind sagging lids, the teeth visible behind the drooping lips.

His legs wobbled beneath him and he felt shocked, sick. Having always prided himself on being stronger than others, he was surprised at the strength of his repulsion. Okay, okay, he said to himself, it's just a head. No worse than seeing a pig's head in a butcher's window. They're both just dead pieces of meat.

He straightened his back and made himself look at the things. Studied them. He leaned closer, making sure he missed nothing. The stump of bone at the center of the neck. The pipes of the throat, cut through. The hacked flesh. A musty, slightly sour smell, with a tang of iron, filled his head. That's the smell of blood, he thought, and swallowed hard again. A picture formed in his head, of himself in his smart suit, coolly looking these things over, and he nodded, feeling proud of himself, even though his fists were clenched. He doubted if many other FUP executives would have been able to do it.

But the Sterkarms must have cut off this head and hand. Who else? The hospitable, kindly Sterkarms, who were all around him, who had mischievously robbed his research teams but not done them any harm. He felt, all in a moment, a good deal less safe. And even less able to trust Toorkild than before. How could you make any kind of deal with the—savages—who would do this?

Someone barged into him, staggering him, yelling in his ear. He turned, heart skipping, and it was Andrea. He was glad to see her. He pointed to the bloody thing hanging from the saddle. "Have you seen that?"

She didn't even look. "You've got to, you've got to!" she said.

Being told that he "had to" always set him against whatever it was. He told other people what they had to do—they didn't tell him. They asked him, at most. The annoyance helped him recover a little from his shock. He tried to turn away from the horse, so that he couldn't see the head, but found himself peering from the corners of his eyes, keeping it in sight as if it might get up to something behind his back. "What have I 'got to do,' please tell me?"

"He's dying!" she said. "We've got to take him through!"

"What are you talking about?"

Instead of answering, she took him by the arm and dragged him along, using both hands to pull when he resisted. He went with her, and the crowd parted to make way. Windsor looked around at them, not altogether happy at being surrounded by Sterkarms who, with their helmets and beards and rumpled clothes, all looked so—so *other*.

They stopped, and Windsor looked down on a robe spread on the grass, with pretty Mrs. Sterkarm kneeling by it. Toorkild, for some strange Sterkarm reason, was lying at full length on his side, with the robe over him, as if he'd decided to sleep on the hillside outside his tower. So many people were standing or kneeling around the robe, getting in the way, that it was a moment before

Windsor realized that Toorkild was holding someone else, pillowing the other's head on his shoulder, and talking as he stroked and kissed the other's face. Mrs. Sterkarm kept stroking the head of the person Toorkild was cuddling and bending down to kiss it. All Windsor could glimpse of this person, as people bobbed in and out of his view, was a face as white as vanilla ice cream, streaked and smeared with blood.

"He's dying!" Andrea said.

"Who is?" Windsor asked.

With both outflung arms, Andrea indicated the still figure under the robe. "Per! For God's sake, we've got to be quick!"

Bryce rose from among the people gathered around the robe and came over to them. "We're keeping him warm, but . . ." He shrugged.

Windsor was looking around at the gathering of horses and people, at the men who were wearing helmets, at the long lances stuck into the turf. He remembered the severed head and hand, the very smell of them. It all came together, and he realized he was looking at a ride—a raid. Which FUP had forbidden. Even while he'd been making a deal with Toorkild about leaving the survey teams alone, Toorkild's son—who had robbed the survey team—had been on a ride. God, what people!

Andrea pulled at his arm and yelled at him again that someone was dying. Her yelling and dragging at him jangled his nerves. "I'm not a doctor! What do you expect me to do about it?"

She was waving her clenched fists in the air and yelling, her plaits falling down. "A blood transfusion!

We can put him in your car! Take him through to the 21st!"

"No," Windsor said. "Absolutely not."

Andrea lowered her hands. Her face lost its anger. She stared at him, openmouthed.

Bryce's head made a bobbing motion. He said, *"What?"*

Windsor was disappointed in him. He would have expected Bryce to see reason. He had thought that Bryce lived in the real world.

"He's *dying*!" Andrea said.

"You don't know that. Stop being hysterical. I should think getting him into a warm bed instead of leaving him lying out here in the rain would do him a power of good."

Andrea and Bryce looked at each other, then faced Windsor again. Bryce said, "We *do* know he's dying." He took no notice of Andrea's start. "He's in shock from blood loss."

"They all know he's going to die!" Andrea said. "That's why they're keening!"

"I don't know exactly how bad he is," Bryce said, "but I'm telling you, James, in my opinion, from my knowledge and experience, if he doesn't get treatment soon, he *will* die."

"I'm sorry," Windsor said, "but whose fault is that? The very reason we forbade these rides is that people get hurt." In his mind was another image of himself: cool, detached and smart in his dark suit, the only adult among a rabble of overgrown children. The only one adult enough to see beyond the pathetic, white-faced, dying boy to the larger issues. That was what he was paid the Big Ks for: to put things into clear, cold, adult perspective. "If you play with fire, you get burned. Perhaps a lesson will be learned here." He became aware that the conversation was attracting the attention of the Sterkarm thugs who stood all around him, and he was sorry he'd come so far from his car. He took a couple of slow, sidelong steps toward it.

"We're wasting time!" Andrea yelled. She actually stamped her feet in a kind of dance.

Several of the Sterkarm men around her, though they couldn't have understood what she said, stiffened at her shout and looked at Windsor. He turned, to make for his car, and found that a couple of men were in his way. Both were tall and bulky, both bearded. They glowered at him from beneath the shadows of their helmets. One held a lance that had to be something like eight feet long; the other had his hand on his belt, at which hung a long knife. Windsor hesitated. He could, of course, just walk around them, but he wasn't sure they would let him.

"Mr. Windsor," Andrea said. "If you'll take Per through, I'll tell Old Toorkild that you tried to save him—and if you do save him, you'll be able to make any deal you please, anything, Toorkild'll do anything for you if you save his son. But if you leave him here, leave him here to . . . if you leave him here, I'll tell Toorkild what you've said—"

"Andrea!" Bryce said.

"I'll tell everyone here, now, what you said!"

Windsor saw, behind her, the Sterkarm men gathering closer, all armed, all staring at him. These were the men who had hacked through a man's neck and wrist and brought the parts home with them. Windsor disliked few things more than having to back down, but he wasn't fool enough to die first. He looked at Andrea. "I hope you're at home here, because you don't have a job 21st side." He felt in his pocket for his keys. "I'll get the engine started."

He started toward his car, and the two big Sterkarm bruisers moved into his way. He saw them glance past him to Andrea, like dogs to their trainer. Behind him, Andrea called out something in Sterkarm, and the thugs stepped aside. His keys in his hand, he made for the car. I'll start the engine all right, he thought. I'll get in and drive off. Then he saw one of the Sterkarm thugs run past him, a long, long lance in his hand, and reach the car first.

Andrea had run back to the people gathered around the stretcher, crouching to take one of the poles herself. "Carry him to the Elf-Cart!"

Toorkild scrambled from under the robe and took one of the poles nearest his son's head; and Isobel, Sweet Milk, Gobby and others all made to help lift the stretcher. "Why to the Elf-Cart?" Toorkild said.

Andrea was opening her mouth to answer when Per gave a small cry. Up flew one side of the fur robe that covered him, and Cuddy, snarling, quivering, planted herself astride him. Her black, trembling lips were drawn back from inches of teeth, her neck ruff bristled, her ears were laid flat and white showed all around her eyes. People moved back so fast that the stretcher was all but dropped, and as it hit the ground, Per cried out again. Cuddy's growl grew louder. She whipped around, facing them all off. Cuddy wasn't a dog to take chances with. She weighed almost as much as a man, and was more powerful.

"You stupid hound, we haven't time!" Andrea made a grab for Cuddy's collar from behind—and leaped back as the dog spun with frightening speed. The big white teeth clacked, actually scraping her arm and leaving it wet.

Both Sweet Milk and Gobby moved in, trying to catch the hound, but she leaped at them, coming up on her hind legs as tall as a man, then thumping down to stand over Per again. She growled even at Toorkild, who stubbornly kept his grip on the stretcher pole and bared his own teeth at the hound.

Andrea was pulling at her own hair. "Hurry!"

A couple of Gobby's men succeeded in catching Cuddy by the collar while Sweet Milk held her attention. She snarled and snapped and struggled as the two of them, with difficulty, dragged her away.

People had pounced for the poles of the stretcher, and lifted it up as soon as the hound was clear of it. "The Elf-Cart!" Andrea said again, and they obeyed her—because she was an Elf-Woman, she supposed, and only the Elves could save Per now.

"What power's in the Elf-Cart?" Toorkild asked breathlessly. Andrea just nodded her head to tell them to go on.

When they reached the car, it hadn't been started, hadn't even been unlocked. "They won't let me in!" Windsor said when Andrea looked at him. Several of the Sterkarm men, all armed, from both Toorkild's and Gobby's bands, had ranged themselves around the car. Andrea couldn't blame Windsor for being afraid to try and push past them.

"Stand aside!" she said. "Let him open the doors—oh, give me the keys!" While the stretcher was held up by the several people around it, she took the car keys from Windsor, pushed Sterkarms out of her way—and dropped the keys in the grass. Toorkild was asking, over and over again, why they'd brought Per to the Elf-Cart. Andrea, scrabbling for the keys, felt like screaming, especially as she still had to sort out the key for the doors. At least the car had power locks. It was a joy to hear all the locks spring as she turned one. Pulling open the door, she tossed the keys onto the driver's seat and reached over the back of the seat to open the back door. "Inside! Put him inside!"

Bryce was one of the stretcher bearers, and he climbed into the car. He was trying to pull the stretcher in, but Toorkild was holding it back—halfheartedly, but he was still hindering.

"We're taking him through the Gate to Elf-Land," Andrea said. "We'll make him well—we'll do our best—I promise—"

Windsor had got into the driver's seat and turned on the ignition. The car throbbed and growled. Several of the Sterkarms sprang back from it, and Toorkild moved as if he were going to grab Per up and carry him away bodily.

Andrea hugged Toorkild's wide back, trying to contain his fear. "It's all right, the Elf-Cart does that, tha knows it does. And we can heal, tha knows it—we've got magic. Please, Toorkild, let us take him!"

Isobel gave her husband a hefty punch on the arm. "Let her take him!"

Toorkild stopped resisting and helped shove the stretcher into the car, where, being narrow, it fitted on the wide floor. Between them, Bryce and Toorkild lifted Per onto the backseat. Toorkild settled himself on the car's floor, his arm resting across Per. Isobel, unable to climb past her husband's bulk, ran around the car to the other door.

Andrea ran after her. "No—tha can't come." Isobel was yanking at the unfamiliar handle on the door. "Toorkild, get out, tha must get out—we can't take you all."

Windsor had been watching through his mirror, his teeth gritted. While Andrea and Bryce had been scrambling half in and half out of his backseat, he hadn't had a chance to drive off, and now that the meat was loaded into his car, he supposed he was committed, but he was damned if he was going to take half the Sterkarm tribe through the Tube. He turned off the ignition, and the car stilled, startling the Sterkarms all over again. "Tell them to get out," Windsor said. "Out, or the Elf-Magic doesn't work."

"Isobel!" Andrea said. "The magic's stopped working! We can only take Per, or the magic won't work and he'll have to stay here." Oh, for God's sake! she thought as Isobel gawped at her. We haven't time for this. She had an impulse to slap Isobel hard. "Get out of the Elf-Cart, Toorkild, please. Let us take him and heal him, please. I promise I'll look after him, I swear it, I vow it. Tha don't think I'd let owt happen to him, dost?" She shook both clenched fists. "Oh, God's teeth, Toorkild, get out of the Cart or we can't take him!"

Toorkild's big face, seen through the car windows, was set. Andrea stared at him for an age. The Sterkarms believed that the Elves could heal and that they sometimes did kindnesses for mortals, but they also believed Elves to be unpredictable and untrustworthy, as likely to blight as to heal. It was well known that Elves liked to steal handsome young men, who were carried into Elf-Land and never returned or were kept until a hundred years had passed.

Isobel let go of the car door, ran around the car again, set her foot against the body and began hauling Toorkild out of the car. Toorkild allowed himself to be dragged, stumbling, out onto the grass, but as Bryce reached over and pulled the door shut in his face, he said, "Bring him back alive or don't come back!"

Andrea opened the door Isobel had been struggling with and climbed in beside Bryce. Windsor started the engine before she had the door shut. Bryce was tucking the robe closer around Per and propping up his feet. As the car slowly started rolling forward, Andrea settled herself on the floor and slipped her arm beneath Per's head. The car lurched, and she braced her feet against the front seats, braced her back against the backseat, struggling to hold Per still on the seat and cushion his head against the jolting and swaying.

She could hardly bear to look at him, he was so unlike himself. His face was so pale and damp, it had the ghastly, greasy quality of candle tallow. He was working hard to breathe, straining and gulping. They heard every breath he took. His left arm was bundled in the robe and trapped against Andrea, but his right hand pawed and clutched at her. She caught hold of it, and it was icy. "All's right, all's braw. Thou'rt safe, all's well, I'm here."

"You're all right, son," Bryce said. Copying Andrea, he said, *"Braw, braw."*

Andrea was thankful that they were moving at last, until her eye was caught by something outside the car, and she was shocked to see it was Toorkild, Isobel and many others, keeping pace with the car. Her heart squeezed with fright—why had they been so quick to assume the car would be faster when, on this ground, a horse might be? But then, the car might make up for its slowness on the hillside when they reached the valley. She bit back the urge to yell at Windsor to hurry. He had enough to do managing the car on this slope.

Windsor's teeth were clenched tight, and he breathed hard through his nose. He was concentrating on getting his car back down the hillside in one piece, and trying to put aside the anger he felt at the way he'd been railroaded into this piece of stupidity. He could have done without the heavy breathing from the back; he could have done without the memory of the severed hand dangling from the saddlebow. His hands felt weaker than they should on the wheel, and the muscles of his legs trembled. His eyes were beginning to ache from their fixed stare.

Keep your foot off the clutch, right off. Second gear is all that's needed, acceleration low. A sudden level bit of ground and ease up the acceleration, ease it up, keep the engine revs level—and then another steep bit. Christ, nearly bloody vertical! A vertiginous view through the windshield into the valley below, but keep your foot off the brake. Don't lock the wheels on this surface, for God's sake! Ease up on the acceleration—

but then it would get so steep that gravity began tugging the car downward, pulling the engine over faster and faster—then he had to risk a touch of the brake, but not slamming them on. God's sake, don't panic and slam them on! A light touch, ease off, ease on again, keep the wheels free.

It began to seem that time was being rewound, and played over and over again, to prevent them ever reaching the bottom of the mountain, but each slow revolution of the wheels dragged them closer and closer to more level ground. . . .

Windsor changed into third gear, and the car bounded forward, jolting, lurching, jouncing, despite its superb suspension, leaving the walkers behind. Per bounced on the backseat, and his hard-caught breath was knocked out of him. His head slumped, open-mouthed, against Andrea.

"Christ!" Bryce said. "Give us some warning!"

"Do you want to get there fast or not?"

Andrea was searching for the pulse in the hollow of Per's throat, and holding back tears and panic as she failed to find it. Then it jumped against her fingertips, so fast that each tiny beat crowded on the next in a light butterfly flutter. "Per? Per?" Her only comfort was that the harsh, noisy breaths had started again. His eyes weren't fully closed, but he wasn't conscious. "Don't argue! Just *hurry*, please!"

Bryce put his hand on her arm. "You do realize . . . even if we get him to a hospital, it might not be any use."

She looked at him, tears running from her eyes, Per's head under her chin.

Bryce's remark struck Windsor too as he rocked and

jolted the car over the rough ground beside the river, heading for the ford. His brain was working fast, keyed up by the effort of guiding the car. It jumped backward and forward between the ground and boulders ahead, the mechanics of the car, and what had been said earlier. *Save his son, and Old Sterkarm will do anything you want.*

He should have seen—would have seen if it hadn't been for the all the confusion—what a great idea it actually was to bring young Sterkarm through to the 21st. It would give him all the leverage he most needed with Old Sterkarm. He didn't trust the old savage's gratitude, but what was Old Sterkarm going to do while his son was with the Elves? Sit up and beg, roll over, play dead and anything else he was told to do, that was what.

It didn't really matter if Young Sterkarm lived or died. Not in the short term, anyway, though obviously, in the long term it would be better if he lived. He called over his shoulder, "How is he?"

It was Bryce who answered. "Alive."

Windsor drove the car along the riverbank as fast as he could, which was still little more than ten miles an hour except for short, jolting bursts. He slowed right down again to negotiate the slope down to Bedes Water, and bounced the car slowly over the rocks in the bottom of the river, before grinding up the opposite bank in bottom gear. Then there was more slow maneuvering around the boulders beside the river before the big steel fence of the FUP compound could be seen through the windshield. As the car crawled up the slope, Windsor pounded on the horn. The blaring noise made Per gasp and move his head on Andrea's arm.

The guards opened the gates of the compound and

waved them through. Windsor drove across the compound and up the ramp onto the platform. He leaned across the car and wound down the window as a guard opened the door from the office. "I want to go through now! Now! Is that okay?"

The guard leaned back into the office, shouted at someone, and then nodded. The green light came on beside the Tube at the same time. Windsor drove forward, and the plastic strips slithered and scratched over the car. They were in the Tube, with its white tiles and gray lighting, and the plastic strips at the other end screening the twenty-first century.

Andrea felt none of the awe she usually felt for the Tube. She just wanted to be out of the other side while Per was still alive.

Seconds, and five hundred years later, when the plastic strips were rustling over the car again, and its nose was tipping down the ramp toward the gravel drive of Dilsmead Hall, she could still feel the fast, light, fluttering pulse under her fingers.

At the bottom of the ramp, Windsor changed gear, put his foot down, and the car sped away along the smooth, flat drive. "Now we'll make up time! Still alive? Here." From the dashboard he took a mobile phone and passed it back over his shoulder. Bryce took it. "Phone the hospital. Let 'em know we're coming."

Crouched in the space between the seats, Bryce dialed the operator and asked to be put through to the hospital. Andrea barely listened. She was mindlessly counting Per's breaths, losing count constantly, but starting again. Her legs were cramped, her arm and shoulder ached from Per's weight, their flesh bruised against her bones, but she would stay in that position for the rest of the day and night if she had to.

Windsor broke the speed limit in the suburban streets surrounding the Hall, until he reached the ring road that encircled the city. The hospital was built on the ring road, a little out of the city center, and Windsor drove so fast that they pulled in through the hospital gates scarcely more than ten minutes after arriving at Dilsmead Hall.

Windsor drew up outside the entrance to emergency. Orderlies, nurses and a doctor were already waiting, with a wheeled stretcher. An orderly opened the car's back door.

Andrea found people pressing against her as they leaned into the car. She was still trying to support the weight of Per's head and shoulders, but another man was trying to take him from her. Bryce was lifting his legs and saying, "Let me take him. Andrea, let me—"

There didn't seem to be anywhere she could squeeze to get out of the way. "Oh careful, careful—don't drop him!"

She didn't quite understand how Per was got out of the car, but obviously the nurses and doctors knew what they were doing. When there was space for her to stumble out onto the concrete, Per was on a gurney, and she was in time to see a breathing mask clapped over his face. The gurney was pushed away, fast, into the hospital. As if she were tied to it, Andrea ran after. Even if the thought had entered her head, she couldn't have stayed behind.

Windsor jumped out of the car, ready to give orders, but found that no one needed them. Everyone, including

Bryce, had vanished into the hospital. He turned back to his car, meaning to drive it away and park it—and saw that his hubcaps were missing.

The Sterkarms, the damned, light-fingered, conniving, ungrateful Sterkarms, had stolen his hubcaps.

8

21st Side: In Elf-Land

PER WAS IN HIS father's hall, drifting among the people there like the smoke, like a ghost. He could see their mouths opening, laughing, shouting, but heard nothing.

He must be drunk, the walls and ceilings spun so, and he wasn't standing, but lying. Under his back, solid, holding him up, was the earth. A bird was calling *chip, chip, chip,* on and on and on. The sun was shining red through his closed lids, and he lifted his hand to shade his eyes, but it was held, tangled in his sleeve.

Quite clearly, a little irritated, someone said, "Don't rile about." A touch on his forehead. "Go back to sleep."

He tried to open his eyes, but the light was too dazzling and his lids too heavy. He sighed and shifted, dozed, and then knew he was wrapped in his blankets, in his bower.

But all the sounds were wrong. There was that insistent *bip, bip, bip.* . . . He had never heard the sound before. He lay listening to it with closed eyes, frowning a little. It wasn't a bird: No bird made that call. It wasn't a wind or water sound, or an animal sound, or anything he could tell.

And everything else was too quiet. There should have been a murmurous din made of voices talking and shouting; animals moving and bleating, lowing, barking, clucking and screeching; pots and pans being walloped, buckets clanked. There should have been small, close sounds of birds and mice moving in the thatch above, and Cuddy sighing and shifting as she kept guard beside his bed.

Instead, beneath that monotonous *bip, bip, bip* was a discomforting silence, like the silence in the hills when you stood still, and the noise of your own movements, which had been loud in your ears, stopped too. Then there was nothing but the deep, soft, echoing silence that the hills held among their folds.

Bip, bip, bip.

Everything was wrong. Under his back was something firm but soft—it was neither a hillside nor his thick, hard palliasse, prickly with straw and spread over wooden chests. Nor was there any musty, sweet smell of hay rising with his every slight movement; and no fug of old sweat, old smoke and wet Cuddy. Instead—he wrinkled his nose—the smells were stinging and sharp.

And too much light. Even with the shutters open, there was not so much light in his bower, shadowed as it was with the tower walls and overhanging thatch.

He was half minded to hunch on his pillow and go to sleep again, but the *bip, bip, bip* and the too-bright light were insistent, and he opened his eyes.

The light dazzled him, and he squeezed his lids shut against it and lifted his arm to shade his face. Something fine tugged at his elbow.

Someone was in the light, blocking it. A voice that

158

made him want to smile, even before he knew it, said, "It gladdens me to see thee."

From behind the shade of his hand, he saw Andrea. The sight of her gladdened him. Her heavy, shining hair was slipping out of its pins and falling in thick tresses over her shoulder. The light, behind her, made a golden halo around her head, so she shone and dazzled. His Elf-May! Her face was all plump, smiling warm curves—like the body beneath, all plump, warm curves. He felt her take his other hand, where it lay on the bedding, and she stroked its back while holding it in her warm, soft clasp. It made him feel peaceful, like a cat in the sun. "All is right, Per; all is good."

For sure it was; why should it not be? He opened his mouth to tell her she was beautiful, and like the Queen of Elf-Land herself, but found that even his face was weary. The arm he had raised to shade his eyes slumped back to the bed. He felt heavy and hazy, half numb and half asleep. He smiled at Andrea, and she pressed his hand between both of hers and smiled back—but her smile was wobbly. Tears spilled from her eyes.

"Oh Per, I'm so gladdened—to see some color in thy face again."

He was surprised. Had he been sick then? Some memory, too quick to be caught, shifted in the back of his head. But seeing her in tears made him forget all that. Something was wrong, something was upsetting her, and he should put it right. His own eyes filled in sympathy. "What?" he said. His voice was a whispering croak. "What's the matter?" Her tears pleased him too, giving him a little stab of pride that he couldn't help. It was said that Elves, like witches, couldn't cry, so she must care for him a great deal if tears could run down her face like this. Maybe it wouldn't be so easy for her to leave him without a look back, as the Seal-Mays and Swan-Mays did.

"Per? Canst understand me, lover? Thou must harken to me now." She leaned further over him, so that she filled his sight. "I have to tell thee something . . ."

He raised a hand, trying to reach up to touch her hair, and she took both his hands and folded them together on his chest, holding them there. She said, "Careful of the drips." Drips? He thought of rain dripping from the eaves of thatch; droplets flying as Fowl shook his head after drinking; snot hanging in a drop on the end of a man's cold nose . . .

"Per?" She smiled. "Thou'rt not quite awake, art thou? Harken, love. Dost remember the ride?"

His eyes kept slowly shutting, and slowly opening again. "Grannams," he said.

"That's right. The night before Elf-Windsor came, remember? Tha led a ride after the Grannams."

"Gobby," he said, on a sigh, as his eyes closed again.

"What? Doesn't matter. Per, dost remember being hurt?"

Memories moved in Per's mind, like fish in a deep pool, flashing into view and vanishing again. A big white moon in a dark sky over dark hills. A cold, damp wind and a smell of earth and grass. Great noise and yelling, and a dreadful, hot, sick ache . . .

"Thou wast hurt badly, Per, and lost blood, lots of blood. Thee all but died. Tha would have died."

He blinked at her, feeling drowsily warm and comfortable, and having no clear memory of his life ever having been in danger. It was like being told about someone else. His head, when he tried to lift it, felt extraordinarily heavy, like a cannonball; so he pushed his chin up toward her, hoping she would take the hint and kiss him.

"Lie still and harken."

"Entraya."

"Hush. We saved thee. We, the Elves—"

"Who's thy prick?" He pulled one hand out of hers, meaning to catch at a dangling strand of her hair.

"Per, thou'rt no harkening. I'm trying—"

One of his hands had fumbled up to her shoulder and her hair. "Is it me? Am I?"

She kissed him. "Ssh. Thou'rt my brave prick." Another kiss. "And my bonny cockhorse. Now lie still, shut thy gob and harken. We saved thee from dying, Per. We put blood back into thee."

"Aye," he said. The Elves were famous for healing. "Thou gavest me espirin."

"Nay, no aspirin, something stronger. Per. Harken. I have a big thing to tell thee. But thee mustn't be feared."

"I'm no feared."

"Nay, never be. Per, we brought thee into Elf-Land."

He blinked at her again, slowly.

"If we'd left thee in Man's-Home, tha'd have died, lover, died. So we—I—I brought thee into Elf-Land. Thou'rt in Elf-Land. This is Elf-Land."

She felt his whole body convulse under her. The drowsiness left his face. His head turned, trying to see past her.

"Per, Per." She cupped his face in her hands, leaning

close over him. "All's right, tha'rt safe. Nowt shall hurt thee, I swear."

Per was staring up into her face and snatching at breath. Above and behind her head he could glimpse white walls and ceiling, shining with a harsh, wet gleam, like milk. The smooth, straight whiteness of the surfaces proved the truth of what she said. No such walls, no such ceilings were anywhere to be found in Man's-Home.

"All's right, Per. I brought thee here to make thee well. When thou'rt whole and healed, shalt go home again, I swear."

Her hands still held his face, and he gripped her wrists with his own hands. Strange little pulses jumped in his elbows. What a fool to have trusted an Elf! What a fool to have trusted that, because there was love between them, she would do him no harm!

> I set my back against an oak,
> Thinking it a strong and trusty tree,
> But first it bent, and then it broke,
> And so did my true love to me.

Elves were, and had always been, uncertain and tricksy creatures, blessing with one hand, blighting with the other, as the mood took them. All the stories taught that an Elf's love was dangerous—you might be drawn away into Elf-Land to be a toy, or a slave, or mere coin to pay the tax that Elf-Land owed to Hel. . . . But love blinded, deafened and tied the hands.

"Per, my own prick, be no feared."

"I'm no feared."

His eyes were straining sideways as he spoke, trying to see more of the room, and he looked so bewildered and so scared that she would have cried for him if she hadn't felt like laughing. She stroked his hair. "All's right. Would I do owt to hurt thee? Would I? Lots of folk have come into Elf-Land, thou'rt not the only one. Tam Lin came—"

Aye. Tam Lin had fallen asleep while out hunting and the Elf-Queen had found him, fancied him, and had taken him into Elf-Land. But the tax to Hel fell due, and the queen's love for him having cooled, Tam feared he would be part of the payment. Tam escaped, but barely, and the Elf-Queen cried after him:

> "Tam Lin, Tam Lin, had I but known
> That thou wouldst so betray me,
> I would have cut out thy pretty gray eyes,
> And put in two of tree.

> "If this betrayal, Tam Lin, Tam Lin,
> If this betrayal I'd known,
> I would have cut out thy living heart,
> And put in one of stone."

"And True Thomas, he went into Elf-Land. . . ."

True Thomas had spent seven years in Elf-Land, taken there by the Elf-Queen to be her lover—her silent lover, for she forbade him to speak. At the end of seven years, the tax to Hel fell due, and the queen loved Thomas well enough to send him back to Man's-Home, with the gift of second sight. His prophesy made him famous and rich, but also feared, and he was never again at peace in his own world, and lived only for the day when he was called back to Elf-Land. . . .

"And there was—"

"Why hast brought me here?"

"I told thee, Per. To make thee well. Look—"

"I want to go home."

"Thou shalt. Thou shalt, as soon as thy leg's healed. Lie still, keep still. Look, let me show thee—there's nowt to fear."

With her fingers she was gently moving a black thread that seemed to be dangling from somewhere overhead. As she moved it, he felt something brush against his arm, and the odd little pulse jumped at his elbow again.

He looked up, following the black thread with his eyes, but was distracted by the pole that stood beside the bed, shining like polished silver in the sunlight. There were bars at the edge of the bed too, and they were silver. So much silver! Worth a fortune. The Elves were truly as rich as was said. But it would be hard to carry the silver away.

"Per."

He looked up again and saw that at the top of the silver pole hung a—he didn't know what to call it. A soft bag that sagged with the weight of its contents, like a sheep's stomach filled with meal or water. But this bag was so thin that its contents could be seen through it. The great mass of the stuff was dark and thick, not quite black, but almost so. Some of it had smeared thinly and greasily over the inner surface of the bag, and here, where the light shone through it, the color was a dark red. It looked like blood. What was blood doing in a soft bag at the top of a silver pole above his bed?

The thin black thread was attached to the bag. It led down to his arm, to his elbow, where the pulse jumped. At the end of the thread was a little—he didn't know what it was, but it was sticking into his arm. *Into* his arm . . .

He gasped for breath and pushed himself up in the bed.

Andrea gripped his arms before he could snatch at the drips or jump out of bed. "All's right, never fear. I told thee, things are strange, but thou'rt safe."

Now that he was sitting higher in the bed, he could see more of the room, and everything was uncanny . . .

"Per, Per, harken to me."

A whole wall was missing. He looked out through the hole at green grass and treetops, from an angle that meant they must be high in a tower, and felt that the room was tilting and they would slide out. He gripped fiercely at Andrea's arm.

"Per, it's Elf-Work. What else wouldst find in Elf-Land but Elf-Work? It won't hurt thee; none of it will hurt thee." He was breathing in snatches, his chest was rising and falling sharply, and he stared at her fixedly, his teeth gritted.

"Look." She drew his attention again to the drip line. "This is how the blood is being put back into thee. See, it's running out of the bag up there, and down this little pipe and into thine arm. It's making thee better, not hurting thee. And this one"—she showed him the drip line that led from the stand on his other side, from the bag of saline solution—"this one has Elf-Work in it to make thy leg heal faster." The doctor had explained to her that it held one of the healing accelerants that had recently been approved for use. "And this"—she pointed to the electrode stuck to his chest—"this is Elf-Work to count thy heartbeats. Listen!" Raising a finger, she wagged it in time to the beeping of the machine. "The faster thy heart beats, the faster it beeps. Now calm down." She stroked his arm. "Calm down, and it'll beep more slowly. Listen."

He pushed himself up further until he was sitting. He still breathed fast, and his heart beat fast, but he didn't know what to do, or say, or where to look. "All's right," Andrea kept saying, and her hand stroked on the bare skin of his arm, and her voice and touch held his fear in check—but she had brought him into Elf-Land. . . .

"How long have I been here?" He hated the pipes in his arms, but they must have been there when he woke, and didn't seem to have done him any harm—and the beeping of the box did keep time with his heart.

"Only a day, Per. Well, getting on for two. But—"

"Why do they count my heartbeats?"

Andrea wasn't exactly sure herself. She kept her hands on his shoulders, stroking, soothing. "It's just so they know thy heart's still beating. It's Elf-Work. It's—"

"How. How long's passed? In Man's-Home?" A year True Thomas had spent in Elf-Land, but when he reached home, he'd been seven years away.

"Per, Per." She put her arms around him, hugged him carefully. "I promise, I promise thee, time is passing the same there as here. Thou shalt not turn to dust when tha goes back, I promise. How canst think I'd do owt to hurt my own prick, my only prick?"

He pushed her a little away and looked into her face,

studying her, searching her face and finding nothing there but honesty. He returned her hug, drawing her close again.

She felt him relax. "Lie down again, Per, lie down." He did, and she stroked his hair back from his face so that it spread out about his head on the pillow. "Listen now; the beeping is slowing down. It's counting thy heartbeats."

His eyes grew vague as he listened. It was true: The beeping was slower. But how did the box count? It must have a spirit inside it. The beeping grew faster again as the eeriness of the thought, the idea of being so close to such Elf-Work, made his heart race, but he deliberately calmed himself, drawing in long, deep breaths. The beeping slowed again. Everything was going to be strange here, he told himself. Elf-Work on every side. He would be a fool to flutter and squawk like a chicken at every new thing.

The fine little pipe felt warm where it touched his arm. "What blood is it?"

Andrea saw the sparkle of fear in his eyes. "Not Elf-Blood, Per. It won't turn thee into an Elf, I promise."

"Pig's blood?"

"It's blood like thy blood, a man's blood. It'll make thee well, it shan't do thee any harm."

"How do Elves get men's blood?"

That was the trouble with simple people, Andrea thought. They understood things simply, and asked devastatingly simple questions. "Never worry about it, Per. It's Elf-Work."

"But whose blood was it?" He looked up at the bag of blood, as if he might be able to recognize it.

"Thy blood, Per." That might shut him up, she thought. "It's the blood tha lost, being put back into thee."

He blinked, remembering his blood, black in the moonlight, dripping from him to earth below and soaking in. He opened his mouth to ask the obvious question.

"By Elf-Work," Andrea said. "Art hungry?"

He was, but there had been so many other claims on his attention that he'd hardly noticed it. Now his hunger seemed to increase moment by moment. He opened his mouth to say yes, and then remembered . . .

> Oh no, no, no, True Thomas, she says,
> Our food must never be touched by thee:
> If ever a crumb goes in thy mouth,
> Tha'll never win back to thine own country.
>
> Oh no, no, no, True Thomas, says she,
> Our drink must never be touched by thee:
> If ever a drop goes down thy throat,
> Tha'll never again see thine own country.

Andrea saw his eyes take on that scared glitter again. "I promise thee, Per, the food I give thee'll do thee no harm."

But, Per wondered, did she want him to see his own world again? "I'm no hungry."

"Per—"

"Be I here alone?"

"Tha'rt with me," she said, sounding hurt.

"But Daddy?" he said. "Sweet Milk?"

"We could bring only thee through the Gate, Per. They wanted to come, but they had to stay behind."

He stiffened his muscles against the new fear that went through him, but the Elf-Working box gave him away, beeping faster. Again he made himself calm, and the beeping slowed. A whole world away from home and too weak to fight for himself—if he raised a cry of "Sterkarm!" here, who would answer him?

He couldn't afford to be afraid. And he needed to know the worst.

He threw back the bedcovers—and was astonished to see nothing but a small strip of cloth around his leg. He had expected much stained padding and wrapping. This gauzy little strip seemed stuck to his leg. It didn't even wrap all the way around it.

"Now, Per—" Andrea said.

He caught the corner of the gauzy strip and ripped it off.

"Per!"

There was no wound on his leg. Though it was sore, and hurt when he moved it, the flesh was whole. He looked up, startled, at Andrea. She had lied to him. And yet . . . He remembered something of being hurt, of the ride home, his uncle cursing because the bandage kept soaking through with blood, the endlessness of it. . . .

But he had seen the wounds of others, and there had been red, inflamed flesh, weeping pus, and the puckered edges of the wound had been clumsily held together by big stitches of black twine, which had themselves inflamed the flesh around them.

Andrea, without actually touching the wound, pointed with her finger to a thin, bright-red line that ran across the side of his thigh. If a wound that had nearly killed him had healed to no more than that . . . "Tha said I'd been here but tyan days!"

"Tha's been here no—"

"My leg's whole!"

"Nay, Per—"

"It's no gone bad-ways!" He stared at her.

He meant it hadn't become infected. In his world almost every cut, however slight, became infected. The infection, rather than the wound itself, was often what killed. "It was cleaned," she said. He looked blank. There was no connection in his mind between dirt and disease. "Elf-Work. We have Elf-Work to stop it going bad-ways." He moved, and she saw that he was going to get up. "Per, no!"

He ignored her, of course—it was his biddability that made him so lovable. By holding on to the chrome stand beside the bed, he managed to get to his feet but then looked around, confused, as he felt the line from the other drip tug at his arm. The line stretched taut across the bed, and he didn't know what to do about it.

"Per." Going close, Andrea put her arms around him. "Thy leg's no as healed as it looks. Lie down again. Rest it—and tha must eat something."

Per had no choice but to drop back onto the bed. The Elf-Box was beeping fast because just the effort of getting to his feet had made his heart beat hard. His muscles had felt like dough. They would hardly hold him up. He didn't think they would have lifted his knees to let him take a step.

Andrea sat on the bed beside him. "I know thy leg looks healed, Per, but that's because of Elf-Work—"

Startled, Per looked at the smooth, closed flesh of his leg again. Was it all a glamor, made by Elf-Work, as the Elves could make dead leaves look like gold coin? Was his leg really stitched up with black twine, swollen and bad-ways?

Andrea put her hand on his knee. "It was a very deep gash, so they—the Elves—have put some stitches deep inside to hold it together. Elf-Work stitches," she added, as he looked up in alarm. "They won't go bad-ways. They'll melt away as if they'd never been there."

"Inside my leg?" He whispered. She felt him shiver. "What are they made of? Where do they go?"

"They . . ." She fluttered her hands, not knowing how to explain to him that the stitches would be absorbed by his body. "They'll do thee no harm, Per. It's Elf-Work." What a useful phrase that was, explaining everything while explaining nothing. Per accepted that "Elf-Work" could achieve almost anything but didn't expect to understand it. "And the rest they glued together!" she said. "They stuck the edges of the wound together, really neatly."

"Glue?" Per said. He had laid himself down and seemed almost to be making himself small in the bed.

Andrea threw the covers over him. "It's a sort of glue. It holds the edges of the wound together really strongly, it's better than stitches, but tha shouldn't try to stand on it or walk about yet. Soon tha'll be able to, soon. In a couple of days." She saw his eyes widen, and stroked his hair. "Only a couple of days. That's not long."

But two days in Elf-Land could be two, or twenty, or two hundred years in Man's-Home.

Andrea got up from the bed and crossed the room to

the shelves and cupboards along one wall. She brought a tray back to the bed and set it on the mattress beside him. "Tha'd get better quicker if thee et something."

There was a smell of food from the tray, a milky, yeasty smell, and he pushed himself away from it. The sides of his stomach seemed to rub emptily together, and the ache reached up his gullet into his throat. It brought tears into his eyes because he dared not eat.

Andrea was moving plates on the tray, clattering them. Per reached out and touched the tray with the tip of one finger. It was of a hard, smooth, dazzlingly white material that he had never seen before. It didn't feel like anything he knew, it was whiter than anything he knew and, when he scratched and tapped it, the sound was strange. Not wood, not metal, not horn.

The plates weren't made of turned wood or earthenware or metal either, but of some other smooth, hard, white substance, even smoother and glassier to the touch than the tray. And there was a tall, straight-sided glass filled with . . . something Elvish. The glass itself was a wonder. So straight, so unflawed, so clear. Worth a fortune but, if he tried to carry it away, he would most likely break it—and how could he get even himself out of Elf-Land?

On the white surface of the tray lay . . . a thing. It was long, thick, curved and as yellow as a coltsfoot flower. He leaned to the left and right as he peered at it. He had no idea at all what it could be. It didn't seem to have any use.

From a small white plate, Andrea had picked up something brownish and flaking. It looked like a large, fat grub with a ridged body, half curled up. Andrea broke it in half, releasing more of the yeasty smell, though it didn't smell quite like anything he'd smelled before. Flakes fell from the thing onto the plate and tray.

"This is a croissant," she said. He couldn't have repeated the word. "It's like bread." She put most of it back on the plate and broke off a smaller piece, which she put in her mouth. Another piece she held out to him. He snatched his head back before any crumb of it could get onto his face and so into his mouth. But his belly wanted it, and his mouth watered.

Andrea dusted her hands, sending flakes of croissant flying, and then picked up a cloth so white that Isobel would have been envious, and wiped her hands with it before picking up a little block from beside the plate and unwrapping it. Inside was something greasy and yellow. "Butter."

Per kept his distance at the edge of the bed. The yellow stuff looked nothing like butter. Butter was white and hard, and came to table in big lumps inside a crock.

Andrea picked up a tiny round pot and peeled a covering from the top of it. She held it so that he could see the smooth, glassy red substance it held. It was pretty. He leaned forward and she held the pot so he could sniff at it. The smell was sweet but sickly. It mystified him.

He drew back, and Andrea sighed and picked up a blunt, clumsy, useless knife that was made all of metal, even its hilt. She stuck it into the little pot, and what had seemed smooth, glassy and hard seemed to melt before the knife and turned into a soft goo. He saw the glass of the little pot flex in her hand and drew back further. Was the knife hot?

She daubed the red goo that had been hard on the flaky, yeasty thing, and bit off a little piece herself. "Jam," she said. It was an Elvish word he didn't know. She held the stuff out to him. "It's sweet. Nice. Tha'd like it."

Careful not to touch the food, he pushed her hand away. Hungry as he was, though his head was beginning to ache with hunger, he would never, never eat anything that had been touched by that hard red stuff that turned to goo. And that strange, greasy, flaky bread . . . Some folk said that Elvish bread was made by grinding men's bones to flour. What was that red goo then? He said, "Where's my pouch?"

"Never mind thy pouch. Eat something, please. It won't hurt thee, Per. Look."

She pushed a small bowl to the edge of the tray. It was heaped full of small, whitish, rounded things, like a heap of large insect's eggs. He didn't know what they were, and they didn't look edible.

"And this is milk to go on them." She touched a small jug.

"Milk?" He leaned forward. The jug was full of a white liquid that looked very like milk. He put his nose down close to it, and for a moment Andrea thought she was going to get him to drink some milk at least.

Then he reared back, wrinkling his nose and saying, "Milk?"

"Cow's milk, Per."

He had drunk cow's milk very rarely. Goat's milk, and sheep's milk, often straight from the tit, were what he'd been raised on. He watched her pour the cow's milk over the insect's eggs. They bobbed and shifted, making popping, snapping noises, as if hatching. Per pulled a face and drew further back. Did the Elves really eat such scrapings?

He looked about the room, with all its brightness, the silver-framed bed, its glass boxes and cloth on the floor. Was it all a glamor, fooling his eyes, while all the time he was lying on a heap of rags in a muddy cave? Some accounts of Elf-Land said that all the riches were nothing but glamor, and their feasts nothing but dry leaves and dung—and insect's eggs floating in cow's milk.

Andrea pushed the tall glass of orange juice toward him. "Try it. It's sweet. Tha'll like it."

Per shook his head. The filled glass was beautiful. There was an old story about a beautiful woman whose tears were liquid gold, and it was as if she'd caught her tears in a glass. Never had he seen any liquid that color before. In the bright light that came in through the hole in the wall, it glowed. He wasn't sure that he'd ever seen anything of such a bright and glaring color.

"It's the juice from . . ." He wouldn't recognize the word "orange." She remembered an older form. "From a narange."

He went on turning the glass with his finger and admiring its color in the play of light but showed no understanding of what she'd said. She'd thought that he might possibly have seen an orange—a small, hard, wrinkled, long-traveled specimen—strung on a ribbon and stuck with cloves for use as a pomander. But it seemed not. She looked at the glass herself and was struck by the thick, smooth, almost creamy appearance of the drink and its artificially colored brilliance. For a moment it looked so weird, even to her, that she put her hand to her forehead as her mind seemed to rock.

"Where's my pouch?" Per asked.

"It's safe. Don't worry about it."

"I want it."

"What tha wants is something to eat."

He shook his head and frowned. It was annoying to have food pressed on him when he was hungry but couldn't eat. "Give me my pouch."

"The food doesn't hurt me, Per."

"Tha'rt an Elf."

"But when I was in Man's-Home, I ate thy food. I trusted thee. Thy food didn't—"

"Tha'rt an Elf," he said. "Give me my pouch."

"A banana!" Andrea picked up the yellow thing.

Curiosity silenced Per. He watched as she pulled at the thing's top. The yellow came away in a long strip, white on the inner side. Long, sprawling white and yellow legs fell over her hand, leaving a white, curved stem standing up. It was like a dead man's . . .

"Thou ates it," she said, offering it to him. He recoiled sharply, and she smiled and shook her head.

She broke off the pointed tip. He was surprised to see how easily it broke. Before his eyes, she put the tip into her mouth and ate it. She pushed it at him again. "Try some. Tha'll like it."

He shook his head.

"It's good. It's fruit."

Strange Elvish fruit. He shook his head.

"Oh *Per*!" In his world, she had made no fuss about eating a boiled sheep's stomach stuffed with oatmeal and the sheep's own heart, lungs, liver and kidneys. "Tha've got to eat something!"

"Then bring me my pouch!"

"Wherefore? I'll bring thee thy pouch when tha've eaten the croissant!"

Per sat up. His blue eyes turned silver, just as if two tiny lights had turned on behind them. He put his hand under the tray and flipped it. The tray rose in the air, turned over, and crashed onto the carpet. Streams of milk ran from the jug, cutlery clattered, orange juice spread from the broken glass, Rice Krispies rolled everywhere.

"Now the mice shall eat it!"

Andrea stood, hands on hips, looking at the mess on the floor. Her teeth were set, keeping back all the angry things she wanted to say. Per wasn't well yet, she had to remember that. He was in a strange place and scared. "I'd better get this up, hadn't I?" She rang for an orderly and, crouching, gingerly picked up shards of glass.

"Call a may," Per said. He could tell he'd made Andrea angry, and he was sad for that. Throwing the things on the floor, too, was unmannerly behavior in a guest—even an unwilling guest. His mother would have said, "Have I taught thee no better than that!" and given a slap to his face that would have rung his ears. But . . . if he'd let Andrea go on and on arguing, while he got hungrier and hungrier, she would have talked him into eating that bone-bread sooner or later. He'd had to throw it on the floor.

"I have called a may," Andrea said, still angry.

The door opened and the "may"—an orderly—came in. "What's been going on here then?" she said, walking across the room.

Andrea saw Per abruptly lie down and cover himself

with the blanket, hiding even his head. She almost forgave him for throwing the things on the floor. He'd always seemed so brash in his own world, and she'd often wished that she had some of his self-confidence. To see him fluster and hide from a stranger was laughable.

But then, everything must seem so alien to him, and he was so far from home. Poor kid, you had to feel sorry for him. To show that she forgave him, she went to the closet and found the pouch he'd asked for. It was a soft leather bag that hung from his belt on loops and held . . . anything he might want to carry. A tinderbox, money, dice. Now it was heavy and she could feel, through the leather, the shape of a bottle. Slipping it from the belt, she took it over to the bed. "Here. Art happy now?"

The orderly came out of the bathroom with mop, bucket, dustpan and brush, and began clearing up the mess. Per wouldn't come out from beneath the covers while she was there, but lying on his side, he fumbled with the buckled flap that closed the pouch. Reaching inside, he pulled out the remains of the rations he'd carried with him on the ride. Andrea stared. So that was why he'd wanted it.

There was a big lump of cold porridge, partly eaten. It was a meal that the Sterkarms commonly carried with them when they traveled, or were working in the hills and fields. Oats were stirred into water, or skimmed milk, until they made a thick mess. A little salt might be added, to lend savor. Then it was poured into a flat wooden tray, or a drawer, and left until it was cold and set, when it was cut into squares.

The pouch also held a lump of hard cheese, a leather

bottle of small beer and, because Per was Isobel's treasure, an apple and a handful of small red plums.

Per lifted the bottle and shook it, listening to the sound and judging how much it held. Then he carefully tore the sticky lump of porridge in half, and put half back inside the pouch, together with the cheese, the apple, and all but two of the plums.

"Per. That isn't going to last thee long."

He began to eat the porridge. It was rubbery and sticky, and took a lot of hard chewing, but he obviously enjoyed it. Andrea shook her head. She couldn't think of anything less appetizing than a greasy lump of cold, salted porridge.

But at least he was eating something. She sat on the bed beside him and wondered if she could get some food sent from the 16th for him. Would he believe her when she said it had come from the 16th?

She nodded and smiled at the orderly as the woman left. The best thing, she thought, was for Per to be sent home as soon as possible. She'd be with him, to make sure he didn't use his leg too much too soon. She'd have to phone Windsor's office and ask him about it.

"Where are my things?" Per asked. He took a sip from his leather bottle.

"In the closet over there. I'm sad for it, but they ruined thy boots and britches. Cut them to pieces."

He stopped eating. "Cut my boots to pieces?" Money, real hard money had been paid for those boots in Carloel. They were part of his riding gear.

"They would have hurt thy leg more if they'd tried pulling them off, so they cut them off. Never mind—"

"Wherefore did they not fetch off me boots with Elf-

Work, and not cut them?"

"I'm not sure there is an Elf-Work for taking off boots, Per."

"Where's my sword?"

"It was left behind, Per. But—"

"My dagger then? My jakke?"

"They're all safe."

"Bring them to me."

"Oh, Per, thou hast no—"

"I want them. Bring them here."

"Per, tha canna wear a jakke in bed, and . . ." She remembered the tray falling to the carpet and wondered why she was arguing. Why distress him again? If he wanted the dagger and jakke, let him have them.

When she brought him the heavy jakke and the dagger in its sheath, he hadn't quite finished the lump of porridge. He put it down on the bedsheet while he sat up and spread the open jakke over his chest, since he couldn't get it on over the drips in his arms. He placed the dagger on the sheet, where he could reach it easily with his left hand. Then he began eating again.

"Tha'rt in no danger here, lover."

Per knew better. He ate the plums, thinking of his mother, and spat the stones out into his palm. Not knowing what to do with them, he put them back into his pouch. At home, he would have thrown them on the floor for the mays to sweep up, but here, having already thrown the tray on the floor, he didn't want to offend again.

"Dost feel better now?" Andrea asked.

He nodded, and lay down, the jakke over him. He felt his eyes closing. The excitements of the day, the effort to stand, had exhausted him again.

Watching him struggle against drowsiness, Andrea said, "I'll try and get some food from Man's-Home for thee," she said.

He said nothing, and she leaned over to see his face, to see if perhaps he'd gone to sleep.

"Came I through the Elf-Gate?" he asked. She nodded. "Where is the Elf-Gate?"

"If I told thee, thou'd no understand."

"But which way is it?"

"When thou'rt well, thou'll be sent back through it. Art sleepy? Sleep, then. It'll be good for thee, to sleep."

"But where is it, the Elf-Gate?"

She thought he would relax, and go to sleep quicker, if she gave him some sort of answer. "At a place called Dilsmead Hall, Per. Now sleep."

"Dilsssmid Oll. Dilsssmid Oll." He settled himself on the pillow and placed his dagger carefully in his hand. It took her by surprise when his face twisted. "I want to be home." He turned his face into his hand and wept.

"Oh Per, Per! Oh!" She crawled onto the bed, close to tears herself. The drip lines were in her way, but she carefully, gently lifted them and moved them aside until she could get under them and lie next to him, easing her arm under his head. "I'm sad for it, lover, I'm sad, but we had to bring thee, we had to, thee'd have died else." She kissed his face. "I promise, I promise, all shall be right." She kissed him again. "I'm here, I shan't go away. My own prick, thou knows I love thee, I wouldn't let owt hurt thee."

But so must the Elf-Queen have assured Tam Lin. And how could she prevent anything hurting him? Was she a man? Could she fight with sword or axe?

But her soft warmth, so close, and her kisses and assurances calmed him. And he was very tired. The Elves had let him live so far; why would they not let him live until he woke?

Dilsssmid Oll. That was what he had to remember.

He drifted into sleep, his head against Andrea's shoulder.

9

21st Side: A Hospital Visit

THE NEXT MORNING Andrea breakfasted on a croissant and coffee and watched Per. He sat up in the bed, the jakke discarded for the moment, and carefully rationed out the food he had left in his pouch. The tray of cereal and croissant meant for him was on the table beside Andrea's chair. Per had refused to allow it near him.

The apple, most of the plums and the greater part of the cheese Per put back into the pouch; then he closed it. On the bedcover he arranged the last of the porridge, a small piece of the cheese, a plum and the leather bottle.

Andrea opened her mouth to speak, and then made herself be quiet. She didn't want to begin another long, exhausting argument.

That morning, flattering herself that she could sweet-talk Per into anything, she'd set herself to coax him into agreeing to eat the hospital breakfast. *"Nigh,"* he'd said, which always sounded more emphatic than "no."

So she'd pleaded and begged, looking close into his face and holding his hand, growing more shameless as his face showed that it did distress him to refuse her. She pelted him with endearments, swore on her life and love and honor that it was safe to eat, kissed him, made promises.

"Entraya! Yi seet nigh!" I said no!

It was not only disappointing but hurtful, to find that she couldn't persuade him after all. She lost her temper and called him stupid, telling him that he was only delaying his own recovery and return home. What was he scared of? Was he a *coward*? She had shouted this, thinking that of all things she could say it was most likely to hurt him, and make him want to prove it untrue.

Per had grinned. He knew that he wasn't a coward and, anyway, didn't much value a woman's opinion on what did and didn't make a coward. Her anger was much easier to bear than her pleading. *"Honning min, nigh."* Honey mine, no.

Andrea had knelt beside the bed and reverted to pleading. "Per, it's only because I love thee. I can't stand by and see thee make thysen sick." She reached for his hands. "When thou wast hurt, I was so scared, and now I'm scared again and—"

"Nigh! Yi seet nigh!" He turned on her so fast, his eyes making that silver flash, that she thought he was going to hit her. "Quiet, woman! Or I'll close thy mouth!"

She'd withdrawn to a chair in the far corner of the room, picked up a magazine and pretended to read, though she'd been too angry and upset to follow a word. If he wanted quiet, he could have it. She'd never speak another word to him until he apologized.

"Entraya. I'm sad for what I said."

She'd lifted her chin and kept her eyes on the magazine, affecting not to have heard him.

"Be no angry, Entraya."

It was an appeal not to be left alone in this strange, strange land. She'd thrown down the magazine, gone over to the bed, and hugged him.

Now, while Per nibbled at his bit of cheese, Andrea looked at her watch and put her tray aside. The office would be open. She went to the phone on the wall and dialed for an outside line.

"Vah air day?" Per asked. What's that?

"It's a—a far-speak. No, sshh, Per! I'm trying to talk." She was dialing the number for FUP as she spoke. "Quiet, Per, please!" The switchboard answered. She asked for Windsor's office, and was put through to his secretary. Windsor, of course, was in a meeting. She asked if she could leave a message for him, and started to explain why she thought it would be best to send Per home as soon as possible—tomorrow, or even today.

"Vorfar tala thu til ayn vegg?" Per asked. Why do you talk to a wall?

The secretary promised that she would pass the message on to Windsor the moment she saw him. "Ssh, Per! I'll explain in a minute." She dialed again, this time for Dilsmead Hall and, when she got through, asked for Bryce.

"Hello, Andrea!" Bryce said, when he came on. "I've been meaning to come over and see you, but you know the way you get bogged down. How's the lad?"

"Well enough to be awkward." She explained why Per wouldn't eat. It was a relief to be able to explain it to someone. "I wondered—is there any way you could get hold of some food from 16th side? If he could see it was—"

"Not before this afternoon. Would that be okay?"

"Yes! Thank you! Anything will do," Andrea said. "Bread. Porridge. Whatever."

"I'll do my best. Dunno when I'll be able to get it over to you, though. Look, leave it with me and I'll see what I can do."

"Vah air day?" Per said. He was standing right by her, wearing nothing at all except the dressing on his leg, peering at the telephone. He'd brought the drip stand with him, using it as a sort of crutch.

"Per, I don't think you should be standing—"

"Vem tala thu meth?" Who are you talking with?

"Is that the lad?" Bryce asked. "Put him on."

Andrea held out the phone to Per. He pulled his head back from it but then, his eyes widening, allowed her to hold it to his ear. She heard Bryce's voice, sounding tinny, shout, *"God dag, Per!"*

Per's eyes flew wider still and he stepped sharply back. He said, "Is that the spirit?" He looked toward where the heart monitor had stood.

"He thinks you're a spirit," Andrea said into the phone. Bryce laughed and said that he'd do his best to get the food sent over.

Andrea put the phone back in its cradle. Per had retreated to the bed, where he was sitting, unable to take his eyes off the phone.

She went to sit beside him, her hand naturally slipping around his. His hands always felt hot to her—and big, thin, and very strong. "It wasn't a ghost. It was a man."

"A man?" There was surprise in his voice.

"I mean an Elf. It's a far-speak. It's for talking to

people who're a long way off. The Elf we were speaking to was about a mile away, maybe a bit farther, in a place called Dilsmead Hall."

"Where the Elf-Gate be," he said.

Andrea was startled. She'd forgotten telling him that, and hadn't expected him to remember it. She looked into his face, unthinkingly raising a hand to touch his cheek, and thought: I underestimate him. Because he was a few years younger than her, she thought of him as sweet and naïve and rather silly—but was he, in fact, any of those things?

She was wondering whether to kiss him, or to wait for him to kiss her, when he got up from the bed and went over to the window, dragging the drip stand with him. "Per! I don't think you should be walking around so much. . . ."

He approached the big window with caution, still not sure that it wasn't a hole in the wall. As he came close to it, he saw that there was something filling the hole, something that caught the light like . . . ice? He put his hand out and touched a cold, hard surface. His fingers told him it was glass. Startled, he looked up at the top of the window, and to each side, seeing the glass shine here and there. Such an expanse of glass! Flat, thin, utterly clear.

"Per, come away from the window. Per, thou'rt not fit to be seen."

He allowed her to pull the lower end of the curtain across between him and the window. Stepping closer, he looked beyond the glass. He saw green: a stretch of neat lawn, with some widely spaced and spindly trees, surrounded by beds of bright flowers. It ended at a wall built of red bricks that were strikingly large and neat, all the same size and almost the same color. To Per, who had never known anything but the hills, and the one small city of Carloel, the sight was almost as alien as the sheet of glass he looked through.

It was all glamor, illusion, he decided. The grass was so even, so smooth, the flowers so large and garish, the trees so much the same and neatly spaced, that it was obvious they weren't real, and the Elves had created them all by Elf-Work—just as they made those neat bricks.

Immediately below the window he could see a gray path, seemingly made of stone—a road such as the old giants used to make. Leaning close to the glass, he followed the gray road with his eyes and saw that it led into a wide area of grayness, very dispiriting to look at, even though it was full of Elf-Carts of every bright, shining color.

Andrea was saying, again, that he should lie down and rest. He said, "Which way is Dilsssmid Oll?"

"I don't know," she said. "At least sit down." He looked at her in exasperation. "I don't know, Per. I think it might be over that way. . . ." She waved vaguely toward the wall, and where she thought the city center might be. "But I might be wrong." He gave her another ill-tempered look. It was all right for him. He'd had a lifetime's training in finding his way over almost trackless hills. She just got on a bus and never gave a thought to which way she was going.

Per was looking out the window again. "Can the Elf-Work only be heard in Dilsssmid Oll?"

It took her a moment to understand what he was

asking. "No. If thee had far-speaks, thou couldst talk to Gobby when he was in his bastle house, and thou wast in thy tower. Tha could speak to folk in Carloel and—London. And Ireland."

Per turned to her, his mouth open. *"Ireland?"* He had never seen London, and had no idea of where it was except that it was somewhere to the south. Ireland, he knew, was even farther, because you crossed the sea to reach it.

"Per, come and sit, and rest thy leg."

He was so struck by the thought of Elf-Worked voices shouting across the sea that he let her tow him to the bed. His leg did hurt, despite the fact that the wound could hardly be seen. He said, "It'd be better than a beacon."

She'd gone over to the other side of the room, and had reached up to a glass-fronted box hung high on the wall. Looking over her shoulder, she said, "What?"

"The far-speak. Better than a beacon. Tha'd talk into it and say . . ." He gave some thought to what you would say. "Sterkarm!"

Andrea blinked at the vision of a ride of lancers in iron helmets and jakkes being summoned by mobile telephone. Then she couldn't help but be impressed by the speed with which he'd grasped how useful a telephone would be. "Better than that. You could tell whoever you were calling exactly what was wrong, and how many men you needed and where you wanted them to go, by which way."

She heard him gasp and looked back at him again to see him sitting on the bed, in the full light from the windows, his mouth open and his face delighted. The sunlight caught his fair hair, polished his skin and, she thought, made him look just beautiful. It was a shame to have to say, "FUP will never let you have far-speaks, Per."

He turned and gave her a long stare. His eyes caught the light and turned silver. There was a lot of thought behind that stare.

"I'll put the far-see on," she said, and reached up to switch on the television. Distraction was called for, she thought, for both of them.

Per looked up at the glass-fronted box, and watched it fill with colors. He didn't understand why Andrea seemed to think so much of it. True, if you studied the ever-changing shapes and splotches of color carefully enough, a picture would suddenly form in them—but as soon as it was glimpsed, it would whirl away as the shapes melted and the colors changed. The thing was noisy too, blaring and yelling with sounds that made him jump.

Andrea was flipping through the channels, looking for something that might interest him. She happened on a news station, and the screen filled with angry, yelling people struggling against soldiers armed with shields and batons. There was no fancy camera work, and Per sat up straighter, exclaiming. He pointed as a mounted man leaned down from his horse and laid his baton hard across a man's shoulder.

"Wherefore is it called a far-see? Is it like the far-speak? Does it see this happening?"

"This is happening a long way away, Per."

"What, London?"

"Farther than London. Over the sea."

"Farther than . . ." He fell silent as the picture changed. He didn't know how or why the picture kept changing. The box hadn't moved, so it wasn't looking in another direction. Maybe there was a spirit in it, and the spirit was turning its head and looking at something else. . . .

Big carts moved through a crowd of people, making them scatter. Some men on the carts held long—Per didn't know what they were, but they flashed fire and made a clattering noise, and the people in the crowd ran away when they did. He guessed that the things were weapons. They seemed to be a little like pistols, though they could be fired faster and more often than any pistol he knew. But Elf-wrought things were always better.

The spirit looked at something else. This time it was seeing corpses, and seeming to turn its head slowly as it looked at more and more of them. Per knew they were corpses, because he recognized the peculiar broomstick stiffness of the dead. No one living lies as rigidly as that, even if senseless.

"Are they Elves?" he asked.

Andrea nodded, feeling ashamed. "It's a war."

The spirit was looking at dead women and dead bairns, toppling backward from a heap. "The Elves fight hard wars," Per said. Women and bairns were always in danger if captured . . . but to deliberately seek out women and bairns in such numbers as this, and to kill them all and pile them up . . . "Tha means a feud," he said. A bitter blood feud, one that had dragged on so long that the families were half ruined and desperate to finish it . . . But you would have to be desperate. He had good reason to hate the Grannams, but he wouldn't have the stomach to stand and butcher even Grannam women

191

and bairns in such numbers, not even if he was drunk on festival ale.

"No, a war," Andrea said, changing the channel. "I don't even know which one." She'd lost touch with who was killing who these days while she'd been in the 16th, and the commentary hadn't given many clues. "Oh look, Per! A tiger!" A wildlife channel. That was more like it.

Per, looking up at the screen, saw only that it was a dazzle of black, gold and green, while new noise blared from it. But then the spirit stood back, and what it saw made sense—of a sort. Per sat up straight again and his mouth fell open. A big animal, more vividly striped than a ginger tabby, strode through greenery. Leaped into a river. "What is it?"

She sat beside him on the bed. "A big cat. It's called a 'tiger.'"

"How big is it?"

"Oh . . . big. As long as one of your horses. And about half as high. Look at those teeth!" The spirit had moved close, and they saw the tiger open its mouth. It was the skin that Per admired, though. To go home with a skin like that!

"Are there any nearby?"

"There aren't any left anywhere, not anymore." He looked at her blankly. "They're all dead." Raising one hand, he pointed toward the television. "Well, that tiger was alive once, but it's dead now, like all the others."

He seemed puzzled. "Every one? Every last one?"

"It's what we call 'extinct.' It means that, yes, every last one is dead. There are no more tigers."

The screen was showing a tigress rolling on her back, playing with her cubs. "How can the far-see show us a tiger if there's no tiger for it to see?"

What a good question. She wasn't sure that she would have thought of such a good question. Difficult to answer, though. If she spoke of "film," Per would think of something thin and fine, something "filmy" like a cobweb or gauze. And "recording," if it meant anything at all to him, would mean something written down. "It's like a memory. The far-see can show us memories as well as real things. There aren't any real, living tigers anymore, just these memories of them."

He gnawed at the skin around his thumbnail and watched intently as, on the screen, a tiger reached high up a tree to sharpen its claws, tearing through the bark. "How are all the tigers dead? What could kill them all?"

"We did," she said.

He looked at her. "The Elves?"

She nodded. "We Elves did."

"Wherefore?"

Was there a more disconcerting question than "why?" She began an explanation of jungles cleared for farmland, and the trade in tigers' bones, flesh and skins. The more she explained, the more irritably guilty she felt. "Oh look! You killed all the wolves in your country, didn't you?"

"Nay. There are wolves still."

"But you kill them, don't you? And sooner or later you'll have killed all the wolves, just like we have all the tigers, and there won't be any wolves left."

He gave a long, considering stare, and then took the remote control from her hand. He handled it carefully, with many glances at her, to see if he was doing the right thing. He pressed one button after another. On the screen, a woman whipped eggs in a basin, a shark swam through a skein of blood, a water cannon was turned on a crowd, an actor pretended to shoot another actor who pretended to die, a car overturned at high speed, and then Per found the news channel which was showing, again, the heap of bodies.

Per dropped the remote on the floor and retreated to the headboard of the bed. Andrea got up and wheeled his drip stand after him. "What's the matter?"

He flicked the drip line away from his arm. "I want this taken away. I'm not a hound to be tethered to a post!"

"Be careful of it. They'll take it away soon. They took the other—"

"I want to go home."

"Per, I know, but—" He held out his arms, and she sat beside him, still careful of the drip line, and put her arms around him. His back and sides felt hard and soft at the same time—stone covered with lambs' wool—and his skin glowed with warmth. His smell of spiced musk rose around her as his arms squeezed her tight, and his cheek, almost as downy as her own, nuzzled her face. She was just sinking gratefully into the moment when he said, "Thou knows the road, Entraya. Tha canst show me."

Wary, she pressed her hands against his ribs, pushing herself back from him. "I know the road where?"

"To Elf-Gate, Honey. Tha can—"

"Oh no. Forget that, Per." She tried to get out of his arms and stand up, but he held on to her.

"Be so kind, Entraya, harken. Tha could— harken!"

Perhaps, after his time in hospital, where he'd eaten so little, she was as strong as he was, or stronger, but she

194

could still only get away from him by hurting him—and she was worried about pulling the drip from his arm. So she didn't fight him very hard. "No, Per! I am not going to be sweet-talked. We'd both get into trouble—"

"Tha'd be in no trouble, Sweet. I'd—"

"I would be in trouble! I won't do it!"

It was then that James Windsor breezed in, his arms full of shopping bags, to see her and Per sitting on the bed, Per naked with his arms around her and she struggling to get away from him.

"Oh dear! Am I interrupting something? Should I go out and come in again?"

Per, startled by the sudden entry of a stranger, let go of Andrea, and she was able to stand up, nervously pulling her skirt straight and touching her hair to check that it was tidy. "Mr. Windsor! Hello!"

He very obviously looked her over. "Well, Sexy! You've changed your look!" Instead of the frumpy jackets, skirts and big boots she usually wore, she was dressed in a calf-length, long-sleeved dress that flowed loosely over her large curves, with low-heeled pumps on her feet. She didn't seem to have on any makeup, but her hair was pinned up, with only a tendril or two falling down. In a tall, imposing, matronly way, she was almost elegant, almost attractive. If you liked room darkeners.

There was no answer Andrea could make, so she tried to look as if she hadn't heard.

"Vem air thu?" Per said, speaking to Windsor and addressing him as an inferior—"Who art thou?" not "Who are you?" He didn't understand what Windsor had said but could tell that Andrea hadn't liked it. And the man was dressed soberly, all in black and white, and

was carrying parcels—a servingman who thought he could take advantage of Andrea's gentle nature. Per didn't like that. He didn't like anything of the stranger's manner toward Andrea at all. Getting up from the bed, the drip line trailing from his arm, he went to stand slightly in front of Andrea and reached behind him to take her hand. He stared at Windsor. *"Entraya, vah sayer han?"* What says he?

"Nie ting, Per. Olla air rikti." Nothing. All is right.

Windsor looked at Per, shook the shopping bag from one of his parcels, and slapped a pair of folded blue jeans against Per's chest. "Maybe you can find a use for them." Leaning past Per, he gave Andrea a large box of chocolates. "And I'm sure you'll know what to do with them."

Andrea took the chocolates and dropped them onto the seat of a chair behind her without looking at them. It was like Windsor to generously buy presents and then insult you as he gave them to you. Perhaps he was just paying for the right to insult you.

"Vah sayer han?" Per asked again. She hushed him, patting his back so he wouldn't take offense.

"Fraternizing with the natives?" Windsor said.

It had been written into Andrea's contract that she wouldn't "fraternize" 16th side. She'd signed it without a thought, thinking it would never be a problem. "We were just talking."

"Talking?" Windsor said. "Not what my mother would have called it. Your lucky day, eh, Andrea?"

"Vah sayer han? Vem air deyn karl?" Who is this guy?

Windsor was tossing the other things he'd bought onto the bed: a large bouquet of flowers, crackling in its cellophane wrappings and tied with a wide yellow ribbon, and a big basket of fruit, decorated with a blue ribbon. The gigantic blooms with their garish colors held Per's attention. There was nothing like them in Man's-Home.

He was still looking at them when Windsor slapped a scarlet baseball cap onto Per's head. Startled, Per fended it off and knocked it to the floor. "Texas Longhorns" it said across the front, in white letters. Windsor stuck his right hand out at Per. "James Windsor. I'm glad to see you looking a lot better than the last time we met!"

Andrea translated, and added, "This is Elf-Windsor, the Elf who came to see thy father. He brought thee through the Gate—he saved thy life," she added generously.

Per turned a long, considering stare on Windsor. He had no clear memory of his life ever having been in danger, so he wasn't filled with gratitude. This, he thought, was the Elf who had trapped him in Elf-Land. This was the Elf who gave his father orders, forbidding the Sterkarms to ride or hunt in their own country—and had the impertinence to think he would be obeyed.

But Per knew his manners. In Elf-Land he was a guest, even if an unwilling one. He offered Windsor his right hand and turned his left cheek toward him, so that the older man could give him the greeting kiss. Windsor took his hand and tried to crush it, but made no attempt to kiss him. Per half turned his head toward Andrea in surprise. Plainly, this Windsor was a boor, with no idea of how to behave. But it wasn't Per's place, as by far the younger man, to offer the kiss first, or to correct Windsor's manners.

"No mistaking whose son you are!" Windsor said. "If

his mother grew a bit of bum-fluff round her chin, they'd be twins!"

"Mr. Windsor says tha looks very like thy mother," Andrea told Per, who merely nodded, while continuing to stare at Windsor.

"His mother can smile, though," Windsor said. There was no good humor in the boy's face. His eyes were just as big and striking as his mother's, their blue as silver-pale, but Per's straight stare translated into something like "Get lost." A sulky teenager—who'd have thought it?

The boy's obvious hostility rather amused Windsor—at least, while the boy was alone, here in this 21st hospital room, it was amusing. Impossible to imagine this boy tying a man's head to his saddle. He would be more credible in the Upper Sixth, well scrubbed and demure on Parents' Day and afterward smashed and sick on cider. It wasn't going to be as hard to keep young Sterkarm on a leash as he'd feared. A few shiny toys and a good bawling out if he overstepped the line should be enough.

Thinking of toys made him remember a present he'd forgotten, and he slapped himself to find which pocket he'd put it in. From his hip pocket he brought a folding leather wallet, and opened it to show a wad of notes inside. "It's unlucky to give an empty wallet, I was always told, so I went to the cash machine. Here." He held it out to Per. "Maybe you can buy some clothes. Get him to put something on, Andrea. Even if you like the view, we should spare the nurses' blushes."

Per had taken the wallet, out of curiosity, and was rubbing his finger on the paper inside it. He pulled out a slip of it and admired the beautiful patterning.

"*Penya*," Andrea said. Money.

Per looked at her and laughed. Money was coin, copper, silver and gold. Not worthless paper.

"*Sootha*, Per. Truly. It's a present from Mr. Windsor. So that you can buy things while you're here."

Per looked at Windsor sidelong. "*Tahk skal thu har.*" Thanks shalt thou have. "*Herr Erlf, nor gaw yi hyemma?*"

"What's he say?" Windsor asked.

"He says, Thank you, and he wants to know when he's going home."

"Ah," Windsor said. He put two fingers on Per's arm and pushed him toward the bed, leaning past him and pulling the bedcovers back. "Why don't you hop back into bed, old son? Rest up as much as you can." Per looked over his shoulder at Andrea, and she nodded to him, so he got onto the bed. Windsor threw the covers over him, put the baseball cap back on his head, and passed him the basket of fruit. "Get stuck into that." He looked around for the chocolates, picked them up and passed them to Per as well. "There. Enjoy yourself."

Per didn't understand what Windsor said, but he read his face and manner easily enough. Windsor didn't wish to answer him—that told him a lot. It was also quite clear that Windsor had no respect for him. He tossed the wallet and its Elf-Money to the end of the bed.

To Andrea, Windsor said, "I hope you've got your bags packed?"

Her face brightened. "Most of my stuff is still 16th side, so—"

"Well, the Tube's going to be up again this afternoon, and I want you on the other side as soon—"

"Oh *great!*" She looked past Windsor to the bed. "Per! Harken—" Per was watching her attentively, but she broke off as Windsor waved his hand before her face.

"You, I said. I didn't say anything about him. He stays here."

"Oh, but his leg's as good as healed and—I don't know if your secretary told you about his not eating." She saw no understanding in Windsor's face. "I explained it to her."

"Andrea, Andrea. Watch my lips. He's not going back. He's more use to me here. And you—you're more use to me 16th side, earning your pay."

"*Vah sayer han?*" Per asked.

"*Nie ting, Per. Sssh!*" To Windsor, she said, "You *can't!*"

"I can't? What can't I?"

"You can't just— He's not eating! He won't eat our food. He'll *starve.*"

"Oh, he'll get over that soon enough."

She wanted to clench her fists in the air and yell. He hadn't watched Per refusing the hospital meals and rationing out his tiny supply of food, and yet he could complacently brush her fears aside. "What if he doesn't? What if he makes himself ill?"

"Get a grip," Windsor said. "The day a big healthy teenager starves himself to death, pigs'll fly."

"But you can't keep him here by himself!"

Per could see that they were quarreling, and he got out of bed again, bringing the drip stand with him. "*Entraya?*" He edged himself slightly between her and Windsor, looking at Windsor with a frown.

Windsor gave him a look from the corner of his eye. "Should I be worried? Look, Andrea. You're employed as—" He raised his hand to wag a forefinger at her. Per put his own hand over Windsor's and pushed it down. Per thought pointing was rude. Pausing, Windsor tutted, and said, "Can we talk about this outside? Without Sunny Jim?"

"Per." Andrea turned to him, pushing him to the bed with both hands. "Lie down and rest thy leg, love. I have to talk with Mr. Windsor." The back of his knee struck the bed and he sat down heavily. She kissed his cheek. "I won't be long."

He caught her wrists. "I'll come with thee."

"Nay. I haven't time to tell thee everything that's said. Best if tha stays here. I'll be back in an eye's blink, truly. Per, let go."

"What is he to thee?"

She looked over her shoulder at Windsor, who was standing with his arms folded, amused by Per's glower. "I work for him. He's my . . . master." She couldn't think of another word that Per would understand, but it was all wrong, suggesting that she was bound in service to Windsor as the Sterkarms' hired men and kitchen maids were bound in service to them.

Per had been letting her go, but now his grip tightened again and he pulled her back, his frown deepening. "What work?"

She was stuck for an answer. She cupped her hands about his face, her wrists still gripped by his fingers, and kissed him. "Per, let me go. I'll be back in a few minutes—"

Behind her, Windsor said, "How sweet."

"—and I'll explain everything then, I promise."

Per looked from her to Windsor. "When do I go home? Ask him!"

She looked over her shoulder. "He still wants to know when he's going home."

Per watched Windsor as Andrea spoke, his wide stare taking in the man's whole figure, his face, his movements. He saw Windsor tilt back his head, as he stood with folded arms, and smile a tight-lipped smile.

"Soon," Windsor said. "Tell him very soon."

Per went on watching Windsor as Andrea translated his words. He saw the man look aside and grin. Watch a cat, and you can tell when it's going to jump, and which way. Per knew Windsor was lying.

"Go with him and talk, then," Per said to Andrea. He kissed her cheek, but she pulled back and looked at him, puzzled by the hurt tone in his voice. He ducked his head forward and kissed her on the mouth, startling her, and then, when she thought he was going to release her, hugged her hard.

"Per! I shall only be gone an eye's blink."

"Go then."

She gave his cheek a kiss, got up and followed Windsor.

As soon as the door closed on them, Per took hold of the drip feed in his arm and pulled it out. Bright red blood welled up in the crook of his elbow, and he stanched it with the sheet, bending his arm over it. The needle made a fine, sharp pain as it left the vein, but he'd felt worse a great many times, and it balanced the pain under his ribs. His Elf-May did not love him so much as she sought the favor of her Elf-Master. She had brought him into Elf-Land to please her Master.

The pain swelled under his ribs. It felt as if his heart would burst, filled as it was not only with the grief of losing his Elf-May, his wife, his future, but with the humiliation of having been tricked, of having loved and trusted her when she hadn't loved him. All the kisses she'd given him, all the assurances and promises, the accounts of his having been near death—the wound on his leg looked as if it had never been more than a scratch—all lies told for her Master!

It was clear to Per why Elf-Windsor wanted him. He hardly had to think about it. As a child, he'd played at riding with his cousins and the other children of the tower, games that had taken days to play out, as they'd fought battles with wooden swords and lances, driven off real or imaginary sheep and taken prisoners. They'd held long ransom negotiations, with hard-driven terms, the ransoms paid in pebbles, buttons and shells.

And then hostages had been exchanged, to make sure the terms would be kept. Haggling over the hostages had been fiercer still. Your enemies always demanded as their hostage the person you were known to love most dearly—and even in play, it was hard to give that person into a captivity that was likely to be harsher than that of a real hostage.

The next stage of the game, inevitably, was the breaking of the terms, the renewing of hostilities, and the vengeful killing of the hostages.

Per was surprised that it had taken Elf-Windsor so long to see the only way to make Toorkild obey his orders.

The duty of a hostage was to escape if he could. And

for every day he stayed a hostage in Elf-Land, a year or ten years or a hundred years might pass in Man's-Home.

When he thought of leaving Andrea, and perhaps never seeing her again, he knew he should feel glad and angry—well rid of her! But it felt as if another long needle were being withdrawn from his heart, and he had to keep touching his eyes to take away the blurring of tears.

Free of the drip line's tether, he got up and looked at the britches the Elf-Man had tossed at him. They were of good, strong, tightly woven material—would be good for riding—but went all the way down to the ankle in Elvish style. Still, he would be noticed less in Elvish clothes. He pulled them on, but had difficulty with the fastening.

The button at the waist was simple enough, but you had to be an Elf to fasten them below that.

In the closet where Andrea had fetched his dagger, he found his shirt, doublet, and belt. From the bed he took the jakke, with its layers of leather, cloth and iron plates. It slumped weightily from his hand. He didn't waste time putting on the clothes but slung them over his shoulder. From beneath his pillow he took his dagger, and his pouch with the very last of his food and beer.

The wallet Windsor had given him was lying on the floor at the foot of the bed, where it had fallen. He picked it up and put it in his pouch. Money was always useful in his own world. He supposed that Elf-Money would be useful in Elf-Land. He reached back to the bed for the baseball cap too, and put it on. The more he dressed like an Elf, the better.

He was at the door of the room, ready to go, but still

it was hard. He thought of Andrea, coming back and finding him gone. She'd think he'd gone without caring, without thinking of her—well, serve her right, and what would she care? But though he tried to be angry, a hope persisted that he'd misunderstood, that she hadn't, after all, betrayed him.

He turned back to the bed, to the big bunch of flowers the Elf had brought. They were wrapped in some Elvish stuff, as transparent as water, that crackled like flames on wood. He didn't want to touch it, though the Elf had held it without harm.

There was an opening at the top, and he reached through that and pulled out a large red flower, gaudy and blowsy. Its thick stem was thorned, and it reeked. He carried it over to the chair where Andrea usually sat and left it on the seat, hoping she would see it and guess he had left it there as a good-bye. He only wished he had a rose to leave for her, like the ones that grew in the woods near the tower.

Going back to the door of the room, he opened it and looked out into the wide corridor. The walls out there were smooth, without plaster or beams, and in color something like dried grass. Though only a corridor, it was brightly lit, as Elvish places always were. There were many doors, and many Elves walking here and there—he saw Andrea, her back toward him, and Elf-Windsor standing several yards away. People passed them by, but they were paying attention only to each other. Andrea was all eyes for her Master, the Elf-Man. The sight held Per by the door a moment longer than he should have stayed.

He stepped out into the corridor, bare chested and

barefoot, carrying his clothes over his shoulder, walking away in the opposite direction from where Andrea and Windsor stood. People passed him and glanced at him, but no one tried to stop him, as he'd feared they might. Within a few feet he came to a staircase and paused for a moment, awed.

Huge windows filled the stairwell with light, so the pale walls shone. The stairs were covered with cloth, and had delicate handrails of polished wood and polished silver. In its beauty and wealth, the stair was truly Elvish.

Then he remembered that the important thing about the stair was that it went down, toward the ground, and he started down.

* * *

"It's illegal!" Andrea said. "It's kidnapping!"

"What a stroke of luck I've got you to advise me. Since young Sterkarm doesn't officially exist 21st side, tell me, exactly what law am I breaking by putting him up in the lap of luxury and making sure he has everything he could possibly want?"

"He hates it here! He won't eat! And you expect me to go back and carry on while Per stays here! Didn't you hear what Toorkild said?"

"I think you should keep your voice down, young lady. We are in a hospital."

"'Bring him back alive, or don't come back!' That's what he said! How do you think he's going to welcome me if I go back without Per?"

"Now you listen to me, Miss. I've got billions of pounds' worth of technology lying idle, and personnel drawing wages for sitting on their arses. And why? Because the bloody Sterkarms are camped around our

206

office, 16th side, like a picket line, and my survey teams won't go out past them!"

"Yes, but—"

Windsor raised his voice slightly and easily shouted her down.

"So what are you paid for? FUP is filling up your bank account every month, and in return you're supposed to liaise for us 16th side, isn't that right? And you have them eating out of your hand, don't you? So I'm told. Did you think it was all going to be a walk in the country, writing your little book on our time and snogging your toy-boy back there? Well, sorry to tear you away from him, but we'd quite like you to actually earn your money now, please. I want you back there this afternoon, squaring it with the Sterkarms. And if that's too much to ask of you, there're always the Job Centers, dear."

Windsor's closeness, his loud voice, his height and sheer bulk, were intimidating. She wanted to stand up to him but could feel herself shaking with anger and nerves. If she tried to speak, her voice would squeak. And his accusations that she'd coasted along on FUP's time, his assertion that he only wanted her to earn her wages, were hard to argue against. . . . But even while she hung her head in silence, she *knew* that keeping Per 21st side was wrong. She tried to think of something to say but couldn't. She needed a notepad, a pen and a few hours to draft and redraft her arguments.

Windsor, seeing that she'd fallen quiet, said, "We could rig up a video in the office, I suppose. Let them in a few at a time to see—I don't know—film of young Sterkarm looking happy and wearing a party hat."

Andrea let a moment pass in silence, and then said, "You can't keep Per here by himself. He'll go crazy. He'll be so lonely. It would be cruel."

"He'll have the time of his life," Windsor said.

"Mr. Windsor . . . you don't even begin to understand, do you?"

"I understand very well that while young Sterkarm is here, old Sterkarm will do exactly what I tell him, how I tell him, when I tell him, for as long as I tell him—and that will make a refreshing change."

"And if he doesn't, what then?" Andrea said.

Windsor looked at her as if she'd made some incomprehensible noise.

"Mr. Windsor, if Toorkild calls your bluff about Per, what will you do?"

"Well," Windsor said, "I doubt if he's really going to want to find that out, is he? Be at the Tube at three."

10

21st Side: Joe Sterkarm

THE ELVES' SICK HOUSE was big. Per descended one staircase of two long flights and came upon another corridor just like the one above: brilliantly lit, lined with doors, the floor covered in cloth, and pictures hung on the walls. A thumping and twittering inhabited the very air about him, and was louder as he passed under boxes high on the walls, as if the boxes held yelling spirits. Elves, many Elves, came and went in both directions, with an incessant din of chattering voices and trampling feet. So many Elves, all swirling by, their mouths all working, their eyes all darting at him, bewildered him, made his heart beat faster, until it was hard to think. So many. More than leaves in the wood or stones in the stream, more than crowded Carloel on market day—and this was but one corridor in a sick house.

There were so many *kinds* of Elves. Some dressed all in white, some all in blue, some all in black. Some Elves had skins as brown as peat water, and dark, dark hair and eyes—those, he supposed, were the Black Elves he'd heard tell of, though he'd always thought the "black" had meant they had dark hair or wore dark clothes.

There were small Elves, children—and he had always heard that Elf-Children were few. Why else did the Elves steal mortal babies? But these children seemed healthy and were dressed in brilliant colors, as were the women. Yellows brighter than gorse, reds brighter than holly berries. Gold and gems dangled from their ears. The women all had their skirts hiked up to their knees, as if they were working in the fields; and all wore their hair uncovered, as if unmarried. So many of them had their hair cropped short that he supposed it must be an Elvish custom and not a punishment.

An Elf-Woman went by him, seated in a chair that moved along by itself, humming as it went. An Elf-Man walked by the other way, talking into a—a far-speak, but one that had no leash fastening it to the wall. Two Elf-Women each carried huge bunches of giant, fiercely colored Elvish flowers. And all the time the air twittered and beeped and hissed and buzzed.

On and on the corridor went, an endless straight line, and all the Elves stared at his bare chest and his bare feet. He opened one of the many doors, hoping to find some refuge where he could put on his clothes, perhaps even a way out of the building.

Behind the door was another brightly lit room, like the one he'd spent the past days in, but luckily empty of Elves. He closed the door after him, dropped his things on the bed and dressed, quickly pulling on his shirt, which hung loose almost to his knees. Its side was stained brown with his blood, and the linen had dried hard. The doublet was hard to put on because he had to thread his arms through the ribboned sleeves, and it, too, was ruined with bloodstains. His mother would not be pleased—but he'd welcome her displeasure, since he'd have to reach home before she could shout at him.

He put on the jakke, shrugging its weight onto his shoulders and fastening its large hooks and eyes. Wearing it, he felt safer, and a little more confident.

He threaded his pouch back onto his belt and would have slipped the belt through the loops of his dagger's sheath too, but then thought it better not to let the Elves see that he was armed. Instead, he pushed the sheath inside his right sleeve, buckling one of the sheath's straps around his wrist. It was difficult to push the dagger's hilt past the narrow opening of his doublet's cuff, and the blade was so long that the sheath's point pressed out against the elbow of his shirt. But he was able to hold the pommel in his right hand, and keep the weapon both ready and hidden.

The room, like all Elf-Rooms, had big windows of great, flat, sheer sheets of glass, and even from close by the door he was able to see that he was still high above the ground. He went back into the corridor, where he drew fewer stares, and kept doggedly on past the closed doors until the passage opened out into a big room with such huge windows, stretching from floor to ceiling on either side, that he had to raise his hand to his eyes against the light. Here there were thickets—indoors, above ground—of lush green bushes, and crowds of Elves sitting on chairs that were all cushion. The cushions were of such violent colors—yellow, violet, scarlet, green—that to look at them was to feel needles in the eyes. And here again was all the din of Elf-Land redoubled: crashes, clangs, twitterings and the laughing of staring Elves.

He kept close by the wall, meaning to make his way around the edge of the room to the other side, but this brought him against one of the windows. He looked down to the ground below, and the view was so clear, he felt that he might fall. His back still to the wall, he edged away from the window.

To get to the other side of the room he would have to walk across the open space in the middle, leaving his back exposed to attack. He leaned against the wall, his heart thumping heavily, trying to find the nerve.

Opposite him, he saw an Elf-Man's head come up through the floor. Per jumped and stood stiff against the wall, watching. An Elf-Woman's head came into view beside the man's—then their shoulders appeared, and the rest of them, sliding upward. They were inside a little room with walls of glass that slid up through the floor. Its door opened, and they stepped out and walked toward him. He watched them until they passed by him into the corridor. Then he looked back at the little room and saw more Elves get into it. The room slid down through the floor and disappeared.

It took him a few heavy beats of his heart to work out that the room was going through the ceiling to the floor below. Was that how he had to get to the ground? Rather than trust himself to Elf-Work in a box like that, he'd break a window and jump.

But he caught sight of Elves going up stairs beyond the little glass room. The only way he was going to reach the stairs was by crossing the open room. So he ran. He reached the other side feeling unsteady, as if a little drunk, and with the muscles of his wounded leg twanging. To feel so weak so soon dismayed him, but he refused to think of it. Leaning on the handrail, he went down the stairs, favoring his hurt leg.

At the bottom was yet another long corridor, with yet more doors. Per opened the nearest door. An Elf-Man, in a long robe, was sitting in a chair near the bed and stared at him. Per looked at the windows and saw that they were open, and that he was on ground level at last.

"Good day," he said to the Elf-Man, with a slight bow, as he closed the door behind him. The Elf-Man continued to stare, watching Per as he crossed the room, turned his back to the window, set his hands on the sill and boosted himself up.

He was astonished at how much effort it took, used as he was to finding such things easy. He wondered if it was some Elf-Work, a spell laid on him to prevent his escape. If so, it failed, because he got onto the sill and swung his left leg over it, even though his arms shook.

He glanced back at the Elf-Man's startled face, and raised a hand. "Fare you well." The muscles complained in his hurt leg as he tried to lift it over the sill, and he had to help it with his hands—but he managed, and dropped to the grass.

Under his bare feet, the earth felt cool and the grass soft and damp, and it was a relief to be outdoors again, though it was a strange world. Nearby was a planting of the big, gaudy Elf-Flowers, redder than blood and glaring as gold as narange juice. The air drummed and roared.

But if he'd been blindfolded and his ears plugged with wax, he'd still have known he was far from Man's-Home. The very air felt different as it touched his skin, as he breathed it in, though it was hard to say how. It smelled wrong, somehow.

He paused a second while he cast about in his mind for the direction of the room he'd lived in for the past days. From the window of that room Andrea had waved, saying, "Dilsmead Hall is that way. . . ." And that was the way he had to go.

He reached the corner of the immense building and stopped, stooping forward to lean on his knees. He felt slightly giddy, and his leg was aching, not badly, but steadily. Still:

> What can't be cured
> Must be endured.

In front of him was a gravel drive leading toward a gateway in a wall. As he approached it, a box on wheels—a box of a glaring, brilliant blue—a noisy, groaning box of metal on black wheels— moved toward him, its wheels thrashing in the gravel and throwing up stones. Its metal sides flashed in the sun, and it had windows of glass as sheer and flat as those of the building, and they too flashed. Per stopped short, alarmed, watching as the thing sped past him with weight and power.

He stood still, on the verge of turning back to the sick house. Never had he missed Sweet Milk so much, or so much wanted the company of his cousins.

But he either went back to be Elf-Windsor's hostage or he went on, no matter how hard his heart beat. He clenched his hand around the pommel of his dagger and went on, walking on the grass beside the graveled path, moving as quickly as he could because he was more likely to be seen leaving by the gate—but, that day, he didn't think he had the strength to climb the wall.

The gate had no guards, though the sick house was walled. But from beyond the gate came such a din, such a savage roaring and screeching and whirring, that Per came to a halt again. The din struck him about the head and made him shake. He had never heard the like of such noise. Even the sounds of battle, of yells and shrieks, and swords banging on shields and clanging on helmets, was nothing like this.

He came to a stop. He couldn't go on, into that din. He couldn't go back. Maybe this was his fate, in Elf-Land, to stand frozen in that spot forever.

* * *

Andrea, her face red, her blood pumping fast, hurried back along the corridor to Per's room. Windsor was the big boss; what he said was law. At three o'clock sharp she was going to be at Dilsmead Hall, ready to go back 16th side. What Windsor didn't know was that Per was going with her.

What happened after that—well, there was no point in thinking about it or worrying about what would happen. She just flat out wasn't going to abandon Per, whatever Windsor or anyone else said. Or did. When she asked herself what was more important—her job, FUP's dealings 16th side, or Per—then she felt no doubt at all. She was scared when she thought of the trouble she would be in, but being scared didn't alter what was important. When the balloon went up, she would just have to cope.

She barged into the room, saying, "Per!" Not seeing him in the bed, she looked around at the armchairs, the corners. He wasn't there.

Going over to the door of the bathroom, she tapped,

and then opened it. The bathroom, too, was empty.

For a moment she was dizzy with fright and anger, and thought: Windsor! He'd had Per moved somewhere. Then her mind started to work, and she asked herself how he'd have had the time. She saw the drip stand still beside the bed, the line from it now dripping healing accelerant onto the carpet. The bedcover was stained with blood. The line hadn't been removed by a doctor. Per had pulled it out himself, as he'd been threatening he'd do.

The big bouquet of flowers and the basket of fruit were still on the bed, but the jeans and baseball cap and jakke were gone. Andrea turned from the bed and opened the closets. Per's doublet, shirt and belt were gone too. Standing, she threw back the bedcovers, letting the flowers and fruit fall on the floor. She pulled aside the pillows. Per's pouch and his dagger were missing. Per had done a runner.

He hadn't waited for her. He hadn't trusted her at all, but had gone haring off. What was he going to do in Elf-Land? He'd only the faintest idea of where he was going, and no idea at all of the dangers he would meet on the way. The ring road, the railway lines, muggers.

She clutched at her head with both hands, trying to hold together the panic and half-formed plans that filled it. Hospital security—if she got them to search the hospital building and grounds, Per might still be on the premises somewhere. Or would that make it official that Per was missing? Would Windsor be alerted?

How long a start did he have? That was the important thing to decide. She tried to estimate how long she'd been arguing with Windsor. Ten, fifteen minutes?

Certainly no longer, and probably less. She knew the general direction Per was heading in. If she hurried, she'd catch up to him.

She got her coat from the closet, putting it on as she left the room, and ran down the corridor to the elevators.

* * *

Per stood on the grass at the edge of the gravel drive, peering out through the hospital gates. He glimpsed a dashing blur of bright colors, blinding flashes. The noise was the noise of an immense river rushing by in high spate, mingled with the rasp of a grindstone, the tumbling crash of falling barrels and shrieking, roaring.

Though his heart still beat strongly, and he was breathing fast, Per could make sense of the din and the blur. It was a race of Elf-Carts, more and bigger Elf-Carts than he had thought there could be, moving at great speed, faster than a storm wind, faster than witches, their glass and metal catching the light.

He knew the longer he stood there, the more likely he'd be caught. He knew that he had to go forward, through the gate, closer to all that hurtling weight and noise. His legs shook under him, but gripping his dagger's hilt, he followed the grass right up to the brick pillar of the gate. He put his hand on the bricks and could feel them vibrating with the power of the Elf-Carts passing.

He stepped into the gravel, which was sharp to his bare feet, and looked around the gatepost. Flung grit, dirt and fumes hit him in the face. He pulled his head back, grimacing, but looked out again. Beside the Elf-Carts' racetrack was a clear path, seemingly made to walk on, since there were Elves walking coolly along it as if the Elf-Carts weren't roaring and snarling a foot from them.

Seeing that, Per stepped out from behind the gatepost and walked on the footpath himself, following it uphill toward the bright sky that was more like the sky of Man's-Home than of Elf-Land. He moved awkwardly—not only did his hurt leg ache, but his every muscle was tensed with fear—and he kept close by the sick-house wall, as far as he could from the Elf-Carts. The dust and grime they flung up got into his mouth and up his nose, and his eyes smarted and ran with tears.

The stories had always said that the Elves were rich and powerful, that they lived for three hundred years in palaces lit by gems, wore colored clothes every day and never went hungry—but as he leaned against the wall and felt it thrum while a great wagon crashed by, he realized that the power and wealth of the Elves went far, far beyond anything he had heard or imagined.

The path beneath his feet wasn't of dirt or grass, but of large flat paving stones, or a dimpled black stuff he didn't know, or a gray stuff. He stooped to touch it, and it felt like stone but it looked like stone melted. There were seams and patches of paving stones, and black stuff, and gray stuff, all pitted with puddles, in which gaily colored scraps floated. Scraps blew all about. There were pieces of valuable metal, oblongs of flat, crinkled metal that would make an arrowhead, just lying abandoned on the ground, thrown away. He picked one up and was able to bend it in his hands, it was beaten so thin—but he didn't think it was iron. Elves feared iron, so it was said, and it didn't have the feel of iron. Still, he was half minded to take it with him for the tower smith, but maybe such Elvish gear would be unlucky. He dropped it again.

He stopped to spit dirt from his mouth, and to wipe at his eyes with his shirtsleeve. With freshly dried eyes, he looked up into the blue sky and saw a tiny dot speeding over the sky's bowl, drawing behind it a double white line—of smoke? His heart beat faster again as he watched the dragon pass overhead. Lucky for him, it was flying high and heading far off.

And then he came in view of the castle.

It was a castle. There was nothing else it could be. And something about the way it hugged the ground of its low hill and held its towers against the sky plucked at his memory. Yet it was nothing like a castle.

It was hard to study it because the Elf-Carts still raced and roared beside him, and Elves were passing by, and they were walking down a ramp into a hole under the Elf-Carts' track. But he saw that, instead of stone, the castle was built of brick, and was surrounded by smooth green lawns, cropped short as if grazed by sheep. The castle's ditch was all grass-grown, and was filled with neither water nor stakes, and a brick bridge was built across it. A castle without defenses.

He turned away, meaning to look again at this hole in the ground, but his eye was caught and drawn upward. The Elf-Carts careering by had seemed so fearsome that he had hardly looked beyond them to the other side of the broad road. The more Elvish buildings, even now, he scarcely saw except as blocks. But there rose above them, into the sky, a square tower of reddish, grayish stone.

He looked over his shoulder at the castle, his heart

skipping with alarm, and again turned to look at the tower.

It was the tower of Carloel Cathedral. He'd seen it against the sky many, many times, and he had good reason to remember it. Beneath that tower, a bishop had cursed all Sterkarms living, dead and as yet unbegotten. . . . Nothing had come of it, and they had laughed and said, "Not even God dares meddle with us!"

Carloel Cathedral, where his family had been cursed, stood almost at the gates of Carloel Castle, where they imprisoned any Sterkarm found within the city walls after sunset. The defenseless Elf-Castle behind him stood just where Carloel Castle would be if the tower was the cathedral. And the tower was just where the cathedral would be if the castle was Carloel Castle. But in Carloel there was no racing track of Elf-Carts between the cathedral and the castle. There were no dragons flying overhead. And the castle wasn't built of brick, defenseless and unguarded.

Per stood by the ring road and the underpass, looking from the castle to the cathedral, thinking "Elf-Land," thinking "Carloel," and unable to think anything else.

* * *

At the hospital gate, Andrea turned uphill, trusting Per's sense of direction to have taken him that way. Shading her eyes, she looked up the road ahead of her—and saw him! He was well ahead of her, almost at the limit of the road she could see, before it topped the hill and disappeared down the other side. She cupped her hands to her mouth and shouted his name, but she'd never been much good at shouting, and he didn't hear her above the traffic. She wasn't sure that he would have stopped if he had.

She ran to catch him up, but everything was against her: She was no runner, the road was uphill, and she had on pumps which, even if low-heeled, were not designed for running. After hopping on one foot to recover a shoe that had slipped off, she settled for walking as briskly as she could, even though out of breath.

Per had disappeared over the brow of the hill. She knew what lay beyond it. There was the castle, which was still in use as an army barracks and bore little resemblance to the castle Per had known; and there was an underpass that led under the road and allowed pedestrians to reach the city center. If Per wandered through there, and got among the crowds, she'd never find him. "Oh hell!" She took off her shoes and, carrying them in her hands, began to run again, dodging the flattened tin cans, puddles and broken glass as well as she could.

* * *

On a piece of cardboard torn from a carton, Joe had written "Homeless. Please help." It lay on the wet tiles of the underpass floor in front of him, beside a plastic cup holding a few coins. People gave more readily if they could see that others already had, but if there was too much money in the cup, they thought he'd already got all he deserved and wouldn't give him any more. Whenever the cup held about a pound, Joe put all but a few coins into his pocket.

He hated it, sitting there on his arse, asking people to give him money. He used to be the one with a job and plenty of money in his pocket, dropping money into charity boxes. When people passed him by without giving him anything, and gave him a look, he could see them thinking, "Why isn't a big lump like you working for his money?" It made him feel sick. But he'd tried being proud. Pride went hungry.

His sneakers were still wet from a heavy rainstorm the day before, and his feet were sticky and damp inside them. The floor was hard and cold under his bum, and he couldn't get his back comfortable against the wall—but the underpass sheltered him from rain squalls and, for a while, it had been a good place to catch office workers on their way to the city center for lunch, and tourists on their way to and from the castle. Things had gone quiet, though. Joe was trying to decide whether to stick around and see if the office workers who hadn't given him anything were in a better mood on their way back after lunch, or whether to just go and get something to eat himself. He probably had enough for a hamburger. He was sick of hamburgers. He never had liked them much.

Sausage sandwiches were what he'd like. He'd like to fry the sausages himself until they were almost black and splitting, and then halve them lengthwise and arrange them on the bread, and dribble brown sauce along them. And to go with it he'd like a big mug of tea that he'd made himself, the way he liked it, and not cat's piss in a squeezy plastic cup.

But to eat like that, you had to have a place of your own, with a kitchen cupboard you could keep a package of tea and a loaf of bread in, and a little gas ring to cook it on. A studio would do. He liked to keep his daydreams realistic—then there was more chance of their coming true.

Not that he could see much hope of getting even a studio anytime soon. He could make twenty, thirty pounds a day, begging—and then, every day, he had to spend it all. The money soon went when you had to buy your breakfast, dinner and tea at fast-food joints. He could buy cheaper food in a supermarket, but he had nowhere to cook it and nowhere to keep it. At the end of every day, there wasn't anything left to save up for rent.

A front door with a lock and his own key. And a bed. And a kitchen cupboard and a gas ring. That's all he'd need, to start with. He could sit on the bed.

No more sleeping on concrete and cardboard. No more being cold all night, and having wet feet for days on end. No more drunks pissing on him, or giving him a kick, because they had a job and a house and he didn't, and somehow that was good reason to kick him.

And when he had the studio, he'd get himself a lady friend to share it all with him. Snuggle up in the bed together. Get up and make her a cup of tea. And a sausage sandwich. A woman with some meat on her bones, one who'd enjoy a sausage sandwich. Heaven on bloody earth!

Voices shouted near him, sharp and angry. He tipped his head forward and opened his eyes. At the bottom of the ramp leading down into the underpass from the pavement above, a young couple were squabbling. Joe was about to close his eyes again when he noticed that both of them had bare feet.

The man was backing away from the woman into the underpass, but then gave a sort of cringing upward look at the underpass roof, swung around, and backed out again. He had a bright-red baseball cap on his head, a sort of sleeveless, quilted body warmer worn over a long, loose shirt that hung to his knees, a pair of blue jeans and nothing on his feet at all.

The young woman, who was alternately snapping and pleading at him, was a nice big buxom lass, a bit older than the lad. If she was going to break up with him, it was a pity Joe hadn't managed to get that studio yet. Her face was all pink, and her long brown hair, which had been pinned up on top of her head, was falling down in long strands. She wore one of those long, loose dresses that always looked so womanly, with a light coat over it, and had a nice shapely pair of calves in dark stockings—but her feet were bare because, for some reason, she was carrying her shoes in her hand, and her stockings' feet were shredded.

Joe felt like some entertainment. He linked his hands around his knees and watched.

* * *

"It's only me," Andrea said. "There's no one with me, tha canst see there's nobody with me. I'm going to take thee home, Per."

"Nay," Per said, pulling away from her.

"I'm going to try anyway. It's all we can do. If we go quickly—"

"Go back to thy Master," Per said.

"Per, come *on*!" She tried to pull him into the underpass, but he twisted his wrist against her thumb's hold and easily broke her grasp.

"Nay," he said, stepping back from under the overhanging shelf of the underpass, with an apprehensive upward glance.

"What do you mean, nay?" For the first time since she'd caught up with him, she began to listen to what he

224

was saying. "We're going to the Elf-Gate! That's what tha want, is it no? Now come on!"

"I know," he said to her. "I know tha brought me here to be a hostage for thy Master! If I go—"

"I brought thee here to save thy life!"

"—thou'lt lead me into ambush!"

"Per! I never heard such . . . How canst *think* that?"

"I'll no go with thee," he said, and looked past her, at the way she'd come, as if he still expected to see people following her.

"Oh? And where be thee going?" She went to take his arm again.

He stepped back, lifting his arms out of her reach. "I'll find my way."

"How? How? Per, don't be such a sheep's head—"

Angered, he pushed her away. She stumbled back a step or two, and hurt her foot by treading on a flattened tin can. Looking down, she saw her white feet sticking out of her ruined black stockings and remembered that she had her shoes in her hand. "Oh, *Per!*"

He had backed out from under the underpass again and stood at its entrance, looking up at the pavement above. It was plain that he hadn't an idea what to do but still wasn't going to do what she wanted him to do.

Andrea dropped her shoes to the ground, put them on, and marched over to him. She grabbed his wrist in both hands. "Come *on*! Stop—playing—silly—" She dragged at him with all her strength and weight, and because he was still weak—and because, she had an awful suspicion, he was lighter than she was—she managed to drag him forward a few steps, even though he leaned back and braced his heels against the tiles.

Then he stopped leaning back, and came toward her, closing the arm's-length gap between them. She started to lose her balance and stumble backward, and he used her grip on his arm to swing her around, and then she was tripping over something—his foot—and thumping down on her backside on the cold, hard, damp tiles of the underpass floor. She gave a squeal more of surprise than hurt, and then another of exasperation when Per wrenched his wrist out of her hold and drew back from her again.

"Hey!" Joe said. Both Per and Andrea turned to him. Joe got to his feet. "Hey, have a care!" Even as he spoke, he knew he'd made a mistake, but too late now. Anyway, he couldn't just sit there and watch a girl get roughed up when calling out might stop it. He walked over to her, to offer her a hand up. The lad pulled a knife on him.

Joe didn't see where the knife came from. It was just there, all of a sudden, in the lad's fist, pointing up at him. It was black and wicked, its triangular blade damn near as long as Joe's forearm and narrowing abruptly to a needle point. It was such a vicious-looking knife that Joe was half afraid it might attack him of its own accord, whatever its owner decided. My big mouth, he thought, raising his hands, and backing off. "Okay, okay. Forget I spoke."

Oh my God! Andrea thought, and floundered to her hands and knees, scrambling to her feet. "Per! Put up! Don't!"

"Quiet!" Per said. "Stay back!" His eyes were on Joe. He'd seen the big Elf-Man sitting against the wall when he'd first looked into the underpass, but he hadn't seemed to offer any threat. Now he wondered—was he part of an ambush? Had Andrea used a far-speak and behind his back quickly arranged an ambush, here in this defile under the road? He glanced quickly over his shoulder, to see if anyone was coming up behind him, and down the length of the underpass, to see if anyone was waiting there.

"Love," Joe said to the girl, "you clear off out of it, quick, go on!" As soon as she was clear, he'd leg it himself, and forget the few coins still in his plastic cup. He wasn't shy of getting into a fight if he had to, but he had a policy about knives: Run away!

The knife remained steady, pointing up from the lad's fist, but the lad raised his right hand and knocked his cap back, to get a clearer view of Joe. The face under the cap was so disconcertingly pretty that, for a moment, Joe wondered if it was a tall, strong girl he was facing, not a boy at all. That bulky body warmer and baggy shirt hid a lot—there was a nasty stain on the shirt.

The kid yelled, making Joe jump, rocked back on his heels by a bellow like a sergeant-major's. The voice was certainly male, but it was hard to understand what it said. Something that sounded like "Stairrick-arram!"

"Eh?" Joe said. Maybe he should have been running, but the girl was still standing there—and besides, after the first shock of seeing the knife drawn, the sense of threat lessened. The lad seemed more wary and concerned with holding Joe off than with attacking him. Joe kept his hands raised to assure the kid that he wasn't going to mess with him. To the girl, he said, "You all right, love?"

"Oh, I'm all right, I'm fine," she said, in perfectly clear English, not at all like she'd been speaking earlier.

"I'd get out of here, if I was you," he said.

"Oh, no," she said. "It's all right; he won't hurt me. But thank you. For your help. Pair," she said to the lad, and added something that Joe didn't catch.

Joe began to back off toward his sign and his money, thinking that he might as well collect them before leaving the girl to the thumping he was pretty sure she'd get as soon as he was out of sight. He'd heard that one about "he won't hurt me" before. But it was none of his business. He should have known better than to get involved in the first place.

The lad came after him, and for a moment Joe's heart skipped. But though the lad kept the knife steady, he was pointing at Joe's chest with his other hand. "Stairrk-arram," he repeated, at a shout.

Joe looked down at himself. His oversize T-shirt had been given him by the landlord of a big city-center pub, The Sterkarm Arms. It was printed, in black on white, with a picture of the pub's sign: an upraised arm brandishing a dagger. All the bar staff had worn them. "That's my coat of arms," Joe had said. "I never said you could use it." The landlord had laughed and given him a spare shirt from behind the bar.

It dawned on Joe that the kid was trying to say "Sterkarm," but had got the pronunciation a bit off, and was rolling all the Rs.

"That's me," Joe yelled, as a bus passed overhead. He pointed at himself. "That's me name. I'm Sterkarm."

Thu air Sterkarm? Per looked again at what he'd taken for an Elf. Certainly, the man wore Elf-Clothes, but Per himself was wearing Elf-Clothes. And all the Elf-Men he'd seen had been clean-shaven, with short

228

hair, but this man had a thick beard and long hair falling to his shoulders. And on his chest he wore the Sterkarms' badge. "Art thee Sterkarm? Did they bring thee here, into Elf-Land? How long hast been here? Didst come through Elf-Gate? Dost ken where it be?"

"Per," Andrea said, "he's no one of thine. Come away." He ignored her, and she didn't quite dare to drag at his arm again. He'd been gentle about putting her on the floor the last time; he might not be the next.

Joe could feel his own face knotting into a frown as he listened to them. They were speaking in foreign again, and yet he kept catching at meaning in the words. *Thu air Sterkarm? Kommer thu av Erlf-Yett?* Listening to the kid was like tuning a radio through the different frequencies. Among incomprehensible foreign speech there were sudden bursts of words you could understand. Not all of them made much sense though. Elf-Gate?

Per saw the expression of puzzlement on Joe's face and realized that he'd been too eager to believe this stranger was one of his own. *"Vem ridder thu meth?"* Who ride you with? *"Vem air thine yarl?"* Who is your lord? *"Fra vilken tur air thu?"* From which tower are you?

Joe shook his head. He couldn't understand, but had the troublesome feeling that if, somehow, he could adjust his hearing slightly, he would. There was something about the kid's speech that, weirdly, reminded him of his Granddad Sterkarm. It was the sound of it, the throatiness, the rolled Rs, the rhythms. "Where do you come from?" Joe asked.

The girl interrupted. "We should be going," she said, and added something to the lad, in words that sounded like a slightly twisted version of what she'd just said in English. The lad continued to stare at Joe, with something of Joe's puzzlement.

Joe had an idea. Instead of trying to speak clearly, he spoke as much like his granddad as he could. "Whor thee come fro'?"

Per leaned toward him, his whole face brightening. He understood! The words were a little strange, but— "*Yi?*" He pointed to himself. "*Fra vor kommer yi?*"

"Aye." Joe leaned forward too, even took a small step closer, just as the kid lowered the knife slightly. "Fra whor come-a thee?" He pointed at the kid.

Per was filled with relief and happiness that warmed him all through and made him dizzy, like mulled festival ale. Holding the knife so that Joe could see it clearly, Per shoved it back into its sheath and then jumped at Joe, crashing into him and throwing his arms round him in a tight hug. "*Day glayder migh a finner thu!*" It gladdens me to find thee!

The girl cried out, and Joe squawked and staggered back, grabbing at Per and trying to shove him away, afraid he was being attacked. Per only clung to him the tighter. The man could be no Elf—he wore the badge, he was bearded and longhaired, and he spoke English! True, he was a little hard to understand, but the more distant Sterkarms often spoke oddly.

"Hey, all right, okay," Joe said, still trying to push the kid away, even when he'd realized he wasn't being mugged. "Steady on. What the hell's this you're wearing?" What he'd taken for a body warmer, instead of being soft, seemed to be full of bits of old scrap. As he pushed the kid away, he could feel the hardness and hear the metallic scratching and clinking.

The kid let him go but still kept close as Joe backed away. The kid's pretty, girlish face had turned pink and was bright with a huge, delighted smile. Joe was surprised to see that the blue eyes were shimmering with tears. The girl had come close to them, and was saying something urgently, but the lad had the more carrying voice, and he spoke intensely, excitedly.

"*Vor kommer yi? Fra Bed-des-dahla, fra tur.*" From Bedesdale, from the tower. "*Yi air Sterkarm, yi hite Per.*" I'm called Per. "*Min far air Stoor Toorkild, oh min fars-bror air Gobby Per.*" My father is Big Toorkild and my uncle is Gobby Per. Per searched his new friend's face for any sign of recognition. "*Yi air Stoor Toorkilds Per—Per Toorkildsson, av tur, av Bed-des-dahla. Yunker Per. Lilla Per. Per May.*"

Still Joe showed no sign of recognizing the names or places. But maybe he'd been in Elf-Land a hundred years or more. Maybe he'd forgotten his own speech. Per turned to Andrea, who was pulling at his sleeve and telling him that they should go. "Ask him how long he's been here—ask him! Has he eaten Elf-Meat?" If he had, he would be trapped here forever. Tears pricked behind Per's eyes at the terrible sadness of it. "Ask him!"

Joe's face was screwed up in bafflement. Again, he'd caught odd words. "Stoor" . . . was that "big"? It sounded like the local word for "big." And "yunker"—his grand-dad had called him "yunker." It meant "young," "a youth."

And "Pair," which seemed to be the kid's name. It sounded a bit like "Peter," said with a local accent, with the T swallowed. "Lilla Per"? "Little Peter?" Joe asked, signing "little" with his fingers and pointing at the kid.

"*Ya, ya.*" The kid turned from the girl and went all serious, looking at Joe with something like concern. "*Vah air thu namma?*"

"What's my name?" Joe pointed at himself. "Joe. I'm Joe Sterkarm. Joe."

"Chyo."

"No. Joe."

Per nodded, and tried harder. "Shyo. How long hast been in Elf-Land, Shyo? Hast eaten Elf-Meat?"

"Elf?" Joe said. "Elf-Meat?"

Andrea had refused to believe it at first, but the longer she listened, the more obvious it was that this Joe Sterkarm *understood* Per—at least to some extent. To a greater extent than she liked. This could be trouble.

"Didst come by Elf-Gate?" Per raised both his hands and made a circle with his fingers.

"Elf-Gate?" Joe said. His granddad had called a gate a "yett," but he still wasn't sure about this "Elf" business. He made one hand into a gatepost, and the other into the gate, and opened and closed it. "Yett?"

"Aye! Came you by Elf-Gate? Dost ken where it be? Tilsmid Oll!"

Andrea gasped. She took hold of Per's upper arm and pulled at him. "Per, I'm going to take thee through Elf-Gate. I told thee I would—come on!"

"Deelssmeed Holl," Per said to Joe, and then turned on her, shaking her off. "Stop it! I'll no go with thee! Th'art an Elf!"

"Per! He's an Elf!"

"I'm an Elf?" Joe said.

"Oh, shut up! Keep out of this. Per, I promise—"

"He's one of my own," Per said.

"He's not, Per, he's—"

"Dealsmaid Hole," Per said to Joe.

"Dilsmead Hall?" Joe said.

"Ya!" The kid tried to hug him again, and Joe had to fend him off. *"Kenna thu vor day air?"*

"Aye. I ken whor it are."

Andrea put a hand to her head and turned away from them.

Joe said, "Be that whor thee come from? Near there?" Dilsmead Hall itself was a big building on the outskirts of the town, a big stately-home sort of place that had been built by some rich bloke years ago. Now it was owned by some firm from down south, who'd turned it into offices. They were supposed to be developing all sorts of technological wonders, and there'd been articles in the local papers about how many jobs they were creating. There hadn't been one for Joe.

The kid grabbed two fistfuls of Joe's waterproof and stared at him so hard Joe couldn't see anything but blue eyes. *"Tar migh der, Chyo!"*

"Take you there?" Joe said. He didn't fancy the idea much. Dilsmead Hall wasn't on his beat.

Then the girl grabbed at his arm. Joe felt things were getting out of hand. "Joe, don't. Don't take him, don't."

Joe immediately liked the idea more—but still, it was out of his way.

"Kommer hyemma, Chyo—kommer hyemma meth migh oh yi skal giffer thee ayn hus oh lant."

"What?" Joe said, stooping his head toward those blue eyes. He knew he'd heard, knew he'd understood, but couldn't believe it.

"Don't listen, Joe," the girl said, and pulled hard at

the lad's arm. "Per, come with me! I'll take thee. Joe, he's talking rubbish, don't listen."

Joe would have thought so too, except he was struck by the girl's anxiety to convince him that the lad was talking rubbish. The lad turned on the girl, gripped her arms with both his hands, shook her and said something angrily that Joe couldn't catch. Then he turned back to Joe and repeated what he'd said before.

"If I go home with him," Joe said, glancing at the girl, "he'll give me a house and land?" And home was Dilsmead Hall? "Yeah, right, sure."

Andrea had retreated a little from Per after the shaking. She said, "He can't go with thee. He's eaten Elf-Meat—he can't go back through the Gate. Come with me—if I meant to trick thee, I'd have brought men with me—oh!" Per wasn't listening to her at all. He was staring at Joe.

"*Kom, kom,*" he said to Joe. "*Sitta.*" Leaning against the wall of the tunnel, he slid down it until he was sitting on the floor. It would be only a few minutes, but it would be a chance to rest his hurt leg, which, though he ignored it, was steadily aching. Curious, Joe crouched beside him, watching as Per pulled his pouch to the front of his belt and opened it.

The only food left inside it was a small plum that was getting overripe, and about a quarter of an apple, going dry and brown. Looking at them made Per's own belly tighten in a knot, and he couldn't resist taking a small bite of the apple. The rest he held out to Joe. "Have it. Eat it."

Was there a loony bin near Dilsmead Hall? Joe wondered. The kid was as daft as a brush. The bit of apple was fit for nothing but being thrown in the trash. He looked over at the girl, who was standing with her hands on her hips. Her hair was falling down and her tattered stockings were in frills about her ankles. The pair of 'em must have escaped from somewhere.

"It's no Elf-Meat," Per said, when Joe was hesitant about taking the apple. "It's from home, it's the last I have. It'll break the spell. Maybe." In all the stories Per knew, it was said that eating Elf-Food trapped you in Elf-Land, but none of the people in the stories had ever been able to get their hands on food from home. Maybe eating men's-food would break the spell and let Joe go home. It was worth trying.

The kid was looking at him so earnestly, and plainly wanted him so much to take the apple, that Joe couldn't find a way to refuse it. You never knew how Looney Tunes the kid was anyway. He might turn nasty, and he had that yard and a half of knife. So Joe sat down beside him, leaning against the wall, took the bit of apple and put it in his mouth, grinning at the lass as he did so. The apple was tart, and he could taste the brownness, but his eating it seemed to please the kid no end. He watched Joe closely as he chewed, with a smile and shining eyes.

Per took a bite at the plum in his hand and bit half of it away, letting a dribble of plum pulp run down his chin. He handed the other half of the plum, the stone exposed, to Joe. Taking the soft, oozing bit of fruit, wet with the kid's spit, Joe said, "Oh, thanks." He put it into his mouth, chewed, and spat the stone as far as he could across the underpass. It rattled on the tiles, and the kid laughed.

Andrea said, "Per, if tha'd come with me, we could be

through the Elf-Gate by now."

"Quiet, woman," he said, sounding just like his father. From his pouch he took the leather bottle and pulled at the stopper. His fingers didn't have their usual strength, and he couldn't get a grip on it.

Joe reached across and took the bottle from him. Holding it, he turned it, puzzled by what the material might be. He'd never seen a bottle made from leather before. He pulled the stopper free.

"*Tahk*," Per said.

"You're welcome." Joe swirled the contents of the bottle, and sniffed at its neck. There was the unmistakable whiff of alcohol. He passed the bottle back to the kid.

"Per," Andrea said, "trust me! There's nobody looking for us. If we go—"

Per raised the bottle, said, "Sterkarm!" and took a sip from it, wetting his mouth, leaving most of what little was left for Joe, though his belly squeaked for it. He held out the bottle.

Joe took it. "Sterkarm!" He put the bottle to his mouth and drank. Whatever was in it was . . . more like cider than anything else, though it wasn't cider. Quite sweet. Alcoholic, but weak. "Good stuff," he said, handing it back. He wasn't really keen on it, but the kid seemed pleased that he liked it.

"Good?" Per said, as he put the bottle back in his pouch. His eye fell on a zipper in the sleeve of Joe's waterproof jacket. He touched it with his fingertip.

"What's up?" Joe twisted his head around to see what had taken the kid's interest.

Per caught hold of the zipper's tab and gave it a pull.

He made a small sound of surprise when the zipper's teeth began to part.

Andrea, seeing another source of trouble, said, "Per, we really, really—"

"Quiet!" he said. He was studying the zipper as Joe pulled it open and shut. As soon as he released it, Per took the tab and pulled it open again. Joe could see by the kid's face that he was truly astonished. "Haven't you never seen a zipper before?" The kid looked at him questioningly. "A zipper. Zipper."

"Sssip." The kid got awkwardly to his knees, pulling a slight face, as if it were painful, and pulled up his shirt, revealing that his jeans were fastened only at the top, by the button, and that he wasn't wearing anything underneath. After a bit of trouble in finding the zipper's tab, he slowly pulled up the zipper, and looked at Joe with a big, bright smile.

Joe grinned back, nodding. "Well done," he said. "Congratulations." He looked up at the girl who was standing by and said, "Where's he escaped from?"

"What?" she said crossly.

"Where *is* he from?" Joe asked.

Startled, Andrea tried to control her face while she thought of an answer. It would be suspicious not to answer readily, and just as suspicious to say she didn't know, or to be rude and tell him to mind his own business. "Denmark!" she said, feeling that she'd left too long a pause. Per's distant ancestors had certainly come from Denmark.

"Oh, right," Joe said. "I'd have thought they'd have had zippers in Denmark." Where on the face of the planet, he thought, could you find someone else who'd never seen a zipper? In the rain forests, in the Australian desert, in the wastes of Siberia, people wore clothes with zippers.

Per started to get up, but as his weight came onto his hurt leg, the part-healed muscles gave a strong twang and, in moving suddenly to ease it, he fell back to the tiles.

Joe said, "You okay? Want a hand?" He got up and offered a hand. Per reached for it, and Joe took him by the hand and elbow, bringing him to his feet with one strong pull. "Something wrong with your leg?"

Per kept hold of Joe's hand and put his other hand on Joe's shoulder. *"Naw vi gaw hyemma."*

Joe laughed. The meaning of the words came straight to him, as if there'd been some magic in the ciderish drink. "Now we go home, do we?" He shook his head. "Sorry." Tempted though he was to annoy the glowering young woman, he just couldn't be bothered to go all the way out to Dilsmead Hall for nothing. "Go with her. Her wants to take you."

"Nigh, Chyo, nigh. Thu maun kommer. Thu skal!"

"I don't think so," Joe said. "Not even for a house and land."

"Yi sverer, Chyo, pa min fars hodda, yi skal giffer thu ayn hus oh lant."

Joe hissed through his teeth and shook his head. Loopy kid! He really believed that he had houses and land to give away. "You're two or three short of a six-pack, you are, son."

Per frowned at him, not understanding, and wondering desperately what else he could do to get Joe's help. If he wouldn't help one of his own from fellowship . . . If the promise of land when they reached home couldn't move him . . . Per thought of drawing his dagger on Joe again, but alone as he was, he would rather have a friend than an enemy and anyway, Joe was a big, heavy man. Per wasn't sure, in his present state, that Joe wouldn't take the dagger off him and use it against him.

He had only one thing that he was willing to give away and that Joe, having been so long in Elf-Land, might think of value. He moved out of Joe's reach and, from his pouch, took the small leather case Elf-Windsor had given him. Unbuttoning it, he pulled the paper money halfway out, so that Joe could see it. Watching Joe's face, he could tell he'd done the right thing. Joe wanted the Elf-Money.

"Oh—no!" Andrea said. "Per, no. Joe, no!"

Per glanced at her, more certain than ever that he was going to get his own way, and more certain that he'd been right not to trust her.

Joe stared at the money. Tenners. Making a quick count up, he guessed the wallet held at least fifty pounds.

"Kommer til Dilsmaid Hole oh yi giffer thu deyn."

Fifty quid. I could open a bank account with that, Joe thought. Nowhere near a week's rent, not even for a tiny little studio, but it's a start.

"Kommer meth migh," Per said.

"Per, no!" The girl went to him and tried to take the money. He pushed her away, held her off with one hand, and held the wallet high in the air with the other. "Joe, don't, you mustn't go there, you'll be in trouble!"

Even without the girl's protests, Joe knew that taking the money would be wrong. Where did a loopy kid, with no shoes and socks on his feet, get fifty quid in a nice leather wallet? He'd either nicked it, or . . . If it belonged to the kid, taking it from him was even worse, in a way. He took a step forward. "Now, where did—"

The kid moved back fast, from both him and the girl. He stuck the wallet between his teeth and brought his hands together again—only Joe knew what that movement meant now. The kid's hand was on the hilt of his knife, ready to draw it.

Joe lifted both his hands. "All right! Calm down. I'm not going to try and take it from you. Tell you what, give me half."

"*Halv?*"

The young woman darted at him. "Joe! No, you can't!"

"Half now." Joe pointed to the ground at his feet. "Half when we get to Dilsmead Hall. Fair?"

"Joe, don't."

Per backed off a little further, took the wallet from his mouth, then hesitated. If the money had been in coins, he could have thrown it to Joe, but if he tried to throw these bits of paper, they would drift in the air. He pulled all but two sheets of the paper from the wallet, put the folded paper between his teeth, and then tossed the wallet to Joe. It landed on the tiles at his feet, and Andrea stooped, grabbing at it. Joe caught her wrist and Per stiffened, his hand going to his dagger's hilt again. But Joe, though he held her wrist tightly, only twisted the wallet from her hand—he couldn't be blamed for that—and then let her go.

"Joe," Andrea said. "Don't take him there. Don't. I don't mean to be rude, but . . . why don't you just take what you've got there and go away?"

Joe opened the wallet and saw the twenty pounds inside. He looked at her. "I want the rest."

"Quit while you're ahead—easy money. If you go to Dilsmead Hall, you're only going to get into trouble."

It was true that, even if he cut out now, he was still twenty quid ahead, but . . . Well, Dilsmead Hall wasn't *that* far away, and he had nothing better to do, and all these hints and threats made him bloody curious. Besides, fifty quid was a lot better than twenty. Trying to sound like a tough guy from a film, he said, "Happen I like trouble."

Per had come closer again and said, impatiently, *"Gaw vi?"*

"Aye," Joe said, and beckoned. "Come on."

Per grinned, darted over to Joe and took his hand. Joe, startled, tried to pull away, but Per held on. "Let go," Joe said, and began prying his fingers loose. Per, to whom it was natural to hold hands with a friend, was puzzled and hurt, and looked to Andrea for an explanation.

Oh, don't look at me, she thought. I'm an Elf and not to be trusted. Why should I help? She was trying to think ahead to what would happen when Per and Joe reached Dilsmead Hall. Of course, if Joe collected his money at the gates and went off, nothing much, probably. Especially if she could keep up with them. She could join up with Per again and try to get him through the Elf-Gate with her.

But the thought of the security guards worried her. Some of them had guns, and she couldn't predict what Per and Joe would do once they reached the Hall.

People were always doing stupid things. Per, convinced he was close to the way home, would draw his dagger and fight. . . . "Joe, you don't know what you're getting into. Please don't go. You're going to get hurt."

"We can look after oursen," Joe said.

"Oh, *Joe!*" Macho men who could look after themselves! She'd like to line them all up and slap their silly faces. "Listen, Joe, listen!" She shouldn't say this, but . . . "You're not going to believe this . . ." She was trying to think of any other way she could dissuade Joe from going to Dilsmead Hall, but nothing came to her. "You're going to think I'm mad, but I don't want you to get hurt, and—"

Joe stopped moving away, and looked at her, Per standing beside him. "Well?" he said. "What aren't I going to believe?"

"What Per calls the Elf-Gate . . ." Why am I saying this? she thought. I signed an agreement to say I wouldn't tell anyone, and he's just going to laugh anyway. "It's a time machine."

Joe looked from her to Per and back again. He looked about at the dingy, muddied tube of the underpass. "A time machine."

"*Kom, Chyo,*" Per said.

Joe held up a hand. "Hang on."

"We call it the Time Tube," Andrea said, "because it's a tube." And she formed her fingers into a circle, just as the lad had done when trying to describe an Elf-Gate.

Joe came back toward her and then stopped, feeling that he was never going to move again. It was bats, what she'd just said, it was alien abductions and talking with fairies, but it made sense. He'd seen pieces in the newspapers about time-travel research. In one, some scientist would be saying that in fifty years' time there'd be practical, working time machines and we'd all be taking vacations with the dinosaurs. In another, a different scientist would be saying that time travel was impossible, and that no reputable scientists believed it could ever be achieved. "You telling me that somebody's done it? Built a time machine? A real one, that works?"

"Here," she said. "In the labs at Dilsmead Hall. FUP's done it."

Per came to stand beside Joe, looking curiously at them. He'd caught the mention of Dilsmead Hall.

FUP, Joe thought. Dilsmead Hall. There'd been stories doing the rounds about what had been going on in Dilsmead Hall. Gruesome animal experiments, new forms of nuclear power that would poison everybody, the building of genetic monsters . . . Joe had never taken much notice, and nobody, that he could remember, had ever said the project was a time machine.

But things came together in Joe's mind, making sense with such speed he couldn't keep up with his own thoughts. He looked at Per, who stared back at him and said, *"Vi gaw?"*

Joe pointed at him. "You mean—?"

"Five hundred years ago," Andrea said.

The peculiar, clinking jacket and the thick, broad speech, often more impenetrable than that of Joe's granddad. The puzzled air with which the kid handled money. The funny-looking knife. The odd bottle made of leather, and the unfamiliar drink it held. The ignorance of zippers.

Joe felt as if a bright, bright light had turned on inside

his head. It must, he thought, be shining out of his eyes and ears. So much made sense if you just accepted that the lad standing beside him was five hundred years old.

"*Chyo?*" Per said.

Joe shook his head. It was hard to look at that bright young face and think that it was—or should be—or was?—nothing but a skull in a forgotten and unmarked grave.

"*Chyo? Vordan staw day?*" How stands it? Per was puzzled by the stunned look on Joe's face as he stared at him.

Joe said, "He's one of *them* Sterkarms!"

The old-time Sterkarms were a local legend, forever galloping about at full tilt, up to no good. Always being arrested and locked up in the castle dungeons, and then the rest of the ferocious family would swarm over the walls and rescue them. Joe had often been teased about his surname.

"He's only a bit of a kid," Joe said. All the stories gave the idea that the old Sterkarms were about seven feet tall, four feet wide, scarred, armed to the teeth, and had beards you could lose a horse in.

Andrea shrugged.

"Bloody hell," Joe said. "I mean—bloody hell! He could be me great-great—ever-so-many-greats-great-granddad!"

Andrea laughed. "If he's not, it's not for want of trying."

Per stepped away from Joe and toward her. "*Vah?*"

Joe said, "Elf-Land?"

"He thinks he's in Elf-Land. He thinks we're—he thinks *I'm* an Elf. He thinks you're one of his own, lost in Elf-Land, like him. When he says 'Elf-Gate,' he means the Time Tube."

"Bloody hell!" Joe said. "And this home he wants to go back to, this—"

"He means his own time."

"So. He really *could* give me land and a house. No kidding." Not just a studio, from which he could be evicted. Not just some low-paid job, where he'd be turned off as soon as it suited his boss. But a house and land, as a gift, a reward, his forever. Freedom.

"Joe!" Andrea said. He never heard her. He grabbed Per by the arm and jerked him backward, never noticing that Per reached for his dagger. "If I take you—to the Elf-Gate—if I go home with you—you'll give me a house?"

Per relaxed, realizing that Joe meant him no harm. He frowned as he listened, watching Joe's face, and caught enough of the words to more or less understand. *"Ya. Oh lant."*

"You mean it?" Joe asked. "You really mean it?" He didn't want to go back five hundred years for nothing.

"Joe!" Andrea said. "Think! You don't want to do this!"

"I do!" Joe said.

"We're talking about five hundred years ago! And in a very remote, backward part of the country. Think what that means! So he'll give you a house! It'll be a drafty hut with the rain coming in and no furniture at all! You'll sleep on the floor! You'll be hungry most of the time, and cold, and wet, and there'll be no medical care, and it'll be dangerous—"

"You mean just like now?" Joe said. He stared at her, and she hadn't a thing to say. Joe turned back to Per.

"D'you mean it? About the house and land. Can you really do it? Do you mean it?"

Per understood, and his face lit with a smile. Taking Joe's arm, he tugged at him until they were squarely facing each other. Joe, moving obediently into place, noticed some passersby glancing at them and saw that the kid was at least half a head taller than he was. He'd thought that people in the past were all short. He stood as tall as he could and straightened his own shoulders, to make his heavier build obvious.

Per took both of Joe's hands, pressed them together as if in prayer, and placed both of his own around them. His left foot he placed on top of Joe's right foot, bare toes on soggy old sneaker. He looked into Joe's eyes, his own wide with the seriousness of what he was about to do, and the anxiety to get it right. *"Yi, Per Toorkildsson Sterkarm, tar thine hander—"*

Joe lost him after that, but Per sang the words out in such fine style that, looking into the boy's intent face, Joe felt his hair prickle. The clasped hands, the foot on the foot . . . This was no joke or game. The lad was nervous but serious. Joe had never seen a clergyman perform a wedding or funeral with as much conviction. Without taking his eyes from the boy's face, he said to the girl, "What's he say?"

She didn't answer. Per went on, speaking with emphasis and swing, until he ran out of words and finished with a solemn, wide-eyed nod.

"What's he say?" Joe demanded.

Andrea didn't want to answer, but refusing to translate was as hard as ignoring a ringing phone. "He said, 'I, Per Toorkildsson Sterkarm, take your hands between my hands and place my foot on your foot, and swear to be your lord, to guard you and guard yours until the day I die.' Happy?"

"*Naw thu*," Per said, and shook Joe's hands between his own. "*Yi*—" He nodded to Joe.

Joe, his hands still between Per's, and his foot under Per's foot, said, "I, Joseph Sterkarm, put my hands between your hands—"

My hands are between his, he thought, because I'm giving them and their use to him.

Half guessing, half prompted by Per, he stumbled on, "—and my foot under your foot—"

My foot's under his foot because he's top dog, that's what I'm agreeing to. What the hell am I getting into?

"—and swear to be your man, to guard you and to guard yours, until the day I die."

The words seemed to take on such vivid meaning, they were like solid, heavy objects, taking up space and pressing in on him.

Swear to be your man. Like a belonging, a useful tool.

To guard you and guard yours. But now more like a dog. He felt the hackles rising on the back of his neck and his teeth baring, like faithful Gelert standing over the fallen cradle of the little prince.

Until the day I die. God, that had a long, distant and doomy ring!

Andrea said, "He believes every word of it, Joe. How about you?"

Joe could see the belief in Per's face. He thought: But he swore to guard me and mine too—if I ever have anything to call mine. And he means every word of that as well.

247

Per took his foot from Joe's foot, dropped his hands and, stepping closer, put his arms around Joe's shoulders and hugged him.

Joe's muscles stiffened and, without actually rebuffing the hug, he tried to hold himself away from it. More people were walking through the underpass—the office workers were returning to work—and they looked at the kid hugging him and hurriedly looked away, some of them smirking.

To hell with them! Joe thought. This ceremony was more important than what some crowd of house livers thought. He even half raised his arms, meaning to hug the kid in return, but wasn't sure that he was supposed to. He stood there, awkward, his arms held up.

Per kissed Joe, first on one cheek, then on the other. He did it bashfully. It was the first time he'd taken a man into service, and though he knew it was his place, as the master, to offer the kiss, he felt shy at presuming to kiss a man as old as his father.

Joe felt the shyness and thought it funny that his new lord and master was shy of him. As Per drew back from him, he put his hands on the lad's shoulders.

"Lant," Per said. *"Oh ayn hus. Yi giffer thu min urd."*

Joe had worked for other masters, schoolmasters, who'd promised that if he worked hard and got qualifications, he'd get a good job. He'd known they were lying at the time. He'd left school, been unemployed, and then got a job in the building trade. Work two weeks, off for six.

He'd worked for another master, a building contractor, and he'd been known as a good worker. In return he'd been laid off at the first sign of a slump in trade.

Good workers came expensive.

He'd paid taxes to his masters in the government, paid tax on everything he'd bought. In return he'd got to sleep in all the cardboard boxes he could beg, and a police force to move him on at three in the morning.

None of those masters had held his hands, looked into his eyes, and solemnly sworn to guard him and guard his until the day they died. Joe squeezed Per's shoulders between his hands, then whacked him on one shoulder and pulled his baseball cap down over his eyes. "I'll take you to Dilsmead Hall. And if there's any such thing as an Elf-Gate there, we'll find it!" He started off along the underpass and when Per, coming after him, took his hand again, he didn't pull away.

Andrea ran after them. She said, "All right, all right, you win. Why don't we take a taxi? I'll pay."

Joe stopped and looked from her to Per. "Okay. Sure. Why not?" It had been a long time since he'd ridden in a taxi. All in all, this was turning out to be an interesting day.

11

21st Side: Per Gaw Hyemma

THE TAXI PULLED UP at the gate of Dilsmead Hall, and the green-uniformed security guard came out of his hut. Andrea wound down her window to show her pass. "I've got two guests with me. We're all expected."

The guard nodded and, taking her pass, went back into his hut to phone reception.

"This might be your last chance, Joe," Andrea said.

"I'm sticking," Joe said. He wasn't sure it was the right thing to do. He suspected that he was making a bloody fool of himself, but between curiosity and the hope of gain, he was stuck. Besides, Per, though leaning over the driver's shoulder and examining the steering wheel and gear stick with interest, was keeping a grip on Joe's hand that was likely to leave bruises. Joe doubted if Per would allow him to leave.

The barrier across the drive lifted, and the security guard stepped out of his hut, returning Andrea's pass with a smile and a touch to his peaked cap. The taxi moved forward into the long driveway. "Here we go!" Andrea said, and crossed her fingers.

It hadn't been too difficult for her to convince Joe

that they stood a better chance of reaching the Time Tube with her assistance, especially when she'd shown him her pass. Joe understood how security worked. It had been harder to persuade Per, and to her vexation, Joe's words had counted more with him than hers. If Joe thought they should go with her, he eventually conceded, then so be it, but Joe was to lead the way, not Andrea. Per feared an ambush.

"You know the office for that taxi company that's just along here?" Andrea had said to Joe. "Just take us there." Going around the ring road would mean they avoided the city center, keeping Per away from the old buildings that he might recognize. She couldn't see that it would be helpful, at that moment, to puzzle and confuse him any more than he was already.

Joe had led the way around the ring road, and Per had gone happily with him, holding his hand. The noise and rush of Elf-Carts so close beside them was still fearful, but Per took courage from Joe, who'd been in Elf-Land longer, and had obviously learned what should and shouldn't be feared. Joe didn't seem bothered by the Elf-Carts at all, so Per ignored them as much as he could. His hopes of reaching home rose, and still holding Joe's hand, he turned and offered his other hand to Andrea. She'd taken it, smiling.

At the taxi office, the woman controller had invited them all inside, to sit on a broken sofa, among piles of old magazines. She'd offered them cigarettes and either didn't notice that Per was barefoot, and holding hands with Joe, or didn't care. When Andrea asked if she could use the phone, the woman waved her hand, puffed on her cigarette and said, "Knock yourself out!"

Andrea dialed reception at Dilsmead Hall, and confirmed that she was coming in for three sharp. She'd be bringing a couple of guests with her. "It's all arranged. I'll be signing them in." She held her breath, but reception just said, "Very well, Miss Mitchell, that's noted."

When the taxi arrived, getting Per into it was a small problem. He went out to it calmly enough, hand in hand with Joe and Andrea, but when Joe opened the back door, Per pulled back and let go of Joe's hand. He stooped, peering into the car's small interior. The idea of getting into an Elf-Cart and riding away in it was thrilling, but actually climbing into that tiny space and being enclosed, trapped, by the magic was something else altogether.

Andrea's reassurances had been soothing; it was good to feel that she cared about him. But however much she cared, she was an Elf, bound to an Elf-Master.

Joe had climbed into the car and beckoned to Per from inside, repeating, *"Air rikti, air rikti."* It's all right. Joe was picking up words from Per pretty quickly.

Per didn't wish to appear afraid in front of Joe, and if Joe thought the cart was safe, then it must be. Folding himself up far more than was necessary, Per climbed into the backseat. Andrea quickly shut the door and got in beside the driver. She wondered if without Joe she could have persuaded Per to get in at all.

After telling the driver where to go, she'd turned around to watch Per, and reached between the seats to offer him her hand. For the first few moments after the car pulled away, he'd looked terrified, but after that, realizing that they were still alive and in one piece, he'd begun to grin and to look through the windows, even kneeling on the seat to watch the road and the cars behind. At all times he kept hold of Joe's or Andrea's hand, or both.

Now the taxi was crawling up the long graveled drive to Dilsmead Hall itself. The house hadn't existed in Per's time. Per ducked to peer through the windshield, and was obviously impressed by the size of the house, its marble pillars and the marble steps leading up to the door—another Elf-Palace. At the last curve of the drive before the house a big flower bed was planted on a sloping bank. Blue lobelias made the letters FUP against a background of white alyssum. Per pointed and exclaimed, recognizing FUP's logo from the 16th-side office.

The taxi rounded the drive's final bend and drew up at the door. Andrea paid the driver and they got out, Per seeming as reluctant to leave the Elf-Cart as he'd been to get into it.

"Listen," Andrea said, as they stood at the foot of the marble steps. *"Per, lutta.* There'll be guards inside. I think some of them have guns. Pistols, Per, Elf-Pistols. Don't do *anything* to alarm them. Don't look at them funny. Per, are you listening? This is important. If you want to to get through the Elf-Gate, you must do as I say. Joe, tell him to do what I say."

Joe pointed at her and said to Per, *"Air rikti."*

Per nodded. He understood that if they could reach the Elf-Gate and go through it without having to fight, that was much the preferable choice, especially as his leg and his head both hurt. But no matter what anyone said, it might still come to a fight. He knew that he would have to keep careful watch about him as they went into the Elves' den. He would have to listen to the voices, even though he couldn't understand the words they spoke. He would have to watch the faces and the movements of all those in sight. He would have to watch, and listen, for the approach of others. His hands would have to be kept free, ready to fight, so there could be no more holding hands. *"Yi forstaw."* I understand.

"Joe?" Andrea turned toward him. "I can't stop you, but do you really want to do this? If we don't make it through here, you're going to end up in jail; you might get hurt. If we do make it through—Joe, you'd better be really sure this is worth it."

Joe's heart beat quicker. He felt slightly sick. She spoke so seriously that she convinced him all over again, just when he'd begun telling himself that this was all a hoax, being filmed for some TV program. Run away, he thought; it's always safer. Yeah, run back to sleeping in a cardboard box and eating out of trash cans. He gestured toward the steps. "After you."

Andrea shrugged and led the way into the reception area of Dilsmead Hall. Per and Joe followed.

They pushed through the double doors at the entrance and came into a cool, shadowed hallway. The floor underfoot was mosaic. Couches and soft chairs were arranged around low tables and screened from the door by racks of potted plants. On the far side of the room a receptionist sat behind a curved wooden desk furnished with a computer and several telephones. A security guard in a green uniform leaned against the desk, chatting to her. Doors led from the hall on either side and at the rear of the room, next to the desk.

Andrea said, "Keep by me and keep calm, whatever happens. Don't run, don't fight." Rapidly, she repeated it for Per. Then they were at the desk, and the receptionist and the guard were looking at them. Perhaps they'd noticed that Per had no shoes or socks on his feet, and that Joe had slept in his clothes.

"Afternoon," Andrea said, and showed her pass. "I'm Andrea Mitchell, and these are my two guests."

The receptionist picked up a clipboard and looked through the papers on it. The guard studied them with what Andrea felt to be suspicion, though he didn't say anything. "I did phone . . ." she said nervously, when the receptionist seemed to be taking a long time.

The woman looked up, smiling. "That's fine. If your guests can just fill out these badges . . ." She pushed the sheet of security badges across the desk, with a pen, while she prepared the clear plastic holders and clips.

Joe and Andrea glanced at each other, and then Joe moved forward and picked up the pen. Andrea, feeling her chest tighten and her mouth turning dry, said, "Oh! This is embarrassing. Um. I'm afraid Mr.—Armstrong"—she nodded toward Per, who was standing silently at her side without any understanding of what was going on—"Mr. Armstrong is—sort of—dyslexic. You know? Would it be all right if I filled in his badge for him?"

The woman looked at her blankly.

Leaning forward, Andrea said, "He can't read or write."

"Oh, I'm sorry," the woman said, looking aside, embarrassed. "Of course. Yes. That would be all right."

"Thank you."

Joe was finishing filling out his badge. He'd given his real name. Why not? With any luck, he wasn't going to be around after today. Against "Company/Institution," he filled in the name of the last construction company he'd worked for; it sounded official, and hopefully no one would check on it in the next hour or so.

Per had been looking at the receptionist and wondering at her extraordinary, uncanny Elvish beauty—her hair, her lips and the skin around her eyes such strange colors! He was distracted when Joe began to write and watched him with admiration. Joe must have been a man of some standing before he'd been taken into Elf-Land, if he could read and write. Maybe that was why the Elves had taken him.

While the receptionist folded Joe's badge and fitted it into its plastic holder, Andrea filled out the badge for Per, giving "Peter Armstrong" as his name, and "Bedesdale Holdings" as his company. As she watched the receptionist tear off the badge and fold it, she thought: We're getting away with it; we're getting away! She glanced at her watch. It was five to three.

* * *

The meeting was the usual séance, where idiots who couldn't string two words together, and idiots who could drivel on for hours without ever making a point, competed to see which could render Windsor comatose sooner. He could see Bryce, sitting on the other side of the circle of easy chairs with a dreamy expression that proved he hadn't heard a word that had been said for the last twenty minutes. It was understandable. Accounts had fielded one of each kind of bore, to try and prove that the 16th Project wasn't viable.

Windsor bided his time, knowing that as soon as his chance to speak came, he could sway the rest onto his side. He looked at his watch. Just after two. If he was going to check up on Andrea Mitchell, he'd better make his move.

The next time the driveler from accounts paused for breath, Windsor rattled his own notes and said, "Could I put in a word? Thank you, Martin." He saw relief on several faces around the circle, and Bryce brightened and sat up in his chair. "We needed to hear that, but time marches on, and I'm sure we've all grasped accounts' view of things."

There was some laughter. Martin from accounts subsided.

"If I could just hit you with some other figures that you might find of interest . . ." Briefly, in a way he knew to be accomplished, Windsor went through some figures he'd obtained for the South American Project, where FUP was already bringing through hardwood and plant samples. "I know that with my present audience, I don't have to mention the price we could charge for mahogany if the market's managed properly."

There was more laughter, a further perking up of interest, and knowing looks from one to another. Bryce looked around at the other people in the room with him. He didn't know how much could be charged for mahogany, and was suddenly keenly aware of how he was regarded by his present company: the stupid security man, all brawn, no brain.

"Furthermore," Windsor said, "the science boys are confident that, in the next few years, the plant samples we're bringing back are going to yield a cancer vaccine. I'll just mention two facts, gentlemen. One, a cancer vaccine will be more profitable even than mahogany." A burst of laughter recognized that. "And two, many of these plants are extinct here, 21st side, where we haven't, let's face it, always taken the greatest care of our natural assets. Now, it's true we aren't going to get any mahogany from the 16th Project, and probably no cancer vaccine either, but we don't know what other vastly profitable folk medicines we might be overlooking. And we know for certain that, 16th side, we have gold, we have oil, we have natural gas, just for starters. And yet, because of a few teething problems and a few unexpected expenses, accounts wants us to abandon the project. Gentlemen, this would be throwing away a million to save a fiver. Let me—let me just tell you something about what we've got 16th side. I have an advantage over accounts—instead of reading columns of figures, I've actually been there."

This produced a buzz of interest and made the faces of the men from accounts go hard.

Windsor launched into a description of the 16th. Bryce, listening, noted that he mentioned not a word about the problems that had actually taken him through the Tube. Instead he spoke confidently about the beauty of the place, the colors, the freshness, the clean air, the peace, until several people at the table looked as if they might inquire about package tours. Then he made them laugh by describing the Sterkarms' charming but pressing hospitality and contrasting it with the discomfort of their home and the vileness of their food.

"They live in this paradise, and they don't have the slightest appreciation of it! Really, we'll be doing them a favor by taking it over and showing them what it can be!"

There was more laughter. Bryce looked from face to face and concluded that none of them had stopped to consider what "taking it over" from the Sterkarms would really—*really*—entail. Perhaps they thought the Sterkarms would hand over their land with a smile.

"Ah, coffee!" Windsor said, as the urn was wheeled in on a cart. Shall we adjourn for a few minutes? After that, I'm sure marketing will be glad to enthrall us."

The people were glad to rise, to stretch, to gather around the coffee urn and chat and laugh over what Windsor had said. Windsor quietly left the room. Just time to nip over to the Tube and check on whether Mitchell had reported, as instructed. If she had, his checking up in person would impress everyone. If she hadn't, he could make a note to have her guts for garters sometime in the immediate future, and that would make everybody else pull their socks up.

Slipping along the corridor, he took the stairs that would lead him down to reception. From there he could cut back through the house, and leave it by a back door almost directly opposite the Time Tube itself.

* * *

Andrea took the name badge from the receptionist and tried to clip it to Per's jakke. It was difficult, as the leather of the jakke, even where it wasn't full of old iron, was too thick for the little jaws of the grip to bite on. She was fiddling with it when a voice demanded, "What the *hell* is going on here?"

She jumped and almost dropped the badge. Windsor had just emerged from a hidden stair at the side of the reception hall. He stood there, very tall, the expanses of suiting across his chest and shoulders glowing with the dark, smooth beauty of the cloth, his dark hair brushed up into a peak above his forehead.

Annoyed as Windsor was, it was gratifying to see the way they all turned toward him with their mouths open—Andrea, young Sterkarm and the tramp they'd somehow acquired. Alarm and dismay: that was what he liked to see.

"What is he doing here?" Windsor demanded, waving toward young Sterkarm. He looked at Joe. "And who's he? Call security."

"No, don't!" Andrea said. "Mr. Windsor, please don't call security."

"Call security," Windsor repeated. He pointed to the tramp. "I want this person removed now. How the hell has he been let in here in the first place?" He glowered at the receptionist, who began trying to explain. "Save it. Tell them at the Job Center." Windsor beckoned to young Sterkarm. "You come with me." Windsor didn't know what he was going to do with Per if he came, but certainly he had to be separated from his girlfriend. "Come. With. Me. Miss Mitchell, will you tell him, please?"

Double doors crashed open on the other side of the reception hall. Two security guards in green uniforms came through. Joe moved away from them, and backed toward Per. "Come on," one of the guards said to Joe. "Time to leave. Easier if you just go quietly."

"*Vah sayer han?*" Per asked. He was standing with his back against the reception desk, trying to look in all directions at once.

Andrea said, "I think we'd better give up, Per. There are too many of them."

"Come on now," one of the guards said, beckoning to Joe invitingly. They seemed wary of actually starting a fight.

Per looked at the nervous guards, at Joe, and at the Elf-Laird, Windsor, standing back, so sure of himself. One thing was clear in Per's mind: He wasn't going back to the Elves' sick house. That was a fact as simple and unchangeable as the stone floor under his feet. He wasn't leaving this building except through the Elf-Gate.

It was easy to see in the Elf-Laird's face what pleasure he had in having them cornered. Per remembered how the Windsor had spoken to Andrea, ordering her about. It made him want to turn things around, so that the Elf-Laird was the cornered one. It would make sense. Without needing to understand what was being said, he had no doubt that Elf-Windsor was the kingpin here. Remove him, and all the rest would fall.

As the green-coated guards edged a little closer, Per raised both his hands, palms outward and, looking across at Elf-Windsor, catching his eyes, said, "Stay an eye's blink, stay."

No one except Andrea understood. Joe's eyes flickered nervously between Per and the guards. The guards looked to Windsor for instructions. Windsor said, "What's he say?"

Joe was thinking: I put my hands between your hands and my foot under your foot—I could end up in the cells for this. I'll guard you and guard yours until the day I die—for a house and land.

Keeping his hands raised, Per came forward a little from the desk, placing himself between Joe and the guards. Looking into Elf-Windsor's eyes, he said, "Be so kind, Master Elf, forgive me. I made Entraya bring me here, it's no fault—"

"There's no need to make excuses for me!" Andrea said.

His hands still raised, Per turned to her, his eyes giving that silver flash of anger. "Tell him what I say!"

"Mister Windsor," Andrea said, "Per asks you to forgive him." She looked at Per sidelong, wondering why on earth he was saying this. They were caught, fair and square, in the act of defying Windsor, and it wasn't like Per to humbly beg for forgiveness.

The security guards had stopped their advance on Joe, hanging back until this conversation with their boss might be finished.

That was all Per wanted for the moment. Looking at Windsor, he said, "Be no angry with Entraya. It was my wrong, and I am sad for it." He took another step forward, but his whole stance was so unthreatening that the security guards tensed only slightly, and Windsor merely folded his arms and stood watching. "Tell him, Entraya!"

Andrea began to speak. Per, though he averted his face slightly and looked up from the corners of his eyes, watched Windsor and knew by the man's reaction that Andrea was passing on his words. He let his head hang down, as if too shamed to look Windsor in the face.

Windsor wasn't sure what all this was about but didn't care much. If young Sterkarm thought he could make bargains, let him. It made it easier to string him along. Meanwhile, it was undeniably sweet to see this spoiled and arrogant sprig of an arrogant family hang his head and beg for forgiveness.

"Tell him," Windsor said, "to come along with me now, and I'll consider how much you were to blame later." He smiled at Andrea. The woman was a bigger fool even than he took her for, if she thought she had a job with FUP after this.

Per took the baseball cap from his head, scrunching it in his hands as he took another couple of steps toward Windsor. One of the guards even moved backward slightly, to make room for him. Per's hands were occupied by the harmless cap, his head hung meekly down, and he was going over to Windsor, as Windsor had ordered him to do. "I've no been a good guest, Master Elf, and I'm sad for it." He glanced up at Windsor, took another step closer, and hung his head again. "Be so kind, Master Elf, forgive me." Sincere apologies were the only kind that gave Per trouble.

As Andrea translated, she saw Joe cast her a bemused look that asked: What's going on? In reply, she rolled her eyes and shrugged.

Windsor's smile was smug. A Sterkarm, one of the crew that carried severed heads at their saddlebows, was admitting that Windsor had beaten him. "Tell him that when he's back in the hospital, where he should be, then we'll think about forgiveness."

Per paused while he listened to Andrea's translation, and then gave a small shrug, admitting his helplessness. *"Yi kommer."* I'll come. Another couple of steps brought him to Windsor, and he turned to stand beside him with lowered head. The guards saw a boy, unarmed and humbled, trying hard to ingratiate himself with their boss by good behavior. Their attention shifted once more to Joe.

Per dropped the baseball cap and drew the dagger

from his sleeve. He locked his right arm around Windsor's neck and, with his left hand, set the point of his dagger beneath Windsor's jaw. He jerked Windsor backward, choking him and dragging him farther from the guards.

The guards did a double take, their attention swinging between Joe and the scuffle. Joe said, "Bloody hell!" and seemed to dance in place, not knowing where to run. Andrea realized that she'd just seen the Sterkarm handshake in action, and felt simultaneously honored and horrified. You had to wonder about someone who could deceive that well.

Per took a deep breath, his chest swelling and his heart beating against Windsor's back. While he had Elf-Windsor, he was in charge—but the big Elf outweighed him, and his leg ached, his head ached and he could feel his own weakness in his grip on Windsor and his grip on the dagger. But now he'd drawn his dagger, he had to win or he was dead. His voice shook as he said, *"Naw, yi gaw hyemma, ya?"* Now I go home, yes?

Windsor gripped the arm that was choking him and pulled at it. Not right! To be grabbed and manhandled like this, to feel Per's body and legs against him—it was humiliation, insult! Holding Per's arm, he bent forward, even though he was choked, trying to wrestle free.

Per was lifted by Windsor's back and felt his feet leaving the floor. Desperate not to lose, he heaved back on his arm and jabbed at Windsor's neck with the knife.

"Mr. Windsor, keep still, please!" Andrea shouted. "He's got a knife—you're bleeding!"

Windsor hadn't seen the knife; it had been drawn behind his back, and he'd been most conscious of the hard bar of Per's arm across his throat. Now he squinted down at himself. He couldn't see much except Per's arm, but from the corner of his eye he glimpsed something of Per's other hand, blurred, clenched in a fist, holding something. Then the pricking pain at his neck, and the warmth there, made sense. A knife. Oh God. He was bleeding. A cold, like cold water, rushed over his scalp, ruffling through his hair. He caught his breath, his heart swelled, his belly and buttocks clenched, and he saw, in his mind, a clear image of the severed head, all stained with blood. Panic began to mix with his anger. "For God's sake!" he said.

Blood was trickling down Windsor's neck through the dark stubble, staining the collar of his shirt. The security guards looked at each other. They knew they ought to rush Per and disarm him—but how, exactly, without getting Windsor killed? They hadn't been trained to deal with knifemen. They weren't *paid* to deal with knifemen.

Per, his feet back on the ground, shouted, *"T'Yett!"* The Gate!

The question Andrea asked herself was: Would Per *really* hurt Windsor? The answer, little though she liked it, was: In this mood, yes. She darted over to the doors at the back of the reception hall and pushed them open. "Through here!"

Joe went over to her and took the door, holding it open. "Go on!" he said to her. She went through the door into the corridor beyond.

Per dragged Windsor backward toward the door, keeping the point of the dagger at his neck. The one security guard in his way, finding Per's eyes fixed on him, got out of the way.

Windsor's feet stammered at the floor as he stumbled backward, his legs bumping into Per's, while Per's arm dragged at his throat. Ridiculously, even as he worried about what would happen with the knife if he tripped, he found himself trying to help Per by keeping up with him. At the same time he was thinking about grabbing Per's knife hand and twisting it, about using his greater weight to slam the boy back into a wall, about— But all these plans ended with the thought that if he didn't quite get it right, he'd have a knife through the neck.

Per dragged Windsor backward through the door, and Joe quickly followed, pulling the door so it swung shut, hiding the reception hall and the staring guards from sight. He ran down the corridor, passing Per and Windsor and joining Andrea. He was aware that he might have just made the worst decision of his whole life.

Per was finding it awkward to go backward down the corridor while keeping a tight hold on Windsor and pointing the dagger at his neck. He wasn't trembling yet, but he could feel the weakness in his muscles that would soon become trembling. He had to keep glancing backward over his shoulder to see where he was going, and he was afraid that while he was turning to look, Windsor would break free. Then Joe came close and set his hand on Per's back, guiding him, so that Per no longer had to look behind.

The doors from reception opened and the security guards came through, speaking into radios. Slowly, they followed them into the corridor.

"Those things they're talking to," Andrea said,

"they're like far-speaks, Per. They're going to tell people to lay for us." She was thinking, I should *do* something before someone gets hurt. Or say something. But she couldn't think of anything she could say that Per would listen to, or of anything she could do that would stop him.

The corridor divided into three, going straight ahead, to the left and to the right. As they arrived at the junction, security guards arrived at the ends of the side corridors almost at the same time.

"We go straight ahead anyway!" Andrea said. Joe pulled at Per's shoulder to urge him on, Per dragged at Windsor and, together, a six-legged monster, they lurched across the junction of the corridors.

With a clatter of boots, another couple of security guards appeared at the end of the corridor they were following, blocking it. Joe came to a halt, stopping Per, who jolted Windsor and jabbed his neck with the dagger. Andrea looked around wildly, wiping hair from her eyes.

One of the security guards said, "Come on now. Stop playing games."

"*Stilla!*" Quiet! Per said.

Andrea made little "keep it down" gestures with her hands and said, "I think it'd be best—"

Per pulled Windsor back harder, choking him. "*Yi skyera han nakka!*"

"He says he'll shear—I mean"—Andrea clutched at her own head—"cut—he says he'll cut his neck—throat! Please be careful!"

All the guards kept still. Windsor's eyes rolled, white edged, in his red face.

Per was breathing fast, excitedly. He was winning and

alive, but knew how quickly both states could end. "Tell them all to go away!"

Try to be calm, Andrea thought. And calming. For Per to be so excited was probably not a good thing. *"Yi skal, Per, yi skal."* Raising her voice, she called, "You'd better let us through. Just go away and let us through!"

Per tightened his arm around Windsor's neck, using his knee in the man's back to pull him backward and jabbing the dagger into his neck. "Tell them to go! Tell them!"

He's going to kill him, Joe thought, and looked around for somewhere to run. Unless he ran over to the security guards and allowed himself to be arrested, there was nowhere. God help me if he kills him and I'm here! He looked at Per and wondered if he could overpower him—but he'd sworn to guard him and anyway, if he tried, he'd probably only make sure that Windsor was killed. So he just stood there, sweating and feeling like an idiot.

Windsor choked and gagged and gasped for breath. His heart hammered in fear and the blood swelled in his temples, half blinding him. He was in the hands of a barbarian. Through all the panic, he reached out for calm. Keep calm or end up dead. Gripping Per's arm to ease the choke hold, he tried to speak. Per relaxed a little, to let him speak, but Windsor could feel the tension throughout Per's body. He could feel the dagger's point at his neck.

Windsor couldn't see Andrea, but knew she was close by somewhere. Breathlessly, he said, "Cut my throat and, and"—he didn't think threatening Per with a custodial sentence, with time off for good behavior, would have much effect—"and they'll kill you. So you can't win, can you? We can talk about this. If you give up—"

"*Stilla!*" Per said. "*Entraya!* What says he?"

Andrea was taken aback by Windsor's courage. In his position, she was sure, she wouldn't have dared to say anything like that. She wasn't sure it was wise to translate, but what excuse could she give for refusing? She hadn't time to think of one. While she translated Windsor's words, she watched the security guards and noted that her mind was working smoothly and quickly while she and everything around her seemed to have slipped into some other dimension of craziness.

Per's eyes widened when he understood what Windsor had said. He shifted the point of his dagger, setting it behind Windsor's ear. With a flick of his hand he snicked the earlobe from Windsor's head, releasing a copious flow of blood down Windsor's neck. Windsor cried out and struggled, and Per rode him and choked him, setting the point of the dagger back at his neck. Windsor and the guards—who had taken a step forward—froze again.

Per's voice, broken with breathlessness, shook with both fear and the excitement of being prepared to do anything to win. "Won't cut his throat. I'll cut off his ear. Then his nose. Carve off his cheek like a pig's! I'll take out his eye. Tell them to go away!"

Joe, catching some of this, said, "Bloody hell!" He looked around again, for an escape. Following Per had been a mistake.

Andrea was sickened. She was too close to what the words meant to feel at all casual about them. She didn't even want them in her mouth.

Per looked at her. She saw by the glitter in his eyes that he was very scared. It was clear to her then that whatever he said he would do, he would do. She hurried to tell Windsor what he'd said, to let him know the danger he was in. All the time she was speaking she was thinking: I should be doing something to stop this.

Windsor hadn't understood Per's words, but he'd understood the tone and the shaking in the voice, the tension in the body that held him. When Andrea told him what the words meant, the severed head floated in the air before his open eyes, so vividly did he remember it. The panicky, rackety mixture of anger and fear he'd felt before took a sideways lurch into a colder, slower kind of fear altogether.

"Go away!" he said. It came out in a croak. He dragged in as much breath as he could with Per hanging around his throat, and yelled, "Get out of their way! Let them through! Move!"

Joe and Andrea looked this way and that, looking to see what the guards would do. The men looked at each other, shifted from foot to foot—and backed off. What could they do? They were merely strong-arm men, poorly paid and not trained at all. They didn't know what to do. The guards blocking their way to the Tube fell back down the corridor and vanished through a pair of fire doors.

"They've gone!" Andrea said to Per. Her heart was beating so fast and hard, she felt sick. Especially when she thought that they had to follow the guards through those fire doors, and the men might be waiting on the other side.

"*Kom!*" Per said, and dragged Windsor on again,

choking him. He swung Windsor around and made him walk in front of him, so that Per could look over his shoulder and see where they were going. With the length of that dagger at his neck, Windsor cooperated. To Joe, Per said, "Watch our backs!"

"I'll watch!" Andrea said, seeing Joe look puzzled. "All's clear."

Per's heart raced, his breath came fast, and he felt giddy, exhilarated, tall and very strong and very weak at the same time. He was going home. Nothing was going to stop him. He knew that with great conviction and simplicity.

Leadership, Andrea thought, as she and Joe scuttled after Per, was mostly knowing your own singleminded mind. When you did, other less singleminded people followed you, even though they might be brighter than you, even though they had serious doubts about what you were doing.

Per stopped before they reached the fire doors. "See what's behind there," he said to Joe.

Joe understood enough, together with Per's intent stare at the doors, to know what was wanted. He wasn't happy about going near the doors. He pictured big security men lurking behind them, with clubs. Going closer, craning his neck, he tried to peer through the windows—but the men might be crouching down. Standing back, he booted one door open hard, and it swung back enough for them to see that there was no one behind it. Joe kicked the other. "All clear!"

"Klahr?" Per said.

Joe held the door open and Per hustled Windsor through, Andrea following. She was sick with fear that this was going to end with Windsor being murdered by Per and she would have to see it done. She hadn't meant it to happen this way. Where were the police? Surely they should be here by now and *doing* something?

It seemed to take forever, and they had to go through another pair of fire doors, but they came in view of the doors that would bring them outside and close to the Time Tube. Per was out of breath from the effort of holding on to Windsor, half supporting his weight and shoving him along with knee and hip. Per could feel his grip loosening, and found every step a greater effort. He was wet with sweat and closer than ever to trembling. Windsor shifted within his hold, and Per called out, "Tell him I'll cut him into collops!" He pressed the edge of his long blade against Windsor's cheek, let him feel its sharpness. "I'll burst his eye!"

Andrea couldn't say it.

Joe pushed open the doors, letting in brighter light. He peered out onto a graveled path, and looked across the path to a portable office on the other side, with a strange round tube thing stuck at one end. With a shock—he actually felt his hair rise—he realized that was it. That was the Tube. If he was going to change his mind, it was going to have to be soon.

Some security guards were standing near the Tube, at the foot of a ramp leading up to it, but they didn't look like men who were ready to do anything. Joe waved to Per and Andrea to come on.

Per dragged Windsor out onto the path, stumbling on the step, their feet crunching in the gravel. Per ignored the pain to his bare feet. Windsor was sweating, almost purple in the face, spluttering and gasping. His tie and hair were awry, his shirt pulled open to show the black hair on his chest.

Per looked left and right, noting the guards. The little prefabricated office and the Tube beside it he saw with relief, recognizing them from the similar office in his own world. As Andrea followed them out onto the path, he shouted at her, "Tell them to go away!"

Andrea began to shout and wave at the guards. Windsor, who had heard the shake in Per's voice, shouted too. "Let them through!" he yelled. "God's sake, get—" His voice choked off as Per's arm tightened across his throat. Windsor's heart lurched as he felt the point of the long dagger sting his neck. But then the guards shuffled back from the ramp, leaving it clear, and Per relaxed.

They crossed the gravel to the foot of the ramp. Andrea saw faces at the window of the control room, peering at them. This is when they're going to try and stop us, she thought. This is where they have to stop us.

Per went sidelong up the ramp, holding on to Windsor and holding the knife at his neck, so that Windsor scrambled to keep up with him. Andrea followed, and Joe dropped back into last place, pushing Andrea on ahead of him and watching the guards, who were slowly coming nearer again.

On the platform at the top of the ramp, Per hesitated, made uncertain by the rustling strips of plastic that hung down to screen the Tube's mouth. Andrea went over to them, gathered several strips together in her hands, and lifted them, so they could see into the Tube itself.

Per froze. There it was—the Elf-Gate. Its great round mouth gaped. His eyes roamed around the curve of the opening, and around the curves of the tiled inner sides. He had no memory of ever being so close to it before, and it was frighteningly strange to him, even smelling strange. It was supposed to be a gate, but he couldn't see his own world at its other end—only a smaller circle and another hanging screen of strips. His hold on Windsor relaxed, and the dagger wavered in his hand.

Joe, seeing Per falter, and also aware of the guards coming up the ramp behind them and the people gathering at the door of the adjoining control room, stuck his finger in Windsor's face and said, "Don't move!" He clenched his fist in Windsor's face and said to Andrea, "What do we do now?"

"It's shut down," she said. The lights at the side of the Tube told her so. Beyond the screening at the other end of the Tube was the rest of the 21st: the Tube was "at home."

"Boot it up!" Joe yelled at the people gathered in the control-room door. He'd never seen a Time Tube before and had no idea how one worked, but he was used to machinery. Since Per was still nonplussed, Joe grabbed Windsor by his lapels and hauled at him, dragging him closer to the Tube's opening. Per was dragged along with him, his hand holding the dagger jolting against Windsor's shoulder.

"The knife!" Windsor said breathlessly. "The knife!" The long blade was waving wildly in front of and beside his face.

"Shut up!" Joe shook him, hoping Windsor took him for some terrifying, half crazed brute from the gutter. "Tell 'em to start it up, or I'll kick your effing head in."

With the head-hunting young thug behind him, and this fierce, stocky, bearded yob spitting in his face, Windsor knew he'd be a fool to do anything but play along. He drew a breath but could hear his voice shaking as he spoke to the people in the control-room doorway. "Boot it up. Do as they say. Do it now."

Some of the people turned and struggled to get back into the control room. Within a minute or so of their going, a humming, whining noise began to come from the Tube. Per started.

Andrea came close to him, pressed herself against his back. "It'll make a lot of noise. It's going to be deafening. But it's all right, it's all right. It's the Elf-Work."

The humming rapidly increased to a roar that made Per duck his head and twist it from side to side, trying to avoid the noise. The noise rose to a jagged scream that beat about their heads, and then abruptly stopped as the sound passed beyond hearing. The lights at the side of the Tube changed, flashing from red to green.

"Go!" Andrea shouted. "Go, we can go!"

Per gave her a shove that sent her staggering into the Tube. "*Gaw!*" He thumped Joe and yelled at him. "*Gaw!*"

Joe, startled, looked over his shoulder at the guards and the technicians, and then ran into the Tube, not really knowing what he was doing. Andrea, seeing Joe run, ran because he was running.

Per shoved Windsor hard, pitching him across the platform toward the ramp. Turning, Per took a jump into the Tube and raced for the other end, catching at Andrea's arm as he overtook her and pulling her along with him.

They burst through the screening covering the other

end of the Tube, running onto the platform and pelting willy-nilly down the ramp. Before them was the trodden, worn grass of the compound, startled guards, the steel fence, smoking fires, and the great wide open bowl of the surrounding hills.

Joe stumbled to a halt at the foot of the ramp and raised his eyes to the hills' peaks and then on up, into the deeps of the gray skies above. A wind came and ruffled his hair and beard, traveling from God knew how many miles away. A minute ago he'd been in a city, hearing the ever-present rumble of traffic, with telephone wires overhead, brick buildings and tarmacked roads pressing all around, bringing sight up short. And now silence, acres of silence, echoed and reechoed, and he looked clear across a wide valley to tiny black sheep moving on the farther hill, following silent, drifting cloud shadows. The air he breathed was damp, chill and almost searing in its clarity. It stunned him.

Per felt the damp wind touch his face and smelled the rich smell of the wet grass and earth, and his eyes filled with tears. He could have wept with thankfulness if he'd had time. Already guards were coming toward them. "Careful!" Andrea said to both him and them. These guards, 16th side, carried pistols in holsters on their hips. One was fumbling to open the flap on his holster. Andrea remembered more than one guard grumbling to her that their pistols were nothing more than ornaments; they hadn't been trained to use them or issued with more than one bullet each. But, just at that moment, it was hard to be comforted.

Per scanned the chain-link fence that surrounded the compound and saw what he looked for. The smoke that rose just beyond the fence came from the fires of a Sterkarm encampment. He could see men standing, peering through the mesh of the fence. Seizing Joe's arm and shaking him, Per filled his lungs and, in something between a bellow and a shriek, yelled, "Sterkarm! *Sterk*arm!"

The guards patrolling the compound whipped around in alarm. Outside the fence, more Sterkarms started to their feet, then snatched up bows, quivers, axes. They knew the shout was a call for help, and they answered it.

With a crash of iron, a man climbed the fence. A guard fumbled at his holster, thought better of it and looked around at his companions to see what they thought he should do. The Sterkarm was over the fence—others were climbing it—and was opening the gate.

In came the Sterkarms, through the gate and over the fence. Longbows were drawn and arrows pointed at the guards. Men ran, shouting, toward the office, carrying spears, long knives, axes, swords. Per ran forward to meet them, and when Sweet Milk suddenly appeared, he threw his arms around him and hugged him as if he were home itself.

Sweet Milk hardly had time to recover from surprise, hardly had time to recognize Per, before Per had him by the hand and was dragging him across the compound, back toward the ramp. At the bottom of the ramp, looking scared, were a thickset strong-looking man in Elvish clothes—but, unlike an Elf, bearded and shaggy-haired—and Andrea.

Per leaned around Joe to take Andrea by the arm and pull her forward, shoving her at Sweet Milk. "Take care of her—and him. He's a friend." He dragged at Joe's hand. "Away from here!" Andrea opened her mouth and Per said, "Go—go!" He leaned close and gave her a quick kiss before turning and running away toward the Elf-House.

Several other men, yelling, running, all armed, were heading for the hut. Joe glimpsed a green-uniformed security guard turning to face them and reaching for the holster at his hip. A Sterkarm, behind him, felled him with a blow to the head from an axe. The guard's peaked cap was no protection. He went down, and Joe saw the axe raised again.

He turned back toward Andrea and the big man in the helmet. He didn't know if Andrea had seen the guard struck down, but judging by her face, he thought she had. The big man had her by the arm and was pulling her away, and she was reaching out for Joe. He grabbed at her hand and was towed after her. From behind came a sound of smashing glass and a wild, panicked yell. Looking back, Joe saw a green-coated man running to the top of the ramp and diving through the door into the office.

Sweet Milk dragged them across the compound, through the opened gate and onto the open hillside, where small, smoking fires of heather and dung burned bright against the chill gray of the day. Stocky little horses grazed, hobbled or tethered at a distance, while around the fires were saddles and blankets and abandoned food. Lances, eight feet long, stood up from the ground.

"Stay here," Sweet Milk said, gesturing with the axe in his hand. The wooden haft was thick, and the axe-head, thick and heavy, narrowed to a sharp edge, its gray surface pitted with black hollows. It seemed less a cutting tool than a bludgeon, especially as it was hefted in the big-knuckled, big-veined hand that held it. "Stay," Sweet Milk repeated, retreating a few steps. He gave Joe a glower of pure suspicion from under his helmet, turned and ran back through the gate and across the compound toward the shouting, running men about the Elf-House.

"Can you see Per?" Andrea said. "Where is he?"

"I wouldn't look," Joe said. "Don't look."

"We should stop it," Andrea said. "We should find Per and—"

She actually moved toward the gate. Joe yanked her back angrily. "Don't be a bloody idiot. There's nothing you can do."

"But they'll—"

"What's going on in there"—more yells drifted back to them, sounds of chopping and smashing glass—"you're well out of. Well out of. There's nothing you can do, believe me. There's nothing you can do to stop it."

A shout rose, pealing above the other yells, and Joe felt Andrea stiffen as he held her arm. Her head lifted. It was Per's voice, raised jubilantly, trumpet-shouting to reach across the valley.

"Brenna day! Brenna day!"

"Oh, nigh," she said. *"Nigh,"* and tugged forward against Joe's hold.

"What?"

"Hura han nigh? Han kaller, brenna day!"

12

16th Side: Burning Down the Elf-House

BURN IT!" PER SHOUTED. "Burn it down!"

Per's shout was caught up and passed from one to another, and those nearest the fence came running back to the gate. Joe and Andrea stood back, watching as three men went from fire to fire, hunting for sticks substantial enough to carry a flame. They lifted them up, and Joe and Andrea turned away, shielding their faces as the wind showered them with fountains of red sparks and clouds of eye-stinging smoke. Then the men were running back across the compound, carrying the brands.

"Joe, they're going to burn it down!"

Joe still held her back. "You go in there, you're going to get hurt."

"But we'll be trapped—we've got to try and stop them!"

"Not me," Joe said. "Stay here."

"They wouldn't hurt me!"

"Don't you believe it, kid." He held on to her arm, and looking at the Sterkarms in the compound, all armed, running, shouting, she hadn't the nerve to go through the gate after them.

In the compound, Per took one of the flaring brands from its carrier, feeling the heat tighten the skin of his hand and face. He carried it toward the steps leading up to the Elf-House, though he didn't know if he could climb the steps. They seemed long and steep. His legs were shaking under him, and he was nearly spent—though rather than admit it, he would go on until he dropped where he stood.

Sweet Milk caught his elbow as he reached the steps and pulled him back. Per tried to shake him off, but Sweet Milk towed him away easily, shouting something about the Elves inside.

"They're away!" Per said. Why else had they run into the house but to run through the Gate to home?

Sweet Milk still dragged at him. Bowstrings plucked close by, and glass shattered as arrows went through the windows. Other arrows thudded into the woodwork. Another man carrying a firebrand started up the ramp and Per, seeing himself being beaten, swore and wrenched himself away from Sweet Milk.

The eaves of the Elf-House wouldn't take the fire, nor would the wooden rails at the stairs, or the steps themselves. They charred and smouldered, but wouldn't burn. Per's legs faltered under him, but he made it to the top of the steps, and was the first into the Elf-House.

Broken glass lay on the floor, and arrows stuck out from the wall. A panel of the wall was decorated with papers hung in fluttering bunches. Per tried to pull out one of the arrows, but it was wedged too tight for him, and he hadn't time to struggle with it, or dig it out with a knife. Instead, he held his brand to the papers. The fire caught in a rush and roared up the wall to the ceiling, where it caught the ceiling tiles with a soft explosion. The Sterkarms cheered, and Per raised his arms above his head, scorching the ceiling with the brand in his left hand.

A second man kicked over a basket, spilling crumpled paper on the floor, and set his torch to that, before firing the papers on the desk. Over their heads, the ceiling was burning, and pieces were falling. A thick black smoke oozed from the burning tiles.

Sweet Milk, looking in from the door to the platform, shouted, "Out! Out!" The two other men threw their brands into corners, but Per stayed to set light to the cushioned seat of an easy chair. He retreated toward the platform door, where Sweet Milk was yelling, but stopped to raise his brand to light the ceiling just inside the door. The black smoke, falling down from above, was filling the room now, making it impossible to see anything, making their breath catch and their eyes sting. Sweet Milk pulled the brand from Per's hand and threw it into the smoke, and then dragged Per through the door by the scruff of his neck, giving him a shove down the ramp that pitched him to his hands and knees in the grass at the bottom. Two passing Sterkarms, one shouldering a longbow, stopped to take Per under the armpits and boost him to his feet.

As the fire took hold, the Sterkarms retreated toward the compound fence, and Per was carried along with them. More windows smashed in the heat, and flames lapped through the holes and seared the outer walls. The roar of the fire grew louder, and the Sterkarms sent up shouts of "Who dares meddle with me!"

Most of them had reached the fence when from behind came a din such as they'd never heard: an eldritch cacophony of screaming, grinding, snapping. The steel girders and scaffolding supporting the great round Elf-Gate twisted, groaning and screeching, and snapped. There was a cracking and roaring of breaking stone and then a crash that shook the earth under their feet as pieces of the Elf-Gate fell to the ground.

The Sterkarms were silenced by the din, shocked and awed by their own success. Then they cheered, a small, ragged sound on the open hillside. "Who dares meddle with me!" Something inside the Elf-House went up with a bang and part of the roof fell. Laughing, the Sterkarms poured out through the compound gate, or climbed the chain-link fences, and came crowding back to their fires. Sweet Milk took the time to go over to the Elf-Men and cut their throats, to make sure they were dead. He gained nothing by it—the Elves had already been stripped to the skin—but he wouldn't have left a dog or a deer to suffer.

Andrea and Joe, standing together outside the fence, looked at each other. Andrea had always known that the Sterkarms were killers, but somehow she'd kept the knowledge hazy and not quite real. Their killings had always, before, taken place at a distance from her, and she'd only heard talk of them. She'd been able to argue to herself that they killed enemies, people who would as eagerly kill them, given the chance; or they'd killed in defense of their livelihood, or in order to survive. . . . Her favorite excuse had always been that she couldn't judge their behavior according to her own beliefs. To them, to kill in revenge was a duty; to forgive the killing of a kinsman a sin.

But she'd just watched Sterkarms—men she knew and liked—club down and hack with axes men whom she also knew and liked, men she'd chatted with as she'd passed through the Tube. She could see the guards lying in the compound. She'd never seen a throat cut before, but Sweet Milk's movements, though at a distance, were unmistakable. Sweet Milk, her friend. Sweet Milk— good-natured, funny Sweet Milk.

And the Elf-Gate, her only way home from this place, was burning down. Destroyed. You're trapped here, she told herself, but didn't seem, by her own reckoning, to be as frightened as she should be. Scared, worried, yes, but not terrified. She thought "killed" and "destroyed," and the words didn't seem to mean enough. "Killed" might as well have meant "decorated with ribbons" for all she could feel about it.

Joe was standing close beside her, pressed against her, as he uneasily watched the Sterkarms returning to their fires. One or two had knives and axes stained with blood, which they set about cleaning. Coming here, he thought, really had been the worst decision of his life. And now he was stuck.

Andrea saw Per looking for her, and his face lit up when he saw her. He tried to reach her but was hindered by the men he passed grabbing hold of him, hugging him, kissing him and then, as often as not, shoving him into the arms of another man. She saw Joe watching dubiously and said, "That's just the way here." Then she felt faintly bemused that she could still think such unimportant things worth saying. "Come on." Patting Joe's arm, she led the way toward Per. She felt strongly, all of a sudden, that if she *had* to be here, then she wanted to be as close to Per as possible. Per, at least, was no threat.

Her way was blocked by men who wanted to welcome her back with a touch to her breast and kiss to her cheek. She didn't want them to come close, let alone touch her—any one of them might have killed those guards. But she didn't know how to refuse their greetings without being rude. No, it wasn't that she didn't wish to be rude—she was afraid of them.

She reached Per, and he squirmed out of Ecky's arms to embrace her. As she put her arms around him, feeling the iron plates in his jakke, she realized that he was shaking, and crying too. She immediately cried herself, and they put their heads together and wept on each other's shoulders. They patted and kissed each other, trying to give comfort, each with a vague idea that the other was crying for the same reason.

Andrea was dimly aware of others standing close by them, who laughed, and pushed and pulled at them. She and Per clung together as they stumbled a few steps sidelong. She felt the heat of a fire, and raised her head from Per's shoulder, afraid of her skirt catching in the flames. The men around them—Sweet Milk was one—pushed them down by the fire and then wrapped a blanket around them. A dirty, damp and sour-smelling blanket, but it still made them feel much warmer.

How can they be so kind? Andrea thought. How can they kill men, and laugh, and then be so kind? She felt utterly confused and insubstantial, as if she dreamed.

Per was wiping at his eyes with the heels of his hands. She had her arms round him and could feel that he was still trembling. It came to her—a relief from her own thoughts and fears—that he had eaten hardly anything since he'd gone through to the 21st and that, after all the excitement and exertion of the past few hours, he must be close to exhaustion. No wonder he trembled. She turned to Sweet Milk as she hugged Per closer and said, "He needs food!"

The crowd around them immediately thinned, but only for the length of time it took for the men to go to their own campfires and fetch back whatever food they had. Soon there was a press around them, with arms reaching over shoulders and pushing through between other bodies, offering horns and leather bottles of small beer, lumps of crumbling hairy cheese, shriveled dried fish, lumps of cold porridge, greasy sausage, rounds of flatbread, a sheepskin cap full of mushrooms.

"This be good."

"Take it all, I got plenty."

"Get that down thee, it'll put thee right."

"Eat up now."

When Per accepted a lump of sausage, bit a lump from it and held it for Andrea to bite, there was a general "Aaah!" of sentimental approval, and some ribald laughter. Andrea thought: These are dangerous men, killers? Instead of biting the sausage, she said, "Where's Joe?" She'd lost him in the crowd.

Per looked up at Sweet Milk and, his mouth full of sausage, said, "Where's my new man, where's Chyo?"

Joe hadn't managed to follow Andrea very far into the crowd before he was stopped by Sterkarm men, who spoke to him in their throaty snarls. He didn't catch what they said, but he guessed that they were asking who he was and what he was doing there. They didn't look the types you wanted to argue with. One had a raised white scar from under his eye to his jaw, parting his beard because hair didn't grow on it, and he had his hand on the hilt of a long knife at his belt. The other held a staff taller than himself, topped with a truly frightening blade and spike.

"I'm with Per," Joe said. He'd just watched two men murdered, right before his eyes, and he was anxious that they understand he was with Per.

They frowned and he tried again, pointing to himself. "*Yi air*—uh—with Per. *Lilla Per?*"

The scarred man said, "*Per? Vilken Per?*" and shoved at Joe's shoulder. They seemed offended that he tried to speak their tongue. The man with the staff said, "*Air thu ayn Erlf?*"

Joe understood that, and also understood, from the tone, that he'd be a fool to admit to being an Elf. "*Yi air Stairrk-arram!* Friend! Friend!"

The two men grabbed him by the arms, their fingers gripping painfully tight, and hustled him into the crowd, shouting for others to make way. Now I'm in for it, Joe thought. He shouted, "Andrea! Per!"

The crowd parted and he was pulled to a small fire, but one that gave out a lot of heat with its choking smoke. On its other side, Per and Andrea sat cuddled together with a blanket wrapped around them, looking very cozy. Per was in the act of putting something into Andrea's mouth when he looked up, startled, at their sudden arrival. His face instantly became angry, and he threw off the blanket and tried to stand up. Two of the men crouched near him lifted him up.

Per pulled the men's hands away from Joe and shoved them away. "Leave him! He's one of our own—and my sworn man!" Per hugged Joe, holding on to him when Joe tried to pull away, and then kissed him first on one cheek, then on the other, so that all the Sterkarms gathered around saw.

There was a momentary silence, and then a murmur of surprise. Even Andrea was impressed. By kissing Joe in front of them all, Per had claimed him not only as a friend but almost as family. Sweet Milk, who, as Per's foster father, was next thing to family, seemed taken aback and perhaps not very pleased.

Per put what was left of a piece of dried fish into Joe's hand, and then pulled him and Sweet Milk closer together. "This be Chyo; he brought me out of Elf-Land. Showed me the way, and watched my back, and fought for me, and I could never have come through the Gate without him."

Sweet Milk's grim face broke into a wide smile. He took Joe's free hand in his own, and slapped him on the shoulder. Hanging around Sweet Milk's neck, and kissing him, Per said to Joe, "This be my little daddy, Sweet Milk."

Joe gave the big man—the throat cutter—a nervous smile, and looked to Andrea, hoping for a translation. He thought he'd caught the word "little," but it wasn't a word he'd have used to describe the man shaking his hand. Perhaps it was a joke. And Per, patting the big man's chest, had seemed to say that he was called "*Sertha Melk*," which didn't make any sense to Joe at all.

But Joe had no chance to listen to translations. Men were pressing at him from all sides, hugging him and kissing him, tangling their beards with his. Joe didn't suppose he smelled like a rose garden himself, but some of these Sterkarms were *ripe*! He found himself holding his breath. They started pushing food at him, and leather bottles of drink like the one Per had shared with him. A grayish, scrunched-up bit of thing that turned out to be a dried fish. A sort of crispbread, very thin and brittle, which was good if insubstantial. And something yellowish and hairy, a bit like a bedraggled ball of wool, which smelled and tasted like—there were no words. It was bad, but in its own unique way comparable to nothing else. The Sterkarms called it *"urst."* If it hadn't been for the hairiness, Joe would have taken it for a nasty, crumbly sort of cheese.

But everyone was grinning at him and nodding, patting him on the back, shaking his hand and then pressing something else—a sausage, an apple—into it. He grinned back. They were murderers, but the security guards were beyond help now and he had to think of himself. It was better to have these murderers grinning at him and offering to share their food than drawing their knives.

When he'd been kissed and hugged at least once by every man there, he was allowed to sit down by the fire. Per was stretched out full length, his head in Andrea's lap, his eyes closed and with one hand holding Andrea's against his face. His other hand was in Sweet Milk's, who sat beside them.

Behind them, inside the chain-link fence, the fire was still consuming the Elf-House, and could be heard roaring and crackling. Now and again there was a crash as some other part of the building fell, or the metal twanged in the heat. Sparks and smut showered about them. Silently, Joe and Andrea looked at each other:

the only two Elves in Man's-Home.

Andrea looked down at Per's face in her lap. He was asleep, and looked very young and beautiful. She wanted to ask him, Why kill those men? but didn't dare. Instead she told herself that there was no need to ask. Per hadn't actually killed them. He'd only ordered the Elf-House to be burned down; he hadn't shouted any orders about killing people.

She looked around her at the armed, helmeted men, drinking from bottles and horns, laughing and congratulating each other, and realized just how alone and helpless she was. Trapped, in one of the sixteenth century's poorest, hardest, most lawless and godforsaken parts of no-man's-land, with the notorious Sterkarms. Her bones felt as if they were filling up with ice water. Far from questioning Per's actions, she thought, she'd better keep on very, very good terms with him.

The idea made her want to stand up and dump him on the grass. Instead, her mind lurched out of the tracks it had become lodged in. I'm not *trapped*, she thought. If FUP built the Tube once, they can rebuild it. And they will.

It was with that thought that she felt the first jab of real fright.

Some of the men stood, pointing down into the valley and calling on others to look. Andrea, sitting on the ground with Per dozing in her lap, couldn't see, but Sweet Milk and Joe stood, and both reported that horsemen were coming up the valley toward them.

"Is it trouble?" Joe said. The wariness of the men around him was worrying.

Sweet Milk said, "It's Toorkild. Coming to see what

the fire is. Per!" He nudged Per with his foot until Per opened his eyes. "Keep out of sight."

Wearily, Per sat up. He turned a sleepy face to Andrea, leaned over and kissed her. They had no need to move in order to hide. The men standing in front of them and around them screened them from view.

Toorkild, with two other horsemen and a couple of pikemen on foot, came picking his way up from the river, rounding boulders and hollows. He'd been told as soon as the big fire had been sighted from the tower, and had left as soon as his horse could be saddled, to join his men already encamped on the hillside. He was full of anger and anxiety, and at the sight of the Elf-House collapsing in flames, he thought his son lost forever. He kicked his horse to a trot, careless that it was trying to carry him up a steep slope, and yelled, "Why does it burn? What happened here?"

His men answered him by laughing and grinning at each other. Incensed by their stupidity and insolence, Toorkild reined in, and dismounted and made toward the nearest men with his fist clenched. They dodged away from him and he yelled for Sweet Milk.

Andrea heard the panicked note in Toorkild's voice and got to her feet, thinking the joke cruel. Toorkild saw her. He gave a start, and his face as he looked from her to the burning Elf-House and tried to work out how she came there sent the men around him into loud laughter.

Toorkild was already looking for Per when Sweet Milk gave Per a hand and pulled him to his feet. Toorkild's face filled with gladness and relief. He didn't wait for Per to go to him, but started forward, opening his arms. Per abandoned all dignity, broke into a big smile and ran to him.

Toorkild clamped Per to him as hard as he could, with an arm at the back of his son's neck and an arm about his waist. "A thousand thanks!" Toorkild said. "A thousand, thousand thanks!"

Per was trying to ask about his mother, about Cuddy and Fowl, but his face was pressed into his father's neck, beard and hair, his chin and mouth pressed against the iron plates in Toorkild's jakke. He pushed, trying to get free, until Toorkild wrapped his cloak around them both, enclosing Per, after the chill of the hillside, in a warm fug that stank of his father and his parents' bed, of peat smoke, horses and other homely things. Per gave in then and leaned against his father, letting Toorkild hold him, if that was what he wanted. "My little lad," Toorkild said, making Per laugh. Toorkild's hands were pressing against the back of his head and patting all over his shoulders and back, as if to check that he hadn't been cheated of any of his son's substance.

"Per's father," Andrea explained to Joe, who was staring. Looking around, she saw all the Sterkarms watching fondly, axes and spears in their hands. Sweet Milk had a big soppy grin on his face and, she was almost sure, a tear in his eye.

Toorkild let Per lift his head from his shoulder, so he could see his face. "Tha've all thy color back!"

"The Elves put new blood in me." Leaning on his father as he might on a doorpost, Per raised his injured leg, showing how easily he could flex it. "They stuck it with glue! And it never went bad-ways. There's no scar."

Toorkild patted the raised leg wonderingly. "Well, well. There's Elf-Healing for thee." He wrapped his cloak more closely around his son, almost hiding him from sight, and nodded to a man who happened to be in front of him. "Thee. Back to the tower and tell the good-wife her bairn's home and safe. Tha've been a worrit to her since afore tha was born," he added to Per, and then declared to the hillside at large, "If the Grannams come and take all my kine this night, I'll no care. Entraya!" He spread one arm for her. "Me bonny lass!"

Toorkild, in his time, had certainly killed, she thought, but she went forward anyway and was pulled into Toorkild's strong, warm and reeking embrace alongside Per. She'd forgotten, even in her brief leave, the full fug of sixteenth-century stink: the breath-pinching mixture of old and new sweat, of leather and horses, of old cooking and smoke and damp. Per had probably missed it.

Toorkild smacked a prickly kiss on her cheek. "For bringing my little lad back whole to me." Another squeeze, another kiss. "And for bringing back thysen." Growing wet eyed and sentimental again, he pushed her and Per together and kissed each of their heads in turn. "My little lad, my little lass. When shall the wedding be?"

Oh my God, Andrea thought. In a dizzying moment, she lived through years of marriage to Per: a small amount of pleasure and happiness offset by sixteenth-century childbirth and—if she survived that—all the humiliations of Per's infidelity, the grief of children's deaths, the frights and shocks of constant petty warfare and daily drudgery. She thought: That isn't the life I wanted. Not even near.

It wasn't likely to happen, though, not once FUP rebuilt the Tube. But something worse might.

Toorkild was looking over their heads, at the smoke and flames that had brought him out there. "Who fired the Elf-House?"

Despite the food and rest, Per was still tired, and had been resting his head on Toorkild's shoulder. He lifted it and said, "I did."

Toorkild grasped Per by the shoulders and pushed him away, shaking Per's head on his neck. "What? Without yea or nay? Without a by-your-leave? *Thee* fired Elf-House? I'll—" He raised his hand to slap.

The raised hand was no more than a threat, and Per easily stepped back out of reach. "I did it to save thee from the Elves!"

Andrea was startled. She'd supposed that Per had burned down the Elf-House because it was there rather than for any reason, still less this reason.

"Whiles tha was sitting on tha fat arse, scratching thasen and belching," Per said, in the manner typical of Sterkarm arguments, "I saved thee!"

Shocked by this ungrateful insolence in the son he made so much of, Toorkild smacked Per across the mouth—a meaty sound. Per was still for an eye's blink, from pure surprise, and then threw himself bodily at his father, as if to shoulder-charge him off his feet. Toorkild's greater bulk allowed him to stand his ground, and Per was bounced back before being hauled forward again by Toorkild's grip on his jakke. Father and son then began swinging wild slaps and blows at each other.

"Clod-head!"

"Fat old dotard!"

"Tha milky-mouthed dizzart!"

"Half-dead old—"

"Shitten-arsed—"

On the open hillside, the shouts were braying and harsh like the cawing of crows. The occasional slap that connected had the sharp crack of a twig breaking.

Andrea folded her arms, feeling a mixture of exasperation and dread. Was this the company she was doomed to for the rest of her life? Joe's face, as he watched the scuffle, was confused and a little scared. In the space of a few minutes he'd seen Per and Toorkild go from being—to Joe's twenty-first-century way of thinking—embarrassingly affectionate to hitting each other. Leaning her head next to Joe's, Andrea said, "Don't worry. This is business as usual."

Sweet Milk, thinking the quarrel had gone far enough, locked his arms around Per from behind and swung him clear of the fight, while Hob and Sim got in Toorkild's way, saying, "Now, now," and "The lad thought he was doing right."

Toorkild's enthusiasm for the fight had evaporated as soon as he'd smacked Per across the mouth harder than he'd intended, but he put his hands on his hips and stumped about aggressively, saying, "Thought he was right? I'll give him right. What's he know about right?" His stumping took him farther away from Per.

With Sweet Milk still holding him by one arm, Per shouted, "Tha never *listen*!"

"Listen? What be there to listen to?" Toorkild shoved his way grandly past Hob and Sim. "Nowt but the bleating of milky-mouthed lambs!"

At Toorkild's approach, Sweet Milk placed himself in

front of Per. Trying to get around him, Per said, "The Elves are too strong! *That's* why I burned 'em out! But tha'll never listen!"

"They were going to trade!" Toorkild and Per circled around Sweet Milk as if he were a pivot, without seeming to notice him. Sweet Milk turned and turned with them, pushing now one away, now the other, though there was no longer any serious threat of violence between them. "Burned wine I was going to get! Wee white pills for the pains! How will I get them now?"

"Listen!" Per said. His brief anger burned out, and he sat down suddenly on the hillside, hanging his head. "Listen."

Toorkild, clucking anxiously, hurried over and crouched by him, unfastening his cloak and throwing it around Per's head and shoulders.

"The Elves put new blood in me," Per said. "And look!" Though Toorkild told him to sit still, he got to his knees, unbuttoned his jeans, struggled a little with the zipper, but eventually pulled it down, and pushed down the jeans to show the faint red line across his thigh.

The Sterkarms crowded around, bending low to get a good look, jostling each other, some even touching the faint scar. Those who saw it urged friends to push through from the edge of the crowd and get a look. Andrea and Joe kept well back from the scrum and glanced at each other.

"The flesh was hanging open like a mouth," Sim said. "I saw it, me." Sweet Milk nodded, so everyone knew it was true.

Everywhere, men were shaking their heads. "Elf-Healing, eh?"

"Elf-Work."

Toorkild reached around Per and pulled up his jeans but didn't know how to fasten the zipper. As Per pulled it up, the Sterkarms pressed close again, to watch. Diverted, they began to feel the cloth of the jeans approvingly, and to comment on their strange cut, and to ask Per to run the zipper up and down again.

"Listen," Per said, but something was being murmured and whispered through the crowd, until Hob shouted out, "No bugger else is going to be Elf-Healed! Tha've made sure of that, burning down the Gate! Toorkild, fetch him another clout!"

"Listen!" Per said.

Toorkild, standing over him, yelled at Hob, "I'll clout thee, tha gobby sheep's-get! Nobody tells me—"

Per got to his feet and elbowed his father in the chest. "Daddy, listen! Everybody, listen! The Elves are—*listen!* The Elves are like the king of Ireland." The Sterkarms looked at him suspiciously. "Who had the cauldron." His listeners all knew the story, but weren't sure what he was getting at. They folded their arms or leaned on longbows or lances, waiting. "And when his men were killed, he put them in the cauldron and they came back to life again. So he couldn't be beaten until the cauldron was broken. See? The Elves have Elf-Work that takes away pain, better than the espirin they give us!"

"Aye, and we'd like some of it!" a man said. Sweet Milk, arms folded, stared him down.

"The Elves can take away their own pain as well as ours," Per said. "They feel no pain. They can stick together their own hurts, and put new blood into *themselves*, and raise themselves up when they're all but dead!

297

And they outnumber us! I was in their town. There are more of them than leaves in the wood or ripples in the stream. Let them come as they please, and we'll be overrun. How can we fight them when they feel no pain and mend themselves? It'd be like fighting the king of Ireland."

"Break their cauldron!" someone called out, and guffawed.

Per pointed to the collapsing, burning Elf-House. "I did break their cauldron." He sank down to the ground again, weary. Andrea left Joe's side, pushed her way through to Per and sat beside him. He smiled at her and took her hand, and she kissed his cheek, grateful that, for now at least, she didn't seem to be included among the Elves.

Above them the Sterkarms murmured and nodded and argued. Toorkild sat down behind them and made himself into a support for Per's back.

"Every Elf has an Elf-Cart," Per said, "and some of these Elf-Carts, some of 'em can go over water! Aye, water!" Men began to settle down on the grass, sitting, lying, leaning on each other. Sweet Milk passed Per a bottle of small beer.

Look at them! Andrea thought incredulously, as smoke and sparks and smut continued to fly from the burning of her only way home. They're settling down for a good listen. Food and drink were being passed around.

"They have Elf-Carts that can go over any ground, over rock, over bog—and they have cannon on the front. They use 'em to break down buildings." He pointed across the valley to where the top of the tower could be seen poking above a hill spur and didn't need to say more. The Sterkarms growled.

"I saw it on a far-see. That's an Elf thing. It's like—like a window, but through the window you see things that are happening far, far away. In London! Or Ireland!"

Men who'd been lying down sat up. They turned to each other, gaping.

Toorkild had his hand on Per's head, and Per irritatedly shook it off. "The Elves have these far-sees everywhere, watching all the time. If we let them come here, they'll bring far-sees with them and watch *us*, and they'll always know when we ride—we'll never be able to ride again! And they have—listen! Listen!"

Per's audience had begun to exclaim and chatter. Toorkild raised his voice and yelled, "Listen!"

Per put his hand to a deafened ear, but went on. "They have far-speaks too. They're like a—like a stick that goes from your mouth to your ear, and you speak to them and it carries your voice to someone else's ear, and you put your ear to it, and you hear someone else's voice. I've done this: I've heard one speak."

Toorkild hugged him and said, to everyone, "He put his ear to one, my bairn. He listened to the—"

"Quiet, Daddy! You can—"

"What do they sound like?" a man asked. "Is it shouting from far off?"

"It sounds like someone standing at your shoulder. Listen, listen!" His listeners had all begun to talk among themselves again. "With these far-speaks you can talk to people in Ireland like they were next to you—" Another outburst of exclamation and chatter. "Listen, listen!

They'll bring far-speaks here, but they won't give 'em to us. They'll use 'em against us! They'll see us ride on their far-sees, and they'll talk to their friends on their far-speaks, and we'll ride into an ambush!"

A silence fell over the hillside as the men considered it all.

"On their far-see," Per said, "I saw bodies, dead bodies—women and children too, piled in heaps like leaves in a drift. More folk than in Carloel, all killed. The Elves love to kill. They had a creature in their land; they called it a tigger. It was like a—like a big—a big—big cat—a beautiful, beautiful beast, all yellow and striped like a wasp. Big and fierce and beautiful. And the Elves, they killed all the tiggers. All. Killed them and killed them until there was never a one left." He pointed around them, at the hills and the black sheep that wandered on them. "They want to come here and kill our sheep, and all our deer, our wolves. The Elves love to kill. Not Entraya." Realizing that Andrea might be blamed along with the other Elves, Per turned to her and put both arms round her. "I should have trusted thee," he said.

In a spurt of affection, she put her arms round his neck and kissed him. The men around them set up a chorus of half-joking jeers and coos. Andrea wished that the affection she felt for Per weren't so mixed with relief at the protection he offered from the other Sterkarms.

"The other Elves," Per said, his cheek still leaning against Andrea's, "they love killing so much, they have their far-sees look at the women and children they've killed and heaped up, so all can see. They're proud of it—of killing children."

The Sterkarms shook their heads.

"No!" Andrea said. "No, they're not *proud* of it. It's on the far-see so that people will know about it and—well, stop it. Not do it anymore." She looked around at the faces that stared at her. It was plain they would rather believe Per than her. Thinking over what she'd said, and of how much television had done to stop wars, she wondered if he wasn't right.

Per half turned to look at his father. "Thy wee white pills and thy burned wine! Elf-Promises! They took me away to heal my leg—they said! But they meant to keep me a hostage. Entraya will tell thee! A hostage, Daddy!"

Toorkild wrapped his arms around Per again. From within the embrace, having fought an arm free, Per continued. "Chyo there, he's one of our own, and they took him into Elf-Land long ago, and how did they treat him? I found him begging in the streets of Carloel. The Elves gave him nothing, not a place by the fire, not a mouthful of beer, not a piece of bread. Daddy, when those Grannams were lost, tha took 'em in, fed 'em, gave 'em a bed—"

"Aye, he did," men in the audience were saying.

"Bad weather that year, deep snow."

"Three days they stayed. Grannams."

"Grannams," Per said. "We owed 'em nowt but blood. But, see, the Elves—they take Chyo to Elf-Land, he's their guest, and they leave him to live like a masterless dog, like a wet fox on the hill. And their guest-promises to me! They made me a prisoner and a hostage. There's no trusting the promises of Elves. They promise us burned wine—aye, to make you all drunk and stupid. They promise you potions to take away

301

aches and pains—aye, to send you all to sleep, like the Irish witches send their enemies to sleep. Let them in—" Fighting off his father, Per got to his feet. "Let them in, and they'll cast us out and down. They'll take our tower from us, and all our kine, and we'll be out on the moor, crying like curlews, while the cold wind blows and the rain comes down. There'll be no fighting 'em, not with their far-sees and their far-speaks. Their carts'll outrun our horses, and it'll be their pistols and cannon against our lances. They'll call us friends, but they'll take our all and thrall us—so I ran 'em back into their own place and burned their house and closed their gate. That's why I did it. To save us from 'em."

The men were silent. Many of them got to their feet as if wishing to stand ready. Toorkild got up, wrapped Per in his cloak again, kissed his head, patted his back and said, "My clever, canny lad."

Andrea got up too and stood beside Per and Toorkild, feeling at a loss. She couldn't think of anything to say. She'd never thought the Sterkarms stupid merely because they were from a time five hundred years before her own, but still, she was astonished at what, and how much, Per had noticed in the 21st, and how he'd put it together. Things she'd mentioned to him casually while trying to keep him amused in the hospital, and which she thought he'd forget. He'd understood some of it in his own way, but he hadn't forgotten much at all.

Joe had edged through the crowd to Andrea's side and nudged her. "What did he say?" He'd caught the odd word here and there, but most of Per's impassioned speech had been too fast for him to follow.

Andrea shook her head, feeling such a mixture of

things that she didn't think she could explain anything coherently. Besides being astonished at Per's perception, she was unhappily aware that his assessment of FUP's aims was right on the money. A few of the details might have been skewed or misunderstood, but he had the big picture framed just right. Then her feelings would whip angrily around, and she'd think: Wouldn't the Sterkarms be better off if the constant raiding and petty warfare were ended? Wouldn't they be richer, better fed, better off altogether under FUP's management? She was embarrassed to find herself feeling indignant on behalf of FUP, but after all, they were People Like Her. Weren't they? Certainly more like her than savages like the Sterkarms. Savages? Is this me thinking this? she asked herself in amazement. And she'd better learn to love these savages, and she'd certainly better act as if she loved them and keep on their good side.

She saw, with a shock, that Toorkild was pointing at her. "Thee! Tha knowed they meant to keep my bairn hostage."

"No!" she said, and took a tight hold on Per's arm.

"It was thee talked us into letting him be taken away, and all the time tha meant to make him hostage."

"He was dying! Remember? I wanted to save his life!"

Per pushed his father away, holding him off. "Entraya helped me to escape—and if I'd trusted her more, I think I'd have been home sooner."

"She knew all this tha've told us," Toorkild said, "these far-sees and far-speaks and magic cauldrons, but she told us nowt of 'em. It seems she's no friend to us."

"She'll be one of us," Per said, "when we wed." Feeling Andrea start, he put his arms around her. "I've

303

captured my Swan-May. Tha doesn't want to fly away, dost?"

Andrea put her arms around him and thought: No, at exactly the same time as her mind was screaming: Yes!

"I'll hide thy wings where tha'll never find 'em," Per said.

Toorkild pulled at his shoulder. "I'll see thee dead afore thee wed that Guthrun!"

Per swore and moved around Andrea, out of his father's reach. He was opening his mouth to shout at Toorkild, and they would soon have been into another argument, if Andrea hadn't pulled at his arm. Per looked at her.

"I'll tell you all this as a friend," she said. "You think you've got rid of the Elves. I don't think so. I don't think they'll stay away just because you've closed the gate. They'll open it again and come back, and they'll come back with—with pistols." To the Sterkarms, "guns" meant cannon. "And guns too probably. And other things—worse weapons than you can imagine."

Toorkild glowered, and she clung to Per's arm and wondered why she was helping them. Wouldn't it be better for her if they were taken by surprise? But then Per might be hurt or even killed. And scowl at her as he liked, she didn't want Toorkild hurt either. Even with the bodies of the security guards lying in the compound, she still liked these people—she couldn't help it. They'd always been good to her.

And she was afraid that people were going to be hurt. Bullets were going to tear through flesh and shatter bones into vein-piercing splinters. Arrows were going to break jaws.

A cold, damp wind blew across the hillside. A little below them Bedes Water ran, and the herdsmen rode among the sheep. Above and beyond rose the hills, to the moors and the sky, and up on its crag Toorkild's tower overlooked it all.

"You don't know what you've done," she said, knowing it would mean almost nothing to them. "You've just declared war on the twenty-first century."

13

21st Side: A Short, Sharp Shock for the Sterkarms

BY THE TIME security called Bryce from the meeting, things were out of control, and there was nothing he could do except stand and watch. He certainly wasn't going to threaten Windsor's life by further panicking an already panicked and dangerous Per Sterkarm.

He'd felt his caution was vindicated when Windsor, at least, was released. "Nobody move!" Bryce yelled above the excited chatter that immediately broke out. He didn't want any heroes chasing Per Sterkarm through the Tube and straight into a Sterkarm ambush—not that the security guards showed any disposition to be heroic, despite Windsor's ranting.

Bryce looked to the security monitors, to try and get some idea of what exactly was going on 16th side. One showed a distant corner of the compound fence, one the sky and the others various shots of the Sterkarms outside the compound. While he was still cursing, a couple of guards from the 16th side came running to safety through the Tube. Bryce's hopes rose.

But then smoke came drifting through the Tube and

the control room shook to a crash so loud that Bryce ducked forward, clapping his hands to his ears. A sound like an immense car crash, of metal wrenching and shearing, of concrete cracking and falling.

The shaking stopped, and Bryce straightened, realizing that the control room was still standing. People had fallen to the floor, but a quick look around showed him none who seemed to be seriously hurt. As his numbed hearing recovered, he heard people whimpering, computers bleeping, and debris still falling.

The Tube had torn in half. People grabbed fire extinguishers to deal with the flames. Bryce moved through the control room and out onto the platform in front of the shattered Tube. The facing of its curved inner wall was in tatters, like wallpaper in a demolished house. Circuit boards hung out of cavities on wires. The cement of the roadway was cracked. Scaffolding was twisted and sheared. The whole farther end of the Tube, the half that had once opened into the past, was missing. Smoke drifted about them.

Windsor's voice rose above the other noise. "How was this *allowed* to happen? I want answers!"

Windsor was a sight. His hair, usually combed and oiled into place, had fallen in a tangle about his face. He had buttoned his shirt and put his tie straight, but both still looked mussed and wrinkled. Blood from his cut ear had dried on his face and run down his neck, marking the collar of his shirt with an ugly stain.

"Where were you?" Windsor said. "You're head of security, where the hell were you? What use are you?" Windsor's heart was still racketing within him, from the many shocks and humiliations he'd undergone—the sight of Bryce, calm and unmolested, was enraging. So was the sight of the wrecked Tube. He pointed at it. "I want that up again! Up and running! By the end of the day!"

No one was listening to him. Several of the technicians were talking to Bryce. "The fire—it's shorted out—"

"There's been a temporal-spatial dislocation—"

"They've got Andrea—"

"And serve the bitch right!" Windsor said, which at least shut everyone else up and made them look at him. "She helped him, she brought him here, she put him up to this! Serves her right!"

"Okay," Bryce said. "So Andrea and four men are 16th side. Where are the two who came through? The med room? I'll talk to them."

"That's nice!" Windsor said. "Have a chat!" Anger was replacing his fright, swelling his heart and brain, reddening his face and making him clench his fists. "In the meantime, the Tube's destroyed, billions down the drain . . ." He ran out of breath and saw them looking at him, staring at him in surprise and disapproval.

Bryce said, "James, get a grip on yourself!"

Windsor's mouth clamped shut. He breathed through his nose, breathed deeply, and yet still seemed to be stifling. The anger inside him was beginning to scald, to roll in his guts. And it was Andrea's doing.

Andrea and her murderous toy-boy. All their doing. "Don't tell me to get a grip."

"James, I only meant—perhaps you should come across to the med room with me?"

"I'm not interested in your opinion! I want to know when the Tube's going to be up again." He shoved his hot, angry face into the face of the supervisor. "When?"

Her degrees in physics didn't, he was glad to see, prevent her from shrinking and stammering. "I. Don't. It'll be. We shall have to—"

"The end of today! I want it running by the end of today! Understand?"

"That's. I'm sorry. That's—"

Windsor took the woman by the arm and swung her away from her friends, out into the middle of the platform. She gave a cry of shock.

"Don't give me excuses!" Windsor said. He could hear young Sterkarm laughing at him. Five centuries away, but he could still hear him. "Don't just stand there staring at me with cow eyes, you stupid mare! Get moving!" The effort of shouting swelled his brain in his skull until it was an uncomfortably close fit. He felt veins pop in his eyes. He was pulling at the woman's arm, to shake her, when Bryce stepped up to them. Bryce prized Windsor's fingers from the woman's arm and pushed him away from her.

"James, that's enough," Bryce said. "Go to the med room."

The intervention, and the silent stares of the technicians, infuriated Windsor. He took another deep breath, and it made his mind spin. The blood beating through his head said, "Make them, make them, make them do it!" He wasn't able, clearly, to think anything else. He wanted to hit somebody. He could feel his muscles moving in that thrust of the fist—

Bryce said, "Don't! Take me on!"

He and Windsor stared at each other. It made Windsor want to hit him more, but some faint little voice at the back of his mind cried out to him that he'd be a fool, a big, egg-splattered fool, to do it.

"Go to the med room," Bryce said.

Windsor turned and walked away down the ramp to the gravel drive below. At the bottom he turned and, pointing, yelled, "I want it up and running by the end of the day, or a lot of people around here will be looking for jobs!"

* * *

Bryce looked around the door. "Can I come in?"

"Come in, come in!" Windsor said, and waved him toward an easy chair. "Want a drink?"

"No, thanks."

"Oh, come on, we both need it."

"Whiskey, then." While Windsor poured the drinks at the bar in the corner of his office, Bryce wondered at the man's good temper. It was after six now—no getting home early that night—so he'd had a couple of hours to recover. Still, he'd practically been frothing at the mouth. Now he'd cleaned himself up, combed his hair back into place, put on a fresh shirt, and seemed as smooth as ever, except for the dressing on his ear.

"And what have you managed to establish?" Windsor asked, as he brought Bryce his drink.

Bryce drew a long breath while he ordered his thoughts. "The two men who got back to our side are okay. I saw them to the hospital, but they aren't hurt, just badly shaken up. The Tube, by the way—not strictly my business, but I thought you'd like to know—is a mess. Best estimates for getting it up again are a—"

"A week," Windsor said. "I know. I've been looking into that. I've given them three days."

Bryce said, "I'm concerned for our personnel who were 16th side when the Tube went down."

"There's no need to worry about our Miss Mitchell."

"Oh?"

"She's where she wants to be, with her bit of rough! She set it up, and—never mind."

Bryce left a short silence. "I'd like to hear her word for it. And I'll tell you now, so you know. I'm putting in a report, and it's going to say what I've been saying all along, that security isn't being taken seriously enough, and not enough's being spent on it."

"It's your department."

"And I have a budget! There's bloody thousands spent on painting offices and that kind of nonsense!" He pointed to the beautiful framed photograph of Toorkild's tower hanging on the wall. "But they expect me to run security on a shoestring, because—oh, the Sterkarms, they're only a lot of ignorant bumpkins . . ."

"You sound like you need a drink," Windsor said, smirking as though he'd never gone scarlet in the face and threatened employees with the sack.

"James, you could have supported me more on this. If you pay night watchmen's wages, you get night watchmen. You can't expect a night watchman to deal with the Sterkarms."

"Yes, yes."

"It's no good giving men guns if you don't train them to use them. The Sterkarms have been training with their weapons since they were children, and they've no hesitation about using them. Our men didn't know what to do. They weren't confident, and FUP's policy isn't clear. They didn't know if they were *allowed* to shoot.

Not that it would have done them much good if they had, with only one bullet each, and they'd probably have—"

"All right!" Windsor said. "I take your point."

"Do you?"

"Absolutely. We've tried asking the Sterkarms nicely. We've tried bribery. This is the result." He pointed to the dressing on his ear. "To say nothing of the Tube being in ruins. And," he added as an afterthought, "personnel stranded 16th side." He pointed to his ear again. "This was done by a—a lout, whose life I'd personally gone to a lot of trouble to save. Ungrateful, treacherous—I think it's time the Sterkarms got a short, sharp shock."

Bryce raised his brows.

"When the Tube's up again, I want you to take some men through. Armed. And show the Sterkarms exactly where they stand vis-à-vis the 21st."

Bryce, his hands clasped as he leaned on his knees, pursed his mouth and nodded. "You realize this could get a bit outrageous? I'll do it if you authorize it, but I want you to know what you're asking. People are going to get slotted."

"Slotted?"

"Killed," Bryce said.

Windsor wavered. The picture Bryce called up was rather brutal, like something from a news report. It would be bad publicity, and Head Office would be on his back—but no, who would ever hear of it? There weren't many investigative journalists 16th side, and, personally, he could tolerate a good deal of brutality being dished out to Per Sterkarm. If Andrea Mitchell caught a smack or two, he wouldn't complain.

"So long as none of our people are—slotted. If the ringleaders among the Sterkarms get hurt, well, they chose to play hardball. But let's not get carried away here. We don't want any massacres."

With a slight effort, Bryce kept his face expressionless. Typical civilian reaction! Wanted him to go in and do the dirty work, but didn't want anyone to get hurt. "James, I'm not into massacres myself. I won't be leading any atrocities. But let's be clear about this from the start. If we go in there armed, I can't give you any guarantees about who gets hurt, and who gets killed and who doesn't. I shall aim to get in and out as quick as possible, with as few casualties as possible, but once we make contact, anything could happen."

Windsor spread his hands. "So be it."

Bryce looked across at the photograph again. "Take the tower. It's their stronghold. Take it and use it against them. Psychologically, devastating."

In the photograph the tower looked grim. "Could you do it—with a small force?" Windsor didn't want Bryce to get expensively carried away.

"If the aim is to beat the Sterkarms, we have to take the tower. It's well sited, but the defenses haven't been built to withstand our kind of weaponry. I'll need maps."

Windsor nodded. "We have some maps that the research teams made. They're not complete because they kept being interrupted by the Sterkarms. I could put you in touch with some of the team members. They may be able to tell you more."

Bryce nodded. "That would be useful."

"I'll get Beryl onto it."

"Good. Thank you. Ah—I don't know how seriously you meant that about getting the Tube up again in three days, but I could really do with a week—better still, a fortnight."

"Why?" Windsor asked.

"To put out the word. To call in the men I need."

"You've got your men," Windsor said. When Bryce looked at him, he said, "On your payroll. Pay them double time, and they'll be fighting each other for the chance."

"*Security?*" Bryce said. "James, what was I just saying? I'm talking about professionals. I need time to recruit."

Windsor shook his head. He was taking a risk in even suggesting this expedition. If it was successful, if the Sterkarms were cowed, FUP would be suitably grateful. If it failed, FUP would probably cover the cost, to keep the whole story in house. But Windsor would be looking for a job himself. "This has got to be kept small, cheap and fast. I don't see the point of holding things up, and paying for professionals when you could use the men we already have on our payroll."

There was a short silence from Bryce, as he remembered how Windsor had "taken his point" earlier. "It's rough country 16th side. We need men who've got some experience of crossing that sort of country and avoiding an enemy while doing it. Because the Sterkarms—"

"Are peasants, armed with sticks," Windsor said. He remembered the severed head, and determinedly turned his thoughts away. "You'll have automatic rifles. I don't think we have to worry too much about the Sterkarms."

Bryce was silent. Everything he'd said to Windsor had been forgotten as fast as he'd said it. His feelings about the situation were getting worse by the moment. "Rule number one, James: Never underestimate your enemy. The Sterkarms are guerrilla fighters. The worst kind to go up against. They know their country a damn sight better than we do. They move fast and light, come out of nowhere, hit you hard and run away before you know they're there."

"Yes, but how hard can they hit you with bows and arrows and swords? And how hard can you hit them with automatic rifles? The Sterkarms already think you're Elves, for God's sake! But we haven't shown them any muscle, so they've been getting a bit cocky." Like Per Sterkarm. "You'll only have to let off one of your rifles, and they'll fall down and worship you as gods. I can't see that we need crack troops for that."

Bryce sighed, but he kept trying. "I'd feel happier going in if we had professionals."

Windsor stood. "We'd all feel happier if the world were perfect. Unfortunately, it isn't. I'll make sure Beryl gets everything to you ay-ess-ay-pee. I'll let you have some figures too, budget-wise. Now you'll have to excuse me. I still have a lot to do."

14

16th Side: A Council of War

THE STERKARM HANDSHAKE carved on the fire hood shone out clear and strongly outlined in shadow whenever the fire burned up bright; sank into darkness when the flames burned low.

Andrea sat beside Joe on a hard bench close by the fire. Her pumps had been ruined by the walk to the tower, her feet soaked and what was left of her stockings torn into holes. One of her best dresses had been ripped on briers and muddied. But despite the tower being such a den of thieves, nothing had been stolen from her bower. She'd been able to change back into a warm skirt and sweater, into thick socks and hiking boots.

One side of her was roasted until her skin was sore and reddened. The room, packed as it was with people, was too hot. She could feel her own face glowing, and could see others' faces shining with sweat.

The noise and jostle were intense. An old man sitting on the ledge by the fire was telling the story of a long-past battle, since battles were in the air, and his listeners were correcting points of the story or asking for explanations, wishing for another story or telling each other to shut up and pass the jug. Joe kept asking for translations, which

Andrea had to yell into his ear. People got up to go outside and then came back.

Dogs lolloped about, shoving their heads into laps, scratching their fleas everywhere, nosing through the straw on the floor for old scraps.

It was, Andrea thought, dirty, uncomfortable, and more crowded and noisy than a four-ale bar. Of course, that was judging it from the viewpoint of her own century, which was anachronistic, and— Oh, what do I care? she thought crossly. It *is* dirty, uncomfortable, noisy and overcrowded. She didn't want to live like this for the rest of her life.

Nor did she want to be the excuse for FUP coming back 16th side and removing all these noisy, chattering obstacles to making money.

What am I doing here? she thought. Helping FUP rip off my friends. Standing by as these friends murder innocent men.

But what was she supposed to do? She had to earn a living, and this job had been such a great, such a unique opportunity. She'd tried repeatedly to warn FUP about the Sterkarms, and only Bryce had listened at all. She'd tried to warn the Sterkarms about FUP, without breaking her contract, but the Sterkarms hadn't understood— couldn't understand. They understood Elves; they didn't understand twenty-first-century companies.

Every time someone looked at her, she felt they were silently accusing her of not warning them about FUP's aims, and of stealing Per away to be a hostage. It made her uneasy, knowing how vindictive the Sterkarms could be. Joe's presence was little help. As a long-lost Sterkarm restored to his own world, she fancied he was finding more acceptance than she had herself. She even felt a little jealous of him.

And she was lonely for Per. If he'd been sitting with her, no one would have dared look at her oddly.

Beside her, Joe said, "Y'know, I think this'll suit me."

"I'd wait a bit longer," Andrea said, "before you say that." She was thinking of seeing the long, sagging bodies of the security guards being dragged away by their arms and feet, to be buried in some shallow, unmarked grave in the wet, lonely hills. A small party of men had been told by Toorkild to do the work, and they hadn't hidden their displeasure at being lumbered with the chore. She'd caught only a glimpse before turning away, but she'd seen them kicking the bodies, heaving at them, and handling what, an hour before, had been living men, with less care than they'd have given to butchered pigs.

From that sight she'd turned to see Toorkild, his hand buried in Per's hair, kissing his son's cheek. "Tha'rt no walking," he said. "Tha mammy'd have me head if I let thee walk." He'd thrown Per up onto his own horse and walked alongside, looking up at Per, his hand on Per's knee.

Joe and Andrea had walked behind. Some of the Sterkarms lingered to stamp out the fires, but most followed, on horse or foot, eager to be present when Per returned home.

Halfway up the steep path that led from the valley to the tower, they'd met a crowd of people, mostly women and children, led by Isobel. Her eyes had been darting everywhere, searching for Per, her face frantic, as if she half expected to be disappointed after all. When people had called back to him that his mother was there, Per had looked alarmed, had slid down from the horse's back and hurried forward through the men and horses to meet her.

Isobel, seeing him, had burst into tears and hugged him tight, pressing her face against his chest. Then she climbed partly up the bank beside the path, to be able to look down on him. She kissed him, tidied his hair with her fingers and asked was he well enough to climb the rest of the way? Wasn't he tired? Had the Elves fed him properly? He must come and have some hot food and lie down to rest.

Per had lifted his mother down from the bank, swinging her around in the air, to prove how well he was. He had dropped her to her feet on the path, set his hand on her breast, kissed her on the cheek and then brought her by the hand to introduce her to Joe.

Isobel, ashamed of having neglected a guest, had startled Joe by embracing and kissing him. Then she'd turned tearfully to Andrea, had drawn her close, hugged her, kissed her and thanked her several times over for taking care of Per and bringing him back mended and safe.

Andrea had been embarrassed. "It was nothing, be so kind—"

"We're in thy debt forever," Isobel had insisted. "If we gave thee all we had—if the grass of the hills was gold, if the snow in winter was silver, and we gave it all to thee, it would no be enough for what tha've done for us."

Over Isobel's shoulder, Andrea caught sight of Per's face. His idea of the gratitude due to the Elves was no longer the same as Isobel's.

"Mother," he'd said, putting his arms round her and pulling her on up the path toward the tower, "I'm hungry." Isobel had taken him by the hand and, calling everyone else on with swings of her arm, had led the way.

As they'd come closer to the tower, and the wall rose above him, Joe had tipped back his head farther and farther. He'd never seen a castle so whole and new. The wall, fifteen feet high and built of smooth blocks of reddish-gray stone, encircling the crag, cast a shadow down the hillside. They'd climbed the steep path to the narrow, square gatehouse, with its thick, wooden, iron-studded door, backed by a heavy iron yett. The short passageway was dark, chill and damp, with puddles and mud lying among its cobbles. Joe felt the weight of the stone hanging above them as they passed under it. This wasn't a tourist attraction to visit on a sunny afternoon, with your girlfriend and a six-pack. That wall, that door and iron yett, had been put in place because there were people who needed to be kept out.

But once through the tunnel and into the muddy yard, Joe had started to look at the buildings. They weren't beautiful: They were jumbled together, higgledy-piggledy, their thick, untidy thatches of heather hanging low and dripping. The lower, stone stories had no windows and, when he came to look, no doors either. The doors were in the upper, wooden stories, with ladders leading up to them. Funny, he thought, until he realized the reason—and then he felt uneasy again. But however you looked at it—even if these houses were drafty, as Andrea said, even if the narrow, muddy lanes around them were full of muck and puddles and stinks—they were still better than cardboard boxes. A sight better. He could see himself living in something like that: his own thatched cottage. With a real old-fashioned girl.

The tower, with its stone walls, its windowless ground floor, its tiny door and iron yett, had brought back his fears, but once they'd climbed the steep, narrow stair to the hall, fear was forgotten. Isobel had taken him by the hand and led him to the fire burning in a big stone fireplace. She'd urged him to sit on the bench near it and had patted his hands, smiling and chattering, before excusing herself and hurrying away. Joe had felt cheered that this pretty lady had taken the trouble to be so kind and welcoming. Sterkarms had crowded around him, grinning at him, and after the chill of the hillside, the fire's warmth had felt good. Who cared about a bit of smoke? Who cared if his new friends smelled a bit strong?

Per, anxious that his guest should feel welcome, had kissed Joe's cheek and said, *"Naw thu air hyemma."*

Joe had grinned at Andrea. "Now I'm home?" When she'd nodded, his grin had got even bigger.

Two enormous and excited dogs kept bounding around Per, setting their forepaws on his shoulders and slobbering over him, whacking nearby people with their tails and prowling around the bench to come up on the other side and do it all again. Joe wasn't used to dogs so big, and they made him a bit nervous. When Per saw that, he made the dogs lie at Joe's feet, and got Joe to let them sniff his hands, until they jumped up to wash Joe's face with one lick from chin to brow.

Isobel returned, with clothes folded over her arms, and followed by two maids carrying trays, one holding cheese and oatcakes, the other a jug of small beer and many wooden cups. Per jumped to take the trays from the girls and press the food and drink on his guest.

Toorkild joined them, sitting astride the bench and pulling Per down to sit in front of him. Repeatedly stroking down his son's hair, he spoke to him in a low, deep voice that Joe couldn't follow. Per answered, constantly turning to look over his shoulder at his father, but speaking to his mother too, and the other people who gathered around. The big man called Sertha Melk came to stand at Per's side, looking down at him, listening and frequently grinning and nodding along with Toorkild.

Joe looked to Andrea. "He's telling them about Elf-Land," she said. "How we got here—all that."

An account of the ride in the Elf-Cart took some time, with Per holding an invisible steering wheel and changing invisible gears. Wildly waving hands indicated the many, many cars zooming past on all sides and was greeted with incredulous laughter. Oatcakes were passed over people's heads. Someone leaned over Joe's shoulder to fill his cup again.

As the story reached Dilsmead Hall, the listening faces grew more anxious. People moved closer, stooping over or crouching beside the bench. Isobel sat down on Per's other side and gripped his arm, while Toorkild held on to him tighter and leaned around him to watch his face.

Andrea saw how many people were holding their breath as they listened to the account of how Per had got close to Elf-Windsor, and cheers and laughter broke out when Windsor was captured. Isobel looked around at the people about her, inviting them to admire her son. Toorkild kissed him, Sweet Milk squeezed his shoulder and others reached over to rub up his hair or touch his arm or knee—but the congratulations were ended by voices calling, "Go on!"

Per moved rapidly on to an account of how Andrea had guided and translated for them, and how Joe had steered him, and scouted ahead, and had taken the lead when Per himself had weakened. Joe had been startled, even alarmed, by the swooping down on him of Sweet Milk, who roared, slapped his back and kissed him—closely followed by Isobel, who again embraced him and kissed him, and then by Toorkild, who dragged him to his feet and hugged him, and called for the jug and filled Joe's cup again. Andrea was shouting above the whistling and cheering, but Joe didn't need her to tell him that he was now well and truly at home with the Sterkarms. The number of people grinning at him, and pushing through the crowd to get a better look at him, or to grab his hand, or to kiss him, made that clear without words.

He raised his cup in a toast to them all—which pleased them—and thought of all the people who'd walked past him that morning as he'd sat in English Street. Only that morning. Five hundred years in the future, but only that morning. Even the people who'd given him money hadn't looked at him, and had been moving away as they dropped their coins into his box. "Outcast!" said their averted faces, their hunched shoulders and quickened steps. We're frightened of you, we pity you, but we don't want to see you or know you.

Here, though . . . He couldn't remember the last time he'd been made so welcome. It was dizzying, intoxicating, to be at the center of so much good humor. The hugs and kisses took some getting used to, especially the ones from the men, but they showed goodwill. The food was welcome too. Solid, filling. And the beer—well, the beer was strong.

With Per's story over, Isobel tried clothes against Joe's back, and draped the ones she thought would fit over his shoulders. She kept shaking him and saying something which Joe eventually guessed to be "Clothe yourself!" She seemed to think he would change his clothes right there, in front of everyone.

Per had seen the difficulty—or maybe Andrea explained it to him—and he took Joe by the hand and led him up another flight of narrow, twisting stairs to the floor above, with Cuddy, Swart and Andrea following.

Isobel, seeing her chance, sent a girl running to bring more food.

On the third floor, Andrea turned her back and promised she would only translate and not look, while Per helped Joe change his clothes. Sixteenth-century clothing was more complicated than it first appeared, with sleeves fastening to bodies by laces, or strings, which had to be woven in and out of small holes and tied.

"There should be some garters with the stockings," Andrea said. "You fasten the stockings above your knee with garters."

"You just keep turned around," Joe said.

Per had thought Joe's modesty very funny. *"Day air nigh sa lilla."*

Joe had shown him his clenched fist. "That's not so little either!"

There was nothing fancy about the clothes Joe was given. They were of rough, harsh homespun wool, in the natural grays, browns and blacks of the sheep, but they were warm and hard-wearing and, being of natural, hardly treated wool, almost waterproof. A complete set of clothes was a generous gift, but as the clothes, or the wool, had probably been acquired on a ride, it wasn't necessarily costing the Sterkarms anything. Unless you counted the cost of risking their lives against the Grannams and other raiders . . .

The gift pleased Joe, since it seemed to mark his even closer acceptance into the Sterkarm family. He would have liked to have had a bath before changing, but one wasn't offered, so he had to make the best of it. The thought of fleas worried him as he pulled on the gray woolen knee breeches, and the gray woolen shirt, but he supposed he would have to get used to them. It was an especial relief to take off his sodden socks and sneakers, dry his feet in front of the fire and pull on the thick, dry stockings. He thought he would keep his big, hooded waterproof jacket from the 21st: The rest of his old clothes could be burned for all he cared.

Instructed by Per, Joe had rolled his stocking over the top of his knee breeches, and was tying the garter, when Isobel came in, carrying an armful of shoes and boots and wearing a sheepskin cap on her head. Behind her came a maid with a tray of food.

Isobel scattered the boots and shoes about Joe's feet, took the cap from her own head and put it on his, and told him how handsome he looked now he was properly dressed. "I think tha'll find a boot to thy foot among them, but if not, I shall find out some others." While Andrea translated that for Joe, Isobel told the maid to take the food through into the bedchamber and then turned to Per.

"Oh my heart," she said, "tha look so tired. Come and eat in peace now, away from all the noise below. There's some oatcakes and butter, and smoked tongue, and fresh mushrooms, and some honey too. Come and lie on the bed and tell me all tha've done." She took his hand, to pull him up from his chair. "Come on, my apple; come and lie on the bed and close thine eyes for an eye's blink. I've had a jug of festival ale drawn, just for thee. . . ."

As she'd towed Per into the bedchamber, Isobel had looked at Andrea and, with her eyes, had motioned her toward the stairs.

Andrea, trying not to laugh, had suggested to Joe that they go back down to the hall, and had led the way. So Isobel had got Per, and the chance to baby him, all to herself. He was above stairs now, sound asleep on his parents' bed, with Isobel's wolfskin coverlet thrown over him. Both Cuddy and Swart lay on guard beside the bed, while Toorkild had dragged his armchair into the door-way of the bedchamber. Isobel was sitting on the bed, leaning against the headboard and passing the time by stitching and darning while she watched her son sleep.

Though she missed Per's company, Andrea couldn't begrudge him to his parents. Isobel and Toorkild had come so close to what she thought they both dreaded most of all—losing their only son. Now they had him back, whole and well, but both knew that soon after he woke, he would be poaching again, raiding. Fighting the Elves. Indeed, they would be disappointed in him if he didn't. Andrea didn't know how they could bear to live like that.

Down in the hall, by the fire, Joe said, "In my whole life—in my *whole* life, I ain't ever been made as welcome anywhere as I've been here!"

Andrea looked into the fire. She didn't like spoiling his happiness. "And when Per asks you to kill for him—or to be killed?"

Joe fell quiet. He felt a chill like the one he'd felt as they'd come through the tunnel of the gatehouse. "Well, nothing for nothing. If Per gives me what he promised . . . and it might never happen!"

"Joe, here it always happens. What d'you think Per was doing in the 21st? He got hurt on a raid—he almost bled to death. But now he's declared war on the 21st. He's made sure that if you get hurt, you won't have that option."

"I wouldn't anyway, would I?" Joe said. "I'm not the lord of the manor's son. Anyway, what do you want me to do? Go back to sleeping in the streets? Begging for change? I'm here, and it's good, and I'm staying. If I have to fight—well, then."

Andrea sighed again. People were never grateful, she thought, for being reminded of the way things were. "I'm going to my bed," she said. "Has Isobel told you where you're sleeping?" Joe shook his head, and Andrea put her hands briefly over her eyes and smiled. "Oh, she's too taken up with her precious baby boy to think of it. Never mind. I'll fix you up."

Andrea got up and struggled through the people

packed on and around the benches and came back with a couple of grinning, bearded Sterkarm men, whom she introduced as Ecky and Sim. They took Joe back to their corner, poured him more ale, and presented him to a girl named Alsie.

When the fire burned low, and the hall began to be dark and cool, there was a general uprising. Some people were unrolling thin mattresses on the stone floor of the hall, and a strong, sweet but musty smell of dried grass rose from them. Ecky guided Joe to the hearth, where there was a jumble of lanterns and candle jars for those who had to find their way through the tower's lanes in the dark. Ecky lit a candle, put it inside a lantern, and passed it to Joe before finding one for himself. The candles, made of tallow, smelled of mutton as they burned.

Ecky led the way down the tower's steep stairs, and their candlelight washed over the plastered stone walls, turning the bends ahead before they did, and quickly dying behind them.

Horses had been brought into the tower's ground floor, and as the candles' light touched those nearest, they shifted moodily, while others huffed and stomped in the farther darkness. The horses' warmth, weight, size and smell within the small confines of the tower seemed overpowering to Joe, and he kept well back against the wall.

The narrow lanes, with their overhanging thatch, were dark as pitch, and their candles seemed to cower inside their lanterns. Ecky and Sim found their way easily enough, but Joe kept blundering into walls and puddles.

In the middle of one narrow, wet, muddy lane, a

ladder leaned against a wall. Ecky and Sim quickly climbed it, and Joe followed. The room at the top smelled of dust, wood and hay, and was full of shadows. Joe shone his lantern around, and saw small shuttered windows, clothes hanging on hooks on the walls, and big wooden chests. The floor was spread with bedding: straw-filled mattresses and woolen blankets. As far as he could understand, Ecky and Sim were inviting him to take his pick.

"Ah well," Joe said, dropping down on the nearest mattress. "Goo'night!"

In her own bower, Andrea lay awake in the dark, unable to sleep for the thoughts that ran round and round her head, about what would happen when— if—when FUP opened the Gate again. If she was guilty of not having been honest enough with the Sterkarms in the past, she had to be honest with them now.

* * *

The next morning, Gobby, with his two younger sons, Wat and Ingram, and a small party of men, rode into the tower from his neighboring bastle house. Gobby hugged Per, weeping and thumping his back as he said, over and over, how thankful he was to see him alive and well. He'd brought a present for him—a pair of long riding boots, an old pair of Young Toorkild's. They would do until Per could get a new pair made for himself.

Gobby then moved on to Isobel and Toorkild, hugging them, kissing them and telling them how glad he was for them. Wat and Ingram kissed their cousin and tried out various wrestling moves on him. They had kisses to pass on from Young Toorkild too, who had wanted to come, but with both the Grannams and the Elves stirred up, someone had to be left in charge at home.

Joe, watching, thought he could cope with the Sterkarms' hard beds and cold bowers, their early rising and habit of eating only twice a day at long-spaced intervals—but it was going to take him a long time to get used to all this hugging and kissing.

Gobby and his sons joined the tower's company for their morning meal. After the meal, most of those at the lower tables went back to their work, but Gobby, Toorkild and their sons stayed in the hall, at the family table.

"So, tha burned the Elf-Gate down," Gobby said to Per. The messengers Toorkild had sent to him the night before had told him so. "Dost never rest, tha mad hogget? Toorkild, it's no just women, dogs and walnut trees should be well beaten, tha knowst."

"Quiet!" Toorkild said to Per, as Per's mouth opened. "And thee, Gobby. Hast owt to say as to what we should do, or are tha just going to bellock?"

Andrea realized that she would have to speak up. Gobby wouldn't like that. Toorkild probably wouldn't either. But she was going to have to put some words together. . . .

"Be the Grannams quiet?" Per said.

"Ronal Grannam moved on us," Ingram said, and Wat took up the story. Toorkild and Gobby smiled at each other and kept an indulgent silence as the brothers, between them, related how the Sterkarms had been ready for the Grannams, how the beacons had been fired and the bells rung.

Andrea couldn't bear the talk of fighting. Getting up

abruptly from her place beside Joe on a bench, she went to stand before the family table. Toorkild and Gobby looked at her in surprise.

She said, "Master Toorkild, Master Per. You must not fight. Whatever you do, you must not fight the Elves."

Sweet Milk looked around at her. Per, Wat and Ingram, leaning together at the end of the table, looked up. Even Isobel stared at her.

"Tha've much to say now, Madam," Toorkild said.

"Listen to me, then. I'm an Elf-Woman. I know what I'm talking about. I'm telling you, if you start a fight with the Elves, they'll finish it. You can't beat them."

Gobby slapped his hand on the table. "Sit down and be quiet, woman."

Per turned his head sharply to look at his uncle.

"There'll be no fight—only dead Elves!" Toorkild said. "I say we keep a watch on the hillside, and if they open the Gate again, we shoot them as they poke their noses through!"

Andrea hissed in exasperation and stepped closer to the table, leaning on it. Per moved around to her side. He put his hand into the warmth of her hair and lifted up a strand; but she pulled her head aside in irritation and pushed his hand away.

"Be so kind, *listen*, Master Toorkild. I don't want to make you angry, but this is important. If you shoot the first to come through, then they'll send more after them, but this time in an armored car. An armored cart. A closed box on wheels, made all of iron. The Elves will be inside it. You won't be able to hurt them, but they'll kill you. They'll have big cannon on the cart. They'll have bombs—mortars—petards. You know? Elf-Work, Toorkild. It's very powerful. You can't beat them, so you must not fight."

With every word she spoke, Toorkild's face became more mulish. He couldn't think of a way to deny the truth of what she said—yet—but he didn't want to hear it. Why did people never want to hear the truth?

"If we don't fight," Gobby said, "will they leave us alone?"

"No," Andrea said, "because—"

Per, leaning beside her, said, "Will they give us far-sees and far-speaks and Elf-Carts?"

"No. They—"

"Will they stop the Grannams stealing our sheep?" Toorkild asked.

"They *tried* to stop the riding! They tried, and you wouldn't stop!"

"They never stopped the Grannams!" Per said. "They told us to stop riding, but the Grannams came and took our sheep!"

"And you should have gone to FUP and let them deal with the Grannams," Andrea said. "I told you so at the time. But you rode instead."

"We have to fight for what's ours!" Per said, spreading his arms as if this was self-evident. His father and uncle and cousins, the old men and women, all nodded and muttered agreement.

As gently as she could, since she knew what she was saying was not going to make her popular, Andrea said, "But this land *isn't* yours. You've no legal right to it. It belongs to FUP. They hold it by charter from the English and Scots kings—" There was an outburst of denial, of curses and obscenities. She tried to shout above it. "They have the right to keep law and order here! They paid for it!"

"This is *our* land!" Toorkild said. He pushed his chair back, rose and came around the table. He was so angry that she backed away. "It's *our* land because we fight for it!"

Gobby was standing behind the table and leaning on it. "When the Scots riders and armies come south, does the English king fight for us?"

Toorkild, pointing at his brother and nodding, shouted, "No!"

Gobby thumped the table. "Does the English king stop the houses and the fields being burned, the flocks being driven off, the women pricked and murdered, the bairns dying?"

"No!" said Toorkild.

Gobby thumped the table. "When the English riders and the English armies come north, does the Scots king fight for us?" He and Toorkild yelled, "No!" together.

Joe, edging up close to Andrea, whispered, "Steady on. You're annoying 'em."

"When the Grannams steal our sheep," Toorkild shouted, "does your Scots king or your English king get his arse into his saddle in the middle of the night and ride after 'em for us?"

A chorus of "No!" echoed from the walls.

"This is Sterkarm land!" Toorkild said. "Our land! Because we fight for it when no bugger else will!"

There were cheers. Per slapped his hands on his father's shoulders and sprang into the air. Cuddy leaped and pranced about them both, wagging her tail. Landing, Per kissed his father's cheek and leaned on him from behind, hugging his shoulders.

Andrea sat down on the bench beside Joe and leaned her head on her hand.

"We were happy to trade," Toorkild said. "Wool for the wee white pills, that was a good deal. But what do they say? We must not ride. For how long would we have wool to trade if we rode not? And how do they repay me for my trade and hospitality? By taking my son hostage! No, if the Elven set foot on *our* land again, we shall fight them! We shall fight them!"

Andrea listened to the cheers. FUP had never, apparently, saved Per's life. The Sterkarms had never, apparently, robbed any research teams. When the cheers were dying away, she stood again and raised her hands high, palms outward, to show that she didn't mean to argue anymore.

"Be kind," she said, "be so kind, and listen. I'm trying to tell you something important. You think you can beat the Elves by fighting. I'm trying to tell you that you've already lost the battle. It's over, it's done, you've lost. All you can do is to try and save yourselves."

They were silent, staring at her, because they didn't understand. At least they were listening.

"I was thinking about this all last night," she said. "Toorkild, FUP aren't really interested in your sheep. Oh, they'll take them. They're going to take everything you have, believe me. But they were just trading you the wee white pills for the sheep to soften you up—the little white pills are worth *nothing* to them, *nothing*. They were taking your sheep, Toorkild, and paying you in dead leaves and ash."

That was how the Elves always paid mortals in stories,

when they wished to trick them—in trash.

"They want your land, Toorkild. They want to dig up your hills for coal and gold. They want your seas for the fish. They'll catch more fish in a month than you could in a year. They'll empty the seas. They want to dig up the floor of the ocean."

There was a long, long silence. The excitement had gone from the Sterkarms' faces. They were stricken. Per came from behind his father to stand beside him, looking at him as if he hoped that Toorkild knew better how to deal with this than he did.

Isobel came to stand beside her husband and son. "Will they bring the sky down on our heads?"

Dig up the hills? Dig up the ocean floor? It would be the End of the World, when the stars fall into the sea, the Giants wake and the earth is devoured in flame.

"The sea will run away," Ingram said.

"Where will we live?" Isobel asked. "Where will the sheep run if they dig up the hills?"

Toorkild said, "And tha tells us no to fight?"

"You can't win, Toorkild. You can't win." Her voice was fading, growing exhausted. "You have to give in."

The outcry came from all sides, deafening. "Give in!" Gobby and Sweet Milk jumped to their feet. Old men got to theirs. "Give in!"

The noise, the anger, were such that both Joe and Per came to stand at Andrea's side. But even Per, looking at her, said, "Give in?"

"If you don't fight—" She had to shout to be heard. "If you don't make trouble—you might end up better off! Oh, listen! They'll keep the peace. There'll be—there'll be—" She saw it all so clearly. If they didn't fight, if they let FUP in, the Sterkarms would be welcome to any land FUP didn't want. They'd have lots of cheap T-shirts and cheap booze, baseball caps and fizzy drinks and hamburgers.

But they'd be healthier, wouldn't they? They wouldn't need to rob and murder each other all the time. That would be better, wouldn't it?

"But if you fight—listen! I've been thinking about it—it'll be like the American Indian Wars—" What am I babbling about? she thought. They've never heard of America. How could they know anything about the American Indian Wars, when they haven't happened yet?

If only the Sterkarms had known something—anything—about the elimination of the Sioux, the Nez Percé, the Cheyenne, she could have made the desperation of their position so clear to them. An invading people with superior weapons moving in unstoppably. Making deals and treaties and promises, and breaking them all. Using any resistance as an excuse for all-out war and genocide. It had happened again and again.

"They'll kill you all," she said. "Like the tigers, Per!" She saw his eyes widen. "All of you."

She'd thought it all through in the night and it had been so clear, so coldly clear. She hadn't been willing to face up to it before, but now it was so close, there was no choice. Even now, though, she still thought: No, FUP won't do that. Windsor won't do that. He wore a smart suit and had polished shoes. He wouldn't commit—genocide.

But . . .

But wasn't it always the men in smart suits and polished shoes who oversaw the manufacture of the gas ovens and drew up the blueprints for the death camps—and kept their shoes polished all the time?

Because who would know? Who would stand up for the Sterkarms? FUP's twenty-first-century shareholders? They'd know nothing about it. The Time Tube was a secret project. Every employee signed a gagging clause.

And 16th side, who would stand up for the Sterkarms? The Scots king? The English king? The Sterkarms were a nuisance to them both. They'd both wanted the Sterkarms dead for years.

"If you fight, Toorkild, they'll use it as an excuse to wipe you out. That's what always happens. You must not fight."

"What must I do then, Elf-May?" Toorkild demanded. "Kneel down and kiss their feet? Give them back my son as a hostage?" There was jeering mock agreement, and even laughter.

Andrea, looking around, saw that her words had made no impression at all. What had she expected? The Sterkarms held their land by no right of treaty or charter. They held it, in defiance of kings, because they fought for it, tirelessly, against all comers. Ourselves alone.

They knew treaties and charters and promises to be so much trash, never made but to be broken. Their land was all they had, and they knew that if they ever failed to fight for it, they would lose it. Come, who dares meddle with us!

She turned her back toward the family table, and put her hands up to her head, pulling at her hair. Long strands of it slipped from its bun and fell down about her

337

shoulders. She shook her head and wiped tears from her face.

It pained Per to see her so distressed. She was too soft, always worrying about someone getting hurt, as if people could be kept from getting hurt. She needed someone to watch over her and keep her from getting so upset. He slipped his arms around her from behind, and couldn't resist squeezing her to feel how soft and cuddly she was. "Honey-mine, what thinks thou we should do?"

Relief that at least one Sterkarm was prepared to listen to her made her almost sob, and she turned in his arms to face him, but before she could speak, Toorkild broke in.

"We need no woman's thinking! What do women know about fighting? Away with the women!"

Isobel and Per turned on him instantly, together.

"We know our sons get killed, our men get killed!"

Per's voice was louder. "She's an Elf! She knows the Elves!"

Joe sat up straighter on the bench, looking around nervously. Everyone was shouting again. He wished he could follow what was being said. At least, then, the Sterkarms' sudden shifts from good humor to yelling might not be quite so disorienting.

"I'll no be told how to fight by a woman!" Toorkild swung around on Andrea so threateningly that Joe moved, as if to defend her, and Per stepped into his father's way.

"I'll be told!" Per said. "Let her have her say!"

"Thee! Thou wilt! When tha've more than three hairs on thy chin, tha can tell me what tha will and what tha willna!"

Per opened his mouth to shout and moved closer to his father. The loungers sat up straighter. This looked interesting.

Before anything could begin, Andrea picked up a stool and hammered it on a bench. Between the stone walls, it made a resounding din. Everyone looked in her direction.

She stepped up onto the bench. "I'll tell you what you must do. Instead of fighting, you must *talk*."

She watched them look at each other. Talk? What a strange may she was. Per said, as if making sure he'd heard right, "Talk?"

"You must go to them with a white flag and—"

"A white flag?" Sweet Milk said.

Andrea broke off, sighing. "It means 'peace.' It'll let the Elves know that you don't mean to attack them and only want to talk. So they won't attack you."

Per, looking up at her as she stood on the bench, said, "Like a green branch."

"Aye, just like carrying a green branch," Andrea said. "But the Elves will understand a white flag, and they might not a green branch. You have to explain to them that burning down the Elf-House was a mistake—"

"It was no," Per said.

"No, but you must *say* it was. What's wrong with lying? You never had anything against it before."

"But thy Elf-Man, thy Veensa," Per said. "He knows it was no mistake."

"Will tha listen? It would be better if Toorkild went down with the white flag—"

Toorkild said, "We have no white flag."

"Oh, anything white will do! Stop making excuses!

339

An apron, a towel, anything! Toorkild should go—or Gobby. Not Per. What you have to say, Toorkild, is that you're sorry Per burned the place down. Say he got out of hand and did it without your permission."

"That's true enough," Toorkild said seriously, nodding, as if the truth were a matter of importance to him.

"You must say you were very angry when you found out what Per had done, and you're punishing him—"

Toorkild brightened, and clapped his hands together, as if this plan were beginning to appeal to him. Sweet Milk, Gobby, Wat and Ingram all laughed. Per scowled.

"Say you're eager to come to terms with FUP again; that you don't want to lose all the trade they promised you. Invite them back to the tower—"

Per's face lit up, as if he understood at last. Leaving Andrea's side, he went to his father. "Aye! We get them to come back to the tower, all friendly like, and I'm lying in wait!"

Toorkild, grinning through his beard, clapped his hands on Per's shoulders, once more on the most loving terms with his son. Sweet Milk went over to the two of them, saying, "Aye, and if we've Ecky and Gobby in the hills—"

Andrea, standing on the bench, shrieked aloud. "No, no, no! That's not what I mean at all!" She stamped on the bench. "No!"

Cuddy, excited by the shouting, started to bound around them again, her big paws thudding on the floor. Her tail whacked, with a crack, against Joe's hip as she passed him.

"I never meant that I wanted you to lay an ambush," Andrea said.

They stared at her. She was a strange, strange may.

"I want you to *talk* to them! Work out an agreement. Sit down and talk out your differences. Explain that you were disappointed that FUP had kept so much back from you. Ask if you can have far-sees and far-speaks. They won't give them to you, but ask anyway—they might give you something worth having. It's your only chance!"

Per looked at his father. Toorkild looked at Gobby and Sweet Milk. Then Toorkild put his arm around Per and said, "Where wouldst lay up?"

Andrea listened as they talked on, suggesting various places for an ambush and discussing the cover they offered. They gathered around the table again, leaning on it, as they talked over what the Elves might do, and how they might be lured this way and that . . .

"Entraya's plan's the best," Per said. "Go to them with the white flag. Say tha'rt sad for what I did. Ask 'em back to the tower."

The others began to laugh as they saw the way his mind was working.

Andrea tried to hold steady in her mind that these nice people, whom she liked, were planning the ambushing and murder of whoever came through the Elf-Gate when it opened again.

The men coming through from the 21st—men with wives and children, who were just trying to make a living—wouldn't know the rules, the way the Grannams did. If scientists could analyze a sample of Grannam blood, they would find that the DNA spelled out, "Never shake hands with a Sterkarm." The 21st men might have heard the phrase, but it hadn't been bred into them by years of blood feud. They'd believe the white flag. They'd believe the smiles and extended hands. And the Sterkarms would cut them into pieces small—and that was no mere turn of speech.

Andrea realized with a clarity that she had never achieved before that the Sterkarms were murderous, ungrateful and treacherous. They confused her by being, within their own walls, hospitable and generous, kindly and warm. When they smiled, embraced and kissed you, when they pressed gifts on you, it was hard to remember that, not so long before, they had burned down houses, run off the sheep that were some poor soul's livelihood and skewered the sheep's owner with a lance because he objected. They would ride home from the murder, good-humored in success, wash off the blood and become charming once more.

She was through making excuses for them. They were killers, plain and simple. And ungrateful. And treacherous.

She stood again, angry and feeling the shame of having been a fool. Loudly she said, "There isn't going to be any lying in wait or any fighting. I shan't let it happen."

They stopped talking and looked at her with curiosity. How was she going to stop it?

She glared at them, hating them, hating Per the most because he had disappointed her most sharply. "I shall warn them. I shall tell them what you're doing, and you what they're doing. So there won't be any fighting."

She saw the look of amazement on Toorkild's face and realized that she should have kept those last words to herself.

"By my God's arse!" he said. "A woman laying me down the law in my own hall! Per, Dearling, I'll give thee a cudgel for tha wedding gift. Madam, tha'll talk to nobody unless tha canst talk to 'em from the lockup!"

For a moment or two, the words meant nothing to her. And then she thought, No! Toorkild wouldn't do that to her!

The lockup was just one of the outbuildings near the tower, no different from the others. But its lower, stone-built story was often used as a jail. Members of the household caught stealing, or brawling, or otherwise making a nuisance of themselves, would be locked in there with some bread and water and a candle if they were lucky, and left for a couple of days. It wasn't an experience she would enjoy.

She was still openmouthed, wondering whether to try laughing off Toorkild's threat, when Per said, *"No!"* She felt quite warm and weak-legged with relief. If you had a quarrel with Toorkild, there wasn't a better person to have on your side than Per.

"No woman," Toorkild said, "is going to—"

"Daddy, no!" Per went close to his father, who scowled, already wavering. "Not the lockup. It's cold and dark."

Gobby started, "She deserves—" but was silenced by Per's shout of "No!" He pointed to the ceiling. "Lock her above stairs."

"Per!" Andrea felt like a damsel in distress who, having been scooped up to safety by a shining knight, had been dropped on her backside with a thump.

"She'd be in the way up there," Toorkild said.

Per's nose almost touched Toorkild's. "Daddy—"

Toorkild cupped his hand to the back of Per's head. "Above stairs, then. But under lock and key! Up the stairs with thee, Madam!"

"You can't lock me up," Andrea said. Her voice shook.

"Can I no, Madam? Will you walk up the stairs thysen, or will tha be helped?"

She looked at Toorkild, at Sweet Milk and Gobby, and saw that they would make her, even Sweet Milk. When she'd threatened to betray their plans to the enemy, she'd overstepped. She hugged herself, shrinking at the thought of the embarrassment of being dragged up the stairs, or of allowing herself to be locked up.

Per came over to her, his arms reaching out to hold her, his face sad. "I'll come up with thee, Entraya."

She shoved him in the chest, pushing him away hard. "Oh, get away from me!" Turning, she walked up the stairs by herself.

15

16th Side: A Falling Out

JOE KNEW SOMETHING was wrong—he wouldn't take any prizes for that. There'd been a lot of shouting and waving of arms, and then Andrea had gone away up the stairs, hugging herself and looking as if she might cry. Per's father and uncle and the big man they called Sertha Melk had followed her. They hadn't exactly been threatening—Joe didn't feel that Andrea was in any danger. But things weren't peachy keen either. He felt that he ought to follow them, but he might only make things worse and probably wouldn't be able to understand everything they said, and . . .

He looked around for Per. If the lad was going to guard Joe and guard Joe's until the day he died, he could start with a bit of explaining.

Per was standing close by the foot of the stairs, not looking happy. He moved as if to follow the others up the stone steps, then stopped. Just as Joe reached him, he changed his mind again and made a dart for the stairs. Catching at his arm, Joe pulled him up short.

"Is Andrea all right?" Joe asked. *"Olla rikti?* Andrea?"

"Ya," Per said, and turned for the stairs again. Joe held him back and Per, turning to him, frowned.

"Why have they taken her up there?" Joe asked, pointing. "What's going on?"

Per understood his meaning, more or less, but not his concern. "No one will harm her. She's my woman," he added, in case Joe had forgotten. He pulled away from Joe and would have gone up the stairs, except that the other men, returning, blocked the way. Toorkild turned Per and moved him toward the high table, though Per looked back over his shoulder. Sweet Milk and Gobby brought Joe with them.

"We need someone to talk to the Elven," Toorkild said to Per.

All eyes moved to Joe. Warily, he said, "What?"

Toorkild shook Per. "Talk to him, tell him!"

Per had been looking at the stairs and turned sharply toward his father. "What?"

His cousins laughed. "He's above with his Elf-Woman!" Wat said. Per's face reddened, making them laugh more.

Leaning across the table toward Joe, Per said, *"Thu skal spak til Erlven foor oss."*

Here's my chance, Joe thought. He could repay the Sterkarms' kindness and begin to earn more favors. "Tell me what you want me to say." Seeing only puzzlement in Per's face, he tried again. "Tell *migh vah thu* want *migh* to spak."

Per's face brightened. *"Thu maun sye . . ."* But exactly what Joe must say was harder to follow. Per tried many different words, none of which Joe knew. Per tried mime, pulling a sad face and pretending to wipe away a tear.

Joe couldn't understand why the Sterkarms wanted

him to tell the Elves that they were weeping. "Sad? Sorry?"

Now the Sterkarms were puzzled. Per, shaking his head and laughing, went down on his knees and raised his clasped hands to Joe. "Begging? Pleading?" Joe said.

Everyone laughed, even Gobby.

Joe went down on one knee to join Per. "Come on! Concentrate! We'll get it! How many words? Is it a film?"

"*Thu maun sye til dem—*" Per was serious again, staring right into Joe's eyes.

"Yeah, I must say to them—?"

"*—at vi vill spak meth dem—*"

"That you will speak—that you want to speak with them, yeah."

"*Oh dey maun kommer til tur. Hayer. Tur.*"

"Oh—here. The tower. They must come here to the tower. Gotcha!"

They grinned at each other.

Joe's mind was working on the problem of why the Sterkarms wanted the Elves to come to the tower. So they could speak with them, obviously and—Per's sad faces and begging suddenly made sense. The Sterkarms wanted to say they were sorry! For burning down the office place.

"*Vill thu spak foor oss?*" Per asked.

"Oh, aye, *ya*. But wherefore is Andrea . . . up there?" He pointed to the ceiling. "Wherefore?"

Per's eyes flickered away from him, he half turned toward his father and uncle, but then gave Joe his big, bright smile and shrugged. "*Kvenna!*" Women!

The smile was so bright that Joe was grinning back

before he realized that he didn't understand the answer—except that it was dismissive. He wished he could talk to Andrea. He looked over his shoulder toward the stairs, but the Sterkarms were gathering around the table again, and he was drawn into it.

Trying to follow their talk was a frustrating business, and his face was soon screwed up. Whole phrases would come to him easily but, just as he thought he was about to understand, the next several exchanges would be incomprehensible. Toorkild was to do something with something *vit*—white—and the Elf-Gate was mentioned often.

Per and the other two young men were singled out by their elders for something; that much was obvious by the way they drew together and grinned at each other and listened, nodding, to Toorkild and Gobby. Joe just couldn't fathom out what it was they were being told to do, though the Elf-Gate came into it somehow. They were to go—somewhere. They were to take—a lot of things. It was like trying to read a story where half of every page was missing.

The young men left the table, all together, all heading for the tower stairs, obviously intent on going somewhere and doing something. Joe felt a panic. He didn't know what was going on. He chased the cousins across the hall and caught Per just as he was starting down the stairs.

Per looked at him wildly and with a touch of irritation. This was the second time Joe had grabbed at his arm. *"Vah?"*

His cousins pushed past him and went down the stairs. Wat said, *"Per! Kom!"*

Joe didn't know how to put what he had to ask. He could see that Per was impatient to be gone. So he said, "*Hus? Lant?*"

For an instant Per was confused, then he smiled brilliantly, hugged Joe and, before Joe could pull away, kissed his beard. As soon as Per released him, Joe backed off fast. His surprise stopped him from catching the first few words of Per's answer. The next few words he simply didn't understand, though Per, as he disappeared around the corner of the staircase, pointed toward his uncle and father at the other end of the hall.

Joe turned to look toward them. They were seated, deep in talk. He thought Per had gone but heard his voice again and, spinning around, saw him leaning in from the staircase. "*Thu skal har thine hus naw olla air forby.*" His name was yelled from the staircase below, and he grinned and vanished again.

Toorkild and Gobby were still talking, and no one was looking his way. Joe crept out into the staircase and climbed it. Rounding the curve of the stairs, he came in view of the upper door. A man was leaning against it. He stared down at Joe.

Joe smiled apologetically, turned and went back down.

* * *

"Go then, Per!" Wat said. "But hurry!" As Per made off, he shouted after him, "Leaving us to do the work, idle hound! If tha'rt not back quick, we shall come and say farewell ourselves!"

Per ran from the kitchen, where Wat and Ingram were filling a sack with food, back to the tower and up its stone stairs from the bottom to the top, where Ecky sat on the landing, blocking the narrow passage.

"What a hurry to be in," Ecky said, and made no attempt to move aside. Per clambered over him. Finding the door of his parents' room locked, Per wrenched at the handle and rattled it while Ecky, sighing, got to his feet. "Now tha daddy's in the hall and tha mammy's about the yard somewhere, so what canst tha want to go in there for?"

Per saw the key lying on the ledge of the landing's tiny window, leaped for it and got it before Ecky could. Ecky, deprived of a chance to amuse himself by making Per fight for the key, sank down on the steps again. Per unlocked the door and went in.

Andrea was in Toorkild's armed chair by the fire, sitting very upright and staring at the door, braced for whoever was to come in. When she saw Per, she turned back to the fire, leaning her chin on her hand.

He could see she wasn't going to be friendly and stood by the door, wondering whether to leave her alone to wear her bad temper out by herself. If she had been merely a woman, he would have done, confident that he could coax her around later. But she was an Elf, and the Elves had been humbled. It was understandable that her pride was badly hurt, and it would be hard for her to turn to him again without seeming to betray her own people.

He went a step or two into the room, looking for an excuse to be there. The fire was burning well, and the hearth was stacked with peat and wood. On the table were a jug and a cup, and a plate of oatcakes. There was nothing she needed, then; nothing that he could do for her, or fetch. "I've come to say farewell."

Without looking around, she said, "Farewell."

He went right over to her and crouched beside the chair. "Oh, Entraya. Be no angry."

"I'm not angry. Farewell."

She was angry. He tipped his head sidelong, trying to look up into her face. If he could get her to look at him, he could probably get her to smile. "Dost want to know where I'm going?" His mother always wanted to know where he was going.

"You're going to get killed. Farewell."

The harshness surprised him into silence, until he decided to ignore it. "Better give me a kiss for luck then!"

She turned a hard, angry face to him and looked at him with Elf-Eyes, like stone. "Your luck's run out. You're going to be killed."

Even so close to the fire, a cold struck through him, and he rose, moving away from her. When he looked around, she was staring at the fire again and he couldn't see her face. Her being angry with him made him physically uncomfortable, as if he needed to work his shoulders and fidget. And for her to say such things—it was ill-starred. "We're 'thou' to each other, Entraya."

She stared into the fire and said nothing.

"I'm to go with Wat and Ingram to watch for the Elf-Gate opening."

"You'll be the first killed then."

He went back to the hearth and knelt in front of her. "Don't *say* that, Entraya! Touch wood! The Good Old Man's listening." He nodded to the fire. A sort of hob-goblin lived in chimneys, so it was said, and took a malicious pleasure in making such carelessly spoken words come true.

Andrea pulled irritably at her skirt. He would go to fight, no matter what she said. She tried not to care, she tried to think, To hell with him! But she didn't want him to be hurt, and she didn't want him to leave feeling fated. She struggled to make herself say something comforting, but she was too angry. "You've said 'farewell.' Now go away."

Per heard the note of doubt in her voice. He tilted his head to look into her face and pouted, big eyed. "Ah, be not angry, be kind, Entraya. Say 'thou' to me."

"Just *go away*, Per."

His pout became sadder, his eyes wider. "Ah, Honey, be kind, be sweet, Honey-mine."

She turned her face so she couldn't see him, and he leaned farther over. "Ah, Entraya, white flower—"

She was unable to resist looking at him—looked away again instantly—as instantly looked back. His pout began to to dimple into a smile, his silver-blue eyes to glint with laughter.

He had brought her out of bad tempers like this before, going on and on until his persistence and shameless insincerity made her laugh. But now she was so far from amusement that she felt like a lump of the Sterkarms' cold porridge. "May I leave the room?"

"Sweet flower—"

"Am I free to go? If I'm not, then go away yourself. Are you going to ambush and murder my friends and get yourself killed too? Then stop simpering at me and clear off and do it!"

He jumped to his feet, embarrassed and hurt. He didn't like the way she used the word "murder." "Women!"

He sounded just like Toorkild, and even Gobby. "Oh quick—run to Daddy! He's got something for you to do, I bet."

The gibe went by him entirely, only puzzling him. He saw nothing shameful in doing as his father told him, so long as he agreed with it, and in this case, what else could he have done but agree with his father?

He went to the door but, with his hand on the jamb, turned back. To leave her on such bad terms was bad luck and made his heart uneasy. He turned back and knelt again, bringing his head on a level with hers as she sat in the chair. "I be . . ." It was always hard to apologize when it was meant. "I be sad for locking thee in, Entraya. But when all this has gone by, I'll make it up to thee, my word on it."

She looked at him, and was even more astonished when she saw that he believed what he said. He'd burned down the Elf-Gate and trapped her here. He'd stood by and let his father lock her up. But when this little matter of ambush and murder was over, he was going to make it up to her. "And just how are you going to do that?"

Challenged, he looked away, blinking faster, then looked at her sidelong. "When we're wed—"

"When we're *wed*?"

"I'll—I'll get—I'll *buy* you some writings, and—"

She had to laugh. She leaned back in her chair and laughed while Per watched her uncertainly. He started to smile, hoping that her laughter meant she was in a good mood again. Catching sight of him, she said, "Oh, *go away!*"

His smile disappeared. "Entraya—"

She got up. "Go away go away go away!"

He started getting to his feet, talking, so she used the worst insults she'd learned among the Sterkarms. "Cod's head, sheep's head, go away! Sheep's son! Dog's bone! Run away to your daddy the sheep!"

Per's fists clenched and his face flushed scarlet. There were tears in his eyes, he breathed in gasps, his mouth worked and his face was so childishly angry, she almost laughed again. He snorted. "*Yi gaw!*" I am going! He crossed the little room in a couple of strides, snatched open the door and caught at the doorpost with one hand as he swung out and on down the stairs. Ecky was left to shut the door again and lock it.

Andrea went back to the chair by the fire and did laugh, but the tears she wiped away weren't tears of laughter. Poor Per! He was so used to getting his own way, by charm if not by force, that he was bewildered when he failed. Poor Per! Poor Wat! Poor Ingram! They were all going to be killed.

She bent over her knees. Her chest, her throat, her head, all ached. How, she wondered, has Isobel lived with this all these years?

* * *

Wat was singing.

> "Oh, as I came down by Bedesdale,
> All down among the scrubs,
> The prettiest lad that e'er I saw
> Lay sleeping with his dogs."

Per, wrapped in his sheepskin cloak, struggled to sit up against the weight of Cuddy's head, which was resting on his chest. Swart lay close against his other side.

Cuddy, rousing, let him sit up but licked his face with a tongue that felt scalding in contrast to the chill damp of the morning. He pushed her away, because where she licked, the heat soon turned cold.

Ingram, breaking fast on bread and beer, took up his brother's song:

> "The buttons on his sleeves
> Were of the gold so good;
> The good gazehounds he slept among,
> Their mouths were red with—"

Per got to his feet, the hounds rising with him. He spat at his cousins and made the horn sign with his fingers, to avert bad luck. The song, "Yanny o' Bedesdale," told how Yanny, resting from the hunt, was betrayed to the king's officers and murdered. Wrapping his cloak around him, Per stalked off into the trees, the hounds following. All the people he loved best seemed to be conspiring to curse him.

Ingram and Wat jeered him as he went. They had thought to enjoy this time, camping in the little wood above the place where the Elf-House had been burned down. But Per hadn't been good company.

He'd gone to say good-bye to his Elf-May but had come running down from the tower so plainly out of temper that they'd laughed. He hadn't thanked them for catching, bridling and saddling Fowl for him, or for fetching his bow, quiver and other gear from his bower, but had mounted and ridden off in an angry silence.

They'd followed on their horses, and Cuddy and Swart had followed too, loping along on either side of

Fowl. Wat told Per to send the hounds back. They weren't hunting and didn't need hounds. They might prove a nuisance.

Per hadn't been in a mood to respond to orders from a cousin only a few months older than himself, and ignored him. Wat tried to send the hounds back himself, but though they might sit or come to heel at his order, they would only put their tails between their legs when told, "Home!" They wouldn't have gone back readily even at Per's order, and Per refused to speak, either to his cousins or his hounds.

On the hillside above the Elf-Gate, in a hollow where the soil was deeper, grew a small, thick wood of birch and hazel. That was where they were to lie in wait. They crossed Bedes Water at the ford and rode up the valley and over the hillsides, passing close by the burned place, where the wreckage of the Elf-Gate still lay in the grass. Long sections of the chain-link fence had already been pulled down, and some had even been carried off.

On reaching the wood, they took the saddles and harnesses from the horses and turned them loose. Ingram and Wat set about making camp, weaving together living and cut branches to make a frame to support a cloak, to shelter them from the worst of the breeze and drizzle. They wouldn't be making a fire.

Per had taken himself off, with his hounds, to the other end of the wood. Wat felt bad about the way they'd teased him, and it was up to him, as the eldest of the three, to take the lead and make amends. So, at dusk, he'd searched through the trees until he found Per, and told him that they were sad for what they'd said. Per had sulked for a moment longer, but then gave it up and said that he was sad for the way he'd behaved. They'd gone back together, hand in hand, to join Ingram.

But just as they were all friends again, it had unfortunately struck Wat as a good idea to tell the story of Vaylan and his Swan-May. He'd meant it as a sort of rough comfort for Per: See what ill luck Elf-Mays always brought to the mortals who loved them? A man was better off without them. But before he was very far into the story, Per's face had made him realize that telling it had been a bad idea. He would have broken the tale off short, but that would have made his tactlessness even more glaring. Besides, Ingram was enjoying it.

As the murders and cruelties of the story mounted, Per had pulled the hood of his cloak over his head, wrapped himself in it, and lain down to sleep between Cuddy and Swart. Wat had gone on with the story for a little while, but then had said, "Ah, it's a stupid tale, I'm no telling more." So he and Ingram had also lain down to sleep in a bad temper.

So it had gone, for the three days they'd been camped in the wood. Wat had several times set Ingram to talk to Per, either to tease him by insulting his hounds or his riding, or to ask his advice about making bowstrings, training a pup or anything else that might serve. Per, not being plagued with younger brothers himself, would come out of his bad mood to tussle with Ingram, or lecture him, and then would play five-stones or talk, as cheerful as usual. But then, as if his very cheerfulness reminded him of his grievances, he'd suddenly turn moody again, and go off by himself to another part of the wood, or lie down with his head on Cuddy's side and pretend to sleep.

The Elf-May was a handsome lass, Wat thought, but she wasn't worth it.

Now, in the early chill of the fourth morning, Per came back out of the trees and accepted a square of cold porridge from Wat. Cuddy and Swart sat on either side of him and raised big paws to nudge him, asking for a share. Their breakfast eaten, the cousins settled at the edge of the wood for another long day of watching sheep grazing in the valley and hawks hovering over the hills. Per lay on his belly, his chin resting on his arms in front of him, not speaking.

He looked down on his valley, on its fast, rocky river and the many streams that threw themselves down its hillsides. His valley, that the Elves were coming to turn from pasture to broken holes, quarries and mines. What could he do but fight them? But every Elf he hurt or killed his Elf-May would hold against him.

Lovers divided by family and feud made good stories, but in life it was nothing but misery.

Wat dropped down beside him in the grass, and Cuddy reared up to lick him. "Come, Elves," Wat said, yawning. "Come and meddle with us."

16

21st Side: Land Rovers and Kalashnikovs

TWO LAND ROVERS WERE parked on the gravel at the bottom of the ramp leading up into the Time Tube. Men dressed in camouflage sat inside the Land Rovers, or leaned against their sides. In their arms, or slung from their shoulders on webbing straps, were AK-49s—kalashnikovs.

Bryce, also in camouflage, a rifle on his shoulder, stood at a distance, smoking a cigarette. He was listening to the men behind him.

"This is going to be an effing good riot!"

"Walk in the country."

One man—his name was Bates—said, "I'm going to take effing scalps!" He raised his voice, so everyone could hear him. "Scalps I'm going to take! Effing scalps! For souvenirs—effing scalps!" Again and again, the braggart guffawed. "This is going to be an effing good laugh, this! Paid for an' all! A right effing holiday, this!"

His companions laughed, and the more they laughed, the more he brayed.

"What are the girls like?" someone asked.

"They stink."

"What, smelly-bellies?"

More laughter.

Bryce's opinion of them wasn't lowered. It couldn't have been lowered. He thought they were dog's meat. Technology was on their side, and was going to allow them to make dog's meat of the Sterkarms—but it wasn't what they deserved.

They weren't the professionals Bryce had wanted. They were security guards dressed in fatigues and armed with assault rifles. The time limits and budget Windsor had imposed had made anything else impossible.

At the briefing beginning each shift, this "special duty" had been announced, together with a warning that it was dangerous and a reminder of the gagging clause in their contract. Double time for anyone who volunteered.

There'd been plenty of interest. These men earned peanuts. They were going to show interest in anything that doubled their pay, even if only to the amount that Windsor would spend on postcards.

It was Bryce's gloomy opinion that the best men—the ones he would have chosen—were the ones who, when they heard what was demanded of them for the doubled pay, shook their heads and said they wanted no part of it. Some of them had been ex-soldiers.

Their reasons had differed. Some had been quick to point out that the time left for planning and training was bloody short. Others had groaned when they'd heard they'd most likely be armed with cheap kalashnikovs. And then there'd been those who said they didn't like taking automatic rifles against "them poor sods."

Those were the men with the kind of caution and

forethought Bryce liked. The men who, as Cromwell had said of his unbeaten troops, made "some conscience of what they did." They were, almost to a man, the ones who'd walked away.

Three good men, all ex-soldiers, had signed up. They needed the money, they said. What the hell! The three of them weren't enough.

The rest—they were what Bryce had dreaded. Football hooligan types, full of piss and wind and hate. The type who thought a good night out was getting drunk and beating somebody up: a black or a queer, but anybody would do. Some quiet bloke walking down the road— "Get the snotty bugger!" Kick his head in.

Even worse were the fantasizers. The ones who liked to dress up in World War Two and Vietnam uniforms and play war games on weekends, who daydreamed of shooting hordes of gooks and wading through blood, and having chests full of medals, but who couldn't stomach the discipline of the real army. The type who signed up as mercenaries, ready to tear the enemies' living hearts out with their bare hands, but came home two days later in tears because—fancy!—real bullets and real grenades hurt and killed people.

They were such a bunch of losers they deserved their kalashnikovs. Bryce had warned Windsor that, when you had to supply guns fast, cheap and without red tape, what you got were the worst kalashnikovs. They might have been made in Korea or China or Vietnam or Hungary or Nigeria. You never knew what crap they'd been made from, or whether anybody had ever bothered to check if they worked or were safe. Barrels machined from old steering-wheel columns. Stocks shoddily manufactured from plastic, or carved out of whatever cruddy old wood happened to be lying around.

The barrels split and peeled back, the magazines jammed, the stocks broke, the safety catches couldn't be released or couldn't be put on.

But never mind, they were only going up against peasants armed with sticks. The first time they let off a round, the Sterkarms were going to fall down and worship them as gods. Yeah, right.

He supposed it might happen. The effect of Land Rovers and automatic-rifle fire on people who'd never seen or heard them would be demoralizing. Despite all his foreboding, if he had to put money on this little outing, he'd back the 21st. But he'd be willing to bet more money if he'd been able to go in better prepared, better equipped and with better men.

God help the Sterkarms if this shit shower got turned loose on them! No discipline, no esprit de corps, no restraint.

He'd spoken to Windsor about the quality of the men. He'd spoken of looting, rape, maybe the massacre that Windsor himself had feared. "I don't want any of *our* men killed," Windsor had said. "I don't want my backside in a sling because some widows and orphans are dragging FUP through the courts for years, claiming compensation and sniveling to the media. But as for the Sterkarms—they chose to play hardball."

The amazing thing, Bryce thought, was that Windsor was quite open about saying this.

Bates was braying again. "I'm going to have me a piece, I am. What? Got to, aint'cha? Ain't leaving without having a piece; don't care what anybody says."

"Could be your great-great-grandmother," somebody said.

"I'm up for that!"

Bryce rubbed his hand over his face. He hadn't had much sleep over the past four days. If Windsor was insisting on ridiculously short preparation, then he had to give up sleep to cram in what he could. He'd been studying maps and collating information on the tower. Plastic explosive would soon bring the walls down. He had only to get one man to the wall while the others distracted the Sterkarms—and he had his three ex-soldiers to help him.

The staff leisure facilities at Dilsmead Hall included a shooting range, and he'd taken his men there and given them some instruction in using their rifles. A farce, but then, if the best your opponents had were short-range pistols that fired one ball at a time, the kalashnikov was a formidable weapon. When it worked. And they'd been able to find and discard one rifle that had its safety catch permanently jammed on. That was one less thing to go wrong in the field.

The laughter of the men behind him changed its note, became sniggering, stifled. Bryce looked up and saw Windsor coming toward them around the corner of the main building. Windsor was dressed in camouflage too, with polished boots and a beret. Bryce had issued the other men their fatigues. He hadn't issued any to Windsor. He hadn't wanted Windsor to come and hadn't done anything to encourage him. He didn't think that Windsor had ever been in the army. The man had gone somewhere and bought the uniform.

"All set?" Windsor called out, and struck his own leg

with a swagger stick. He had a swagger stick! He'd gone and bought a *swagger stick*!

"All set, sir," Bryce said. He struggled with himself, but then saluted.

"Perhaps I should say a few words—to the men," Windsor said.

Oh God! Bryce thought. He kept his face blank and looked away into the distance. "If you think it's necessary. But I've briefed them."

Windsor wasn't a fool. He saw what lay behind Bryce's strained politeness. "Oh well, perhaps not." He was only trying to do the right thing. "Let's not waste any more time." Giving his leg another thwack with the swagger stick, he went across to the entrance of the lab. Bryce followed.

As Windsor passed, the men whistled quietly and made cooing noises. Bryce glared, and the noise subsided but started again behind them.

Seeing Windsor, the lab supervisor came forward. She looked exhausted and ill. The technicians had been working around the clock too, to wire up the new Tube and make it operational.

"We can't put too much strain on the system," she said.

"Does it work or doesn't it?" Windsor demanded.

"It works," the supervisor snapped back. Weariness made her less easy to intimidate. "But we had to skimp on some of the fail-safe systems. We'll send you through, and then we'll shut down."

"We'll be stranded?" Windsor said.

"Obviously we'll come on-line again at intervals—every six hours for the first day, Mr. Bryce suggested."

Windsor looked at Bryce, who nodded.

"And then every four hours, and then at decreasing intervals—repairs are ongoing. Performance should be improving all the time."

"Is it safe?" Windsor asked.

"For the time it takes to send you through, as safe as it ever was. You won't end up with a fly's head!" Windsor looked at her, and her smile turned apologetic. "Perfectly safe for short spans."

Windsor didn't look convinced, and Bryce hoped that he might decide to stay behind. But he whacked his leg with his swagger stick. "Let's go."

The wreckage of the old Tube had been cleared away and lay on the lawn at a distance. The new Tube was completed but unpainted. The floodlights, on tall scaffolds, erected to allow the laborers to work through the night, hadn't been taken down yet, and ripped bags of cement, heaps of gravel, shovels and wheelbarrows littered the area. The place looked like a construction site.

One Land Rover was already drawn up on the platform at the top of the ramp. The men sitting in it were silent, looking into the Tube.

Except for the roadway, its inner surfaces weren't finished. They could see the steel frames holding the circuitry.

Bryce and Windsor climbed into the Land Rover. Two others drove into line behind them. The lights at the entrance of the Tube changed from red to green. The Tube began to hum, to roar, to scream—and was then silent.

At Bryce's nod, the driver started the engine and drove forward into the Tube. Windsor felt a creeping sensation along his neck as they entered it. Despite the assurances of safety, he could not throw off a suspicion that, this time, there would be no way back.

But the men cheered, and though even with the echo of the Tube, it sounded thin and forced, it raised Windsor's spirits. "Phasers on kill!" one of them shouted, and there was laughter. They were in good humor, then. Morale high. And they had automatic rifles.

The second Land Rover drove into the Tube, and another thin cheer went up. By the time the third Land Rover entered, the first was bumping down from the Tube onto the burned black earth of the sixteenth-century hillside. Windsor's confidence rose again as he looked about at the emptiness. Nothing but bare hills, and air, and sheep. Except for the top of the tower, there wasn't a building in sight. Anyway, not one that could be called a building rather than a heap of turf and mud slowly sliding back into the landscape.

And here were three machined, sharp-angled, powerful vehicles from the 21st, and twenty-four men, and twenty-two assault rifles. Time's up, lads! he thought. We're coming to get you. Per Sterkarm shall draw my chariot. I shall exhibit him in a cage.

There was every chance that the boy would be shot dead. Well, that would teach him to fart in church.

* * *

Per was lying at full length on his belly, leaning on one elbow, with Cuddy and Swart stretched out on either side of him, when the Elf-Gate opened. The great round stone pipe, supported on a cradle of silvery iron girders, appeared from nowhere, silently, blotting out the greens and russets of the hillside.

Swart moved, gathering his long legs under him and giving a yap of surprise. To both hounds, Per said, "*Hold. Stilla.*" Stay. Quiet.

Out of the pipe, out of thin air, came an Elf-Cart, moving slowly down the ramp to the grass. Ingram shifted slightly with excitement. The Elf-Cart was a muddy color, not as shiny and resplendent as the one Elf-Windsor had come in, but it was still awesome. It growled and throbbed. Its back was loaded with Elves, all holding—

"Pistols," Per said softly. He had seen them being used on the far-see in Elf-Land. He was tense with excitement, and a shiver of fear ran through him. Just as Andrea had said, the Elves had come back, fearsomely armed—and the Elves meant to smash their world like an egg, lap up all the goodness and leave them nothing but the dried, shattered bits of shell.

Ingram shifted again, and gasped, as a second Elf-Cart came down the ramp, bringing more Elves and more pistols. And then a third. They watched the Elves jumping out onto the ground, and they picked out the leader easily, by the way he moved, and the places he chose to stand. Elf-Windsor was recognizable too, by his build and movements. Per's bow and arrows lay beside him—if only Cuddy would get off them. He could hit Windsor from this distance. And would, given half a chance.

When the Elf-Captain looked up toward their wood, they knew what it meant. . . .

* * *

The sheer silence of the 16th silenced the 21st men's cheering and catcalls. They raised their eyes to thick gray sky above them and looked round at the wide rise and fall of hill and valley in the sparkling air. Far below was the gray-and-white running of Bedes Water, and the black sheep that grazed its banks. A damp, chill breeze touched their faces; a mist of rain hung in the air. Around the burned area some sections of chain-link fence lay flat on the ground, thrown down. Other sections were missing, carried away.

They looked back at the Tube and, as they looked, it vanished. The green slope of the hill, and a little stand of birch, filled in the space where it had been.

As soon as Bryce saw the little patch of woodland, he knew it was the most likely place for an ambush. He scanned the Land Rovers. "You, you, you." The men he chose were the three ex-soldiers, the only ones with anything like the experience to check out the wood. "Get up there at the double. Safety *on*. No shooting unless you have to. Anybody you find, bring 'em back here."

The three men made off uphill, looking at least something like soldiers, though two of them were well out of training. Bryce would have liked to go with them, but there was no one he trusted to stay behind with the Land Rovers. Certainly not Windsor.

Bryce took his map from his pocket and spread it on the hood of his Land Rover. It was a rough thing, the first effort drawn up from the geologists' unfinished explorations, but it was all they had. He'd hardly got it opened when Windsor said, "They're coming!"

He pointed down into the valley. Bryce tucked the map behind a windshield wiper, unhitched his binoculars and leveled them, leaning his elbows on the Land Rover. He saw a party of mounted men, about ten of them, riding up the hill toward them. "They've got a white flag," he said. Something white, at any rate, was fluttering from a spear.

Windsor had his own glasses leveled. "Surrender," he said. "Without a shot. I told you the Sterkarms weren't going to give us any trouble."

* * *

Per, Wat and Ingram, keeping low so that the bushes and long grass would hide them, took up their bows and quivers and moved back into the wood. They didn't trouble much about the noise they made: The Elves were at a distance and making their own noise. It was movement that would draw the eye and give them away.

Passing through their little camp, they collected their cloaks and pulled down their flimsy shelter, carrying the cut branches away with them. Per's chosen hiding place was a hollow partly filled with the trunk of a thick, fallen birch overgrown with toadstools. Old leaves, bronze and brown, had filled the hollow deeply. Per, with his bow and quiver, burrowed into the leaves, raising a rich scent of earth and decay. Lying on his back, he spread his cloak over himself, its brown, stained, leather side uppermost. He called the hounds under the cloak with him—a wagging tail or twitching ear would be less noticeable under the cloak. The cut branches he dropped on top of the cloak, then he scattered fistfuls of the old, dead leaves over it. The top of his head and his eyes he left uncovered, but he filled his hair with leaves. "*Hold. Stilla,*" he said to the hounds, and then drew his dagger and lay still himself.

The brown of the cloak's leather merged, an earth color, with the browns of the dead and dying leaves scattered over and around it, and with the branches lying on it and growing around it. The stains and dirt of long use, and its crumplings, further broke up the outline of the cloak. Where the black fleece of its inner side showed, it blended with the black markings on the birch log and with that part of Swart's black, hairy back that was uncovered. There was nothing about the wrinkled, brown toe of Per's boot to catch the eye, half covered as it was with leaf mold. The shifting, leaf- and branch-broken light danced over the hollow, melting all outlines. Someone searching for him wouldn't see him even if they trod on him.

It was easy for Per to hear the Elves coming. The birds, which had grown used to the cousins' presence, flew up at the approach of the newcomers, alarmed and screeching. The Elves themselves panted, coughed and called out to each other. Their feet thumped, trampled, crushed. They thrashed through the undergrowth, setting branches swinging and rattling.

Per, lying still under the sheepskin cloak with the big, warm bodies of his hounds pressed against him, grew hot. Cuddy lay partly on top of him, and grew heavier every time he blinked. He could feel growls trembling through her, though she was silent as yet. Hardly moving, he pressed his hand against her and breathed, *"Stilla."* She stopped growling but poked a startling cold nose under his chin and unrolled a hot, wet tongue against his neck. He hoped the noise of slobbering wouldn't carry.

Wat had been right about the hounds: Per should have sent them back. But at the time he'd wanted their company. They wouldn't give him away now by barking.

They never barked. But if the Elves came near, they might snarl, or throw off his cover by leaping up to defend him. "*Hold. Stilla.*"

The Elves came close by where Per lay. One stood within three feet of him, turning his head and looking about at the height of a man. He never thought to look down. Per sprawled in the leaves and watched them through the intervening branches, his heart beating only a little quicker. He saw them plainly, despite their camouflage gear, because their upright shapes were often dark against the light coming in at the edge of the wood. Cuddy and Swart continued to tremble against him with hatred of the strangers but made only the faintest of sounds, unheard among the sounds of trees shifting in the breeze and the stomping feet of the Elves.

The Elves moved away. Cuddy and Swart, thinking the danger past, stopped growling, and Cuddy licked Per's face while Swart licked his ear. He screwed up his face and endured the licking while he lay still and tried to listen through the slobbering. In other parts of the wood birds were chattering as the Elves moved through the trees. Only when all the birds were silent in all parts of the wood, and had been for many heartbeats, did Per sit up.

Keeping silence, he hugged the hounds, kissed and patted them, to let them know how proud he was of them. Shouldering him over, they pressed him down in the leaves, showing him how proud they were of him by thoroughly licking his face and hands. One of them alone weighed almost as much as he did, and he couldn't even sit up with both of them standing on him. He played dead until they were thoroughly bored and wandered a little away. Then he got to his feet fast.

Snatching up his cloak, quiver and bow, he made his way toward their watching place, with the hounds bouncing and panting beside him. Wat and Ingram were already there. Per crawled the last couple of yards, to keep his movements out of sight below the screen of bushes and scrub that edged the wood. The leaves in his hair, as he poked up his head, helped to disguise him.

The new Elf-Gate had gone, vanished, though the wreck of the old one remained. The Elf-Carts were still there too, and the Elves with their pistols.

"Daddy's-brother's coming," Ingram said.

Far, far down in the valley, Per caught a glimpse of the moving black thread that was the troop of horsemen coming from the tower with the white flag.

He wondered what Andrea was thinking at that moment. He wished she might be thinking of him, as he was of her, and that it was something kinder than her last thoughts.

* * *

Bryce held his field glasses steady, watching the approach of the mounted party. He wasn't as sure as Windsor that the Sterkarms were surrendering, despite the white flag.

The three men Bryce had sent out came slithering back down the steep hillside. "All clear!"

Bryce lowered his glasses for a moment and looked them over. "Sure?"

"It's just a little dip," Philips said. "Couple of hundred yards long, half that wide. Trees, bit of scrub. There's nobody in there. We'd have trod on 'em if there had been."

Bryce stared at him consideringly—but there was no point in delegating a job to a man and then refusing to believe him when he said he'd done it. Bryce nodded and looked through the glasses again.

A white flag. He hoped Windsor was right, and it meant unconditional surrender. So much easier on everybody.

17

16th Side: An Elf Hunt

JOE HAD LEFT THE tower on foot, following the horsemen with a few other curious men. For most of the way they'd trailed behind, but when the horses slowed to climb the hillside, he'd pushed himself to walk faster and had caught up with them. Panting and sweating, he walked beside Toorkild's horse, his hand resting on its warm, rough-haired, flexing rump, ready to speak to the Elves as well as he could.

Ahead and above was the 21st wreckage: fallen chain-link fence, broken concrete, twisted and snapped steel girders. Near the rubble were the Land Rovers, great ugly square shapes. Joe was astonished at how unfamiliar these things already seemed to him: how unsympathetic their shapes, how alien their straight, machined lines.

And the soldiers standing there—posing, their black boots planted on the green turf, the outline of their clothes broken by those big, flat patches of green and brown, the helmets on their heads, the rifles in their arms. My own time, Joe thought, puzzled by his lack of any fellow feeling with them. He felt no affection.

But once he'd left childhood behind, the soldiers'

time never had been his. Looking at the soldiers, he remembered being turned away from shopping malls by uniformed guards. "Leave, please. Now I've asked you nicely." He remembered being woken and moved on from station forecourts and shop doorways, grudged even those hard, cold beds. "You can't sleep here. Move along." He remembered being doused with cold water early one freezing morning, his cardboard box soaked and ruined. "You've been told you can't sleep here." These soldiers, with their guns, had stood behind the policemen and the security guards. . . .

He saw Windsor's face smirking under a beret. Joe's "own time" had denied him a job, a home and the vote. It had taken his taxes while he worked and refused to help him when he was broke—and it had taken greater sums than Joe's whole life earnings and handed it to men like Windsor as a payoff after some huge blunder.

His "own time." He'd never been anything but disposable to the 21st—one drop in a great pool of unemployed who could be used to keep wages low and force them lower. "If you won't work for that, I know those who will." His "own time" had never opened its arms and welcomed him in with gratitude, giving him everything—shelter, food, clothing and respect.

I'm a Sterkarm, he thought. In his "own time" his name had been an almost meaningless tag, only convenient for sorting him out from other people—"You're not eligible to claim, Mr. Sterkarm." Here, it really meant something. The mere fact that you were named Sterkarm meant you had a claim. I'm a Sterkarm, he thought, and felt his back straighten and his head come up.

It wasn't Per sitting above him on the horse, but it

was Per's old man. "I'll guard thee and guard thine . . ." Joe patted the horse again and went forward, to speak to the Elves and serve his family, the Sterkarms. Raising his hands, to show he meant no one any harm, he smiled. "Hello!"

Windsor and Bryce saw, emerging from the knot of shaggy horsemen, a shaggy footman. He was bearded and longhaired, and dressed much like the others, in gray wool and calf-length leather boots, except that over his other clothes he wore a long green waterproof that was definitely twenty-first century in origin. And he seemed to speak English, though of course, anyone might pick up "hello."

Bryce opened his mouth to speak, but it was Windsor who said, "Who are you?"

"Sterkarm. I'm a Sterkarm."

"You speak English," Windsor said.

"Aye. Picked it up."

"Where did you get that coat? From one of our survey teams?"

You smug, arrogant sod, Joe thought. Don't remember me at all, do you? He hadn't been worth Windsor's notice. "I paid for it," Joe said, "with me own money. I'm here to tell you what he's got to say." He gestured toward Toorkild, still sitting his horse behind him. "Do you want to hear?"

Windsor's eyes moved to Toorkild, who nodded and, after passing his lance to a horseman beside him, dismounted, coming forward to Joe's elbow.

Bryce said, "You can tell us where our personnel are. A young lady, Andrea Mitchell, and four men: Allmark, Bailey, Colucci and Shepherd."

Joe hesitated, and then remembered that he was a Sterkarm. "They're okay; they're at the tower." Well, Andrea was, anyway. The four men weren't very far from where they stood, as it happened. "Look, Toorkild's come here to say he's sorry. For the fire. It was a mistake. He's really cut up about it, and he wants to make it up to you."

Windsor was frowning. "You speak English *very* well. You're not *from* one of our teams, are you?" Some of the geologists were pretty shaggy.

"I'm a Sterkarm," Joe repeated. "Toorkild wants you to know that the fire didn't have anything to do with him. He didn't order it. It was his son, y'know, getting a bit out of order. If Toorkild had knowed, he'd have stopped it. He wants it to go on like before. How can he make it up to you? That's what he wants to know. He's really sorry about all this." Joe waved his hand toward the burned grass.

A horse stamped its foot, shaking its head with a flourish of long mane and a rattle of bit. "Steady," Bryce said to the armed men behind him.

Windsor was thinking. It was true that, from the moment they'd loaded the boy into the back of the Range Rover to the moment Per had ordered the firing of the FUP office, it was impossible for him to have planned anything with his father. And old Toorkild had been keen to trade.

"How is young Per?" Windsor asked.

Toorkild, catching his son's name, shook his head sadly, saying, "Per, Per," like a sorely tried father.

Joe, with inspiration, said, "He's locked up in the tower. Toorkild was mad—hell, wicked as a wasp. He never said he could light any fires, see. So Per's locked up. On bread and water."

Windsor put his swagger stick behind him, gripped it with both hands and smiled. "Parental discipline, eh? Very good. I approve."

"Toorkild wants to talk things over—he wants to invite you back to the tower—*til tur*," he added, to Toorkild.

"*Ya,*" Toorkild agreed, nodding and smiling. As a courtesy, he attempted English. "Too-wah. Pleese."

"He's inviting you to eat and talk and—" Joe had another inspiration. "He wants Per to apologize to you personally."

Windsor's brows rose, and he smiled. Joe could see that Windsor was going to agree and felt a flash of triumph, but Bryce spoke first. "There have got to be safeguards. And how do we know that our people are at the tower?"

Toorkild hadn't been able to understand what was said, but he'd been watching closely. He turned to his men, waved his hand and said, "*Kaster dem neath.*"

Every horseman, with a creaking of leather and a chinking of metal, threw his lance down on the turf. The horses sidestepped. More movement, more thumps followed, as the horsemen threw down bows, swords, axes.

"Steady!" Bryce said, as some of his own men, startled, began to lift their rifles.

"This is to show he trusts you," Joe said. Joe hadn't known they were going to throw down their weapons, but his brain felt fresh and alert, and he was quick to go along with anything. "To show how much he wants to make things up."

Windsor put his hands on his hips, his swagger stick in one fist. He looked around at the scattered weapons and smiled at Bryce. "Surety enough?"

Bryce was silent but very slightly shook his head. He knew that it paid to be suspicious.

"Toorkild's not asking you to put your weapons down," Joe said. "He really wants to be friends again. He didn't know what Per was going to do, and he's really sorry for it."

"You speak English too well," Bryce said. "Who exactly are you?"

"I learned from Andrea," Joe said. "She's a good friend of mine. We all want to be friends again." He felt the intensity of his own anxiety for them to believe him, and he realized that the 21st men weren't being asked to the tower to talk friendship and trade. He admitted to himself that when he'd lied about the whereabouts of the dead security men, he'd known that. "Andrea'll be glad to see you," he said. "And the others." What was he going to do, tell the truth and see those automatic rifles turned on his friends?

"Tell him we accept," Windsor said.

"Mr. Windsor—" That was Bryce.

Joe said to Toorkild, "*Dey kommer.*" Toorkild opened his arms wide, went over to Windsor, embraced him and kissed him on the cheek.

Windsor endured the hug and the stink, patted Toorkild's back and, breaking from the embrace, said to Bryce, "I'm in charge here. We're going."

Bryce bit his tongue. He wanted to snap back that, on the contrary, *he* was the leader—but this wasn't a military operation, and he wasn't in charge of real soldiers.

Windsor could put them all out of work.

Turning his back on Windsor, he looked over the men. He wasn't going anywhere without first posting guards on the place where the Tube would reopen their way home. He saw the smirking face of Bates, one of the thickest of the football hooligans. A good excuse to leave him behind. "You! And you!" One of the ex-soldiers, Millington, to provide a little backbone. "And you!" Another no-brain, Saunders. All they had to do was stand there and look frightening enough to keep the Sterkarms away, and God knew, they frightened him. "You stay here, you guard our way home. Understand? Millington, understand?"

"Sir!"

"The rest of you, into the wagons! Move!"

Windsor slapped Toorkild's arm and said, "Lead on, Macduff." Walking past Bryce, he climbed into a Land Rover. Toorkild mounted his horse.

The men rapidly and noisily swung into the Land Rovers, with a crashing of boots on metal floors and much laughter. Slowly the two Land Rovers set off downhill, leaving behind a litter of lances, swords and bows, the third Land Rover and three men hugging kalashnikovs.

The horses were frightened by the Land Rovers. Toorkild had so much trouble with his horse, he had to dismount. He pulled the scarf out of the neck of his jakke and tied it around the animal's eyes. He was well behind when he led the horse on.

But he was pleased with himself. Throughout the meeting with Windsor, he had never once raised his eyes to the little wood of birch and hazel that grew higher up the slope, and he didn't give in to the temptation to look that way now.

* * *

Per lay on his belly at the edge of the wood, propped on his elbows, intently watching the men, Land Rovers and horses below. On either side of him lay Cuddy and Swart, their noses on their paws. Often they rolled their eyes to look at him, showing white around the edges, and sighed. They were bored, but hunting always involved long periods of boredom, and Per had told them to lie still. They did, but for the second or third time, Cuddy lifted her head and licked Per's cheek. *"Cuddy. Hold."*

Ingram and Wat were close by. Wat was sitting, leaning against a tree, Ingram lying on his side as if asleep. Their clothes of brown and gray merged into the leaves around them, and they were dappled with shifting light. From a few feet away, they were invisible.

They could hear nothing of what was being said around the Elf-Carts, but they watched the figures closely, their advancing and retreating, the raised arms, the pointing.

Per had picked out his father and Joe and followed them with his eyes. Not once did his father even glance toward the wood, and since Toorkild knew they were there, that must have been hard; but he knew his father would do far harder things for him.

When the Elves climbed back into the Elf-Carts and moved away down the hill, Per clenched his fists and grinned. Slowly—quick movements catch the eye—Per turned his head to look at his cousins. They were grinning too.

The three left on guard watched the Land Rovers jolt away down the hillside, followed by the men leading frightened horses. It was lonely being left there, not knowing what was going to happen. They looked about, at the empty hills and the gray, damp sky above. Nothing in sight was homely or comforting: no roads, no pylons. The sheep were black. The shepherds rode on horseback, carrying spears. Not exactly Bo-Peep.

Bates felt in his pocket for a pack of cigarettes and offered them to the other two. When they each accepted one, he felt better, a little more at ease. "I'm Bates." His rifle was slung on his shoulder while he lit a match.

The others stooped to his hand for lights. "Millington."

"Saunders."

"Godforsaken shit hole," Bates said. Taking his rifle from his shoulder, he pointed it down the valley. "Be a laugh, wouldn't it? Shot-up sheep!"

Millington turned away. Saunders laughed, and Bates laughed harder himself, feeling he'd made a friend.

* * *

The three Elves kept putting their hands to their mouths and taking them away again. Rolling onto his back, Ingram said, "Wherefore do they do this?" He waved his hand to and from his mouth. Per shook his head.

Away down in the valley, the Land Rovers were on the other side of the river's white-and-gray thread, with horses ahead of them and behind.

Soon horses and Land Rovers would be out of sight, lost in the valleys' turnings. Per had seen no sign of far-sees or far-speaks, so those Elves down there would have no idea what was happening to these Elves up here.

On his belly, Per wriggled back from the edge of the wood, drawing his bow and quiver after him. "*Hold.*" The hounds lay still, trembling with impatience, watching him.

When he was far enough back from the wood's edge to be screened by the trees, Per rose slowly to his feet. In the shifting leaf shadows away to his right, Ingram and Wat were doing the same.

"*Cuddy, Swart, kom.*" The hounds uncoiled from the ground and slunk to him, their shoulder bones and hipbones rising above their spines. When he led them off along a narrow path, they frisked and wagged their tails, and he tapped their sides with his bow, to remind them that this was serious. They calmed, and followed him with tails and ears up, alert and happy. He was carrying his bow in one hand, his quiver in the other. That meant hunting. Work for them soon. A deer to run down.

Per chose his spot by a big birch that gave him shadow but had no low-hanging branches to block his view or his aim. He set his quiver on the ground and, leaning his back against the tree, hidden from the Elves, pointed at his hounds. Obediently, they lay flat at his feet. Swart put his nose on his paws, resigned to more boredom, but Cuddy's tail stirred, and she looked up at him with a loving expectancy that made him want to pet her. He knew that, if he did, she would jump up to return his affection, so instead, he set the end of his bow against his instep and strung it. Cuddy's tail wagged a little faster in the grass. A strung bow meant shooting. Shooting meant a deer to run down. Running down a deer meant a feed of deer's guts, and much praise and fuss from Per. She stirred her haunches. *"Hold!"*

Leaning against the tree, Per turned and scanned the hillside below. The Elves could easily have seen him, if they'd known where to look, but with the speckled light and shade of the trees falling over the soft, dull colors of his clothes, he was invisible as long as he kept still.

Without moving his head, he moved his eyes, searching for his father's troop below in the valley. There was no sign of them, or of the Elf-Carts.

The Elf-Cart just below him took an eye's blink to find, so much did its patchy colors disguise it. But the three Elves on guard he saw easily, because they moved unguardedly, walking about, lifting their hands to their mouths, dropping them sharply to their sides again. He considered his aim, not so much calculating it as feeling with his muscles the position they would take as he tilted the bow and arrow to the right angle.

He rolled his shoulder against the tree, swinging back behind it, out of sight. There he took an arrow from his quiver, a broad-headed, barbed hunting arrow, and fitted it to his bowstring. Both hounds watched, tails twitching. Their interest made him smile. "No deer the day, Dearlings."

Per turned from behind the tree and, in one movement, took up the shooting stance, his body turned sidelong to his target, his bow arm outstretched, the shoulder and elbow of his string arm raised high. Once in that position, if he had not been seen, he need only make the slightest of movements to shoot.

He had not been seen. The soldiers were still standing together, their hands going again and again to their mouths, occasionally glancing about, but ignorant of where to look or what to look for.

With one eye closed, Per lined up the point of his arrow with the chest of the soldier who was facing him. He moved the arrow's point higher, unthinkingly allowing for the fall of the ground, the distance and the breeze. His body, not his mind, told him he had the aim correct.

He drew up, pulling with his back, and pushing the bow stave forward with his other arm. He kept his head still, and drew and drew back until his fingers on the bowstring touched the corner of his mouth. His arms, his hands, his wrists, his fingers, his shoulders, were all braced against the power of the bow. He adjusted his aim again, allowing for the strain of drawing the bow having shifted it off. Then he straightened his string fingers, loosing the arrow.

The bowstring twanged, loud to his ear, but he knew the Elves wouldn't hear it. His hand, drawing back, stroked across his cheek. He didn't change his stance or lower his arms.

For an eye's blink he glimpsed the arrow against the gray sky as it sped away, but then it vanished. An eye's blink later, he knew he'd missed. He caught the merest flash of the arrow as it struck the sloping ground short of the Elves and skidded, flat, into the grass. One of the Elves glanced up and around, but then put his hand to his mouth again and looked at his friends.

A bow is no weight to carry. An archer doesn't stand and wait for his position to be found. Per took up his quiver and moved, slowly at first, but more quickly when he was deeper among the trees. The hounds loped after him.

Per's ear caught the soft sound of a bow released. One of his cousins had shot, but he heard no other sound, so whoever it had been had probably missed. Good. He was glad they'd been no more successful than him. With Cuddy and Swart on his heels, Per looked for another place to stand.

* * *

There was a sound near them, a soft *tok!* Millington looked around. He thought he'd seen something, a shadow crossing his vision. There was nothing to be seen but short grass when he looked at the spot.

"Hear anything?"

Bates looked at him and then around at the hills, shaking his head.

"Sort of a—I dunno—sort of a little thump."

"A wild haggis running past," Saunders said.

Tok!

Millington turned quickly toward the soft sound, but, again, there was nothing to be seen. "Sounds like—like somebody's throwing little stones at us. Hear it?"

Bates, scanning the surrounding countryside, suddenly fixed his stare on the little patch of woodland above them. He thought he'd seen something move. The rifle in his arms lifted as his grip on it tightened. Then he relaxed.

"There's animals, wild animals around here, ain't there? Foxes. That sort of thing."

"You reckon foxes am throwing little stones at us?" Millington said.

Bates, not knowing whether Millington was being sarcastic or not, grinned vacantly.

"Where are they hiding?" Saunders asked, looking

around. "We searched the wood."

"Somebody could have got in among the trees since," Millington said. It was almost a question.

Bates pointed the muzzle of his rifle at the trees and put his hand to his rifle's safety catch. "We could give 'em a burst. Just to make sure. Be a laugh, eh?"

"Shut your mouth, you stupid bugger! You heard the boss. We'm only to fire under orders."

Bates thought of telling Millington to shut up himself, but then kept quiet and tried to look tough instead. "What's the matter?" he said. "If there's anybody in there, they'm only smellies."

* * *

Per's second shot was from beside a thick, spreading hazel bush, which didn't give him such a clear view or aim. It was difficult, shooting from a new place each time. It gave him no chance to find the distance and correct his aim. But he drew up and loosed his second arrow.

And saw it—oh, beautiful!—fall into the chest of the middle soldier in a perfect shot. Slowly taking up his quiver, he faded back into the wood and then ran along a path. He came on Ingram, leaning on his tree, his quiver at his feet and his bow in his hand.

Grinning, Ingram put his free arm around Per, thumped his back and kissed his cheek in congratulation. Together, they fitted new arrows to their strings.

* * *

The arrow struck Millington with a deeper, hollower note than the first two had struck the ground. He didn't see it coming. All the weight of the bow, plus all the speed of the arrow's flight, struck one small point on his chest and knocked him clean off his feet, toppling him backward down the slope, heels over head. The impact drove the arrow's broad, barbed iron head and its wooden shaft deep into his chest.

Saunders and Bates swung around and watched him fall and roll in astonishment. They'd heard the sound of something striking, they'd heard Millington's grunt as breath was knocked from him, and Saunders had glimpsed something blurred in the air—a stone? Or had Millington simply stumbled and fallen?

As Millington rolled, the arrow embedded in his chest struck against the ground, making him cry aloud—and then it snapped off. Saunders and Bates scrambled down to the fallen man, and Bates grabbed his arm, dragging at it, to help him up. They saw the blood staining the front of Millington's camouflage jacket, but the broken arrow shaft was lost in the grass.

"What you done?" Bates asked.

Saunders' head snatched around, and he looked up the slope toward the trees.

Tok! Something else hit the ground near them. Alarmed now, Saunders and Bates eyed the grass around them, but saw nothing. "Arrows!" Saunders said, realizing. "Oh God!" He raised his rifle clumsily, fumbling at the safety catch and cutting his fingertips on its sharp edge. Bates stared at him, not having caught what he'd said.

An arrow hit Saunders in the upper arm, tearing through his flesh, spinning him around in a circle and throwing him down.

Bates, seeing both his friends down, bleeding, dead or dying, looked around wildly. He held a rifle in his hands but never gave it another thought. He saw the trees, and ran toward them, to hide. The weight in his arms slowed him down, so he threw the rifle away.

Wat, seeing the Elf running toward him, grinned and held an arrow on his string, letting the Elf come closer and closer until he couldn't miss. His barbed arrow went right through Bates, from belly to back, knocked him from his feet and tumbled him down the slope.

Saunders, his arm bleeding and burning with pain, raised himself up on his knees. He tried to lift the rifle, but it was a heavy weight on his torn arm—and the safety catch wouldn't come off, but sliced his fingers instead. There was no one to help him. His friends were dead. Stumbling to his feet, he tried to get away down the hill, slipping and reeling on the steep slope and thin, slick grass.

Cuddy and Swart, seeing the bows raised and hearing the strings hum, were shivering and whimpering with excitement. Ordered to lie at Per's feet, they quivered, half rose, lay down again, and shifted their haunches in the grass, looking up at Per and making little pouncing motions.

When the Elf ran, Per looked at Ingram, grinned and then crouched between his hounds. He pointed to the running Elf. "Bring him down! *Good* hounds!"

They pushed themselves from the ground, running as they rose. Per, still crouching, gasped to see their beauty. They leaned with their speed, as silent, almost as fast, as the arrows. Ingram raised his bow over his head. "Run, Elf, run!" He left the trees to join the chase, Per following. Both knew the Elf had no chance of outrunning the hounds.

Per and Ingram were always skittish when they were together. Wat let them go and attended to the real business of killing the fallen Elves.

Saunders, slipping on the steep slope and falling on hands and knees, looked behind and saw the racing hounds coming on him with a rippling motion, their heads stretched forward and black lips stretched back from long white teeth.

In a panic of blood beating in his head, of pounding heart, Saunders tried to scramble on. His legs had gone weak, his feet slipped. He was hit by a solid, heavy weight, screamed aloud and rolled on his back, his rifle sliding away down the slope. He threw his arms up in front of his face. A hard, bruising, pinching grip closed on his forearm.

Swart overshot the running Elf, leaped in the air and came bounding back up the slope. Cuddy had her teeth in the Elf's arm, and as he tried to wrench away, her teeth sank deeper. Her tail waved. She loosed her grip and bit again, bit deep for a better grip and, big hound that she was, braced her feet and tried to drag her catch back to Per.

Swart came, filling the sky above Saunders, dripping hot slaver on him, blowing his face full of hot, stinking breath. Biting at his shoulder, at his hands, his face, his leg, wherever there seemed to be a hold, biting and dragging. Saunders screamed like any caught hare. Between them, the big hounds pulled him about on the slippery grass, tearing at him.

Per, slithering down the slope, felt the screams in his own belly and yelled, "*Cuddy, foorlet!*" Leave it! "*Foorlet, Swart, foorlet!*"

It had seemed a good joke to send the hounds after the Elf—Per hadn't even known if they would chase him. He'd never foreseen that they would worry the Elf like this. He'd run with them himself a hundred times. They'd knocked him down, but the worst they'd ever done was try to lick him into another shape.

Hearing Per's voice, Cuddy released her hold on the Elf and turned toward him. Swart, his teeth in the Elf's thigh, didn't let go but only growled. And Cuddy, having jumped up at Per, flecking him with blood and slaver, dropped back to the ground and bit at the Elf again. Seeing Ingram on the slope above her, she glared at him with white-edged eyes and growled through her mouthful of Elf. Ingram wasn't fool enough to go any closer and called out warningly when he saw Per reaching for Cuddy's collar.

Per beat both dogs about the ribs with his bow. "Leave it, leave it! Down! Bad! Bad hounds!" Cuddy was the first to loose, and to cower in the grass, putting back her ears. Swart, even when made to loose, kept trying to go back to the Elf, and even growled at Per, who beat him with the bow and drove him off.

Saunders' face was obscured with blood. Whimpering and coughing, his many wounds burning, he tried to get to his hands and knees. His ripped and bloody hands slipped on the grass, and his shaking legs wouldn't support him.

His struggles excited Swart, who cast back and forth, longing to get at him, if only Per would let him. Cuddy, though lying in the grass, was trembling and looking to Per for permission to spring on the Elf again. Per held his bow poised to threaten Cuddy, and gripped Swart by the collar, though he couldn't hold the hound if Swart made a real effort to break free. To Ingram, he said, "Kill him!"

But Ingram stood and watched the Elf flounder and choke. Per knew that it wasn't right. The Elf should be killed fast. That was something Sweet Milk had told him over and over and again: Kill fast. "Take Swart—take him!" If Per let Swart's collar go, he would be on the Elf.

Ingram pretended he hadn't heard. He didn't want to go near Swart until this was over and the big hound was calm.

Wat came down the hill. The knife in his hand was already bloodied from finishing the other Elves. He straddled the third, knelt on his back, pulled back his head and cut his throat. He rose, panting a little from the effort, and stepped back, his hands and sleeves bloody. He looked at Ingram and Per with an expression that asked why they had waited for him to do such a simple thing. And why did he have to do all the hard work?

Per, shamefaced, began hauling Swart away up the hill, and calling Cuddy to follow. "Bad hounds! Bad!"

Wat, following him, said, "Good hounds, good." Per looked at him. "They did what tha told 'em to do."

"Good hounds!" Per said, to annoy Wat. "Good girl, good boy!" Cuddy began to bound around him, hanging out her long pink tongue.

They came up by the fallen chain-link fences, picking their way through all the weapons thrown down by Toorkild's men. There, lonely and alien, stood the Elf-Cart, the strangest thing in the whole landscape. Not far from it were the bundles of clothes with arrows sticking from them that were the dead Elves.

Per stood over the bodies and felt the high spirits of the shooting and the chase collapse. His blood chilled, and he shivered. He had turned a living thing to a lump of dead meat, and this was his own death, foretold in these slumped carcasses. This was how he was going to die, perhaps soon: choking, struggling, humbled. And that night the ghosts would gather to his candle's shadows, to remind him.

"You should have stayed in Elf-Land," he told the bodies. This hill would be haunted for years to come. That night, he'd get drunk and share his bed.

Ingram was ranging over the slope and, stooping, pulled an arrow from the grass and brandished it. Per drew his knife and crouched, to cut the arrows from the bodies.

"Leave 'em," Wat said, waving to call Ingram. "Get the horses."

"Leave *all* of 'em?" Per asked.

Wat tapped him with his bow stave. "Get the horses."

Per shrugged, dropped his bow and quiver and ran to help Ingram catch the wandering horses. Wat, as the eldest, was in command. If he chose to waste arrows, well, he was the one who'd be blamed when they got back to the tower.

18

16th Side: Windsor to the Dark Tower Came

THE TWO LAND ROVERS came to a halt on the slope below the tower's crag. Out of the tower's gate, and down the crag's steep path, came a crowd of women and children, led by Isobel, who held out her hands to Windsor, smiling and chattering at him.

"She's sorry for everything," Joe said. "She hopes you're going to enjoy the meal." He hadn't caught everything Isobel had said, but he supposed it would be something like that. She'd certainly said something about "*maht*," which he'd at first taken to mean "meat" but had since learned meant any kind of food.

Bryce was looking from his men, climbing out of the Land Rovers with their rifles, to the Sterkarm women and children milling about them. Some of the girls were very pretty, as his men were noticing. The girls, smiling, were reaching out to touch the camouflage sleeves and even touching the rifles, confident that they would be allowed to. Others lifted up small children to see the Land Rovers.

Bryce didn't know whether or not to be reassured. He didn't trust the Sterkarms—but he knew them to be protective of their children and women, as most peoples were anywhere, anytime. The fact that he and his men had been invited here, to the tower, into the midst of the women and children, seemed to suggest that the Sterkarms were, for once, acting in good faith. It might be a bluff—but it was a pretty foolhardy bluff if it got your children killed. And Old Man Sterkarm had been keen on aspirin. . . . On the whole, and while trying to stay wary, Bryce believed the Sterkarms when they said they only wanted to talk and make friends again.

He could see Old Toorkild Sterkarm, his head close to the head of the man in the 21st waterproof, the one who spoke such suspiciously good English. Waterproof came over to them, pushing his way through the curious women and children. "If you'll all come inside," he said, jerking his thumb toward the tower, "there's a feast set in the hall—a friendship feast. You're all invited."

The 21st men at the Land Rovers started grinning. "A party!" one of them called out, and Bryce said, "Quiet!"

"A friendship feast!" Windsor said, and nodded and smiled at Mrs. Sterkarm. "That sounds splendid!" It was the kind of thing you had to say, even though he had clear memories of how terrible Sterkarm food was. Still, the Sterkarms' eagerness to make amends was going to make the food a lot tastier this time around. It was gratifying to see them realize that they'd gone too far. If young Sterkarm could be made to apologize too, it'd be better than a meal at a four-star restaurant. "We accept."

Bryce was startled to hear that but, before he could speak, Joe said, "Don't mind me saying so, but we'd like it—well, it'd look friendlier if you left your guns outside. We laid—"

"Wait a minute," Bryce said. "Where are my men? Where is Andrea Mitchell?"

"Inside," Joe said.

"Let's see them out here," Bryce said. "Let's see that they're alive and unhurt, and then we'll talk about going inside."

Joe's mind was working harder and faster than he'd needed it to work for years. The strain made his heart beat faster. "They're hurt." He saw Bryce and Windsor look alarmed. "Not Andrea. She's—helping get the food ready. But the men, they got a bit hurt."

"How much is 'a bit'?" Bryce said.

"One got bashed on the head." Joe remembered the axe bashing down. "They all got knocked about a bit. You know how it is. Things got out of hand. People got overexcited. Toorkild's very sorry. He wasn't there, or he'd have stopped it." At the back of Joe's mind, he knew that these lies were going to get more men hurt but were going to keep Sterkarms from being hurt. He hadn't time to think about which was more right, or more wrong. "They're being cared for. Toorkild's very sorry about it. But if you want to see 'em, you're going to have to come inside."

Bryce looked at Windsor. "I don't like this."

Windsor tucked his swagger stick under his arm. He saw the risk but hated appearing to be under Bryce's command.

"We ain't going to hurt you," Joe said. "Not with all the women and bairns running about. This is our home. What would we hurt you with, anyway? We left most of our weapons up there, on the hill."

There was a small child standing right at Windsor's

feet, peering up at him. And the Sterkarms had seen the power of the Elves. They'd seen the Tube made operational again after they'd destroyed it. "We're going to get nowhere standing out here, pulling faces at each other," Windsor said. It was undignified, this bickering on the hillside. But strolling into the Sterkarms' den and making yourself comfortable—well, as comfortable as you could make yourself on Sterkarm furniture—that had a certain panache. To Bryce, he said, "We'll go in."

"And leave the guns outside?" Joe said. "To show good feeling. We laid down our weapons." He felt he was pushing his luck too far, but he couldn't do the Sterkarms a greater service than getting those rifles laid down.

Bryce held himself back from refusing outright. That would only antagonize Windsor as well as the Sterkarms. "I'd strongly advise against it, Mr. Windsor. They outnumber us. The safety catches are on."

"But better safe than sorry," Joe said. "It's all these little kids I'm thinking of. This is someone's home you're going into. I'm not asking you to give your guns up—leave 'em here, put a guard on 'em. Just for while you're in the tower. Just to show friendly."

Bryce went close to Windsor. "It's too risky."

Windsor could see Toorkild watching them. He didn't want to give the old savage the satisfaction of knowing that he could intimidate them. He didn't want to give Bryce the satisfaction of nannying him. "Sometimes you just have to take a risk."

You're telling *me*? Bryce thought. "Mr. Windsor, they're taking you in there."

Bryce pointed, and Windsor looked up at the square

gray-red tower rising against the sky. It threw a qualm into Windsor, and at once made him still more determined to prove he was right by going ahead. He refused to behave like a coward. The bloodied severed head flashed into his memory again—but it hadn't been the head of an *Elf*. "We're going in," he said, "and we're leaving the rifles out here."

"James—"

"I'm in charge!"

"Shit!" Bryce couldn't let Windsor go in there alone. Nor could he leave the guns out here with no better guard over them than a few security guards and an ex-corporal. But he had to do one or the other.

He went over to the nearest Land Rover, unslung his rifle from his shoulder and dropped it onto the Land Rover's metal floor. "You, you, you!" Bryce rapidly counted out nine men. "Guns down here." Only one or two of them began unslinging their rifles. The others looked at each other, spoke, muttering. Either they all shared his fears or they just didn't want to give up their toys. Bryce was infuriated by their insubordination. "Do it! I didn't ask for a discussion!" He watched them as, with sour faces, they put their rifles, one by one, on the floor of the Land Rover. "Skipton!"

"Sir!"

Skipton was one of the ex-soldiers, and one of the ten men left still holding rifles. "I'm leaving you in charge here. You guard the guns and the Land Rovers, okay?" Skipton nodded.

Bryce turned to Windsor. "Let's go." Under Bryce's camouflage jacket, in a shoulder holster, he had an old

Browning pistol, thirteen shots in its mag. Could be enough if things got outrageous.

* * *

Andrea had heard the sound of the Land Rovers' engines, and then the sound of the horses being led through the tower's lanes to their stables. She'd gone to the window but hadn't been able to see anything. The windows on the top story, in Toorkild and Isobel's private rooms, were the largest in the tower, but they were still small. If you looked straight out, they gave a good view of the surrounding hills and the valley below, but it was all but impossible to look down from them and see what was happening in the tower's yard, or just outside its walls. The roofs, the wall, got in the way.

She could shout, of course. Take a big breath and yell, as loud as she could: "They're going to ambush you!" Her heart started beating faster at the thought of it, and she felt breathless and ill.

It was what she'd said she would do.

It was easy to talk.

She didn't know who was out there—she couldn't see. If there were car engines, then there must be people from the 21st, but had they come armed, as she'd feared, or did they just have briefcases and five-year business forecasts?

What if she shouted, and alarmed the Sterkarms into turning on the 21st men and killing them?

What if the 21st men *had* come armed, and her shout made them open fire on the Sterkarms and gun them down, women, children and all?

Either way, it would be her fault.

She went back to the hearth and sat in Toorkild's chair. A fire burned in the hearth, and she had a box of fuel to feed it. There was meat, bread and ale on the table. Both Toorkild and Isobel were angry with her, but she was still a guest under their roof. And still thought of, she feared, by some, as their son's future wife.

She got up again. She couldn't sit there, warm, by a fire, while murder might be going on outside. She listened at the window again, and heard voices but not what they were saying. She could see tiny sheep moving distantly, in the valley, but not the people a few feet below.

She walked around the table, around and around. People were going to get hurt. Had Per been hurt? He'd been up on the hill when the Elves had come through.

This whole project must have seemed such a good idea on paper. Go in, get the gold, the oil, the gas, make a profit. It was always people who loused things up.

* * *

Joe's heart was swollen and tight in his chest, and yet it was rattling away in there with a painful rapidity and force. The soldiers had given up their rifles, but he didn't suppose they'd given up every weapon. In a couple of minutes, he could be dead.

They'd come through the tower gate and were getting close to the tower itself. Toorkild was on one side of him, slightly ahead; and Windsor on the other, slightly behind. Bryce was behind Windsor, and behind him came the soldiers and the Sterkarms. Joe, remembering that he should be seeming happy and relaxed, tried to smile at Windsor but felt his face freeze into a grimace.

As they reached the tower door, Bryce called out, "Wait!"

Toorkild stopped in the act of opening the door.

"I'll go in first," Bryce said. Behind him the rabble of Sterkarms and 21st men filled the yard in front of the tower, and crowded the alleys leading to it.

Toorkild must have guessed his meaning, because he grinned through his beard, stood aside and waved for Bryce to go into the tower before him.

Bryce edged to the door, leaning against its doorpost and keeping well back from the opening while he peered into the shadows inside. His hand was inside his jacket, on the grip of his pistol. With his free hand, he beckoned to one of his men. "Go in."

"Me?" the man said.

"Go in," Bryce said. The man looked around at his colleagues, and then at Bryce again. "That's an order," Bryce said. "Were you expecting a walk in the park?"

Slowly, as if his boots were filled with concrete, the man came forward to the tower's door. He hesitated, and looked at Bryce, but then fear of his colleagues' contempt, or fear of losing his job, or both, overcame his fear of what was in the tower. He leaped in through the door.

The Sterkarms standing in the yard laughed genially. Inside the tower, the security guard was walking about, kicking up the straw on the floor. He started laughing himself. "Nothing in here but shit."

Bryce leaned in at the door to check for himself. The ground floor of the tower was dark, lit only by the light from the low, narrow door, which was blocked by Bryce himself. Fragments of light played on the upper walls, and over the curved barrel vault of the ceiling. There was a sweet, rank smell of horse dung.

"Check the stairs," Bryce said. He watched the man come toward him, to the foot of the stairs that rose from just inside the left-hand side of the door. It was a job he should be doing himself. He didn't like sending this poor dim herbert into danger, but if he did the brave thing and got killed, who'd watch Windsor's stupid back?

The stairs were guarded by a heavy iron grid, which the man pulled back with a sound of metal scraping on stone. He peered into the dark, narrow stairway. "Nobody here."

Toorkild, leaning at the other side of the door with his arms folded, grinned indulgently at Bryce and asked him—as far as Bryce understood—whether he was gladdened now. "Not yet," Bryce said. He moved into the cool shadows of the tower's ground floor and took up a position at the foot of the stairs. "Go on up," he said to the guard. "Have a look around the corner."

The man looked at him, swallowed hard but started to climb, moving his hand up the plaster. As he got closer to the turn in the stairs, he moved slower and slower, looking around the bend at the few stairs ahead with nothing but the corner of one eye. Half of him disappeared, and Bryce beckoned another man forward. "Stand here. Yell if anybody moves."

Bryce climbed the stairs after the first man. The first few steps were lit by light from the doorway, but then they curved and became dark, until they turned another curve of the spiral—and then light appeared again, through a narrow slit in the wall. Looking up, Bryce saw light spilling down from the landing, partly shadowed by the man ahead of him. "What d'you see?"

"Nothing," the man said.

Bryce moved up alongside him. Together, they blocked the stairs. Ahead was the small square landing, grayly lit by one slit window. The door into the hall was standing open, letting through a little more light. Beyond the open door, on the other side of the landing, the dark stairs continued up.

A man came to the open door, leaned on the post and grinned at them.

Bryce pushed his man out onto the landing, while he took up a position at the top of the stairs. "Go and check those stairs out." As his man crossed the landing, Bryce watched the Sterkarm in the doorway.

The Sterkarm watched the man pass him with friendly curiosity and then, when the security man had vanished into the darkness of the farther stair, grinned at Bryce instead.

"Down there," Bryce called. "Everything okay?"

"Everything's fine," came the shout from below.

Echoing footsteps on the farther stair, and the 21st man came back down. "Nothing up there," he said. "Just a locked door at the top. Nobody about."

"Fine," Bryce said, gesturing toward the hall door. "Have a look in there."

The security guard was more relaxed now, but he approached the hall door a little warily, because of the man leaning there. Seeing his nervousness, the Sterkarm grinned again, shouldered himself off the wall and went back inside the hall. The security guard stuck his head around the door.

"Anybody near the door?" Bryce asked. "How many people?"

"No. Five or six. Five. And a woman."

Mention of a woman made Bryce feel very slightly happier. "Okay. Come back to the stairs." As his man came back to the top of the stairs, Bryce went forward to look into the hall himself. It was set out as if for a meal, with long trestle tables laid with jugs and platters of bread. A fire was burning in the hearth, and something was boiling in a big pot. But the woman in the hall was Andrea. She was sitting right at the far end, at a table placed across the room. She saw him, she lifted her head and sat straighter, but then she looked at the big man sitting beside her before, again, staring down the length of the hall at Bryce.

When he backed out of the hall, back to the top of the stairs, he still wasn't sure whether she'd been trying to warn him or signal to him that everything was all right. Certainly the hall seemed to be prepared for a meal, just as the Sterkarms had promised.

"Stay here," Bryce said to his man, and went back down the stairs. Just inside the doorway of the tower, Toorkild and Isobel were waiting, their arms around each other. Windsor was beside them. Unable to talk, they were nodding and smiling at each other. "It all seems okay," Bryce said, "but I'd still be happier if we stayed outside."

"Toorkild just wants to be friends," Joe said. He spoke too quickly for Bryce's liking.

Windsor said, "For God's sake, Bryce!" and laughed. He felt much easier now Bryce had checked the tower out, but he wasn't going to admit to ever having felt nervous. "Here's Mrs. Sterkarm, going in with us. How much reassurance do you need?"

Bryce's mind ranged over possibilities. Now that

Windsor had committed them to this, there weren't many options. He stood back and gestured to the stairs.

Toorkild, with a forgiving smile, handed Isobel to the stairs ahead of him, and himself led the way for Windsor, who was followed by Joe. Bryce went next, to keep close to Windsor, but he waved to his men to come on in after him.

So many people were a tight fit on the narrow stairs. Their hands, moving on the wall, touched; they trod on each other's heels and jostled each other with their knees. The musty, sour smell of the Sterkarms was also unpleasantly noticeable in the enclosed space. Windsor was just wishing they could climb faster, when Toorkild stopped at the small window, his large body completely blocking the way. He pointed to the window, smiled at Windsor, and said something.

Windsor smiled back, irritably aware that Isobel was continuing on up the stairs ahead of them. The window was so small that he couldn't look through it until Toorkild leaned aside. When he did, he couldn't see anything except a scrap of sky and some thatched roofs. He turned to Joe, behind him, hoping for a translation.

Joe smiled. He hadn't understood a word Toorkild had said, hadn't really tried. He was too nervous.

"What's the holdup?" Bryce asked.

"Nothing, nothing," Joe said, and Toorkild murmured something in a comforting tone.

Below them the 21st men were pushing in through the tower's door, pushed in by the Sterkarms jostling behind them. Since the stair was blocked, the men had to spread across the tower's ground floor, forming into a ragged line for the stairs. Farther in and farther they crammed, until some of them reached the cold stone of the far wall. And then the small, cold room darkened. Looking up, the men saw a moving shadow—the patch of light on the upper part of the wall was shifting, shrinking as the tower door closed.

The 21st men shouted, lunged for the door. One, reaching it, was punched in the face and went backward into the tower, with a bleeding nose. The tower door was pulled shut from outside, slammed into its stone setting. Its key was turned from outside.

As the voices from below rose in panic, Toorkild turned and hurried on up the stairs to the landing and the door into the hall. Reaching behind, he grabbed Windsor by the arm, urged him on up the last few steps and shoved him into the hall.

Joe, behind Windsor, was yanked upward by Toorkild's sudden, tight grip on his arm. He was almost lifted from his feet as Toorkild shoved him in front of himself, into the hall, and pressed in after him. Men waiting inside the hall flung the door shut.

The door, heavy and wooden, slammed shut, with an echoing din, in Bryce's face. He had his hand inside his jacket, on the grip of his Browning pistol—but he was left without a target.

The man he'd left on guard at the top of the stairs was sprawled on the stone floor of the landing, looking dazed. "Get up!" Bryce said.

From below came the dismally echoing shouts of the men trapped on the stairs. From farther below, on the ground floor, came the sounds of fists and feet banging on the locked door. The sound boomed and rebounded from the stone walls.

Bryce felt the thick stone of the tower enclose him. Sterkarms above them, and Sterkarms outside. Exactly what he'd feared, what he'd tried to warn Windsor about.

He went to the narrow landing window and tried to see what was going on below the tower, but could see little except the thatched roofs of outhouses. A breeze blew in through the unglazed window, carrying a spatter of cold rain. The cold light the slit admitted lit Bryce's face, and little else. Behind him the landing and stair were in deep shadow.

What to do?

He had a pistol, some plastic explosive and some grenades.

They had Windsor, Andrea and the captured security men—supposing that any of those people were still alive.

Things were getting outrageous.

* * *

Windsor, dragged into the hall, jerked half from his feet, laughed, thinking it some sort of horseplay. He didn't like it but thought he ought to laugh along with it, to show that he could take a joke.

Laughing, he turned to find the door of the hall shut, and a thick bar of wood dropped across it, and himself alone among many Sterkarm men, who looked big, hairy, grimy and threatening even when there wasn't any special reason to fear them. Toorkild was looking at him with no trace of laughter. Windsor looked around for nice Mrs. Sterkarm.

Long trestle tables ran the length of the room—but men were already moving the jugs and platters from them and putting them on the floor around the hearth.

Other men lifted the boards and stacked them against the walls, or folded the trestles. As Windsor watched, alarmed, the center of the floor was cleared, exposing a wooden trapdoor at the center of the stone floor and giving him a clear view of the hearth, where a large pot was suspended over the fire. White steam coiled from the pot, together with smoke.

Trying to turn fright into anger, Windsor demanded, "What's going on?"

Joe was feeling hilarious. It was the way Toorkild had yanked him, flying, into the room, and the audacity of what the Sterkarms had done. "You've been stitched up like a kipper, pal, that's what's going on!" He lifted his feet in a heavy dance. "Makes a change, eh? How's it feel? How's it feel to be the one that's stitched up for once?"

Windsor goggled at him, understanding only that he was in trouble, perhaps even in danger—and before he had time to think any further, he spotted Mrs. Sterkarm. She was at the back of the room, standing with Andrea. He shouted at Andrea, "What's going on?"

All Andrea knew for sure was that, a little while ago, she'd been released from the upper floor and brought down to the hall, where she'd glimpsed Bryce in the doorway. When she'd asked what was going on, Sweet Milk had smiled, pointed to the tables and said, "We're going to have a feast."

She'd wanted to be reassured, but the cauldron over the fire made her suspicious. She had never known the Sterkarms to prepare food over the hall fire. Before she could think it over any longer, or answer Windsor, Sweet Milk took her arm and pulled her toward the trapdoor in the middle of the stone floor. Men were stooping, noisily unbolting the trap and lifting it up.

She looked down through the trap into the darkness of the tower's ground floor. The gray daylight coming in through the hall's narrow windows, and the hall's firelight, filtered down through the trap, and the scared, upraised faces of the 21st men could be seen, blinking and shading their eyes. A moment before, they had all been shouting and gabbling, the noise rising into the hall. The moment the trap opened, they were instantly silent. The sudden, abject quiet grated on Andrea's nerves. The Sterkarms around her were stringing longbows or setting arrows on strings. She thought: Terrible things are going to happen, and I'm going to have to see them.

Someone nudged her. She looked up and saw Toorkild. He said, "Tell them to give in. They're our prisoners now."

Andrea looked at the other faces standing around the trapdoor. Per wasn't there, and she wished he were, even though he would almost certainly side with his father.

Joe was there, but he was standing among the Sterkarms as if he were one of them. She bent over the trapdoor and translated Toorkild's words for the men below. She added, "Do as he says. They've got a big pot of boiling water up here. I don't know what it's for if not to pour on you."

The fear on the upturned faces intensified; and then the men began to shove each other, their feet scuttering on the floor, all trying to get as close to the walls as they could, thinking they could avoid the arrows, avoid being scalded.

Bryce leaned forward a little, peering up. "Andrea. Are you all right?"

Tears came into her eyes. "I'm fine, but—"

"And my men?"

"The men who got trapped with me are all dead."

"How?" he said.

Her tears came faster. She didn't want to say that the Sterkarms, her friends, who had spared her, had killed them. "Give up," she said. "Please."

"Are they going to kill us?" Bryce asked. If it seemed they were, then he had grenades and might as well take a few Sterkarms with him.

Andrea turned to Toorkild and began to talk with him. Bryce at first tried to follow what they were saying, but it was too quick. He looked around at the men with him in the half darkness. They were pressing against the walls, each calculating how likely he was to be missed by the arrows. Few of them knew each other. They wouldn't fight for each other.

One of the men said, "They've only got bows and arrows."

"Think an arrow can't kill you?" Bryce said.

"'Tain't a bullet, is it?"

"Chuck a grenade up there," someone else said. "That'll give 'em something to think about."

"Windsor and Miss Mitchell are up there," Bryce said. He didn't see the movement of the man who, without waiting for orders, reached for a grenade at his belt.

A three-foot arrow stuck out from just under his rib cage. It passed clean through him, struck the wall behind him, and, quivering, splintered inside him. Another hit him in the thigh; a third shattered against the stone floor. The man's knees sagged with shock, and he went down to the dirty floor. The other men, staring, were rigidly still.

When they looked up, it was impossible to tell which of the longbowmen had loosed the arrows. All of them had arrows on the string again.

"Brawly done, brawly," Toorkild said, nodding at his archers. He had warned his men of the magic the Elves might be armed with, and he was proud of the way they obeyed him. "Braw shooting." To be quick-eyed enough to spot the movement down there in the shadows had been worth praise; but to shoot down at such close range and hit the mark so well—that was worthy of reward. "I'll remember thee, my lad."

"I'm sorry," Andrea said, to the men on the ground floor. Her hands were to her face and her face was white. "I'm sorry, I'm sorry." Joe, just behind her, felt he'd been turned to stone. What showed of his face, through his beard, was white. He swallowed and looked about at his new family.

Bryce held up his hands and said, "Okay, okay." He had his pistol, with its thirteen shots. But those bowmen were fast. He would be gambling that he could get his pistol out and cock it before one or more of them nailed him. Even if he succeeded, how many could he shoot and how many could they shoot? And there was the danger of hitting Windsor or Andrea, with a ricochet if not a direct shot. Maybe he was making the wrong decision again, but he didn't have much time to think before more arrows came down.

"I told you to give up, I told you," Andrea said. "Oh God, is he all right?"

Bryce wanted to say, Of course he isn't, you stupid—Instead, he said, "We give up! What's going to happen to us?"

"They're going to ransom you," Andrea said. "It's what they usually do with prisoners." She looked at Windsor, who stood on the other side of the open trap, his arms held by Sterkarms, his face pale and sick. "Toorkild wants aspirins. Boxes and boxes of them, enough to last him for years. And whiskey. But aspirins more than anything. If FUP gives him them, he'll let you all go back through the Elf-Gate—but then the Elf-Gate must be closed and never opened again."

"Oh certainly," Windsor said. "Oh yes." Dirty hands held his upper arms in bruising grips, and he was surrounded by a fug of sweat and onions. He could hear the blood thump in his ears, and the beat of his heart was shuddering through him, he hardly knew whether with anger or with fear. "Promise him anything you like. Pile cream. Corn plasters."

"What about this man, this injured man?" Bryce called.

Andrea spoke with Toorkild again, briefly. "They'll take care of him if you give up. They won't hurt any of you if you give up, I can promise you that. Well, no more of you. They aren't a cruel people." The man on the floor of the basement below her writhed as she spoke. "I mean, they're not sadistic." I'm babbling, she thought. "I mean, they won't beat you up just for kicks or anything like that. Please—give up and do just as they say. Don't let's have anyone else hurt, please."

"We give in!" Windsor said. "For God's sake, we give in!"

"What's going to happen," Andrea said, "is, they're going to open the door. One or two of you will go out into the yard. They'll disarm you. I promise you it'll be all right if you don't fight." She put a hand to her head, thinking: I was telling someone else not to fight. Who?

Bryce sighed and lowered his head. Whatever was promised, there was no knowing that the Sterkarms wouldn't murder them in ones and twos as they went out into the yard. "I'll go first," he said.

It was a slow business. Toorkild shouted orders from the window, and the door of the tower was opened a little. Against the light was a shaggy-haired black shape. "*Kom!*" Bryce raised his head, straightened his shoulders and walked out. The other 21st men hung back.

Sweet Milk, stooping over the open trap, pointed at the men nearest the door. "*Ut!*" The two nearest ducked out through the door, and it was slammed shut.

Bryce and the other two, out in the bright light of the yard, were surrounded by people, many of them women, who grabbed at them, shrieking, and pulled them, shoved them, dragged them off their feet into the mud. It was terrifying. Bryce's heart pounded and his body shook. It was the sheer malice of the women that was so frightening, their twisted faces, their shrill voices, and the certainty that they saw no value in *him* but only in his clothes. His jacket was dragged off, revealing the grenades on his belt and the pistol in its shoulder holster. Then men moved in, shouldering the women aside. They held Bryce down in the mud and took off his belt and holster, while the women tugged off his boots.

When both his boots were off, everything went still around him. The Sterkarms had lost interest. Bryce sat up in the mud, moving slowly so he wouldn't alarm anyone. The other 21st men were near him. Both had lost their boots and jackets. One had lost his shirt as well. Their clothing and their boots were now being bundled up in the arms of different women.

A Sterkarm man stooped over Bryce, took his arm above the elbow and dragged at him to let him know he should get up. Another man stood by with a long knife in his hand. Bryce got up.

He and the other 21st men were taken along a narrow alley, paddling through the mud and muck in their stocking feet. The turns and twists of the alleys among the crowded buildings were confusing, and when they stopped, there seemed no reason why they'd stopped at this building rather than another. They all looked much alike. A ladder led to the door in the upper story, and Bryce and his companions were made to climb it.

Other Sterkarms were waiting to receive them at the top, and they were brought into a long, dim room, smelling of wood and thatch. A trapdoor was opened in the floor, and they were made to climb down another ladder, into the building's cold, dark, stone-built lower floor. There were no doors or windows down there. The ladder was pulled up, the trapdoor slammed down, and the bolt shot across. The darkness, except for a few cracks of light reaching them between the floorboards, was complete.

They waited a long time in the dark. Bryce felt his flesh turning to stone in the cold. He couldn't see the others, and was ashamed to speak to them. They must be blaming him. He upbraided himself, screaming at himself inside his head. He should have ignored

Windsor, should have insisted. What was the point of keeping your job 21st side if you were killed on the 16th?

The trapdoor above was opened again, the ladder lowered and three more half-naked men clambered down it. They shuffled about in the dark for a while and then found a place to sit on the floor of hard-packed earth. None of them had anything to say.

* * *

Gobby Per was in charge of the tower yard and had been considering the problem of the Elves guarding the Land Rovers. They were still unsuspecting—the uproar in the tower had been muffled by its thick stone walls. But there were ten of them, and they were armed with Elf-Pistols. Gobby had no time for pistols himself: They were cumbersome, slow and unreliable. A bowman could shoot countless arrows while a pistol was being loaded for one shot. But Little Per had said that Elf-Pistols were different, and sheep-brained though the boy too often was, he did have some sense.

Gobby sent men with bows, to be let down from the tower wall out of sight of the Elves. They made their way quietly around the tower, keeping out of sight below the hill's ridge. Other archers went up on the tower's wall.

A sudden shower of arrows fell on the Elves, some from above, some from the side.

It seemed the arrows came from nowhere, sudden flickers of darkness, whacking into the ground around the Elves, hitting the Land Rover, sinking deep into flesh. Some Elves were hit at once—others, not realizing they were beset with arrows, turned, looked up. Arrows hit them in the face. Down they went, without firing a shot. Others tugged at the arrows in their bodies, found they were barbed, and forgot their guns. Some fumbled at the unfamiliar weapons and couldn't make them fire. One Elf shot two Elves beside him.

A couple of the pistols were fired, with long bursts of terrifying noise that had the Sterkarms ducking below their wall and covering their ears. Stone chips flew. When the noise stopped, the archers bobbed up again.

When it seemed that all the Elves were disabled, Gobby himself led out five men with spears, to finish them off. The archers came out of cover too, drawing knives.

One of the Elves heaved himself up, and again there was that deafening, terrible noise that set the sheep and horses running in the valley below. One of the archers went flying backward. Gobby and his men took cover behind the Elf-Cart.

The noise of the Elf-Pistol stopped. Cautiously, the Sterkarms raised their heads or peered out from behind the cart. Not all the Elves were dead, but none of them seemed to be raising Elf-Pistols. Gobby and his men went forward, kicking the pistols out of the way and spearing the men. When they saw what the pistol had done to their archer, they chopped the Elves into pieces small.

* * *

The basement emptied slowly as the day passed. The men, filing out, passed by the wounded man, who had been moaning, trying to get up, falling back and crying out for hours now. Andrea had begged Toorkild to do something for him, and Toorkild had said, "In a while,"

"When we can" and, finally, "Go where tha canna hear if tha canna stand it."

She'd gone over to the big stone fireplace and, leaning in its corner, she cried, over so many things and for so many people, she wasn't sure, from minute to minute, who she was crying for.

Windsor shouted, "For God's sake, can't you do anything for him?"

When the basement was empty except for the wounded man, the door of the hall was opened and Windsor was hustled down the steps, past the sobbing man, and out into the gray light of a damp, chill afternoon. His escort dragged him straight past the excited women—Windsor's boots, jacket, swagger stick and watch had already been taken from him in the tower.

Now only the wounded Elf lay in the tower's basement. Sweet Milk went down the tower stairs from the hall, drawing his dagger as he went. In the basement, a long stripe of light entered from the open door, showing the straw and dung. The wounded Elf lay in shadow, behind the door. Sweet Milk crouched over him and cut his throat.

As Sweet Milk straightened, with blood on his hands, Toorkild came down the stairs, laughing and clapping Joe on the back. Sweet Milk couldn't laugh.

* * *

Windsor was shoved to the ladder, and shaken and prodded until he preferred to climb down it into the darkness below rather than be pushed down. As he went down, the chill of the stone building closed around him. His feet touched a damp, cold floor, and the ladder was tugged from his hands and pulled up, out of sight. The trapdoor was clapped down. The sound boomed dully between the stone walls.

Windsor stood still, listening to the blood thump in his ears and feeling the beat of his heart shudder through him. Gradually, the worst of the fear began to fade, and anger began to rise.

He saw, clearly, that nothing could be done with the 16th Project while those savages remained in possession. There was no reasoning with them. Offer them all the benefits of the twenty-first century, and because they were too ignorant to appreciate them, they flung them back in your teeth and spat in your face too.

Wipe them out, the lot of them.

I'll kill them myself, he thought. With my own bare hands. He could do it. Any monkey could kill. Look at the monkeys that did.

Aloud, he said to the men huddled around him in the dark, "Well? How are we going to get out of here?"

16th Side: Making Promises

THE STERKARMS WERE triumphant. They had, they thought, taken on the Elves and beaten them again, and they were all, men, women and children, flown with their own magnificence. Their glee had been quite unashamed and, for Andrea, unsettling. She'd half expected to be locked up again, but her earlier treachery seemed forgotten. Toorkild had hugged her and called her "Bonny lass!" Sweet Milk and Sim had kissed her. She'd felt as she imagined a Christian might have, if caught up in a self-congratulatory Roman crowd while the lions were still hungry.

She'd gone looking for Joe. In the yard outside the tower there had been dancing, laughing women waving the 21st boots and clothes they'd taken from the prisoners. Some of the clothing was heavily stained. Bloodstained. It had been her first clue to the fate of the 21st men guarding the Land Rovers.

From outside the tower walls had come a loud, alarming, percussive noise that had made her heart beat though she hadn't recognized it. Only when she went out through the gate did she realize that it was rifle fire. Even at a distance the noise was far worse, far more violent to the ear, than anything she'd heard on television or film.

The rifles were being fired by Sterkarms—mostly men, but one or two women. They were standing on the ridge of the hill, firing out over the valley. Joe had been among them, showing them how. The Sterkarms were thrilled to be handling Elf-Weapons of such power, noise and destruction. They fired into the air, they shot at rocks, sending bullets ricocheting and chips flying.

Andrea had been appalled—if no one had been hurt so far, it was only a matter of time before someone was. She'd begged the men to put the rifles down, but they were too excited to take any notice. Why should they listen to her? She was only an Elf, and they'd beaten the Elves.

She'd shouted at Joe, "Why did you start this?"

"They asked me!" he shouted back. "I thought it'd be better if I showed 'em how to do it instead of just letting 'em fool around; I didn't expect everybody and his dog to join in!"

Some of the rifles ran out of ammunition, but the Sterkarms fetched others from the Land Rovers and started again. Seeing Toorkild coming out of the tower gate, Andrea had run over to him and asked him to stop his men playing with the rifles, but he said, "Away, woman!" and waved her off. "I've other matters to think on." What matters, he didn't say.

It had been Per who'd stopped it. He'd been climbing the steep path to the tower with his cousins, leading their horses, when a burst of fire had startled the animals, setting the horses rearing and the dogs jumping and howling. When the rifle fire had paused for a moment, Per had yelled, "Stop that!" Most of the fire had stopped. Some of the men had even gone down to help with the horses.

Per had reached the hilltop at a run, having left his horse behind. He came among the Sterkarm men, most of them older than him, and had roundly slapped the faces of the first three he'd reached. What business had they with the Elf-Pistols? Did they know nothing about horses? Were those sheep's heads on their shoulders? Pointing to the ground at his feet, he'd demanded that all the pistols be laid down there, now!

Some of the men brought their rifles and laid them down immediately, but a handful of them hung back. One of them said, "The pup yapping when the old hound's quiet!" And then he'd grinned at the other men.

Per had darted at him, dragged the pistol from his hands, and thrown it on the ground. He'd shoved the man in the chest and tripped him, sending him sprawling on the hard, rocky ground. Standing over the man, and looking around at the others, Per had said, "You God-damned, back-jumping, horn-brained, dead-eyed cod's heads!"

The fallen man, plainly furious, had twisted to his knees before he saw that Wat and Ingram had come up behind Per, neither of them in good temper. All the other rifles had been brought and laid on the pile, and one of the men helped up the one Per had knocked down and hustled him away, telling him to calm down. Per had said to them all, "You rut-minded, gutless runts! You should all be bent over tables the night and whipped!"

Andrea had been startled. She'd never seen Per so angry, and couldn't help feeling a little impressed. She'd looked at Joe and had seen by his expression that he was also taken aback. He'd scuttled over to the heap of rifles and started putting the safety catches on, trying to look as if he'd had nothing to do with shooting the bullets off.

While Per had been organizing the carrying of the rifles to a storeroom, he'd seen Andrea and had eyed her, obviously wondering whether an approach would be snubbed. The possibility had been too much for his pride; instead, seeing his father and uncle come from the tower's gate, he'd run down to meet them, followed by his cousins. "We shot 'em all, Daddy! All three!"

Toorkild had opened his arms to him, hugged him and lifted him off his feet. Andrea, coming up, had heard an excited account of the killing of three men, and had watched Toorkild and Gobby proudly kissing and petting their sons as they listened. The cousins had competed vociferously to claim their share in the murders, and Andrea had been quite unable to convince herself that Per had somehow been a bystander, going along for the adventure but holding back from any unpleasantness. The best she'd been able to do had been to remind herself that the Sterkarms had been defending their land against invasion—and she would have found that an excellent excuse if the people they'd killed hadn't been *her* people. And if the stains on Per's clothes hadn't been, quite clearly, blood.

Soon after that, the Land Rovers had been wrecked. Their hubcaps had been taken off, their mirrors wrenched off and seats torn out, their windshields smashed. Someone had accidentally released the handbrake on one, and it had gone careening off down the hillside, the gathering rumble shaking the ground beneath their feet. The uneven ground had sent the Land Rover shooting into the air, and it had crashed down onto its wheels several yards lower down, with an impact that made Andrea cringe almost to the ground. When she'd looked up, it had been to see the Land Rover run into an outcrop of grayish-reddish rock and rear up over it. A crunching, grinding, ripping sound of buckling metal had carried back to them as the Land Rover's underside was torn away.

The Land Rover exploded. Andrea had seen it happen often on film but had never heard such a shattering noise in reality before. She thought her eardrums had been burst as the whole world became muffled in the aftermath—the noise was even louder than the rifle fire. The force of the explosion had shoved at her, and the heat of it touched her. Bits of metal, dirt and rock had pattered down around them. Orange flames had leaped up from the Land Rover, and black smoke spread from it. The first pollution, she thought, that FUP had succeeded in bringing 16th side.

From the Sterkarms there had been a long silence, then wild cheers and screams. The second Land Rover had soon followed the first—it hadn't taken them long to work out how to take the brake off deliberately. They cheered and danced as it went down the slope, tilting and tilting at such an angle that, despite its wide wheelbase, it tipped over on its side. There had been disappointment all around when it failed to explode.

But there's nothing like an exploding Land Rover to set the mood for a party. Isobel had promised to set a feast on the tables, and there'd been more cheering and dancing. People had run off to find fiddles and pipes, and such finery as they possessed. Isobel looked around for Andrea, and beckoned to her. "Tha'll have to learn," Isobel said, "what's in store and where to find it. No better time to start than now."

Andrea had gone with her, not knowing how to refuse, but the words had sent a dart of fright through her. Why should she have to learn what was in store, and why now? Because the Elves were beaten, the Elf-Gate closed, and she wasn't going home.

Now, in the hall, the din rang from wall to wall as people shouted, laughed, sang. At least three different groups were singing "Come, Who Dares Meddle with Me!"

It was a special occasion, and so Isobel was waiting on the tables herself, serving bread and ale. Andrea had elected to help. It kept her away from Per. She wasn't sure this was a good idea. Under the circumstances, she should probably be doing all she could to get back in Per's favor. If her past experience was anything to go on, it wouldn't be difficult—except that it would, because she'd have to pretend to forget all the dead 21st men and her own predicament. She'd have to try and pretend, all over again, that Per was a lover and a loving son, and not a killer, raised to cut throats at his mammy's knee.

A man raised his cup to her. She filled it from her jug and raised her eyes to find him smirking at her. What he was thinking was as plain as if he'd spoken: She was one of the defeated. A captive, as good as. She turned her head and looked the length of the hall, to where Per was, and the man quickly, guiltily, looked in the same direction.

Per and his cousins were defending the family table

from the main hall with scuffles and thrown bread and bones. A crust hit Per, and he was jeered at because he was looking at Andrea instead of paying attention. She looked away quickly, pretending that she hadn't really been looking for him at all.

Per saw her turn away. She was still in a bad temper with him, then. If he tried to go to her, she would call him a sheep's head and a sheep's son again, in front of everyone.

He withdrew from the defense of the table and leaned against the wall behind his father's chair, watching Andrea. If she looked around again and saw him like that, she might feel sorry for him.

Would she have been happier if the Elves had won, and he'd been killed? Or if they'd lain down in the mud and let the Elves use them as stepping-stones on their way to take Sterkarm land? Maybe she would. There was no telling with Elves.

> I stand outside my sweetheart's bower door,
> Where I've stood many times before,
> But I can't enter nor yet win in
> To that pleasant bed that she lies in.

After having killed the Elves on the hillside, he didn't want to spend the dark hours alone. Company he could always find: Ecky, Hob, Sim . . . He didn't want to listen to them braying and laughing. He wanted to be cuddled up with Andrea, in her bed. And he wanted her to want him there. Vaylan stole his Elf-May's swanskin and made her his wife by capture, but she flew away and left him as soon as her chance came.

He made up his mind that he would stop shilly-shallying, go across to Andrea and speak to her. Straightening, he pushed himself away from the wall—and then leaned on it again and slid down it until he was sitting on the floor. Cuddy, lying under the table, saw him and her tail wagged. There was one bitch who loved him!

Andrea moved to a table where most of the men were from Gobby's household. As she leaned over the shoulder of one to fill his cup, their conversation faltered, and one said, "Shut it. She don't want to hear."

She glanced around at the men. Their faces weren't friendly, though a couple held out their cups. She held her jug back. "What don't I want to hear?" They looked at each other, and no one answered. She turned away. "No ale for you then."

Behind her, one of the men said, "Elves should be trod down in water."

She turned to face them, as others at the table nodded and agreed. Some looked away from her, others stared her in the face.

"They trod Grannams down just for cutting the May. The Elves *killed* Luggy."

Andrea moved away, leaving them to be served by Isobel. Looking back, she saw them still talking. Three of them rose, moved to the next table and stooped to talk to the men there. As she poured ale on the other side of the hall, she saw those three and several others pushing their way down the hall to the family table. They leaned across the board, speaking to Toorkild and Gobby.

Toorkild stood up and called his nephews over to him. Strangely, Per didn't seem to be there—but then he rose up from behind his father's chair, with Cuddy leaping up to rest her paws on his shoulders. All of them began to talk with the men of Gobby's household.

It wasn't hard to guess what they were talking about. Andrea stood amidst the noise, holding the jug and watching everyone near the family table being drawn into the argument. She felt queasy. She hadn't lived so long with the Sterkarms without learning how they felt about justice. They expected a life for a life. Or, in exchange for a Sterkarm life, many lives.

They were talking about taking Windsor, and Bryce, and the other 21st men—who all had families, wives, children—and treading them down in Bedes Water.

* * *

Locked in the storeroom, the 21st men were pressed close against each other's sides, arms around each other, trying to keep warm. They breathed each other's breath, listened to each other sigh and snuffle, and were silenced by embarrassment. Close as they were, it was so dark that they could only glimpse an occasional movement of a head.

Hours before, they'd heard rifle fire from outside, and an explosion, muffled to a rattle and a *ker-ump* by the stone walls around them. A rescue party? No rescue had come.

It hadn't taken long to establish that the only way out was up. The walls were of stone, and the floor, though only of earth, was hard packed and they had nothing to dig with. A search, scrambling around on hands and knees in the dark, banging heads and bruising knees, had made certain of that. There was nothing on the floor but straw, and nothing hung on the walls.

But above their heads were wooden floorboards, either nailed or pegged into place. They could reach up and touch them, usually dislodging a shower of dust. Sterkarm guards were above too. They could hear them walking about and talking. Long before the prisoners could succeed in forcing a floorboard out of place, the guards would raise the alarm.

Bryce tried not to remember that he'd warned Windsor, over and over, not to underestimate the Sterkarms. Gibing at Windsor wasn't going to be any help. Nor was anything else he could think of.

* * *

Putting the jug of ale down on the nearest table, Andrea edged and shoved her way through the people until she reached the family table too. Reaching between the bodies of others, she caught at Per's arm. He looked around, and his face took on an expression of wary surprise. Andrea pointed toward the door that led from the hall to the stairs, and then let go of his arm and pushed her way through the crowd.

Andrea reached the small landing outside the hall door first. The only light came from the hall's open door, and the stairs were dark. She climbed a few steps toward the upper story and leaned against the plastered wall, waiting. The stone walls muffled the din from the hall and blocked the heat. Where she waited it was quiet, and chill.

Per came out onto the landing, with the noise and light of the hall at his back, and looked up to see her standing above him on the stone steps, melting into the darkness, only faintly touched by light. He thought she looked very beautiful, and he was afraid to speak in case he said the wrong thing. He didn't know how to hold his face: whether to look pleased, or sad, or indifferent. He was afraid that she'd called him out here to tell him that she was going to use some Elf-Work to leave him. Or that, although she would stay, she would never speak to him or look at him again.

Andrea, on her side, was ashamed to be asking for his help. She held out a hand to tell him to keep his distance: It would be unfair to let him think she wanted anything but help. "Per, what are they going to do with the Elves in the lockup?"

She was interested in her fellow Elves, not in him. The disappointment hurt. He looked over his shoulder toward the hall, and the firelight shining through the doorway lit his face. He gave a slight shrug.

"They're going to kill them!" she said.

"There's talk of it." His voice was hard. If she didn't care how she hurt him, then he didn't care for Elves.

She came down the steps, closer to him. "Per, please don't let them kill them. Be kind, let them go."

Immediately he felt that he'd been cruel, and his chest and throat tightened. He went toward her, meaning to cuddle her, but her outstretched hand still told him to keep away.

"Talk to thy father," she said. "Ask him to let them go."

"It's Gobby wants them killed. It's Gobby who lost a man."

"But they're in your father's lockup. Be so kind, Per. I promised them they'd be ransomed. Be kind, don't make me a liar. I'm one of them: They're my people. Be so good."

"Oh, Entraya." He climbed the steps to her and put his arms around her.

She tried to push him away, but he caught her wrists and folded her arms up against his chest. He was very strong. He hugged her to him tightly, enveloping her in his smell of sweat and sheep and leather—a blunt instrument of a smell, but one that was rich and musky and irresistibly comforting, since it meant Per, and ease and happiness. Instead of pushing him away, she leaned on him and burst into tears. "Oh Per, I'm so scared. I don't want those men to be killed. Be so kind, don't let them be killed."

"Ssh! There's nowt for thee to fear, Honey." He kissed her eye and held her tighter. She seemed so warmly alive and soft in his arms, so easily hurt. So human. "Nobody shall hurt thee—I won't let them."

"But the Elf-Men!" she said. Her face was all wet and caught the little light from the hall door. "They didn't want to come here, Per. They had to come—and they have families—be so kind, be so good, don't hurt them."

Tears came to his own eyes. He wanted to tell her anything that would make her happy. Now that she was in his arms again, looking up at him, asking for his help, he didn't want to fail her or make her angry again—but she was asking him for something he couldn't give. If he promised it, he would only have to break his word, and that would make her angrier than ever. "They killed Gobby's man, Sweet."

"Look how many of them you killed! Men who—"

She was crying too hard to go on.

His hand went to the back of her head, stroking her hair. "But little bird, they attacked us. They'd come to take our land."

She tucked her head hard under his chin, and sobbed, "Be kind, don't kill them, be kind be kind don't kill them, be so kind, don't, Per, be so kind, don't."

Above her head, he grimaced, trying to blink his eyes free of tears. He couldn't refuse her, but he couldn't promise her anything either. It was a joke at the tower that his mother and father would give him anything he asked for, but he knew it wasn't true. If he asked for the lives of the Elves, he didn't think he would be granted them. Largely for his sake, Toorkild and Isobel wished it to be known that the price for taking a Sterkarm life was many other lives. Their slogan, "Come, Who Dares Meddle with Me!" must always be more than mere words.

"Entraya? If we spare the Elves—if we let them go home—wilt thou stay?"

She stopped crying and froze, keeping her head down against his chest. What would life be like, if everyone else from the 21st went back through the Tube, and the Tube was shut down, and she was left here alone? She loved Per, despite everything—with his arms around her, she knew she loved him—but what if he was killed? What about the time she'd spent waiting for him to be hurt again, or killed, and dreading it?

With an uprush of feeling that choked her, she realized with what deep longing she wanted central heating and inner-spring mattresses, supermarkets and intensive care, microwave pizzas and noisy, crowded, polluted cities where you could go out alone for the day without needing a troop of friends, all armed to the teeth, to ensure that you got home again. She loved Per, but she didn't think she was strong enough to stay with him in the 16th.

"Stay, Entraya. Be so kind, stay. Tha've been happy here—tha said it was more green here, tha said people were more friendly than Elves, tha said tha never wanted to go home!"

She had said these things, in her first flush of enthusiasm for all things Sterkarm, in the first drunkenness of finding that Per wanted her—but that was before things had become complicated. When she'd said those things, and meant them, she had always known, at the back of her mind, that it would be easy to return home to the 21st. Nothing was the same now.

"Entraya!" He bent his head down and sideways, trying to see her face. A kiss landed on the side of her nose. "If our folk fight, we don't have to fall out! I ken tha'll be leaving th'own folk, but every may leaves her folk, and she's sad for a while . . ." The Sterkarm women sang laments about it on their wedding day. Andrea had written out some of the songs in her notebooks. "But she settles, and has bairns and is happy! And I'll *make* thee happy, Entraya! I'll do all to make thee happy. I'll buy thee writings." Per was uncomfortably aware that Elf-Land was wealthier, more luxurious and comfortable than anything he had to offer. "I'll buy thee cloths for the floor, and a bed with a feather mattress. Tha shalt have thine own sheep and cow. And a pig—all thine alone. I'll—I'll—" His imagination couldn't stretch to anything else he could give her. "And I'll wed thee,

Entraya. We'll jump the broom—now, this night, if tha'll say 'aye.'"

In the absence of any priest, jumping over a broom together before witnesses, followed by drinking from the same cup and an exchange of rings, was a binding marriage for the Sterkarms. She started shaking her head, feeling overwhelmed by his insistence. "Per—"

"I need a wife." He tried to kiss her again, but she ducked her head. "I must have a wife, and tha'rt better than any! Tha'rt big and strong and clever and bonny. Tha'll be my wedded wife, Entraya, whatever comes."

By which he meant that, big and strong and clever as she was, he would always grant her the respect and status due to his wife, no matter how many mistresses and bastard children he later acquired. "Per—"

"Our first son shall be called Toorkild—but if the first be a girl, I'll no care. She'll be my second Elf-May. And after the first son, tha canst name the others as tha wilt, with Elf-Names."

Tracey, Sharon and Wayne Sterkarm.

"Not thee or our bairns shall ever go hungry, I swear. I'll never let thee go hungry."

No, he would ride instead, steal sheep, and leave someone else hungry behind him.

"There's nowt to fear. I'll look after thee. I'll kill anyone who hurts thee."

"Per—" But it was useless trying to explain to him that she couldn't stay with him precisely because, when he said he would kill anyone who hurt her, he meant exactly that. "Per, be so kind, wilt ask thy father to spare the Elves?"

"Wilt stay?"

433

"Per—" She started to cry again. "This isn't fair!"

He held her tighter and rocked her a little. "Ssh, ssh!" He knew it wasn't fair, but many things weren't fair, and if this was what he had to do to make her promise to stay, then he'd do it. Better to get her to give her promise than to steal her swanskin so she couldn't leave.

She looked up at him and said, "Would thee come and live in Elf-Land?"

In the faint light from the hall, she saw his aghast expression. Then she watched the pretty face that had earned him his nickname turn cold. He said, "They're talking of hanging thine Elves from the walls."

She stared into his face, and he looked steadily back. Though his hand stroked her hair at the back of her head, his expression didn't change. If she didn't agree to stay with him, he would give her no help in saving the 21st men.

She ducked her head and pressed her face against his chest, hiding from him. She felt him kiss her head. He said, "It will be all right, little bird, all right . . ."

She was thinking: How had she got into this, and how could she get out of it? She couldn't seem to untangle the events that had brought her to this moment. At what point could she have turned back, or done otherwise? She could hardly bear to look at what the future held. Was she to watch men, who were guilty of nothing much more than trying to earn a little money, strangling from the tower walls? Was the rest of her life going to be discomfort, squalor and drudgery, without even the consolation of having chosen it for herself?

These couldn't be her Sterkarms, it couldn't be her Per, forcing her into this. These must be those murderous, frightening Sterkarms whom she'd always sensed hiding behind the ones she loved.

"Birdie?" Per spoke with difficulty, through a narrowed, painful throat. He knew that what he was doing was wrong, and it made him afraid, but he had to do it. If he didn't, then his whole life would be spoiled. Everyone at the tower knew he had his eye on the Elf-May, and if he didn't wed her, then everyone would see him snubbed. . . . He would wed some other may, but she wouldn't be an Elf-May, she wouldn't be as beautiful and glamorous, and their children wouldn't be half Elves. He would spend all the rest of his life in regret, and he had no intention of wasting his energy in doing that. "All will be right, honey cake; I'll *make* it right. . . ." He would. If he hurt her now, then he would make it right later. He'd succeed, because he'd try so hard.

She thought: He is so naïve. Lifting her head, she said, "If I stay . . . if I wed thee . . . dost promise tha'll get thy father to free the Elves?"

He drew a breath and held it. "Entraya, if tha'll stay, I'll do my all, but—Daddy might say no."

She slid her arms up and around his neck. "Not if thee ask him."

"Mammy'll be for killing 'em."

Andrea knew that was true. For all Isobel's charm and gentleness within the tower, she was fiercely in favor of killing enemies. And Toorkild, if asked for one thing by the son he doted on, and its opposite by the wife he dearly loved for all his infidelities . . . Andrea felt almost sorry for him.

She kissed Per's cheek. "Promise to do thy best, to try thy hardest, and I'll stay even if Toorkild says no."

435

He let out a long breath and gave his brightest smile, while tears spilled from his eyes, catching the faint light. "I give thee my word I'll do my all to save the Elves. By oak, ash and thorn, by my mother's heart, I swear it."

It was the nearest to a binding promise that anyone was ever going to get from a Sterkarm. Even so, would he keep it? "Then I'll stay." She didn't know if she meant it. She didn't know if she could go through with it.

His arms squeezed tight around her, pulling her up onto her toes, pressing breath out of her. He kissed her cheek, his scanty beard and mustache scratching her skin as he tried to find her mouth. She turned her head, and his tongue slipped between her lips.

It was a roar from the hall that made her jump and bang heads with him. He drew back, his hand to his nose, grinning wryly. She breathlessly clutched at her thumping heart and wondered, was that yell from a lynching party setting off for the lockup?

Per leaned close again, and she smacked her hand against his chest. "No!" She had to think of the frightened men in the lockup, and their families back in the 21st.

Oh, the 21st! Hot showers. Sliced white bread. A happy absence of fleas and lice, and a general use of deodorants. And, despite the tabloid headlines, a tendency not to hack strangers to death right outside your own front door. "Go and talk to thy father, be so kind."

"Entraya—"

"We've plenty of time," she said, and smiled.

His big, bright smile came back. He kissed her cheek. "I'll talk him round!" He ran down the steps and back into the hall, looking back at her over his shoulder, smiling.

Andrea was left in the cool darkness of the stairway, her heart beating uncomfortably fast, her body shaking slightly. She believed that Per would now do his best to persuade his father to free the Elves, but she had far less faith that Toorkild would agree. So what was she to do? Simply wait until Per failed, and then stand by as the 21st men were murdered anyway, and bleat, "I did my best"? After all, she was in no danger of having a noose tied around her neck and being thrown over the tower's wall.

While Per was trying to sweet-talk his father, he wouldn't be wondering where she was, so she had a little time.

And there was Joe. . . . So many complications!

She looked in at the door of the hall. Joe was sitting on the end of a table near the door, a cup in his hand. His face was flushed and he looked thoughtful. She went over to him. "Joe? Joe, if you could go back to the 21st, would you?" He raised his eyes from his cup and gave her a long look. "Would you, Joe? I haven't time for a long discussion."

But, for Joe, it was a hard question to answer. He thought of the men he'd seen murdered. He thought of Per knocking down the man who'd defied him. He also remembered the welcome he'd been given, the gifts, and Per's promises. "What should I go back for? A cardboard box?"

"They're going to kill the men in the lockup, Joe— our men."

"'Our' men?" Joe said. "They're bosses' lackeys. I'm

437

a Sterkarm. I'm staying."

She looked at him. "Okay. I hope you know what you're doing. I hope it works out for you. Listen: If Per should ask, you haven't seen me and you don't know where I am. Will you do that much for me?"

Joe looked at her doubtfully. "You be careful."

"I will." Looking around, she caught the arm of the nearest woman. "If Per looks for me, will you tell him I'm tired and—I've got a headache." The old lines were always the best. "Tell him I've gone to my bower to try and sleep it off."

The woman grinned and said she would be sure to tell him. On her way to the hall door, Andrea gave the same message to three other people. It would be common knowledge that she'd been in her bower, asleep, all the time.

She ran down the stairs in the dark and heaved aside the heavy yett at the bottom. The horses shifted and snorted in the dark, and she could smell their sweet animal smell. Pushing through them, she reached the tower's heavy door and struggled with it, finally shoving it open to emerge in the fresh, damp, cold air of the yard.

Oh God! she thought. Do I want to do this? If it went wrong, she could end up hanging on the tower walls herself.

But she had Per to protect her, even if things did go wrong. . . . If she didn't try, it was almost a certainty that the 21st men *would* hang.

If she did this, would she dare to keep her promise to Per, and stay to face the anger of Toorkild and Gobby—and Isobel? The very thought made her cringe with fright. Far safer and easier to run back through the Tube.

But that would mean breaking her promise to Per, and he was keeping his promise to her. . . .

Oh, did she have to throw her whole life away?

Whatever she did, she was going to have to hurt and betray someone. And however much her betrayal hurt Per, he would still be alive. The 21st men wouldn't be.

She ran from the tower door into the muddy yard.

20

16th Side: Asking a Favor

THE NOISE IN THE HALL, the yelling that had startled Andrea, was the noise of a chanting game, with forfeits for those who couldn't remember the ever-lengthening list of words. Per made his way through the crush of people to the family table, where Toorkild lay back in his chair, a little drunk, red-faced and cheerful. If Per had been about to ask him for a horse, or for fleeces to sell to buy himself a helmet, or for anything in that way, he would have been certain of getting it.

Isobel was among the tables, serving more drink. That was good. She wouldn't overhear and make things more difficult. Gobby, though, was sitting in his place beside Toorkild.

Per leaned over the back of his father's chair, stooping down and putting his head close to Toorkild's. "Daddy?" He spoke quietly, but insistently, to be heard only by his father. Toorkild twisted in his chair and looked up. "Daddy, shalt thou hang Elven?"

Toorkild, who had thought this matter settled, pulled his son's head down, doubling him over the back of the chair. "Why art asking, eh?" Gripping the back of Per's jacket, he shook him. "What's it to thee?"

Per, struggling, slipped sideways and landed on his knees at Toorkild's side. Leaning on the chair's arm, he looked up, his face flushed and his hair on end. "Daddy, let them be."

Toorkild threw himself back heavily in his seat and shouted, "It's kill no Elven! Then it's kill the Elven! Now it's kill no Elven again!" Per raised his hands to hush him, but Gobby had already looked around. He saw Per and nodded to himself, as if everything were explained. "If I'd known how much cussed trouble Elven were," Toorkild said, "I'd have burned the Gate down meself at the beginning!"

"What now?" Gobby asked.

Pulling Per's head against his shoulder, Toorkild shouted, "Now he wants to spare the Elven!" His voice vibrated through his chest and through Per's skull.

Gobby, considering the matter already decided beyond question, turned away. "Pah!"

He never failed to irritate Per. Wrestling away from his father, and pitching his voice to carry, Per said, "It's by cause I'm nesh, like any son of Bella Hob's-daughter."

Gobby turned and glared at him. Toorkild looked down at him, puzzled. From Isobel came a shout: "*What?*"

Per got to his feet. Now that he'd spoken, he wished he hadn't. He never much minded vexing his uncle, but now he'd hurt his mother.

Isobel came close to the table and set both her fists, a jug grasped in one, on her hips. "What *about* Bella Hob's-daughter?"

"Nothing, Mammy," Per said, and Gobby looked grimly pleased, which only irritated Per again.

Toorkild pulled at his hand. "What?"

"It's only something Gobby Daddy's-brother said."

Isobel turned and looked hard at Gobby, hands still on her hips. Toorkild was looking at him too. The hall was falling silent.

"I never said any such—" Gobby began.

"Tha did, Daddy," Wat said. "When we were riding, before Per was slashed."

Gobby, exasperated, looking to Toorkild for understanding, saw Toorkild looking bitter, and shouted, "If I said he's nesh, it's because he *is* nesh! Always arguing, won't be said! Always—"

"Oh!" Isobel said. "Oh! And I suppose *thy* sons—"

And they were away, Gobby and Isobel, both of them calling on Toorkild to support them. Gobby drew in Wat and Ingram, and Toorkild called in Sweet Milk. Every person in the hall packed closer around the family table to hear, and a few of the bolder spirits ventured to give their opinions. Within five minutes so much had been said that no one remembered the argument had started over the question of whether or not to kill the Elves.

Isobel, on hearing that she had given Toorkild only one nesh son while Gobby's Bertha had given him three good ones, screeched and banged down the jug she held.

Toorkild demanded, "Am I nesh? Am *I* nesh?" for no clear reason. Wat infuriated his father by refusing to take his side. Neither would Ingram, who often wished Per had been his big brother, in place of the two he was stuck with.

Ecky and Sim, at the tops of their voices, gave accounts of Per's courage and fortitude, to which no one listened.

Sweet Milk stood by, pulling at his beard and looking unhappy.

Joe had come forward through the crowd to see what was happening, and now looked about bewildered, with no idea of what this quarrel was about, or what might come of it. He caught Per's eyes and was comforted when Per's nod seemed to tell him that there was nothing to worry about. Per was certainly at ease. He had seated himself in Toorkild's vacated chair and, with one leg slung over the wooden arm, was stroking Cuddy's head as the big dog leaned it against his shoulder.

Per was pleased to hear Toorkild declare that Gobby's three gowks all put together weren't worth his Per. In a little while more, when he asked again for the lives of the Elves, both his father and mother would take his side, to spite Gobby. He hadn't planned it that way. His repeating of Gobby's insult to himself and his mother had merely been in the ordinary way of Sterkarm quarrels. But once the row was started, he had suddenly seen how it would work out, and had decided to let it.

At some point well into the quarrel, Gobby shouted that "the May" was a well-chosen nickname—"A may's face, a may's nature—runagate and flighty and not a gnat's turd of sense!" That stung, but Per bent his head to kiss Cuddy's nose instead of jumping up to join in the yelling. It would only go on longer if he did.

It was still going on when a woman crept up behind Per and whispered in his ear, under the noise of the shouting, that she was off to bed now, but first had to pass on a message from the Elf-May.

When he'd heard it, Per kissed the woman's cheek, thanked her, and settled back in the chair to consider that Andrea wanted him to know that she was lying down in her bower.

He looked up at the waving arms, the toing and froing, the gaping red faces above him, and wondered if he could somehow intervene and bring the row to a quick end.

But no, he wasn't much good as a peacemaker. If he stood up and spoke now, they would all turn on him and dress him down. Even his father was likely to ask him if he wasn't happy now he'd started this, and tell him to sit down and shut up. Better to keep low and wait it out.

* * *

It was dark in the yard and, in the narrow alleys between the buildings, pitch-black. Andrea knew the tower well enough to find her way, but she blundered into rubbish heaps, and tripped on uneven ground, and had to catch herself on walls. It made her think again about the distance between the tower and the Elf-Gate. It wouldn't be like walking down a city street at night, over smooth tarmac or paving stones, lit by streetlamps. This was wild, trackless country. By day, going by the shortest way, it was a walk of over ninety minutes. By night, what with the rocks and the tussocks, the harsh tangle of bilberries and heather underfoot, and the river to cross, it would take much longer. It was the kind of country that could break a leg. Or they might go astray in the dark, wander in the wrong direction and become completely lost, to be found and recaptured by the Sterkarms.

But what was the point of worrying? They had a simple choice. They could make the attempt to reach the Elf-Gate, or they could stay and rely on the Sterkarms' goodwill.

A lantern hung from a hook outside the lockup, casting a little faint candlelight into the dark alley. It showed her the ladder leaning in place, and she climbed it, calling out, "Halloo! You, up there!"

One of the men on guard came to the door and gave her a hand into the upper room. The two guards were using a chest as a bench and had set a couple of candles on the top of another. The candlelight showed the strings of vegetables and hard flatbread strung from the roof, and cast deep shadows among the rafters and the jumble of sacks and storage chests on the floor.

"Oh, my head aches," Andrea said, as soon as she was in. She put a hand to her forehead. "I'm off to bed to try and get rid of it, but I just stopped by—Toorkild asked me to tell you to come on back to the feast."

The men looked at each other and then at her again. She could see them thinking that, nice may though she was, she was still an Elf.

"Isobel's idea," she said. "She said it was a shame you were stuck out here on your own. 'What's going to happen?' she said. 'They're in the lockup, the gate's barred, there's a watchman on the tower—why can't they come in and have a drink?'" She saw them glance at each other again as they relaxed. She might be an Elf, but didn't Toorkild trust her enough to let her run around loose? Wasn't she the May's may? "So go on and enjoy yourselves," she said. "Me, I'm off to bed." She turned back to the ladder, as if she had nothing in her mind except her pillow.

"You got no candle?" one of the men said. "Here, have one of our candles." They were studying her closely, but with kindness.

"Get her the lantern," said the other and, coming forward, took the lantern down from the hook.

Andrea thanked him and started down the ladder with the lantern in one hand. Watching her go, the man who had unhooked the lantern said, "You get your head down in the dark and quiet, my love—you'll soon feel better."

"Thanks shall you have," Andrea said. She stood at the bottom of the ladder long enough to see that they were following her down, and then called, "Good night," and went off with her lantern into the dark alleys.

She turned a corner and waited there, hiding the lantern light and peering back the way she'd come. She glimpsed the dark, moving shapes of the men coming down the ladder before she ducked back out of sight. To her disappointment, they lifted the ladder down and set it along the side of the building. She heard them talking as they moved away. One said to the other, "Poor lass, Elf though she be. The May'll lead her a hound's life."

Andrea winced, but it was probably that pity that had saved her from closer questioning.

When the men were out of hearing, she went back to the lockup as quickly as she could without making too much noise in the mud. Setting the lantern down, she lifted the ladder, relieved to find that it wasn't as difficult to manage as she had feared, being neither very long nor very heavy. But as she put it in place, she was keenly aware of danger. Yes, the guards had believed her—probably because they were bored and cold and wanted to—but what if, when they reached the hall, they were asked why they'd left their post?

She hurried to climb the ladder, the lantern in her hand. A gang of Sterkarms, angry and vengeful, could arrive at any moment, gathering around the foot of the ladder, shaking it, yelling. . . . She put her finger into the hole in the door and lifted the iron latch. The door swung inward and let her into the storeroom.

She set the lantern down on the chest, beside the snuffed candles, and didn't bother about being quiet. The bolt on the trapdoor was a little stiff, but she wrenched it back, skinning one finger, and heaved up the trapdoor. From below came a scuffling sound of movement, and then stillness and silence.

She took the lantern from the chest and held it over the darkness of the trap. A little of its light filtered down, showing her nothing much but rafters. "Mr. Windsor?"

The men in the stone room below started to their feet, their hearts beating faster. The light above them was the first they'd seen for hours. But a woman's voice asking for Windsor was not what they'd been either hoping for or fearing.

"Andrea?" Bryce said.

The woman's voice said, in English, "Hang on, I'll get the other ladder." From above came the sound of footsteps and something being banged and dragged on the wooden floor. The light went on shining at the edge of the trap, so she must have set the lantern down there. The end of the ladder appeared in the light, and slid down, racketing on the trap's edge.

Bryce caught the ladder by one of its rungs and took its weight, helping to lower it down. But even when it rested on the earth floor, they hesitated. Bryce called, "Are you alone?"

"Oh, hurry up!" Andrea's face appeared above them, framed in the trap. "I sent the guards away, but I don't know how long we've got."

"Well done, girl!" Windsor called. "I didn't think you had it in you!"

Bryce swarmed up the ladder. At its foot the men crowded to follow. Windsor pushed in among them, and succeeded in being the third to climb.

"We heard gunfire," Bryce said. They had a few seconds while the rest of the men climbed the ladder. "We thought the men with the Land Rovers—"

"They were all killed," Andrea said, as more and more of the men clambered out of the trapdoor. "They"—she tried to keep her voice steady—"hacked them to pieces. It was the Sterkarms letting off guns, but they're all locked up now, the guns I mean. And the Land Rovers. They rolled them down the hill. One exploded. The other's upside down and wrecked."

All the men had climbed out of the room below and were standing around her. They were struck into stillness and silence by her news.

"No Land Rovers?" Bryce said. "Do you know where the guns are?"

She shook her head. "We've got to hurry up—I don't know where the guns are!" she added, as she saw him about to repeat his question. "There are dozens of storerooms—I don't know which one they were put in."

Bryce was thinking: Was it worth trying to escape across this country, barefoot, in the dark? How long did they have before the Sterkarms, coming to feed them, discovered they'd gone and came after them? When the Sterkarms came after them, armed and on horseback, they would catch them barefoot, unarmed, exhausted and half frozen. Better to take their chances of ransom here.

"They're going to hang you," Andrea said.

"Hang us!"

"The men by the Land Rovers killed one of them—"

"One?"

"So they want to hang you—there's no time for this—"

"We need boots," Bryce said.

"We haven't time!" Andrea said. "I don't know where to look for boots—there are too many storerooms, and they might be coming after us now! Come on!"

Bryce nodded, and then kicked the ladder down into the storeroom below. Crouching, he closed and bolted the trap. No one, to Andrea's relief, argued anymore, or asked questions, not even Windsor. She caught up the lantern and went, as fast as she could, down the ladder to the alley. There was no sight of the Sterkarms. Even the sound of them was distant, muffled by the tower's stone walls.

"Bring the ladder with us," Bryce said, when they were all standing in the alley's mud, and a couple of the men picked it up.

"Why?" Windsor asked. "It'll only slow us down."

Bryce drew a breath. "To make it harder for them to check out the lockup. Move!"

The men carrying the ladder bumped its end into a wall. Andrea spun round. "Ssh! Quiet!" She pointed upward. "There's a man on the watchtower." They were probably hidden from his view in the dark, narrow alleys, overhung with thatch, but strange sounds might alert him.

"Put the ladder over there," Bryce said. They'd turned a corner from the lockup, and the ladder, laid along another wall, wouldn't be found immediately.

"This way!" The tower's narrow streets wound in and out of the crowded outbuildings. Andrea was leading them toward the gate, not by the most direct way, but by the way that offered the most shadows and shelter. She wished that she could feel certain she was doing the right thing.

Coming up close behind her, Bryce whispered, "Will the gate be open?"

Windsor's voice chimed in from her other side. "It'll be locked and guarded. How are we going to get past?"

Andrea was shaking her head. The tower wasn't a castle under military discipline. "The gate'll probably be barred. I don't know about guards. With the feast, there probably won't be any."

"If there are," Bryce said, "we can deal with 'em."

That made Andrea feel twice as miserable. More than enough people had been hurt and killed—and what if the Sterkarms caught up with them just as they "dealt with" the guards? Why, she wondered, did I ever take this job?

Huddled at the end of a lane, they looked across a small open space, where stones had been trod into the mud to make a kind of paving. On its other side was the gate. A lantern hanging above it showed them that there were no guards. It also showed them the heavy bar set in place.

* * *

The guards Andrea had dismissed, entering the hall, found everyone gathered around the family table, some standing on benches to see over the heads of others. Several people were shouting above the babble of talk. The guards filled cups from jugs of ale left on abandoned tables, and joined the edges of the crowd. No one took any notice of them, or asked them why they were there.

Joe wasn't making much sense of it all. He could tell that Gobby was pretty much embattled, with even his sons seeming angry with him, but everyone was speaking too fast and shouting too much for him to be able to understand anything being said. He'd almost stopped worrying about it when Per jumped up from his father's chair, shoving Cuddy aside, and started shouting too. Joe's anxiety increased. He felt that the row must be escalating to some higher level, especially as Per was ranging himself alongside his uncle and shouting at his father. Both Gobby and Toorkild looked astounded.

Per had been roused by Sim's announcement that Per's wounding had been all Gobby's fault in the first place. This was an unexpected doubling back to an earlier squabble, and an accusation so shocking that it produced a few eye's blinks of silence, even from Isobel.

Sim, finding everyone staring at him, hurried to explain how Gobby had taken the leadership of the tower's men from Per and had then taunted and snubbed the lad until he'd been driven to do something reckless. All Gobby's fault.

A second silence fell. Sweet Milk, hearing his private opinion so aired, had turned his back on them all. Toorkild had glowered at Gobby, who looked stunned. Sim regretted having spoken.

Per, jumping up, shouted at Sim, "Thine empty head

rattles like a pebble in a pot!" His uncle was a brave and a good man, and to hear him accused of such disloyalty was more than Per could stand.

Besides, his actions were his own, and not attributable to Gobby's taunts. "It was Gobby got me *home*!"

Sweet Milk, who flattered himself that *he* had got Per home, turned around again.

Gobby, deserted by his own sons, and with tears in his eyes, put his arm around Per's shoulders. "Toorkild! Isobel, we've often not been the best of friends—but tha can't believe I'd wish any harm to my brother's-son! I love him like one of my own. I was never so glad as to see him come back to us whole and well."

Isobel looked as if she would have liked to deny it but hadn't the nerve. She turned away.

Toorkild looked confused and tired. He had no idea how things had come to his brother being accused of harming his son. He could think of nothing to say, and shook his head. Moving to his chair, he sat heavily and waved his hand in dismissal. "Into hell with the lot of you!"

The quarrel had worn itself out, leaving behind a listlessness. People went back to the benches and poured ale.

Gobby still had one arm draped across Per's shoulders. "Father's-brother, may I ask a favor?"

Gobby sighed. "What?"

"Daddy's-brother, be so kind, don't kill Elven."

Gobby dimly remembered that, what seemed days ago, at the beginning of this exhausting row, a similar favor had been asked. His eye glinted; he was about to refuse.

"If you kill them, my Elf-May'll be angry with me."

Gobby relaxed and grinned. "Is that it? That's the whole of it, is it?" His arm pulled Per closer. "I'm expected to rile my folk, and let a man's death go by, just so thee—"

"Daddy's-brother, be so kind. We can ransom them, and tha canst have it all, to make up for thy man."

Gobby laughed, hugged Per and thumped him on the back. "I can see thy daddy agreeing to that!"

Per went over to his father, pulling Gobby with him by the hand. "Daddy, Gobby can have all the ransom, can't he?"

Toorkild, who had been leaning his head in his hand, started up. "What?"

Per knelt beside his chair, leaning on its arm, and explained it to him. "Our prisoners," Toorkild said, "held in our lockup, at our cost, and I'm to ransom 'em and give all to Gobby?" He cuffed Per's head. "I'll send thee to deal for me at market."

"But Daddy—"

"It's to please the Elf-May," Gobby said.

"Is that it?" Toorkild and Gobby both laughed, and Per's face reddened. He thumped his head against his father's shoulder. "Daddy!"

"My folk'll no settle for ransom anyway," Gobby said. "They want the Elven's lives for their friend's life. If I took the ransom, they'd still give me trouble."

Toorkild was hankering after little white pills. "What if we hang half the Elven and ransom the others?"

Gobby nodded slowly. "Aye. And we divide the ransom? Aye. I could make my folk happy with that."

Toorkild turned to Per, kneeling at his side, and

pulled at a tuft of his hair. "Will that do for thee, tup?"

Per nodded, smiling. He thought it an excellent deal, the best that could be made, and Andrea would have to be pleased. "Aye! A thousand—ten thousand thanks, Daddy!" He kissed his father's cheek, got to his feet and kissed his uncle before going down the hall toward the stairs. Halfway there, he turned and came back, to bend over his father's chair. "Daddy, hast thou any wee white pills left?"

His father pressed a thick, hot hand over his brow. "Art sick?"

"Nay! It's for Entraya—she has the head pain."

Toorkild heaved at his belt, groping for the pouch he wore under his robe. "And tha wants to cure her head pain, aye."

Gobby laughed again. Toorkild found, in his pouch, a strip of white paper with aspirins sealed into it. Carefully he tore off two and gave them to Per. He gripped Per's wrist as he started away, holding him. "If she uses only one, bring me the other back." Per kissed him again and ran across the hall to the stairs. He didn't bother to take a candle or lantern. Cuddy, under the table, roused with a yap, got up, shook herself and ran after him.

She overtook him on the steps and reached the basement before him, making the horses shift and stamp. Together they crossed the yard toward the bower where Andrea slept. It was dark, but Per knew his way.

Cuddy growled faintly. Looking at her, Per saw her ears cocked and a faint glimmer of teeth as her lip lifted. "What dost hear?" He stopped and listened but couldn't hear anything but the murmur of talk and laughter from the hall above. The quiet and darkness, even the chill, of the yard seemed to increase. If an armed force were approaching the tower, the dogs who guarded the sheep would be hollering from the valley. Maybe Cuddy was growling at the ghosts of the Elven who'd been killed. Did Elven have ghosts? Better to get close to a living Elf than stand in the dark wondering about that. Per ran on into the alleys, and Cuddy hurried after him.

The ladder was in place at Andrea's bower, left for him to climb. He did so, and knocked at the door. Cuddy reared up, her forepaws resting on the same rung as his feet. "Entraya?" No answer. No light shone through the latch hole: She had blown out her candle and gone to bed. Maybe she really had a head pain. He knocked again and called her name. No answer.

He put his finger through the latch hole and lifted the latch, half expecting the door to be bolted, but the door swung inward. His heart began to beat faster as he stepped inside.

> Oh pleasant thoughts come to my mind,
> As I turn back the sheets so fine,
> And her two white breasts are standing so,
> Like sweet pink roses that bloom in snow.

The room was in deep darkness, but smelled of wood and straw, and of Andrea—there was an Elvish perfume that clung to her things. He stumbled against the bed and felt over it with his hands, raising a thicker scent of hay from the mattress, mixed with a stronger whiff of Andrea. The bed was empty.

He straightened. "Entraya?" But the room was empty. The way his voice sounded told him so.

Where was she? Crouching, he felt under the bed and touched the cold earthenware of a chamber pot. So she had no need to go to the privy. Still crouching, he leaned his chin in his hand and said to Cuddy, "Where's Entraya? Entraya!"

In the dim light from the open door he could see Cuddy sitting on her haunches. When he spoke, she cocked her ears and her eyes brightened. Stretching out her neck, she gave his face a couple of gentle licks.

Andrea could only have gone to another bower. At the thought, he seemed to breathe in anger—but she wouldn't, not Andrea. The Elven! She'd gone to see if the guards would let her talk to the Elven, to let them know they might not be hanged. That was like her. She was kind.

He could go to meet her, and give her the pills, offer to see her safely back to her bower . . .

"Entraya! Find Entraya!" Cuddy bounded to the door, and he rose and followed her. Cuddy was a gaze-hound, hunting by sight rather than scent, but like all hounds, she had keen senses of smell and hearing. She would hear a footstep or a whisper when a man wouldn't. Per had taught her to know Andrea by name, and she knew her step and her voice as well as her smell. Leaping to the ground, Cuddy raced away into the darkness.

Per slid down the ladder and whistled for her, and she came cantering back from the dark and jumped at him, knocking him back against the wall, her paws heavy on his shoulders. "Entraya!" he said, and she bounded away again. He ran after her, his boots sticking in mud, trying to keep her dark, moving shape in sight.

Andrea went forward alone, out of the alleyway, across the little open space in front of the gatehouse, into the lantern's light. There'd been some whispered argument about whether this area would be visible to the watchman at the top of the tower. One opinion was that of course it would, another was that the buildings between the tower and the gate would block the view.

"We have to assume it *is* visible," Bryce said. Assuming that, the only one among them with a chance of crossing it without arousing suspicion was Andrea. If she could take down the lantern, so the space was unlit, the rest of them might be able to unbar the gate.

She was tall, and taking the lantern down from its hook wasn't difficult, though she felt that she was glowing in the dark and setting off sirens. Her hands were already trembling in expectation of a shout from the watchtower.

As she left the gate, she heard a scampering and panting behind her, and her heart lurched with fright. She whipped around to face the sound, and a big, dark shape rose from the ground, gave her a hefty shove on the shoulders, driving her back on her heels, panting in her face with hot, stinking breath.

She went staggering back under the thing's weight, but almost laughed, because she knew what it was. "Cuddy! Oh, Cuddy, you gave me a fright!"

Cuddy leaped away from her and leaped back again and, as the hound danced in the dark, Andrea's breath caught and her relief curdled into another kind of fear. Cuddy, unless she was taken and locked up, was never far from Per. If Cuddy was here . . .

She looked toward the alley where Bryce and the others hid. In the darkness, she glimpsed the hazy gray blurs that were their faces.

She glanced back toward the other dark alleys that opened between the many buildings. Out of their darkness came Per's whistle, and the sound of his running feet.

"Cuddy!" he called. "Entraya!"

21

∽

16th Side: "Sterkarm!"

THE ALLEY PER WAS following, pursuing Cuddy, ended at the tower's gate. "Cuddy!" She must still be intent on chasing Elf-Ghosts, or maybe she could hear a fox outside the walls. Andrea wouldn't be at the gate.

But as he emerged from the narrow alleyway, fending himself off the wall, he saw Andrea standing in front of him. She had Cuddy's collar in one hand and was being pulled a few steps this way and that as the hound, growling, made lunges toward the alleys. In her other hand was the lantern that should have been hanging over the gateway, its light swinging low about her feet. As the light briefly swung high enough to show her face, he saw that she looked scared half to death, as if she'd been caught doing something wrong. He went to her, laughing, asking, "What's the matter?" He was startled, and he sidestepped, when Cuddy gave a loud, shivering growl.

A sound behind him, a nudge and, before he could turn, something hard against his throat, yanking him backward against solidity. He made to smack his right elbow backward, but his arm was entangled, held. A man's arm around his neck: He felt the warm flesh, and his fingers slipped on the hair. Sweet Milk playing a joke! But the movement around him in the darkness, Cuddy's snarling, the sounds of breathing and of feet in the mud told him that there were many men, and strangers—Grannams! Inside the tower walls!

He reached for his dagger with his left hand, but the arm was caught and pulled partly behind him. He snatched breath to shout, and a large, heavy hand smacked across his mouth and clamped there, sealing in the breath and reducing his shout to an incomprehensible moan.

Per reacted with fury. That the Grannams should dare! His head was being held against the shoulder of the man behind him, but he smashed his skull sidelong into his captor's face. It hurt, but he knew by the gasp in his ear, and the loosening of the hold on him, that he'd hurt the man holding him more. He kicked backward at the man's shins, scraped the heel of his boot down the shin and stamped hard, hoping to smash the man's foot. With more gasps of pain, the man shuffled backward, out of reach. Per's arms were still held, but he was all but free. He lifted his head, and drew breath to shout.

The darkness moved, in the shape of a big man in front of him. Something was said, in no tongue of the Grannams, and a fist driven hard into Per's belly.

What breath he had left him in a long groan, and the pain and shock of the blow made it impossible to draw another. His legs buckled and the man behind him came close again, leaned on him, and pushed him down into the mud. His arms were twisted behind him, and a weight settled heavily on his back. Somewhere nearby,

Cuddy's growling had changed to a wheezing.

Per strained for air, choking, his face turned sidelong in the dirt. His lungs seemed turned to stone, refusing to open. He struggled, trying to free his arms, but they were at their weakest, pulled behind him. He tried to get his knees under him, to throw off the weight that held him down, but the effort and lack of air dizzied him, making the darkness flicker with white flashes. So he lay still and made repeated hoarse snatches for air. He knew he'd been outwitted, beaten, and had let attackers into his home. He was afraid for Cuddy and Andrea, and then for his mother, his father, his cousins and uncle and everyone he'd failed. It made him furious, and the angrier he grew, the more his helplessness enraged him.

Andrea spoke near him, urgently. He couldn't understand what she said but recognized the slippery, hissing sound of the Elven language. Surprise made him lie still and silent for a moment. His captors were not Grannams. They were Elves. Either the prisoners escaped, or others come to rescue them. And Andrea was helping them.

The realization was another defeat. He felt anger rise in him until, with his already hard-thumping heart, it was like a blockage in the throat, stifling. The lantern light turned dark in his eyes. He gasped for breath, and struggled again. If his heart burst, if his joints cracked, he didn't care. He spread his legs, pressing his knees and toes into the ground, trying to lift up and twist his hips, to throw off the man on his back. He pressed his head into the mud, arching his spine.

Bryce, sitting astride Per, had a glow of pain on his face where Per's skull had smacked into his cheekbone and nose; and another glow of pain down his shin, where Per's boot heel had kicked and scraped. But he'd thought Per beaten, and was taken aback by this sudden and fierce coming to life. He twisted Per's arms higher, but the body beneath him still bucked like a bronco and almost threw him off. "Get his legs, get his—"

One of his men grabbed Per's legs, held them, lay on them. Another pressed Per's head down into the mud. Sobbing for breath, Per subsided again. "Bastard!" Bryce said, and wiped his bleeding nose on the shoulder of his shirt.

Andrea was swinging the lantern erratically. It showed her Cuddy, teeth locked in a man's arm, and another man squeezing her throat between his hands. It showed her Per panting in the mud with three men holding him down. "Don't hurt him! He's only a boy—"

From the darkness near her, Windsor said, with satisfaction, "I've already hurt him." She glimpsed him miming the action of a punch.

She could hear Per fighting for breath, and it reminded her distressingly of when he'd been bleeding to death. "You haven't hurt—?"

"Whose side are you on?" Bryce was out of breath too.

Andrea crouched beside them. Per, his face turned sideways on the ground and masked with mud, was hardly recognizable. His narrowed eyes glittered in the lantern light, and he breathed in strange, hiccuping little gasps. "Don't you know who you've caught? It's Per—Per Toorkildsson. The May."

Bryce's head jerked up.

"Don't hurt him." She meant—the word was large in

her mind, though she wouldn't say it—don't kill him. "Listen, if we don't make it to the Tube—if Toorkild catches us, and you've hurt Per—I can't even bear to think about what Toorkild will do to us."

"Keep your voice down," Bryce said. "Everybody!" The man who'd been bitten was breathing hard with a sobbing sound. Faintly, seeming miles away, came shouting, laughter and what might have been music from the tower. Their struggles, though desperately loud in their own ears, must have been swallowed up among the stone and thatch of the surrounding buildings and had passed as the usual nighttime noises of the tower. Bryce said, "Are you wearing those hiking boots?"

"What?" Andrea said. It seemed a strange question. "Yes."

"Give me a bootlace. Do it!"

She was baffled but tugged at the lace of her right boot, pulling it undone and unthreading it from the six iron loops. It was thick, strong and very long. Pulling it free, she handed it to Bryce.

"Hold him," Bryce said to the men holding Per's head and legs, and he used the bootlace to lash Per's arms together at the elbows.

Per hadn't yet recovered his breath, but knew that once tied, he would have even less chance of getting away. He struggled again, trying to pull his arms free of the lace being wound around them, trying to lift his head, to kick. It was a waste of strength and breath. He grunted as his shoulders were dragged further back and the lace bit into his arms. His eyes filled with tears of rage that mixed with the mud on his face.

463

"Okay, get off him." The two other men moved away, and Bryce, grasping Per by the collar, hauled him up to his knees, his legs folded under him. Bryce felt about his waist, found his belt, followed it and said, "Ah!" as he found Per's dagger. "Good man!"

Their prisoner surprised them all by calling out softly, as if he was quite alone, though his voice was broken by breathlessness. "Cuddy? Cud—?"

Bryce clamped his hand over Per's mouth, pulling his head back against his shoulder, and showed him his own dagger. "Tell him to keep quiet!"

Despite the knife, Per was twisting his head, trying to get his mouth free—but Bryce's hand had sealed to the mud on his face and was glued in place. "You're choking him," Andrea said. "*Per—stilla!*" Quiet! "*Han har thine kneefa!*"

Per was still, and Bryce loosed his hand a little, to let him breathe. Looking straight ahead, not trying to look at Andrea, Per whispered, "*Vordan staw Cuddy?*"

"What's he say?"

"It's his dog, he's asking about his dog." She moved the lantern so its light fell where she'd last seen Cuddy. There was a huddle of men, one clutching his bleeding arm. On the ground in front of them lay a long gray shape, its ruffled fur muddied.

Per made a lurching movement, trying to get to his feet. Bryce dragged him back and clamped his hand hard over his mouth again. He said, "Is it bad?"

The man grimaced. "Hurts."

"You've got to keep going," Bryce said. The man nodded.

Andrea had gone to Cuddy and was running her

hands through the long hair. The hound was still warm, and she thought she could feel the rib cage moving, but that might just have been wishful thinking. "Have you killed her?"

The man crouched beside the bitten one said, "Might have done—dunno."

Bryce said, "It's *his* dog?" He threw Per's dagger over to the men huddled by Cuddy. Per, by the lantern's light, saw his dagger land in the mud and guessed what it was to be used for. He made another convulsive attempt to rise, but Bryce held him and pinched his nose shut as well as covering his mouth. Remembering the word Andrea had used, he said, "Still—or else." Threatened with suffocation, Per stopped fighting, and Bryce let him breathe again. "Make sure it's dead," Bryce said. "Last thing we want is it coming round and following us."

The man who'd throttled Cuddy picked the dagger up but then just held it. He was prepared to shoot people with automatic rifles, it seemed, but not to stab a dog. "Kill it!" Bryce said.

Windsor took the dagger and knelt over the hound. Andrea turned sharply away but still heard the sounds of the dagger tearing into Cuddy, its hilt banging on her ribs. "Cut its throat!" Bryce said.

A painful sorrow for Cuddy filled Andrea. Poor Cuddy, who'd adored Per as a blend of pack leader and pup, and had never known or cared what danger she was in, set only on protecting him. Then she heard another sound: a choked, grunting, coughing sound that, when she realized what it was, made the pain in her heart well-nigh unbearable. It was Per, sobbing.

Windsor walked over to Bryce and handed him back

465

the dagger. He was panting, and his heart was beating fast. Killing the dog had been hard work because he'd never killed anything before, and he'd thought the only way had been to go at it hard, with all his strength. He was shaking, and the sticky, greasy blood on his hands was disgusting. But he'd done it. He felt proud, exhilarated.

Per looked up at him, staring. The boy's face was plastered with mud, but the lantern light caught the eyes, fixed on him. They seemed huge, with only a thin ring of pale blue around the dark centers. Tears were glinting in them.

"You broke off the point," Bryce said.

Windsor laughed, boastful and appalled and scared, but quickly smothered the sound. He gave Per's face several rapid, sharp slaps, and said, "What d'you think of that?"

Per twisted his head and bit at Windsor's hand. He succeeded in nipping the flesh of a finger between his teeth before Windsor snatched his hand away and swung it to deliver a blow.

Bryce swore and hauled Per to his feet, yanking him away from Windsor. He put the edge of the dagger to Per's throat. "Get that bloody gate open!"

The men rose and, leaving the lantern light behind, moved to the gate, dim shapes in darkness. Andrea went close to Per and Bryce, meaning to try and say something to Per—but he gave her such a straight, stony stare that she felt ashamed, even guilty, and looked away.

They heard the sound of the gate's bar being lifted. From above, ringing through the dark upper air, shocking them all into silence and stillness, came a voice from the tower's height. *"Vem air day?"* Who's there?

Per gasped, and Bryce pressed the dagger's blade harder against his neck. Andrea, though her heart thumped, realized that the watchman's voice wasn't too alarmed. He'd heard something but, if answered, would be satisfied. Taking a deep, shaky breath, she cupped her hands about her mouth and shouted, *"Olla air rikti, min fen. Air Per oh yi."* All's well, my friend. It's Per and I! From the top of the tower came a laugh. She didn't dare look at Per.

The men were struggling with the gate, lifting it up so it wouldn't drag and make a noise. Bryce nudged Per forward. With his arms tied and the knife blade scraping his throat, Per went. His mind was racing like a river in spate, too full of Andrea's treachery and Cuddy's butchering and his own failure to think. . . .

The gate was opened narrowly, and they edged through. "Ditch the lantern," Bryce said to Andrea. "They'll see the light." The land in front of them looked terrifying, impenetrably black, but she set the lantern down just outside the gate.

They were at the top of the steep, rough path that led down the tower's crag. The night was colder, now they were out from behind the shelter of the walls. A cold wind whipped past them.

The lantern, flickering behind them, was no help in descending the steep path. Holding their breath, they went forward step by step, feeling for each foothold on the pitch-black ground, never knowing when a loose stone was going to throw them down. We're not even going to make it to the bottom of the crag, Andrea thought.

Bryce slipped, muttered, clutched and dragged at Per's arm. Their feet kept getting tangled. He took his arm from around Per's neck—he didn't want to stumble and slit his prisoner's throat by accident. Keeping a tight grip on one of Per's arms, he pulled him along behind him.

Per sucked in one deep breath after another. The wind chilled the mud and tears on his face; his muscles trembled from effort; his lungs still felt stiff and ached; his belly still felt Windsor's blow; but his mind was set: The Elves were not going to get away. Treacherous Andrea, Cuddy's killer, was not going to get away.

Per knew the path better than any of them could imagine. At about midway was a wide shelf, made by an outcrop of stone projecting from the earth. He knew it when, pulled by Bryce, he half fell, half jumped down onto it. To the left of it, he knew, was a hollow, filled with low scrub, dead nettles and other herbage. In the dark, blind, he leaped into it.

He pulled Bryce off balance, and to save himself, Bryce let him go but still fell, smacking his hands down hard on the gritty rock. His legs, kicking out, knocked the man in front of him flying, with a cry.

Per landed hard too, in bushes that whipped him with their branches and briers that gave him fine, smarting scratches. His arms were fastened behind him, and his shoulders were wrenched as he landed. The fall knocked the breath out of him again, but he gulped for air and yelled, in a voice he'd learned to make carry across valleys, "Arm! Arm!"

Andrea's head jerked around. She was at the bottom of the crag but scrambled back up the path as fast as she could, colliding with confused men, pushing them aside.

They would kill Per, they'd kill him!

Through the darkness, blaring like a trumpet, came Per's voice. "Sterkarm! Sterkarm!"

She heard Bryce's voice ahead, and a scrabbling of hands and feet. "Get him! Shut him up!"

"Don't hurt him!" Andrea wailed.

From the tower's height came a clamor, a ringing clamor, showering down through the air to the ground. The clumsy, tuneless bell was being rung frantically. Another voice, stronger than Per's, less hampered by lack of breath, bawled, "Sterkarm! Sterkarm! Arm! Arm!"

22

16th Side: Hard Going

I N THE HALL, the people were dancing to the beat of a drum and the music of an elbow-pipe. Joe stood among the onlookers, watching the dancers circle and interweave and whirl about. The music was toe-tapping stuff, and he grinned at the people on either side of him, who laughed back.

The shouting of the watchman, even the ringing of the bell, went unnoticed among the stamping of the dancers, the music, the clapping and laughter. It was two tired women, stepping out into the yard on their way to bed, who heard the clangor from the top of the tower. They turned and ran back up the tower's stairs.

Inside they yelled for silence and shouted out their news, but their voices were lost. They caught the arms of people near them and yelled the warning into their faces, but were waved away. One of them fought her way through the crowd and dragged the drum out of its owner's hands.

"Harken!" Some of those nearest, who had seen her struggle with the drummer, fell silent and looked where she pointed. From them the silence spread, and the ding and clang of the bell broke through.

Toorkild banged on the table with his cup and roared for silence. The last chatter died away, the dancers stopped. Joe looked around at faces still hot and wet, but transformed with alarm.

From outside, dulled by the stone walls, came the shout of the watchman: "Sterkarm! Arm!"

Joe was knocked sideways, shoved again, spun as all around him men and women burst into movement and outcry. Watching the people scatter, he thought: Oh God, this is what Andrea warned me about! We're being attacked. They'll want me to fight.

His heart picked up speed. He thought: I swore an oath and I have that house and land to earn. He ran down the tower steps and out into the yard, looking for Per or Toorkild. If he stuck close by one of them, he figured, he'd be most likely to find out what was going on, and he might be noticed, remembered. Rewarded.

His heart still thumped heavily, but he told himself, All through history, thousands of men have gone into battle and survived. And I'm a Sterkarm too. If they can face it—if a kid like Per can face it—then I'm sure as hell big enough and ugly enough to cope.

* * *

Andrea scrambled down into the hollow beside the tower's path, slipping in the dark, scratching her hands, banging her knee on a rock. Bryce was ahead of her somewhere, and she could hear other men crashing through the low scrub beside her and behind her.

"Got him!" Bryce said, ahead, in the darkness of the hollow; and there was the crunching of feet, scuffling, the sounds of blows. Other men—angry men—went leaping past her.

She shouted, "Stop it! Don't hurt him, leave him!" Reaching them, she pulled at their shirts, their arms. An elbow caught her on the cheek and the pain silenced her for a moment, but then she dived forward again. A gap opened in the fence of bodies and she buffeted through it and reached Per. Even in the dark she knew him, by his smell and by his tied arms. She held on to him, trying to shield him from the others. Her chin on his shoulder, she shouted, "They'll be out after us! You need him unhurt! Toorkild will make you pay ten times over for anything you do to Per!"

Per was shaking in her arms, laughing breathlessly. How he could be laughing she didn't know, but he couldn't have done anything better calculated to get himself beaten up. She could feel the anger growing around her as the other men pressed close, could feel the bunching of their muscles. She shook Per as hard as she could.

"Let's get out of here!" Bryce said. He dragged at Per's arm. "Let go of him, for God's sake!" As Andrea drew back from Per, others reached past her to grasp at his clothes and drag him along. Bryce used his arm to block a swing aimed at Per's head. "Haven't you got ears? Nobody touches him. Move!"

The clanging of the bell and the yelling of the watchman still sounded from the tower, but there seemed to be no rush of Sterkarms in answer to it. Blundering into briers, squelching in mud, tripping on rock, slithering on the slope, they clambered and hauled themselves out of the hollow. Per, his arms tied, slipped and fell, and Bryce hauled him bodily to the hollow's lip, where he crouched beside him a moment, to grab a few breaths.

"I lost the bloody knife," he said. "Haven't even got a bloody knife." Ignoring his own orders, he clouted Per's head with a dully ringing thump. Per laughed, amused, it seemed, at having caused so much annoyance. Andrea pressed her hands together and hoped Per's sense of humor didn't get him beaten insensible.

Bryce heaved Per to his feet and pushed him on down the side of the crag to the smoother hillside below. "I'll make you laugh on the other side of your face, friend!"

From behind them, from the tower, came an outburst of shouting, as if a door had been opened, letting sound flood out. They all turned toward it. Per laughed again, and Windsor smacked him across the mouth.

"Move!" Bryce said. He started away, dragging Per with him. Per hung back, allowing himself to fall to the ground as his feet slipped on the short, smooth grass. When Bryce tried to lift him, he made himself a dead weight. "Help me with him!" Windsor jumped to help, taking Per's other arm and wrenching it enough to make Per gasp as they heaved him up between them and set him on his feet.

Bryce was trying to remember the maps he'd studied. To one side was the gentler slope they'd brought the Land Rovers up, following the path worn by the Sterk-arms. If they still had a Land Rover, he'd have gone that way, but on foot it would be fatal. They'd be seen and followed too easily.

To the other side was a steep, narrow cleft in the hillside. He remembered seeing it by daylight, strewn with rocks. Hard travel, but harder for their pursuers too.

More places to hide. To Andrea, nodding toward the decline, he said, "This comes out in the valley? There's a way down?"

"Yes." She went down that way sometimes. By daylight.

"Then come on."

* * *

Joe found Toorkild standing under the tower, yelling up at the watchman, who leaned over the parapet and pointed. Against the luminous dark blue of the night sky, the black shape of his arm could be seen. "By the gate," he shouted. Joe understood that. He didn't catch the rest.

Somebody trying to break in at the gate? Oh God! Joe thought, can I fight like this, with weapons—with axes for chopping and spears for stabbing? Things could get hairy on the streets, and he'd threatened to punch, and had punched, a couple of people. But looking thickset and rough had always helped him to avoid trouble, and he'd never got into anything serious. This would be different. No talking your way out of this. Please don't let me piss meself or run away!

Toorkild shouted for lights and made for the gate. Joe kept close by him. People came crowding behind them, and many others could be heard shouting and trampling their way along other lanes.

Someone with a lantern got there before them, and was shining the light on the gate's bar lying in the mud—but the gate itself was closed. *"Erpent fra i hayer,"* someone said, which Joe's ear caught easily: Opened from in here.

Joe, taking a step backward, caught his heel on something and staggered. He had to lean on a wall to stop himself falling. Crouching, he felt for what had tripped him and touched hairy, solid flesh. An animal. "*Hayer!*" he said, beckoning to the lantern holder.

The light shone on gray fur. A big, lean hound. Black blood, open wounds. Toorkild looked and said, "Where's Per?" When people only crowded around to stare at the dead hound, and no one answered, he raised his voice. "Where's my son?"

"Grannams!" Gobby said. "They climbed over the wall and opened the gate! Why'd tha no set a better watch?"

Toorkild swung toward him and opened his mouth—but then turned away and, cupping his hands round his mouth, bellowed, "Per! Per!" The yells struck some wall and echoed faintly, dully.

Sweet Milk came out of an alley, carrying a lantern. "Prisoners have gone. They was let out."

"I'll hang the guards," Toorkild said. He swung back to Gobby. "They've got him, they've taken him." He pulled open the gate and went out onto the path. Joe pushed forward and got through the gate close behind him.

Sweet Milk went down the path ahead of everyone, shining his lantern at his feet. He stooped, straightened and held up a dagger with a broken tip. Toorkild snatched it from him and showed it to Gobby, pointing to the broken blade and the blood drying on it.

Joe watched both their faces become strained. He looked around and saw, on faces shadowed and distorted by shifting lantern light, the same expressions of anxiety and anger. And something came through the air to him, soaking into him, hardening his muscles, sending blood to his head: an Us-against-Them anger. It was as if the hairs on his head were picking it up as it was being broadcast through the air. Per's a nice kid, he found himself thinking. Helped me, brought me here. I swore an oath to him.

Toorkild seized a man by a handful of his jerkin and shook him, putting the dagger to his face. "Tha left thy guard!"

"The girl—she said—"

"What?"

"Said you'd sent her to tell us to come in—honest!"

"Entraya?" Toorkild said. "The *Elf-May*? And tha believed her?"

"She said you'd sent her!"

Toorkild shoved him away hard. "Fetch horses! I'll kill her too." He ran down the path from the crag to the gentler slope below, never putting a foot wrong even in the dark. At the bottom he filled his lungs and bellowed, "Sterkarm!" The yell rang away into the dark.

* * *

Andrea and Per were wearing boots, which protected them from a lot. One of hers was unlaced and slipped about on her foot in an irritating way that she suspected would soon give her blisters, but the other men were all barefoot, and she could hear them groaning and hissing in the darkness as their toes and ankles were bashed on rocks, as the harsh, strong growth of bilberries scratched them, as the tough bracken stems cut like razors.

Per seemed hardly able to keep his feet. Every few steps he slipped and fell. Bryce and Windsor wrenched at his arms, trying to keep him on his feet, but he would become a limp dead weight. He persisted in it, even though Windsor cuffed his head every time. Andrea winced when she heard another dull thump to Per's skull, or the softer thump as Per succeeded in dragging them down again, often with them both landing on him. Andrea didn't understand how he could go on inviting such punishment. She wanted to plead with him to stop, to behave, but doubted he would listen.

And then came Toorkild's yell. Per twisted his head around and yelled, "*Sterkarm! Hayer! Sterk!*"

"Jesus Christ!" Bryce forced Per down, flat on his back on the slope, pressing his hand over his mouth. "Fill this in! A gag!"

"A little late," Windsor said.

"Yes, a little late! Now how about finding something to— Andrea! Give us one of your socks and your other bootlace!"

Andrea came scrambling back up the slope. "You can't gag him with a sock! Let me talk—"

"Shouldn't we be moving?" Windsor was peering into the darkness above them.

"No discussions!" Bryce said. "Give me the sock and bootlace!"

Andrea took her foot out of her unlaced boot and pulled off the sock, and knelt to unfasten the other lace as fast as she could. Great! Both of her boots would be loose and flapping.

Bryce took the sock—a thick, long, knee-length walker's sock, which Andrea had worn for several days—and tried to push it into Per's mouth. Per turned his head aside and clenched his teeth, and kicked, until Bryce sat on his legs. Windsor pressed on the sides of

Per's jaw but couldn't make him open his mouth. "They're going to catch us!"

"They're going to anyway!" Bryce said. "When they do, *I* want to be the one talking, not him!" He pinched Per's nose shut.

Per resisted as long as he could, and even then tried to open his mouth only for long enough to snatch a breath. But Bryce was ready, and stuffed folds of the sock between his teeth, though much of it was left hanging from his mouth. Per twisted his head, and retched, and tried to push the sock out with his tongue, but Bryce held his jaw. He passed the bootlace to Windsor. "Tie that around."

Windsor obeyed with alacrity, wrapping the long lace twice around Per's head, before tying it. Per retched again, and his nostrils flared as he tried to suck in air. "You're going to kill him!" Andrea said. She imagined that hairy wool stuffed into her own mouth, and felt like retching herself.

"Good," Windsor said. He and Bryce lifted Per to his feet again, and Windsor gave his head another cuff.

"Leave him *alone*!" Andrea said, and pushed Windsor, as one angry child in a playground might push another.

She sat down on the hard earth with a thump that jarred all her bones and put her hand to her smarting mouth. Her eyes filling with tears, she realized that Windsor had backhanded her hard enough to make her lose her footing on the steep slope. His knuckles had cut her lip against her teeth.

Per, stumbling as Bryce dragged him backward down the slope, and retching convulsively over the gag in his mouth, never took his eyes from Windsor.

Joe was standing behind Toorkild and Gobby when they heard Per's answering shout come back from the narrow valley below them. The second shout was stifled.

"He lives!" Toorkild said. He turned back to the tower but found Isobel behind him, with his jakke, his boots and his helmet in her arms. His sword, in its scabbard, was slung over her shoulder, and his lance was carried, awkwardly, by a maid.

Horses, saddled and bridled, were being led down from the tower. Men were putting on their jakkes and helmets, or slinging quivers of arrows from saddlebows.

I can't ride, Joe thought. I don't have a sword or a lance. Couldn't use it if I had. He was surprised to find himself disappointed at not being part of what was going on around him. He was a Sterkarm. Per was one of his; he had a right to be included. He didn't want to be left out, even if it would mean being safe.

Toorkild had struggled into his jakke, and Isobel was bending down so he could lean on her while he stepped into his long boots, which she held for him. She helped him pull them up.

"If they hurt Per," Ingram said. "If they hurt him . . ."

"We can't take the horses down there," Wat said.

"Shut up and listen," Gobby said. "An eye's blink of thought is worth a day's march. Think: Why have they lumbered themselves with Per?"

"No bloody riddles!" Toorkild said. Isobel was helping him on with his other boot. "Say tha piece!"

"They'll no hurt him while they think they're getting away," Gobby said. "It's if we press 'em too close that he'll be in danger."

Toorkild stamped his feet into his boots. "I want my son back!"

"I want my brother's-son back. And I know how to get him back whole."

Isobel, out of breath from her struggles with the boots and from supporting Toorkild's weight, said, "Harken to him, Toorkild."

Gobby said, "We know which way they're going, and we know where they're going. Have tha weapon's stores been broken into?"

"Nay," Sweet Milk said.

"Then they've no weapons. No boots to their feet. It'll take them all night. We can be at the ford long before them." Gobby watched his audience looking at each other and nodding. They all knew there was only one place within miles to cross Bedes Water. "If we don't get Per back at the ford, well, we'll have men sitting at their Gate. We'll let them go right to it."

Toorkild hissed through his teeth. "Let my little lad stay in their hands that long!"

"Tell me, Toorkild," Gobby said, "when we get Per back, what wilt do to Elven?"

"Cut 'em into gobbets no bigger than peas."

"Aye. If thee was them, wouldst give him up? For owt? As long as they think they can get away, he's safe. He's the only thing they have to bargain with. It's when they're cornered we have to worry."

"And that'll be at the Gate!" Toorkild said. "What's to stop 'em killing him then?" Isobel moaned and clutched at his arm.

"Nowt," Gobby admitted. "But they'll have the Gate in sight. They'll think they're all but home. It'll be easier to talk them into giving him up then."

Isobel struck her husband on the chest. "That's sense! Harken to him!"

Toorkild put his arms round her, hugging her to stop her hitting him. To Gobby, he said, "I'm not letting them go."

Gobby laughed. "Think I will? Gobbets no bigger than grain!"

Toorkild nodded, and a short time after that all the men with horses were mounted. Carrying their long lances upright, they rode slowly away down the tower's path, fading and melting into the darkness. Only faint sounds of hoof tread and harness came drifting back.

Joe watched them disappear, feeling as if he'd been left out of a party. You're better off, he told himself. You'll live a bit longer. But his heart beat and his thoughts ran with its beat. What was it like, to fight with the Sterkarms? He was a Sterkarm, but was he brave enough?

Isobel ran back into the tower and opened up storerooms. She armed everyone—women and old men, young lads and menservants—with sickles and scythes, with axes, long knives, staves: anything heavy or sharp that might serve as a weapon. Joe got an axe.

Isobel kilted her skirts to her knees and led her army out of the tower gate and down the hill, following after the horsemen. She stood to one side of the path, watching them go past her in the dark. As Joe went by, Isobel was saying, "And Entraya, that Elf!" She raised the cleaver in her hand. "I'll make dog's meat of her."

481

23

16th Side: Making Up

"PER, BE SO KIND, listen. Per . . ."

Andrea felt wretched. She was shivering with cold, but her hands and knees glowed with the heat of grazed skin. Her hips and bum and thighs ached from falls on hard ground or rock. Her boots had protected her from toe stubbings but, unlaced, had moved on her feet and rubbed them into hot sores. Trying to climb down the steep streambed in the dark had been disastrous.

Worse than her own stumblings and bruises had been listening to Per retching and coughing and gasping for breath through the sock that she'd handed over to gag him. Occasionally moonlight had filtered down into the dark, narrow valley and, in shades of gray and gray-blue, had shown her Per twisting and tossing his head like a fly-bothered horse, uselessly trying to rid himself of the tormenting gag. The cord tying his elbows and pulling them so awkwardly behind his back had to hurt too. All the time they'd struggled over and between the stones and boulders, she'd ached with misery for him and had longed to help, but hadn't even been able to keep up as Bryce tugged Per along by the belt, often pulling him off his feet. Every time Per had fallen, she'd known exactly how much it hurt, from falling herself.

She'd tried telling herself that she should be thinking of the poor men who'd been killed, and of the men with her, who were just as bruised and cold and scared, but she knew and loved Per better than any of those men, and every time she heard him retch or gasp, she wanted to take hold of him and help him, and couldn't.

Bryce called a halt when he was sure no one had followed them into the valley. They'd called softly to each other until they were all gathered in the shelter of a great lump of rock as big as a house. Sitting on the rubble of smaller rocks beneath it, they huddled together, trying to share warmth, since it was a damp, chilly night, and most of them were in shirtsleeves and barefoot. Andrea had squeezed in between Per and Bryce, her bruises painful against the rock.

None of them were comfortable, but Per, with his arms wrenched behind him, had been unable to lean back or sit up straight or lie down—and they could hear him constantly munching at the gag, and retching and coughing.

"Please," Andrea had said to Bryce, "couldn't you untie him? He can't get away with you all here, and the better we treat him, the better—"

"Okay!" Bryce had said. With the other men standing guard, he'd untied Per's arms, and then tied his wrists together. His arms were still behind his back, but more comfortable.

"Thank you," Andrea had said, and had let a few minutes pass before saying, "Could you take out his gag?

I mean, he's not going—"

"Do it," Windsor said. "I'm sick of listening to that noise."

Sighing, Bryce had roughly shoved down Per's head, so he could reach the knot in the cord holding the gag. Unable to undo it in the dark, he'd wrenched the cord over Per's head, tearing at his hair, and tugged a length of sodden sock from between Per's teeth.

After first drawing a long deep breath, Per had coughed and worked his jaw. "*Tahk*."

"What's he say?"

"Thanks," Andrea had said. "He says thanks."

Bryce had been amused. "He's polite, I'll give him that. Tell him the minute he gives me any grief, I'll ram this sock so far down his throat that—well, you get the idea." He stuffed the sodden sock and lace into his pocket.

"*Per, thu maun nigh tala*." Thou must not talk.

Per had refused to answer her then, as he was refusing now. In the faint light, where his head was merely a denser darkness against darkness, she could tell that his face was turned away from her. But her side was pressed against his, her thigh against his, and she could tell by the braced tension in his body that he was aware of her.

"Per, I'm sad for what happened. Harken to me, be so kind. I got them to take the gag away, didn't I? Per—"

"What are you saying to him?" Bryce asked, from her other side.

"Nothing!"

"Shut up then. There's nothing he needs to know."

Andrea wanted to say: I need him to know that I

didn't lay a trap for him. Even if they never saw each other again after tonight—especially if they never saw each other again—she needed him to know that. But she couldn't say that to Bryce. She couldn't say it where Windsor might overhear.

Per worked a bit of wool out from between his teeth and lip, and spat it out. His face ached from his jaws having been held open for so long by the gag, and the retching and coughing had left his throat so strained and sore that he didn't think he'd be able to do more than whisper.

He hunched and relaxed his shoulders, trying to ease the ache in them. Trying to pull his hands apart only made the cord tighten around his wrists. The Elven knew about knots.

"Per?" It was Andrea's voice, spoken hardly louder than a breath, close by his ear. The breath stirred his hair against his skin and he shivered. His throat closed, his eyes filled with tears.

> I set my back against an oak,
> Thinking it a strong and trusty tree.
> But first it bent, and then it broke,
> And so did my true love to me.

He'd been captured because he'd trusted that where she was, there could be no danger for him. Because of her, Cuddy was dead. Even when she'd kissed him, she'd been lying to him.

"Per." They were touching, but only because all of them were crowded so close in the shelter of the rock. Her hand hovered in the dark—and then she determined to stop timidly begging him for some sign of being willing to listen to her. She put her hand on his knee and said, "Per, I didn't plan this, I didn't mean any of it to happen, I didn't—"

He pulled away from her, twisting his upper body and jolting into Bryce, who was knocked into the man next to him, who bumped into others. There were groans and smothered protests as men were startled from uncomfortable, unhappy dozes.

"Per—"

Per was furious that she could be so shameless as to speak to him, and spat at her, "Guthrun!"

"Hey, hey," Bryce said, and grabbed at the scruff of Per's neck.

"Guthrun?" Andrea said. "I'm *Guthrun*? Oh Per! Thou wert in the hall. I thought tha'd stay there. How could I know tha'd come haring—"

Too angry to keep a silent dignity any longer, Per said, "Tha *told* me to come!"

"I told thee?"

"Hey," Bryce said. The other men could be heard moving, shuffling against the rock, disturbed by a fierce, whispered quarrel they couldn't understand.

"I never told thee! I *told* thee to stay—"

Per leaned toward her, and was half choked by Bryce's grip on his collar. "Tha told Yennet to tell me—"

"I never—"

"That thou wert in thy bower—in bed—" He broke off.

Andrea let a couple of breaths pass before she said, "I told her to say I had a head pain and had gone to sleep it off. I meant thee to stay *in the hall*. Oh Per, tha'rt a bonehead." An apt Sterkarm expression dropped into her mind. "Tha've a sheep's head and a ram's—"

He dragged against Bryce's grip. "And tha'rt a *codfish*!"

Bryce shook him. "Hey, hey, hey. Less of it. I can gag him again."

Andrea reached around Per to lay her hand on Bryce's arm. "It's all right. I'm only saying that I'm sorry about his dog."

Windsor's voice came from the darkness. "He doesn't seem to be taking it very well."

Andrea ignored him. "Per, be so kind, believe me, I never meant for thee to be caught." She put her hand on his chest and, when he didn't try to pull away or push her off, she put her hand to the back of his neck and prized Bryce's threatening hand away. "I never meant for anybody else to be hurt, Per. I was trying to *stop* any more folk being hurt."

That struck a true note with him. She was always worrying about folk being hurt, and trying hopelessly to think of ways to stop them being hurt. When she put her face close to his and kissed his cheek, he didn't try to stop her, though he knew he should, if he didn't want to be her fool.

"And Per, tha must believe me, be so kind, I never would have wanted Cuddy to be hurt—I loved Cuddy— be so kind, don't blame me for that—"

"Oh, Entraya." All he could do, with his hands tied behind his back, was to press his cheek against hers, and nuzzle in the hollow of her neck. When she started to shake and sob, tears filled his own eyes, and he knew he would have believed her even if he'd watched her take

487

the dagger and stab Cuddy—he was that big a fool.

"I thought thou'd be in the hall, and she'd be with thee, and you'd both be safe! I was only going to let the Elven loose, and then I was going to come back." She wasn't sure herself if this was true. Perhaps, at the last moment, she really would have turned back. Even if it was a lie, if Per found it comforting, it was a kind lie.

"Entraya . . ." She had her arms round his neck, and he turned his head within her embrace, trying to kiss her.

"But I've made such a mess of it all, and now I'm so scared—"

"Ssh, little one—"

"God!" Windsor said. "This is nauseating. Have we got to listen to it?" There was some murmured agreement from the other men. Cold, damp, hungry, battered and scared, they weren't much in the mood for lovers.

"Leave them alone," Bryce said. "So long as they're quiet."

"We're all going to be killed," Andrea sobbed into Per's neck. "I got Cuddy killed, and now I'm going to get all the rest of us killed! I'm so sorry, Per. I didn't mean it."

"Entraya, ssh!" He whispered in her ear, and kissed it, making the hair stand up all over her. "No one's going to hurt thee, no one."

"But them," she said. "They'll be hurt. And it's all my fault. . . ."

"Ssh! Ssh!" He kissed her ear and her cheek, trying to find her mouth. He couldn't comfort her by saying that the men around them would be unhurt, since if he had anything to do with it, every one of them would be cut into collops, in revenge for Cuddy alone. "*Thu air sikka, Lam. Inyen skahl sawrer thu. Kews migh.*" Thou'rt safe, Lamb. No one shall hurt thee. Kiss me.

They leaned to each other, opening their mouths— and drawing back as the first touch sent darts of pain through their split lips. They both smiled, which hurt more, and moved together again. Andrea licked at Per's mouth, where it was hurt, and he licked back, and the bruises, the cold and the hard rock under them stopped mattering so much. Andrea refused to care about the other men, so close around them, listening. This might be the last she ever had of Per.

There was a sound of scrambling as Windsor struggled up from the huddle of men and stumbled his way to them. "I've had enough of this." He took Per by a handful of hair and tried to drag him away from Andrea—but she clung to Per, and their mouths clung together.

"Leave 'em!" Bryce said.

But some of the other men, as angry as Windsor, got hold of Andrea and dragged her away from Per, their fingers biting hard into her arms. She struck out at them, as angry as she was scared.

"What about snogging *us*?" one of the men asked, and Windsor said, "You make me sick!"

Bryce was on his feet. She could see him, dimly, standing taller than the other stooping figures. "Leave her alone! Leave her! Sit down—now!" Someone was clouted. In the darkness, she couldn't see who, but hoped it wasn't Per.

And then everyone settled down again, though they muttered. Her heart was thumping. And she wasn't sitting by Per any longer.

Per, his head aching worse than ever because of Windsor's hauling on his hair, settled himself to wait. Morning would come, and when it did, he would get his chance.

* * *

Bedes Water was a brown water running fast over many rocks with a constant purling and gushing. It caught what little light there was, making a milky twilight about its banks that, within a few feet, faded to darkness. At the ford, the only place in the whole valley's length where the water could be safely crossed, the Sterkarms waited. The little horses, loose, wandered here and there or stood still, dozing. The men crouched on the ground, wrapped in cloaks, grimly waiting out the night.

Isobel and her foot army came tramping across the springy turf of the valley and joined them. Women, children and men huddled together, sharing cloaks and warmth, breathing in the cold smell of the water.

Throughout the long night, at intervals, riders came in from patrolling the waterside, the horses treading gently. Other men rose as these dismounted, whistled to their horses, mounted and rode off.

Some passed the time sleeping, others in kissing, or telling stories or singing songs, until the darkness over the valley paled, as if water had been added to ink. Joe watched as a patrol rode in, looming startlingly clear from the dawn twilight, the metallic chink of their weapons and harness ringing in the new day's fresh, cold air.

A woman's voice rose, hoarse but tuneful:

"Now Yanny's good yew bow is broke,
And his good gazehounds are slain,
And he's asleep in the deep greenwood,
With all his hunting done, done,
With all his hunting done."

24

16th Side: Back to the Tube

THE ROCKS AND TREES of the valley showed gray against gray, and the trickling of the small stream seemed to grow louder, the smell of earth and leaves stronger. Birds began to chitter. Bryce said, "Let's make a move, before we freeze solid."

Getting up wasn't easy. They were all cramped, and their bruises had stiffened. Andrea saw Per, his hands still tied behind him, hauled to his feet by Bryce. In the early gray light his face, as he looked around for her, was merely a pale smudge, obscured by the mud dried on it.

On tender, sore feet, they limped down the narrow valley, clambering over and around the many boulders, which were at least easier to see in the growing light. Andrea's blisters hurt at every step. She tried not to look at the men around her, who still glowered at her. Ahead, she could see, Per stumbled as Bryce pulled him along by his belt, and as Windsor shoved him from behind. The gag was still in Bryce's pocket; that was one good thing.

The light strengthened, bringing delicate color into the hills above them. Green thornbushes and ferns emerged from the morning dusk, and the birds shrilled louder.

At the spot where the ravine opened into Bedesdale, they stopped to catch breath. It was nearly full light and the valley before them was shining green. Distantly came the sound of the river. Andrea shivered as she looked. It was very beautiful, and cold. She turned and saw Per standing beside Bryce. Per was staring at her, waiting to catch her eye, his pale-blue eyes bright in his mask of dirt. He mouthed at her, *"Thu air sikka."* Thou art safe.

She doubted it. In the clear light she could see three mounted men riding by the river, each carrying a long lance. As they watched, one of the men raised his lance high in the air, signaling to someone, and then used the lance to point to them.

Per smiled. The scouts had seen them, and had told the main party where they were. He looked again at Andrea.

"The Sterkarms are at the ford," she said, for Bryce to hear. The low land near the river was hidden from them by folds of ground.

Bryce, squinting, looked around, wondering if there was somewhere else they could cross, and almost grinned as he realized it made no difference. He must be too tired to think straight. Even if they could afford to walk miles to find another ford, the Sterkarms were mounted. Wherever they went, the Sterkarms would overtake them.

"Well, we've got Sunny Jim here." Bryce pulled his sleeve over his hand, spat on it and, gripping Per by the hair with his other hand, scrubbed the wetted sleeve over his face. When Per turned his face aside, Bryce pulled his head around again. "Not used to washing, eh?

But we want you spruced up and looking your best."

Andrea thought Bryce was making a mistake. As the dirt was wiped from Per's face, the marks on his face showed more clearly. His nose was reddened and slightly swollen out of shape. There was a cut on his left eyebrow, and the eye below it was swelling, darkening and closing. His lower lip was noticeably puffed up, and at the corners of his mouth were grazes made by the cord that had held the gag. Toorkild's people teased Per about his girl's face, but they were proud of his looks too. They would see this spoiling of them as a vandalism of their property.

Still grasping a handful of Per's hair, Bryce studied him. Per stared back, his face blank.

"He's got some bottle," Bryce said. "I'll give him that."

Andrea thought that it couldn't hurt, even now, to try and build a bridge between the two sides. "He says you're brave," she told Per.

Per glanced at her, and then gave Bryce a sidelong look that held all the contempt a Sterkarm could have for the opinion of anyone not a Sterkarm.

From his pocket, Bryce took the sock and bootlace. Per, who'd been silent and obedient for so long, stepped sharply back, colliding with the men behind him. "*Nigh! Yi skal nigh snakka. Min urd, yi lerfta.*" No! I shall not speak. My word, I promise.

"Sorry, Sunshine," Bryce said. The men behind Per took his arms and held him. Windsor came up, ready to help.

Andrea nodded toward the horsemen who still sat, at a distance, watching. "Are you going to do this in front of *them*?"

494

Bryce ignored her.

Per had reckoned on a little while yet before they tried to silence him. He leaned back against the men who held him, craning his neck, trying to see the horsemen. He filled his lungs and tried to yell, but his hoarse, strained throat pinched out the sound even before a hand came over his mouth.

Andrea said, "Per, don't make it harder—"

But Per had suffered the gag once, and that was more than enough. If he could break free, he could run toward the horsemen, and they would ride hard toward him, leveling their lances. . . .

He banged his head into the nose and mouth of the man behind him, sending considerable pain reverberating through his own head. An arm came around his neck and he set his teeth in it. Bryce was in front of him, with the gag, and Per kicked at him, catching him on the hip with the heel of his boot. Bryce staggered and sat down with a grunt of pain. Per was using his heels on the bare feet and legs of those behind him.

Andrea hopped about at the edge of the struggle, feeling scared and useless. "Per! Don't! Oh, don't hurt him!" She looked over her shoulder and saw the horsemen picking their way closer, as if to get a better look. "They're coming!"

Per's feet were kicked from under him; he was pressed to the ground, held down; and the gag was forced into his mouth for all he could do. And then, when he was pulled to sit upright in the grass, he was so breathless from the fight that the gag stifled him—and there were several among the men surrounding him who wanted to punch him.

Bryce, crouching beside him, fended them off. "Nobody touches—get back! See them three on horses over there? Nobody touches him." Bryce pulled most of the sock out of Per's mouth, to let him get his breath back. "But if we didn't need you alive, you little—"

Andrea saw the horsemen riding away at a fast trot toward the ford. They disappeared into the land's folds. What a sight they had to report to Toorkild.

Per's breathing had eased, and Bryce stuffed the sock back into his mouth, then gave him a hefty slap to the face that made a dull thump and rocked his head sideways. A thin trail of blood ran out of Per's nose.

"Nobody touches him!" Windsor said.

"Officer's privilege."

"Right!" Windsor said, and swung back his arm to take his turn. Bryce gave Windsor an irritable shove that sent him sprawling. He scrambled up, fists clenched, to find Bryce waiting for him.

Bryce said, "Yeah? Want to try a shot at somebody who hasn't got their hands tied behind their back?"

"You'll answer for this when we get back," Windsor said.

Bryce grinned. "*If* we get back." He tied the shoelace around Per's head and shoved him, stumbling, in front of him.

Per was making a convulsive, repeated, sidelong movement of the head, chewing at the gag, retching and gulping for air. Andrea, wanting to put her fingers in her ears so she didn't have to hear the distressing sound, thought: Mistake. Big, big mistake.

The sight of Per, bedraggled, bound, dragged along, half choking on a gag, his nose bleeding and his face marked with bruises, was not going to put Toorkild, Gobby or any of the Sterkarms in a happy, reasonable frame of mind.

They had no choice but to go on toward the ford, tramping over the thick, wet grass that gave and bounced beneath their feet, making them stumble at almost every step. Topping a rise, they saw the ground slope down to the river, and they saw the Sterkarms.

The horsemen sat their strong, shaggy little horses with a horribly relaxed air of business as usual, the points of their lances bristling above their heads. Here and there the greased, blackened iron of helmet and lance head dully caught the light. Behind the horsemen was a small crowd on foot. The whole tower had turned out against them.

The Sterkarms were drawn up well back from the ford, leaving the way to it clear for them. But none of them—except, perhaps, Per—were keen to try making it to the water. Andrea knew how fast those thickset little horses could cover ground, and how practiced the riders were with the lances. She wondered how she could be so, so scared and still be standing up and breathing and thinking.

Bryce was holding Per in front of him by one arm and his scruff. Per was trying to push the gag out of his mouth with his tongue, and retching, and twisting his head from side to side. Through a dazzle of tears he could see the horsemen as a wavering dark block. He knew that his father would be there, at the front, and so would Gobby, and his cousins, all watching him. It made him sweat with shame that they should see him like this, helpless and needing rescue. For his father's sake, he should show some fight.

He ducked his head, rubbing his cheek against his shoulder, trying to dislodge the cord that held the gag in place. If he could shout . . .

Bryce took a handful of his hair and pulled his head up and back. With his throat pulled taut, Per's retching became even more choked and desperate. "Oh, please—" Andrea said.

Bryce shook Per's head. "Don't start! Tell him he gives me grief, I'll knock him cold." Bryce hoped the threat would be enough. He could do it; he could drop Per like a marionette whose strings had been cut, but with the Sterkarms watching, it was probably not a good idea.

Windsor said, "E-e-er . . ." like someone politely trying to interrupt.

The horsemen had started moving. Five or six of them were walking their mounts forward from the line and along the riverbank toward them. They came slowly, as if they were nothing more than idly curious, but each rider rested the butt of an eight-foot lance on the toe of one boot. Per strained toward them.

Bryce heaved him the other way. "Right! Go. Go!"

Some of the men realized what he meant, and scattered down the bank for the ford. Some, exhausted and battered, stood gawping at the advancing horsemen. Andrea ran, her boots flapping on her feet, her blisters painful. She was terrified that she was too fat to run and would be left behind and run down by the horses, but she splashed into the cold, shallow water together with three of the men, and one of them caught her hand to steady her against the fast current and pulled her over the river stones toward the opposite bank.

Bryce was trying to take Per with him to the water's edge, but Per dug his heels into the turf. He made himself heavy and sagged toward the ground, watching the horsemen pace nearer. Windsor came back up the bank and helped to heave Per upright.

Bryce spun Per around toward him, stooped and dug his shoulder into Per's midriff, put an arm between Per's legs and—to Windsor's surprise and Per's astonishment—hoisted him off his feet and made for the river.

Per pivoted precariously on Bryce's shoulder. The driving of the shoulder into his belly had knocked the breath out of him, and every step Bryce took jolted him again. The gag blocked his mouth as he sucked for air, and the ground whirled by upside down. He was going to either choke or be dropped on his head to break his neck.

The horses came on faster, the sound of their hooves louder as they struck the turf.

Bryce struggled on with the widest stride he could manage. Per's weight was shortening his spine. Windsor was ahead of him. Andrea and three men were clambering out on the farther bank. Bryce couldn't look around for the others. His own feet splashed into the water.

Every step after that was hampered not only by Per's weight rocking on his shoulder but by the water rushing around his legs. At the middle, the water rose over his knees and the current snatched at his feet. He tottered, clutching at Per's legs, but the water lifted one foot off the stones and he and Per both went down, thrashing and rolling in the water.

Bryce glimpsed horses' legs at the water's edge and

through ears bubbling with water heard shouting. He didn't let himself pay much attention but grabbed Per under the arms and dragged him—Windsor was helping, good, they might make it—to the other bank, where more men came to help drag the prisoner up the slope. Not that the kid was putting up much fight, what between the gag and the ducking. He was choking, his eyes rolling back in his head, showing white. Bryce pulled the gag out of his mouth, bent him forward over his arm and thumped his back. When Per began to cough and wheeze and gasp, Bryce was able to look elsewhere.

The people around him were quiet and still. There was little noise coming from across the river, though there had been some shouting while Bryce had been busy trying to revive Per. Now he saw that not all the members of their party had crossed the ford.

A body floated in the water, and clouds of blood uncoiled from it. He could see the face as the head bobbed—the man who'd been bitten by the dog.

Half beached on the stones of the ford lay another man. As Bryce watched, a long spear jabbed down into him, and another came from the other side. Horses wheeled away, and another horse came in, another lance drove down. Blood ran over the stones and into the water.

It was horrible to watch, because there was nothing they could do. Some, like Andrea, couldn't watch and turned away or hid their faces, and then felt guilty. Everyone in the 21st party knew they were just as deserving or undeserving of dying under those spears. They'd started running a little sooner, or had run faster—those were the only reasons for their being spared. They all knew that they should be doing something to help, but that if they did, they'd be killed themselves.

The horsemen, on their dark, wheeling horses, looked across at them, and saluted them with bloodied lances, but didn't ride into the water.

Bryce put his hands under Per's elbows and heaved him to his feet. Per was shaky and breathless, but alive, and it was important that his friends see he was alive.

Per watched the lancing with professional interest and looked around at the men near him. An hour earlier that look would have earned him a kick, a cuff, an elbow in the ribs or belly, despite Bryce's order. Now no one would even meet his eyes, and no one made any move to raise hand or foot against him. He was suddenly their talisman. While they were close to him, they were safe. The stragglers, on the other side of the river, had died because they'd been too far away from Per.

Filling his lungs as deeply as he could, Per jerked up his head and tried to shout across the river—but could only cough.

"Come on," Bryce said. He and Windsor took Per's elbows and walked him away from the ford. A little farther up the valley, in the shelter of another hill spur, was the place where the Elf-Gate opened.

After them, walking through the river, walking up the slope, came the Sterkarms, on foot and on horse.

Isobel, her skirts kilted up and her legs thrashing through the water, was saying to herself, over and over, *"Oh Per min, min Per, min Per, Per min,"* as if she didn't even know that she was speaking.

Toorkild was among the leading horsemen, wearing his jakke, his helmet on his head, the butt of his lance resting on the toe of his boot. He'd been so angry for so long, he was no longer aware of being angry, and was admiring his own calm as he watched the little party that struggled up the slope ahead. His eyes hardly shifted from the figure of his son.

Every time one of the men on either side of Per dragged at him, Toorkild nodded. Every time Per stumbled, Toorkild nodded. He noticed the cord still tied round Per's head, and dragging at the corners of his mouth. He noticed his son's hands, tied behind him at the wrists. Every time Per looked over his shoulder, Toorkild glimpsed the bruises on his face and realized—with as much shock as if for the first time—that these walking turds, these sheep's gets, these bags of cess, had so forgotten their place among the vermin of the world that they'd tied his son's hands behind him and then hit him in the face.

When I have him back safe, Toorkild thought, when I have him safe, when—

He would have the Elves tied hand and foot.

And give them to Isobel.

The slope was steep, and the Elves panted and sweated as they climbed, their legs and lungs aching, their feet bleeding and painful. Their backs prickled with awareness of the crowd of people and horses only yards behind them.

Windsor's and Bryce's fingers pressed deep into Per's arms as they urged him on. Bryce was worried by the way Per kept looking over his shoulder. The kid was bracing himself to make a break for it, and God help them if he succeeded!

The folds of land opened and showed them the Time Tube ahead, a bizarre and thankful sight. Andrea, pausing, allowed herself the luxury of a long, deep breath and a heartbeat's rest before pressing on. The sight put a new energy into all of them. So little farther to go. Get there, scramble up that ramp, and they were home safe.

The sight of the Elf-Gate startled Per from weariness. Leaning back against Bryce and Windsor, he braced his heels against the slope and stamped at their bare feet until, with the help of three of the other men, they picked him up and carried him like a long parcel. The Sterkarms heard his yell of fury.

Horses passed them. The line of horsemen was lengthening at the ends as some of them passed the Elves, riding ahead of them to the Elf-Gate.

Bryce, looking ahead, saw the Elf-Gate go. It winked out, switched off, disappeared. The burned hillside it had blocked out reappeared.

Bryce stopped, and that stopped everyone else. Per was dropped to the grass, where he sat among their feet.

"They switched it off," Bryce said. The people in the control room probably hadn't even seen them coming. How many times had he asked for those security monitors to be repaired and resited? Typical of FUP! Spend a fortune on security cameras and monitors, and let them be maintained and sited by chimps.

The Sterkarms, on horseback and on foot, had surrounded them, though they kept clear of the place that the Elf-Gate had filled when it had been visible.

Andrea felt herself begin to shake and thought of the lances going into the men at the stream. They'd come all this way, had kept going despite everything, and they'd got here, and— Per had promised her that she would be safe, but she would still have to see the others killed, and go on living after. . . .

Per got to his knees and made to stand up. Bryce put a hand on his shoulder and pushed him down. Per said something, but the cord tied around his mouth distorted whatever it was into noise.

Andrea could see Toorkild. He was staring at Per, and his face was white. It was Gobby who spoke, leaning forward on his saddlebow. He said, *"Naw, vah vill thee?"*

"What's he say?" Bryce asked.

Andrea's heart was thumping and skipping, her breath was coming fast and shallow, and she didn't know how she could manage to think connectedly enough to answer. But she said, "Well—more or less, he says—'*Now* what are you going to do?'"

25

16th Side: Sterkarmer
Gaw i Erlf-Lant

PACE BY PACE, the Sterkarms shrank the space around them.

In Andrea's head, a jaunty, dancing tune was singing itself with the words: We're going to die, we're going to die, we're going to die—

Among the Sterkarms, men drew long knives from their belts. Toorkild kicked his horse, and it came forward at a slow walk. Toorkild, swaying with it, brought his lance down to point at them.

Oh God, Andrea thought. We're going to die, we're going to die—

Bryce dropped to his knees behind Per, hooked his arm around Per's neck and pulled his head back. He shouted, "I'll break his effin' neck!"

Andrea flapped her arms. *"Han brekker Per's nakka!"*

The Sterkarms stopped moving. Toorkild reined in.

Bryce got the point of Per's jaw into the crook of his elbow and clenched the fist of that same arm in the hair at the nape of Per's neck. With his other hand he grasped Per's shoulder, ready to twist head and body in opposite directions.

Per tried to move, but the nutcracker grip of the elbow on his head was too strong, and the twist on his neck was forceful enough to convince him that Bryce could and maybe would break his spine. He kept still, and waited. Eventually, Bryce would have to relax his grip.

Toorkild slowly lowered his lance still further. From the extreme corners of his eyes, Per caught something of its movement. The point passed over Per's shoulder and came to rest against Bryce's chest.

Andrea covered her face, certain that she was going to see Bryce skewered or Per's neck wrung. She heard Toorkild speak: "You'll be dead before he takes his last breath."

Bryce could feel the surprising weight of the lance head resting painfully on his collarbone, and the prick of its iron point. Every time he breathed, it stabbed at him again, scratching. His skin felt hot, and he was sure the lance had drawn blood. Keeping his grip on Per, he looked up at the face at the end of the lance. It was shadowed by the helmet, half hidden by the thick beard, making any expression hard to read, but Bryce was conscious of a steady stare. Through gritted teeth, he asked, "What's he—?"

Andrea, her hands still over her eyes, shouted out and told him.

As the lance pricked again, Bryce said, "Ask—ask him, is killing me worth risking a dead son?" He tightened his grip as Per shifted.

Andrea took her hands from her face. "I can't say that to him!"

"Tell him!" His collarbone ached under the lance's weight.

Andrea tried to find the words. When she spoke, Toorkild's eyes moved to her, and her voice shook so much she stammered and gasped. Toorkild had been kind to her; she knew him, and knew how much he doted on Per. It was not only cruel to say such things to him, but the thought of the revenge Toorkild might take for them made her shake.

The blood left her face at Toorkild's answer, turning her flesh hard and cold. "He says"—she choked—"that you dare not kill Per. If you do, he says, they'll kill all of us." Even me! she thought, despite Per's promises. "He says, Bryce, if you harm Per, he'll build a fire and sit you in it. He says . . ." Her voice failed. She didn't even want to speak the rest of Toorkild's threats. The thought that the kindly man she knew might carry them out created an almost supernatural fear in her.

Bryce hadn't time to worry about the fire. Per was moving his hands, the fingers stretching. Bryce knew what the little bastard was doing—trying to reach his balls, to give them a twist. With his hands tied in the small of his back, it was probably impossible, but Bryce shifted his grip on Per's arm anyway, wrenching both bound arms higher up his back. The thought made him sweat, but he knew he couldn't hold Per in the necklock for ever. "Tell him—whatever he does to me—I'll die happier knowing his son's dead too." He shifted his forearm, tightening the twist on Per's neck just a little more. Per made a choking noise.

Toorkild's eyes flickered at the sound, jumping to his son and back to Bryce. The lance point pressed harder as Toorkild lifted his arm, angling the lance downward for the thrust.

Gobby dropped down from his horse and led it forward. His eyes scanned the 21st men, noting their sagging shoulders and bleeding feet, and he grinned through his beard. Taking off his helmet, he squatted down in front of Per and Bryce, his horse's reins looped over his arm. Bryce saw a broken-nosed man with a front tooth missing, which somehow made his grin friendlier. Bright, pale eyes studied Bryce, rather kindly, from thickets of brown hair and beard.

"Now, now," Gobby said. "Little birds in their nests must agree." Per knew his uncle's voice, though his head was twisted too far around to see him. At another time, he'd have laughed, but now he kept very still, even holding his breath. To his own surprise, he found that he had greater faith in his uncle's ability to free him than his father's.

"We no want our lad hurt," Gobby said, slowly, pausing to allow Andrea to stammer through a translation. "You no want to be hurt. So. We can deal." Gently, Gobby reached out and pushed the lance up, away from Bryce. Toorkild let him do it but continued to hold the lance above Bryce's head.

Bryce heard his own people sigh and was aware of a shifting among them, a relaxing. This new speaker, with his broken-nosed grin, was more dangerous than Toorkild. They were all so knocked about and exhausted, they were ready to believe anything he told them.

"My brother's angry," Gobby said, "by cause that's his bairn you've got there—but I can talk to my brother. And I ken how it is. Many's the time I've felt like blacking that one's eye myself. He'd try the patience of a stone."

Per felt comforted. His bruises had been noted and would be avenged.

"Come on now," Gobby said. "Let the lad go, and we'll let you go. I give you my word."

Andrea translated, and someone among the 21st men muttered, "Only chance we've got."

Loudly, Bryce said, "Tell him I know he's lying."

Andrea did, and Gobby grinned. "You canna hold him much longer. Three choices you've got. Hold him until you tire—then he'll break free and we'll kill you. Or break his neck while you still can—and then we'll kill you." Gobby glanced over his shoulder. "See his mother over there, with the cleaver?" Gobby waited for Andrea to finish translating, smiling gently into Bryce's face. "Or you can let him go, and we'll let you go. What use is he to you? Your Gate's closed. Where are you going to go? Come on; let him go now."

Windsor crouched beside Bryce. He said, "Ask them what guarantees they'll give us." As if he were in a boardroom. As if there could be any guarantees.

Bryce opened his mouth to answer—and it stayed open. Behind the Sterkarms, the Time Tube appeared again. There it was, blotting out part of the hillside with its big pipe and the textured rubber ramp that rose up to it.

There was an outcry from those Sterkarms who could see it, and Gobby, still crouching, swiveled on his heels to look behind him.

"I'll tell you what we're going to do," Bryce said. "Andrea, tell 'em this. We're going through there, going home. We're going to take Pair right to the entrance, and when everybody's gone through, *then* I'll let Pair go. You've got my word."

"—right up to the Gate," Andrea said, looking from Gobby to Toorkild. "But not through it!"

Bryce got to his feet, pulling Per up with him. They had to get to the Tube fast. Bryce was tiring. Moving sidelong, Bryce advanced a step, and Per was forced to go with him. Gobby got out of their way. "Keep up close," Bryce said to his people, "and we'll get there." They crowded around, pressing close to each other. "Andrea, tell 'em I can kill him in a second—and I will!"

Andrea looked at Gobby's face, glimpsed Isobel's in the crowd, and was scared to look at Toorkild. Why do I have to tell them? she thought. Why does it have to be me they remember saying it? But she said, "He can kill Per in an eye's blink. It's an Elf-Power he has!"

Per wasn't listening to the exchange of words. He knew that he was being taken toward the Gate, and to another imprisonment in Elf-Land. He tried moving his head a little, and it seemed to him that Bryce's grip had slackened. If he could turn his head a little more within Bryce's arm, he might be able to bite, despite the cord in his mouth. He stamped at Bryce's feet, missed, and stamped on grass.

Bryce jerked him to a halt and tightened the twist on his head. "I don't want to have to kill him to prove that I can!"

Gobby was keeping pace with them on foot, having thrown the reins of his horse to one of his men. Even while Andrea was translating, Gobby spoke sharply, cutting through her words. *"Per! Slerssa nigh!"*

"What's he say?"

"He told Per not to fight."

The kid stopped fighting. Bryce moved on several

more paces, and the kid went with him, good as gold. *"Tahk,"* Bryce called to Gobby. "Appreciate your help."

Step by step they made toward the Tube's ramp. Not one among the Sterkarms tried to stop them, but Gobby kept with them, and at his side hung a big, gray sword that must have weighed a few pounds, its edges sharpened to cut.

Bryce set his foot on the bottom of the ramp and prayed that the Tube wouldn't be turned off now. "Go past me," he said to the nearest man. "Get going. Not you!" he added, to Andrea. "I need you."

Per, feeling the ramp under his feet, panicked. Gobby's sharp order not to fight had been, in a way, soothing; trust in his uncle had made him obey. But Gobby had done nothing and here he was, on the very threshold of Elf-Land. The way his head was held, he could see nothing of his own people or land anymore—only the ugly, unnatural slope leading up to the Gate.

Bryce's grip on him faltered, and Per was able to shift his head within the crook of Bryce's elbow. He managed to get a thin pinch of Bryce's flesh between his teeth, through the thin shirt, and he bit as hard as he could make his aching jaws close. Bryce's arm thrashed, the fist clubbing Per's head, but that was proof it hurt, and Per hung on. At the same time he made the fingers of his tied hands rigid and drove them behind him into Bryce's belly. It didn't inflict much pain, but it made Bryce move away from him. Per took his teeth from Bryce's arm and spun away from him, back toward the bottom of the ramp and the waiting Sterkarms. But Bryce still had hold of him by one arm, and pulled him up short.

Windsor, behind Per, stooped and gathered his legs together, lifting them up off the ramp, hugging them to smother the kicks. Bryce got a grip on his tied arms and supported his upper body. Between them, they lugged him up the ramp. "Keep going!" Bryce yelled, out of breath, to the men passing him.

Per kicked his knees against Windsor's throat and croaked, from a dry throat, "Sterkarm!"

Bryce, higher on the ramp, looked over Windsor's shoulder and saw the Sterkarms coming forward, the men on foot in front, their knives and sickles and cleavers ready. There was a zinging, scraping sound of iron as Gobby drew his sword. Bryce strained for breath and pushed himself to move faster, forcing Windsor to keep up.

They reached the top of the ramp, its platform and its great open tunnel mouth, with that beautiful glimpse of the 21st at the other end. Such relief rose into his brain, he thought he might faint—but he said, "Put him down, put him down!" Windsor had seemed to be continuing on into the tunnel.

Windsor dropped Per's feet onto the rubber surface, and Bryce steadied him. There were Sterkarms halfway up the slope, Gobby in the lead, but now they stopped. Bryce glanced around and saw that Andrea was already in the Tube, and that the last couple of his men were passing him. There were only Windsor and himself left. He let go of Per and set his hand in the middle of the kid's back, ready to push him down the ramp and into his family's arms.

Windsor grabbed Per by the shoulders and ran into the Tube, dragging Per with him. Off balance, his hands tied, Per could only stagger with him, though looking wildly back at Bryce.

Bryce looked down the ramp and saw Gobby coming on again, lifting the sword in his hand, his face viciously angry. There was nothing to do but pile into the Tube after Windsor as fast as he could and even, when he caught up, help to hustle Per along. No point in trying to explain that the treachery had been Windsor's, not his. He yelled to those running ahead of him, "Turn it off! Tell them to *turn it off!*"

Toorkild yelled, "Way!" and set his horse at the ramp. The horse shied, but Toorkild pulled around its head, kicked it and whacked its rump with the butt of his lance. Men on foot jumped from the ramp to clear the way as the horse started up it with a hollow banging of hooves.

The hooves gripped on the textured surface, and the horse scrambled to the top. Leveling his lance, Toorkild rode into the Elf-Gate. Others set their horses after him, and Gobby jumped from the ramp and ran for his own mount.

Joe ran up the ramp with a pack of other footmen, his axe raised. He felt angry, exhilarated, wild. Dragging in breath and opening his mouth wide, he yelled, "Sterkarm! Sterkarm!"

26

21st Side: Reiving the 21st

I T WAS QUIET AND COOL in the Tube's control room; the windows were screened with blinds, and the whirring of fans and humming of computers made a soothing background noise. But the people seated at the computers were less relaxed than usual, as their eyes flicked from one display to another. The supervisor stood, staring at the monitors high on the wall, now at one, now at another.

From the Tube, beginning abruptly as the dimensional border was crossed, came an echoing yell. Men, shouting, gesturing wildly, staggering, looking behind, broke from the Tube's mouth. They were wet and filthy, their feet bare, dirty and bleeding. They ran straight down the ramp and across the gravel path separating the control room from the main building. Shoving open a door, they crowded into the Hall.

In the control room, startled technicians rose from their terminals and looked at each other, or looked up at the security monitors, one of which showed a beautiful view of the 16th-side sky.

In a struggling knot, Windsor, Bryce, Andrea and another stumbled from the Tube. All were soaked and muddy and scratched. Windsor's usually well-groomed hair had collapsed about his head in an oily, muddy mess; Andrea's hair had come down from its bun and was flying everywhere.

All of them were shouting and struggling as Bryce and Windsor dragged between them a young man whose hands were fastened behind him. He was kicking, elbowing and trying to get back into the Tube. Windsor cuffed his head with the knuckles of one fist, making a hollow sound that was clearly heard by everyone watching and left no one in any doubt as to how the young man's face had come to be so bruised. Andrea yelled and hit Windsor, who yelled and shoved her.

Bryce was yelling too, as he hauled the young man toward the ramp. It sounded as if he shouted "Turn it off!" Then he and Windsor bundled their prisoner down the ramp and out of sight, with Andrea following.

From the Tube an explosion of sound, movement, weight. A dark mass of horse, hooves crashing, drumming, lunged from the opening. People shoved themselves back from their keyboards, jumped to their feet. They glimpsed a rider, leveled lance, helmet on head. The horse vanished down the ramp, thunderous—but others were behind it. One, slewing, crashed into the control room.

Its bulk, the prow of its head, neck and breastbone, the great working muscles of its shoulders, the huge barrel of its ribs and its great, stamping feet, filled the aisles. Carts and computers tilted, beeped, smashed to the floor. Keyboards and mouses dangled at the ends of their cords. The horse, disturbed by the frantic electronic twittering, lashed out with its hind feet. Its hooves struck the doorjamb behind it, splintering wood, shaking the whole room, panicking people into running and setting many more computers bleeping. The rider's lance, driven into the ceiling above him and wrenched out, brought down a shower of plasterboard.

While many fought to get out the door, some went out by the windows.

* * *

Elf-Land was eldritch, infinitely more strange than the Sterkarms ever could have expected. Those who blundered into the control room found themselves between walls of an unnaturally straight, pastel glossiness, and heard their horses' hooves boom as if they danced on drums. A shrieking, as of many startled birds, was all around, and boxes rattled and blinked.

Those who rushed down the steep slope were faced with a building, a long, long building, bigger than Toorkild's tower and Gobby's bastle house put together, and built all of large red bricks. It had huge, shining windows through which a troop could have climbed, and curtains of a deep, rich red hung at the windows—enough cloth hanging there to dress a Sterkarm wedding.

In every direction, Elves were running, and all of them wearing brightly colored clothes. They ran over wide, smooth green lawns and past—even through—beds of brilliant flowers.

Even Joe was startled by the glaring white of a notice on a wall, giving directions, and the bright scarlet of its lettering. A woman was standing, astounded, at the bottom of the ramp, clutching at the handle of a tea cart, her smock a deep, clear blue. Back in the 16th even the brightest of colors were faded, muted, and mostly things were gray, green or brown. For a giddy moment, Joe was simultaneously homesick for the sixteenth and twenty-first centuries.

Bryce and Windsor were at the bottom of the ramp, pulling Per this way and that between them. Andrea was adding to the scuffle, tugging at Windsor's arms, crying, "You should have let him go!" and staggering back as Windsor shoved her. Per's kicking and elbowing had prevented them reaching the shelter of Dilsmead Hall, and now there was a horse between them and the nearest door. Their best defense was still to hold on to Per as they tried to edge along the path to another door.

More horses were thundering down the ramp, swinging around on the path, stamping over the lawns. Toorkild was standing in his stirrups, bellowing to call his men's attention back from plate-glass windows and dragons in the sky.

Bryce quickly saw that the Sterkarms weren't keeping their distance as they had on their own ground. The horses came pacing forward, coming between them and the buildings. The lances were coming down, ready to stab. Here, in Elf-Land, they were uneasy, less willing to hold off or bargain.

Pulling Per's head back by the hair, Bryce twisted him to his knees and dragged him backward through the gravel. It was time, Bryce thought, to give the Sterkarms something to think about, while he and Windsor and Andrea ran for it. It was time to finish with Per.

Toorkild saw Per on his knees in the gravel, his hands tied behind him, yelling. He saw the man standing above and behind him raise both hands, to strike a blow down on Per's bare head.

In wrenching at his horse's reins to keep clear of the horse beside him, Toorkild glanced aside. When he jerked his head back, the blow had landed. He saw Per's head roll back of its own weight, and his whole body slacken as it sank and fell in a heap.

Toorkild's sight turned white. A blizzard cold closed about him. Kicking his feet from his stirrups, he dropped from his horse, still blind. His own breathing roared in his ears. All his thought was: Killed! Killed! Killed!

"*R-u-u-n!*" Bryce yelled and, turning to run, collided with Andrea, who shouted, "What have you done? What have you done?" He shook her and tried to take her with him. "Run!" He could see Windsor sprinting away—but there were people standing on the lawns and the path, staring. He yelled at them, "Get inside! Under cover! Run!"

Andrea, pulling away from Bryce toward Per, broke free of his hold. He looked over his shoulder at her and then ran for shelter himself. She'd made her decision, and good luck to her! Now he had to save himself.

Looking back again, he saw Andrea stooping over Per; saw horses milling in place and lances stabbing the air; saw one horse lunging forward, coming at him. He felt the ground shake under his feet.

Sweet Milk leveled his lance, with his weight and his horse's weight behind it. Bryce was struck, skewered, smashed to the gravel.

Sweet Milk let go of the lance, swung his horse right over Bryce and jumped down. Keeping his reins looped over his arm, he drew his long knife, dropped on Bryce's back, and cut the throat of the worthless carrion dirt who'd killed Per May.

He got to his feet with blood on his hands and shook blood from his knife, bringing shrieks from the Elves pressing into a doorway nearby. Sweet Milk looked at them, and then turned toward Toorkild, and saw him gathering up his son's body.

Sweet Milk wiped his eyes and nose with a bloody hand and led his horse back toward his friends. There was nothing he could do to ease Toorkild's pain, but he could, at least, give him the head of his son's killer.

* * *

Windsor ran hard, without looking around, making for the far end of the long building. He ran straight past the door where others were crowding, trying to get inside. Idiots! Let them jostle together there until the Sterkarms picked them off. He'd run on and find another door.

His mind was on his Mercedes, waiting for him in the parking lot. The quickest way to reach it would have been to run in the other direction, but the Sterkarms were blocking the way, so he was going to have to run all the way around Dilsmead Hall to reach his car.

He rounded the corner of the building, and there was another door. A young man and woman—brighter than most—were just disappearing inside. Windsor followed them. It made more sense to take a shortcut through the building, where horses couldn't follow, than to try running around it in the open.

The young couple were running down the corridor and were almost out of sight as Windsor entered. Instead of running after them, he took long enough to slam the bar down and lock it. That was one door the Sterkarms couldn't enter by.

He couldn't be sure that the Sterkarms hadn't gotten into the building one way or another, and from somewhere came the sound of smashing glass. It must have come from some room nearby, but the sound was muffled by the walls and he couldn't be sure from where. A narrow staircase—what had once been a hidden, servants' stair—opened to his right, and he ducked into it.

The staircase brought him into an upper-floor corridor that ran the length of the house. He was able to look down from the windows and see the cluster of horsemen below. He heard more glass smash, and saw Sterkarms dragging curtains down.

Running along the corridor, he turned the corner at the end. From the windows there he could look down into the parking lot. His Mercedes was on the side farthest from the building, but even so, it was only a matter of a few yards.

Below him, a party of Sterkarms, on foot, appeared around the corner of the building, armed with pikes and axes. He heard glass smash below him as some of them broke a window. Another ran to the nearest car and wrenched off its side mirrors. The distance between the building and his Mercedes suddenly seemed far greater, the space he would have to cross more dangerously open.

He watched the party of Sterkarms move along the side of the house and turn the corner that would bring them to its front entrance. Once they were out of sight, he ran down the nearest staircase to the ground floor. Near the foot of the staircase, he knew, there was a side door leading out to the parking lot.

At the bottom of the stairs, he peered into the corridor—and drew back sharply. The door was standing open, and something lay on the floor nearby.

He hid on the staircase, his heart thumping, wondering whether to go back up the stairs. But if Sterkarms were roaming about the house, he might meet them anywhere. If he could get to the door and run for it . . .

He looked out into the corridor again. The thing lying on the floor was a man in a green uniform. He was lying facedown, clutching at his belly, and blood was pooling on the floor underneath him. Dead, Windsor thought. But he wore a belt and holster.

Windsor went over to him and, trying to keep his shoes and hands out of the blood, took the man by the hips and rolled him over. His gun was still in its holster. Windsor was reaching for it when the man cried out and raised his head.

"I'm—going for help." Windsor took the gun from the holster, and made for the door. On its threshold, he hesitated, afraid to leave the building's shelter, but knowing that the building was no longer safe.

He looked at the gun. It was much heavier than he'd expected, much more awkward to handle—and was sticky in his hands, from the blood. The guard on the floor lifted his head and tried to say something.

"Ssh!" Windsor said. Leaning toward the man, he showed him the gun. "Is it loaded?" But the guard had collapsed again and was silent. Windsor didn't know how to open the gun. It had always seemed deeply uncool to play with guns, and he'd never taken any interest. But he'd seen plenty of actors use them, and if actors could use them, how hard could it be?

There was a lever on the side of the gun, which was hard to push aside and didn't open the gun when he'd managed it. Was it the safety catch? It wasn't labeled. Well then, he'd just taken the safety catch off, hadn't he? Unless he'd put it on. He lifted the gun up and peered at it, but there was nothing to indicate "on" or "off"— and he was wasting time.

Be positive. Just the sight of the gun ought to be frightening. And if he was bold and made decisively for his Mercedes, he'd probably stroll it without seeing any Sterkarms at all. But as he braced himself to step out of the door, he heard a voice calling outside, away to his left. *"Vi maun venda tilbacka!"*

Windsor shrank back into the corner behind the door. In front of him, in both hands, he held the gun.

* * *

Toorkild seized Andrea by her shoulder and a handful of her hair and dragged her away from Per, sending her sprawling on the gravel. Then Toorkild dropped to the ground himself, heaved Per into his lap and hugged him to his chest.

To him Per felt as chicken-boned and fragile, as desperately in need of protection, as when he'd been a day old and had lain between Toorkild and Isobel so they could count his breaths through the night; or when he'd been two, and sick, and had done all his shivering, crying and puking in their arms because they'd feared that in the moment one of them wasn't holding him, he would die. Toorkild tried to fold himself around Per so that nothing could get at him, not even the wind.

Andrea, sitting bruised and dazed in the gravel, watched Joe use the edge of his axe to saw through the cord around Per's wrists. Toorkild gathered the freed arms into his hug. Sterkarms were crowding around Per, on foot and horseback, looking down on him. Ecky slipped the blade of his small, sharp knife under the cord tied around Per's head and snicked it through.

Per came alive in Toorkild's clasp and pushed against his father's chest with his hands and elbows. Toorkild, his heart and throat too swollen for speech, crushed him in a grateful bear hug and pressed his lips to Per's hair and brow. He slackened his hold, but only to change his grip and renew the suffocating hug. Thanksthanksthanks! No having to tell Isobel her son was dead. Thanksthanks!

Per was still fighting Bryce—but as the cramped muscles of his arms and shoulders ached, and the abrasions on his wrists stung, it came to him, dimly, that his hands were no longer tied behind him. Bewildered, he stopped struggling. The arms around him tightened again, and he was rocked.

The bruises on his face hurt as they were pressed into a jakke. He knew it was a jakke: He could feel the small iron plates flexing under the cloth. Elves didn't wear jakkes. Elves didn't smell like this either: like a stable a fox had been kept in.

A gentle pressure on the crown of his head felt like a kiss. Only one Elf had ever kissed him, and she wasn't this strong and didn't wear a jakke. He braced his hand against the iron-filled leather but couldn't find the strength to break the hold around him. A voice grumbled close to his ear, vibrating through him. *"Lilla ladda min, min wey barn."* My little lad, my wee bairn. This could only be his father.

He pushed hard, the muscles of his arms creaking, and pushed himself far enough back to see his father's face. From beneath the shadowing helmet, Toorkild's pale-blue eyes stared at him, while tears and snot ran down into his thick, gray-flecked beard. His hand came up and touched the bruises and scratches on Per's face with thick, hot fingers. "Look at this," he said. "Look at this."

"He's alive," someone said, close by Per's ear. He turned his head so sharply, he went dizzy. Ecky was crouched beside him. Beyond Ecky were horses—and grass, and the legs and boots of other men. Above was a blue sky, and his cousin Wat's face, looking down.

He looked up, astonished and disbelieving. He had been trying to get away from the Elven. What Elf-Work had dumped him down, untied, among his own people and made the Elven vanish? Trying to sit up, he said, to his father, "Entraya?"

People stooped over him, laughing at his confusion. They laughed the more when he scowled, and someone rubbed up his hair.

Gobby's voice said, "Toorkild, up! This is no place for us to be. Back through the Gate—move, now!"

Per was lifted to his feet without his having to make any effort to get up. Toorkild's arm was around his waist, and Wat gripped his other elbow, as if he needed help to stand. "Daddy! Entraya, where be she?"

"Ssh!" Toorkild said, pulling him along. "Ssh!"

Per was distracted from protesting by the sight of a little metal wagon on wheels. It had shelves, loaded with cups and plates and cans that rattled and chinked as the wagon was dragged over the gravel and up the ramp to the Elf-Gate. A man followed it, his body wrapped around with thick folds of cloth—a curtain, torn down from the nearest windows. A third man was carrying a big framed painting and a fourth clutched an armful of brightly colored cushions. And then he saw Andrea, her brown hair falling down her back, and a man on either side of her, gripping her arms, hustling her along.

"Hey!" He lunged out of Toorkild's hold and grabbed at the shoulder of the nearest man. "Take your hands off her!" Both men turned in surprise, and Per pulled Andrea away from them. "Did they hurt thee? Did they?"

Andrea wrapped her arms around Per's ribs and held on to him tight. She wasn't hurt, but she was scared. She shook her head against his shoulder and was glad to feel his arms move protectively around her back and head.

The men were saying that she was an Elf and had helped the Elven, and couldn't be trusted. Others came pressing up behind Per.

"Guthrun!"

"The hounds'd choke on her."

"Any man—" Andrea felt Per's chest move as he sucked in air to shout. "Any man looks at her wrong answers to me! Hear?"

They stared back at him, surprised, even annoyed— but if he said so . . . Especially as Toorkild stood behind him, with his hand on his shoulder.

"Veensa," Per said, looking around. "Where be Veensa—Elf-Veensa?" Their blank faces made Per angry. "You let him go? My small fowl you can catch, but not—"

At the back of the crowd, Sweet Milk lifted his arm above his head. From his hand, by the hair, hung Bryce's head.

Per was swayed slightly as Andrea turned her face

into his shoulder, to hide from the sight. He cupped the back of her head in his hand but called out, "Nay! T'other one! Hast thee Veensa's head?"

Sweet Milk pointed down the length of the gravel path toward the distant end of the redbrick and glass building. "He ran."

"He lives?" Per said. Andrea's mouth was cut where Windsor had hit her. Windsor had killed Cuddy.

Gobby beat the butt of his lance on the ground and said, "Toorkild! Call 'em in. Let's be gone."

Per swung Andrea around and shoved her into his father's arms. "Look after her!"

Toorkild staggered but clutched at Andrea. "What—?" He had to turn his head to see where Per had gone.

Per shoved through the crowd to its edge, where one of Gobby's men held two horses by the reins. Taking the reins of one from him, Per swung up onto the horse. The stirrups were too short, but that he could cope with. What he couldn't bear was the injustice of Windsor being alive. Windsor had slapped his face with a hand covered in Cuddy's blood. Windsor had knocked Andrea down. Insufferable that he should live to laugh at them—insufferable that, when they were home, when it was too late, he would be jeered for letting Windsor live.

A man gawped up at him from the ground, a lance on his shoulder. Per leaned over and took the lance. As Toorkild yelled somewhere behind him, Per kicked his horse, and men scattered out of their way.

"Per!" Gobby's voice.

Per kicked his horse again. "On!" The horse bounded from a walk to a canter, pounding for the far end of the building, kicking up dust and gravel.

"Per! Get back here!" In exasperation at having wasted so much breath, Gobby hammered the butt of his lance on the wooden wall of the smaller Elf-House.

Toorkild let go of Andrea and ran for his own horse. Ingram looked from his father to Per, galloping away, and swung up onto his horse. And then other men, of both Gobby's and Toorkild's households, were mounting up. Sweet Milk dropped Bryce's head on the grass, so he could ride.

Seeing both Per and Toorkild ride away left Andrea feeling lonely and scared, and when she saw Joe running after the horses on foot, waving an axe, she felt that she hadn't a friend anywhere near. She was looking warily around, and wondering if there were somewhere she could run, when she felt a big, strong hand close on her arm and tug her backward. It was Gobby. As he watched his second son, Wat, ride after Per, followed by a run of men on foot, he ran through every obscene and blasphemous word he knew. "If I'd had the rearing of him . . ." He called the men remaining near him to order. They were to stay where they were, and guard the Elf-Gate, so it would still be open if the madheads ever came back. "Some bugger has to think!"

A sudden howling came from the Elf-Gate and made Gobby and every man turn sharply toward it. Only Andrea knew what the noise was, and she felt her heart ache with strain and fear. The Tube was closing down, was bringing its other half home. As the noise dropped from a howl to a roar and then diminished to a whirring, she watched the lights near the Tube's entrance.

Silence fell with a thump. Then Sterkarms came running to tell Gobby that a new length of pipe had appeared. Gobby's grip on Andrea's arm tightened, and he glowered down at her. "What's happening?"

She'd never been on as good terms with Gobby as with Toorkild, and she was too afraid of him to try and lie or make anything up. "The Gate's closed. You can't go back."

He nodded, looking out over the lawns around them, as if he could see the other Sterkarms. "I promise thee," he said, "I promise, if my sons and I die here, thou'lt die too. Thou too."

27

21st Side: The Battle of Dilsmead Hall

WINDSOR CROUCHED behind the door leading to the parking lot in an agony of indecision, afraid to go forward, afraid to go back, afraid to stay put. He knew his best chance of escape was to dash for his Mercedes. Once locked inside that steel box, he could drive away faster than any horse could run. But he was afraid to set foot on the long stretch of open ground between him and the Mercedes.

The shouting band of Sterkarms had passed by his hiding place without seeing him, but they'd shaken his nerve. What if they were still close by, but keeping quiet? They'd spot him as soon as he stepped through the door. But he wasn't safe inside either, because other Sterkarms were in the building and would soon turn the corner of the corridor, and see him, and come running at him, yelling. . . .

A shout, distant and half muffled by the walls, decided him. It was from somewhere behind him, from some spot lost among turns of corridors and walls of rooms. It was enough to push him out the door and across the path that separated the building from the nearest corner of the parking lot.

He'd reached the first cars when he heard the shouting again. Not words, but long whooping cries. They were clear now, and he could tell they came, not from inside the building, but from its other side. With the voices was another, deeper sound that hadn't carried to him inside the building—the sound of horses' hooves, coming closer.

He stopped and looked back at the door he'd left. It was so much closer than the car. But once cut off from the car, he was trapped. He swayed on his feet, undecided which way to run.

A black horse appeared at the corner of the hall, on the farther side of the parking lot from him. It went back on its haunches as it was reined in and then curvetted in a circle, its rider turning in the saddle to look toward Windsor. Raising his long lance above his head, the rider cried out, with a sergeant major's scream: "*Sterk*arm!"

Windsor ran a couple of steps back toward the building—and saw other Sterkarms, on foot, coming toward him, running, carrying pikes and axes. He stopped, his heart a center of pain inside him, his feet stammering in the gravel as he made to run now this way, now that. He lifted his gun, its weight awkward in his hand, and pointed it at the men on foot. It made him happy to see that they stopped. He spun around and ran from them with all the strength and speed he could force from himself, cursing his own slow heaviness, making for his car at the other end of the parking lot.

* * *

Joe, axe in hand, ran his hardest but soon found himself overtaken by Sterkarms who'd never smoked and had

530

spent their lives bounding up and down sodden hills. And not even they could keep up with the ride.

Ahead of him, he saw, horses, riders standing in the saddle, were turning the corner of the house; and by the time he'd panted around the same corner, the horses were out of sight, at the front of the house.

His run slowed to a tired jog, Joe reached the front of the house, with its broad gravel drive, its marble pillars and the lawns and flower beds sweeping down toward the gates. The horsemen were gathered in a knot in front of the hall's marble steps, reined in for some kind of conference.

It was easy to spot Per among them—he was the one without helmet or jakke, the one who, at the cry of "Sterkarm!" turned his horse and kicked it to a trot, pounding over the lawn toward the parking lot on the hall's farther side. As he went, he rose and fell in the saddle, bringing the heavy, eight-foot lance he carried down to the horizontal, managing it with as little thought as he'd need to move his arm. Through a flower bed the horse went, scattering petals. In seconds, the other horses were following, with a great drumming that made the ground thrum under Joe's feet. Despite his fear of what might follow, it was an exhilarating sight, and Joe picked up heavy feet and ran after them.

As Per reached the corner of the hall and saw the great gray square where the Elf-Carts stood in row after row, all flashing and gleaming in the sun, he reined his horse to a walk. A movement on the farther side of this pound for Elf-Carts caught his eye, and squinting against the glare, he saw an Elf-Man—Windsor!

He kicked his horse to a fast walk, scanning the long

line of Elf-Carts, looking for a gap between them wide enough to let his horse through. Windsor was running. Doubtless he meant to climb inside one of these Elf-Carts and ride it away.

Per kicked his horse to a canter, standing in his stirrups and leaning over his mount's withers. "On! On!" He felt the horse stretch to a gallop beneath him, hardly seeming to touch the ground. He balanced above the power, riding it.

The horse carried Per to the end of the line of Elf-Carts before Windsor could cover half the distance—but at the end of the line, Per had to turn the horse. He reined in to a walk while watching what Windsor was going to do, but the horse still wanted to run, and then shied at the other horses coming up—and Per had to tussle with his mount and turn it in a circle.

Windsor, midway along the parking lot's side, looked back and saw mounted men guiding their horses along the path between the cars and the building, toward the clear aisle that ran the parking lot's length. Ahead of him, a knot of horsemen was gathering, though there was still the width of the parking lot between him and them.

Windsor hesitated, gasping for breath. He could feel sweat running between his skin and his shirt. He lifted the heavy gun in one hand and held it out at arm's length. His arm shook with strain and fear, but he hoped the threat of the gun would keep the Sterkarms off.

As the first horse, with a clash of hooves on concrete, turned into the aisle between the cars, Windsor reached into his pocket with his free hand and found his car keys. Thank God for power locks! As he started running again, he held out his keys, pressed the button and heard, with thankfulness, the electronic squeal that told him all the locks were sprung. The passenger door was nearest. He'd get in there, lock all the doors, and crawl over to the wheel.

Per kicked his horse to a fast trot and, rising and falling in the saddle, rode it along the second side of the parking lot, and turned it onto the third side. Windsor was running toward him. Per kicked his horse to a canter and lowered his lance to take Windsor in the chest.

Windsor saw the horse's broad chest bearing down on him, heard its hooves, felt the tremor in the ground, and slipped between two of the cars parked beside him. The angle of the lance changed to follow him, and Windsor ducked desperately, not knowing if crouching would save him. The lance swept over his head, and then horse and rider were past him, and the rider was reining in, and turning the horse.

Windsor lunged for the end of the cars and reached the clear aisle. A clatter of hooves warned him to look up, and he saw other horses coming at him between the cars. He ran ahead of them and threw himself against the sun-heated black metal of his own car, reaching for the nearest door—the back door.

He got his hand around the handle and pressed the button hard. The clatter of hooves was loud and close. As he rolled himself into the car's backseat, he heard a tearing crunch, and the car rocked, nearly tipping him out again. He clung to the front seat to hold himself in and looked back through the narrowing space as he pulled the door shut. There was a sound of gushing liquid, and a stink of gasoline. A long lance shaft protruded from the torn black metal of his car's side.

A lance head, aimed at him, had missed and torn through the car's bodywork, into the gas tank. Metal screeched and tore, and the car swayed as the lance was tugged and twisted free. Stinking gasoline gushed out in a stream.

Slamming the car's door, Windsor collapsed onto the seat and pressed the button on his key ring. The lock of every door snapped shut, and the alarm was armed. For an instant he sagged and heaved for breath, feeling himself safe inside his glass-and-steel box. Then he scrambled over the backs of the front seats to reach the wheel. With luck, even though the gas tank was punctured, there might be enough fuel remaining in a corner to get him away.

Per, turning his horse back to the Elf-Cart, could see Windsor inside, tumbling into the driver's seat, where he would move levers and turn the driver's wheel to make the thing move. Per looked down at the thick, black wheels that the Elf-Cart ran on. Lifting his lance, angling it, he drove it down as hard as he could into the nearest wheel.

It was easier than he'd thought it would be. Maybe the lance head, being cold iron, broke through the Elf-Work protecting the cart. The wheel puffed and hissed, and when Per twisted and withdrew his lance, the wheel groaned, and the whole cart began to list.

Ecky, at the car's other end, his lance still dripping gas, shouted, "Sterkarm!" and drove his lance into the wheel nearest him. The car tilted still more.

Windsor, sweating behind the steering wheel, steadied one hand with the other and managed to insert the ignition key. Even on punctured wheels, he could get away. . . .

A third horseman, coming up behind the car, punctured a third tire. "Never mind," Windsor whispered to himself as the car swayed. On three punctured tires, he'd slam it into reverse, and if the horses were in the way, he'd drive through them.

Per, wheeling his horse so he could get at the other front wheel with his lance, saw the Elf-Cart's face. It had two great glass eyes and, beneath them, a grinning mouth. With memories of heroes plunging lances into the grinning mouths of dragons, Per drove his lance into the Elf-Cart's mouth, wrenched it out, drove it again.

Jesus! Windsor thought. If he's got the radiator . . . He turned the ignition again, and the car's engine started. Windsor's heart soared as the quiet throbbing ran through the big Mercedes. The windshield might be filled with the wet black flanks of a horse, the stamping and clashing of hooves might be all around him, his own heart might be hammering in his ears and throat but he was on his way.

He pressed down the clutch, released the handbrake, shoved the gears into reverse—and the engine stuttered, coughed, growled and died. His hand went to the ignition key, turned it off, turned it on—he was holding his breath. The engine chugged and chugged—and died.

A bang, and the windshield turned white, crazed before his eyes. He didn't know what had happened—and then saw the long, brown shaft, passing just by his arm, passing between the two front seats, and ending in the leather of the backseat behind him. The crash of it punching through the toughened glass still dimmed his hearing and made his heart hop. He watched the shaft twist, glimpsed the shifting of the horse through the shattered, whitened glass, heard the tearing as the iron head was dragged from the leather behind him—and then the shaft blurred past, withdrawing.

Oh God, Windsor thought. Oh God, help me. He remembered the gun in his hand and lifted it. He pointed it at the shifting shapes glimpsed through the shattered glass, found it too heavy for one shaking hand, and tried gripping it with two—then couldn't quite decide which finger should be on the trigger.

An explosion, of noise and of whiteness. Sharp, cutting things, glassy hailstones, flew into his face, and he closed his eyes against them, hit himself in the face with the gun as he instinctively drew back his hands to guard his face. The car alarm whooped and howled. Windsor caught a glimpse of the lance head as it smashed more of the shattered glass from the window frame. Fragments of broken glass were scattered over the car's shining hood, and beyond that, fidgeting at the strange sound of the alarm, was a thickset black horse. Leaning far from its saddle to peer in at him through the broken windshield was the wielder of the lance.

The rider wore no jakke and no helmet. Windsor recognized the bruises rather than the face. The nose and mouth and jaw all swollen and dirtied with bruising, and one eye half closed by the red, darkening swelling round it. The less bruised eye stared at him with a silvery fixity that seemed slightly mad.

Per kicked his feet from the stirrups, swung his right leg over the horse, and slid down from its back. The eight-foot lance was still in his hands as he came toward the car.

Windsor lifted the heavy gun in both hands and pointed it at Per's face, trying to ignore the car alarm's incessant screaming. At this range, could he miss? His hands and arms shook, both in fear of what he was going to do and see and from the weight of the gun, but he tightened his grip and held steady.

Per hefted the lance and held it, one hand over its butt end, ready to drive it forward. The iron head pointed at Windsor's chest. He looked into the barrel of Windsor's Elf-Pistol. He knew that Windsor was preparing to fire it at his face and kill him. But to back down from this Elf, who had hit Andrea and killed Cuddy and punched him—the rage and humiliation would be too great. It would keep him from sleeping for three nights. At that moment, risking a pistol ball in the face seemed an easier choice. Pistols were clumsy anyway. And Windsor was surrounded by Sterkarms. Even if he hit his aim, he wouldn't crow for long. Looking beyond the pistol barrel, into Windsor's eyes, Per said, "*Sa, shoota!*" So, shoot!

Windsor tried. His forefinger hauled at the trigger. His hands trembled. He even changed his grip, the gun slipping in sweat, and tried to pull the trigger with his other forefinger. The trigger wouldn't move. "Shit!" He remembered how he'd played with the safety catch. He must have set it on.

Per drew back the lance—and a banshee shrieking rang out, louder even than the wailing of Windsor's wounded Elf-Cart, a din that rose over the roofs of the Hall, setting the horses prancing and rearing. Per turned away from Windsor, startled, looking to see what made the uncanny noise.

Windsor squirmed in his seat, clutching at the gun, pushing at the safety catch. His heart thumped and pounded. He could hardly breathe, but he was ecstatic. He knew what the noise was: a police siren. Rescue was coming. The safety catch off, he raised the gun again, aiming at Per's body.

* * *

The police car drew up at the pillared entrance of Dilsmead Hall, gravel rattling against its sides. From the parking lot at the side of the hall, Joe ran hard to meet them.

He reached the car, out of breath, and leaned on the hood. A policeman wound down his window and looked out at him.

Glancing over his shoulder, Joe could see one edge of the parking lot and Sterkarms running about on foot, with pikes, and a couple of horsemen carrying lances. "Reenactment," Joe said. "Historical society. Battle of. Battle of Dilsmead Hall!"

Joe backed off as the policeman opened the door and got out. "We had a report—"

"It's all an act!" Joe said. "A family day out."

The driver had got out too. "In the week?"

"Rehearsal!"

From the parking lot came an ear-thumping crack. The policemen looked at each other across the car. "Gun!"

"Blanks!" Joe said, while wondering who had been shot.

"That was real!"

538

The driver was speaking into his radio. "—need assistance. Gunfire. Urgent assistance."

Joe turned and ran back toward the parking lot. God help us! he thought. Any minute now, up the drive, fast-response units with rifles in the trunk and marksmen at the wheel. And who'd been shot?

* * *

Windsor lay sprawled across the car's front seats, toppled by the gun's recoil. It had thrown his arms upward and punched his hands into the roof of the car, crunching and bruising his fingers. The noise had been so loud, he felt he'd been kicked in the head and then had both ears stuffed with cotton. Christ! Guns in films never sounded like *that*. Where the bullet went he had no idea. But the gun worked.

Windsor hauled himself upright again. The car alarm was still whooping, the police sirens were bawling, and through all the din people could be heard shouting. Windsor aimed the gun through the broken windshield. He had to keep the Sterkarms off until the police could reach him. This time he'd be ready for the stiffness of the gun's trigger, its powerful recoil, its noise. He pulled the trigger a second time.

* * *

As he ran, waving his axe, Joe was desperately trying to think of the Sterkarm words he needed. Even if he could think of them, he didn't know if he had breath to speak them. He ran between two parked cars and then along the open aisle toward the black Mercedes where the horses shied and wheeled.

Stopping, he looked back over his shoulder and, seeing no policemen, heaved for breath. "*Gaw!*" he yelled, and made shooing movements in the direction of the Elf-Gate. *"Backa!"*

There was another report, so loud that he tried to cover his ears with his hands despite holding the axe.

In front of the Mercedes, a mounted man toppled from his saddle. The horse went racing away, back toward the Hall.

Joe started running again. *"Gaw! Erlf-Yett! Gaw!"*

* * *

Per's ears were deaf from the gunshot. In ringing silence, he saw his father keel from the saddle, saw his body thump heavily into the gravel—and then the horse raced away and Toorkild was dragged behind, his foot trapped in the stirrup.

In Per's mind there was a collapse, a crash as if the tower had fallen. He watched as the stirrup broke and Toorkild's body lay still while the horse sped away. Per's next breath shook him, and he took a couple of running steps toward Toorkild before stopping, afraid to go nearer.

Per turned, moving without thought or plan, a stillness of fury in his mind. He drove the lance through the Mercedes' broken windshield and into Windsor.

Windsor felt he'd been slammed in the belly with a cricket bat. He looked down and saw the lance shaft, as thick around as a woman's wrist, leaving his belly. He said, "No!" He refused to believe it. His shirt was turning red. He could see the wood grain in the shaft. He could see it resting on the steering wheel and angling up through the broken windshield. "No," he said. His right arm rested on the steering wheel's other edge, and the hand was loosely clasped around the heavy gun, though his fingers were beginning to open and let it go.

Per swam across the smooth hood of the Elf-Cart, scattering pieces of broken glass. He reached in through the window, leaning against the lance as he did so, and moving it. Windsor cried out. He tried to lift the heavy gun, but Per caught hold of it and wrenched it from his fingers. He struck Windsor across the face with it once and then threw the pistol away, onto the gravel beside the car. Pistols were clumsy and unreliable, and he wanted no part of the ill-starred weapon that had shot his father.

Windsor lay slumped in his seat, his head on one shoulder, bleeding from the nose and mouth. Per, on the hood of the car, swiveled on his hip, sat up and got to his feet, the metal of the hood denting under his weight. He was startled when Joe suddenly appeared, yelling, beside the car, and he clutched at the lance shaft for support. "Chyo," Per said. "Give me thy axe—give it me! I'll take his head."

Joe threw his axe onto the path in front of the car. Per, standing on the hood of the car, turned in surprise and stared at it, and wasn't prepared when Joe reached up, grabbed his wrist and yanked him from on top of the car. Per landed, staggering, and only just kept his feet.

Joe looked back toward the front of the Hall as the din of sirens increased. The assistance the policeman had called for was arriving.

Joe caught Per by the arms, spun him around, pushed him forward. In front of him, Per saw his father. Toorkild was looking knocked-about and shaken. He leaned against the flank of Sweet Milk's horse, one hand pressed to his own ribs. A jakke made a good bulletproof vest.

Per ran to his father, slowing only to avoid frightening the horse. "Daddy—thy knife! Give—"

"Mount up." Toorkild's voice was thin and wheezing. He hunched as he spoke.

"Daddy—"

"Mount up!"

Wat, in the saddle, was holding a riderless horse by the reins. Per, instead of mounting it, stood beside it and cupped his hands. Toorkild, moving awkwardly, set his foot in his son's hands, and Per threw him up on to the horse's back. When Toorkild was settled in the saddle, Per stood at his knee, looking up.

Toorkild gritted his teeth against the pain of his bruised and possibly cracked ribs, and looked down at his son's bruised, scared face. Putting his big, heavy hand on Per's head, Toorkild turned his son's face against his own knee, then rapped Per's skull with his hard finger ends. "Mount. Now."

One of the footmen brought up the horse Toorkild had been riding. It was still skittish, and shifted and shied as Per tried to mount.

Joe, hopping from one foot to the other, had been staring over the roofs of the cars at the corner of the Hall. He saw policemen appear, one carrying something long. A rifle?

But the horses were moving, their hooves thumping, the muscles shifting under their shaggy coats. The footmen ran with them, often clutching at the horses' stirrups and going in great bounds.

Joe made to run after them, then turned back toward Windsor. He was a Sterkarm now, there was no going back on that, but . . . The man in the car was a man. And he had a lance stuck in him.

The policemen were coming between the cars on the other side of the parking lot as Joe, already wincing from what he might see, peered in through the broken windshield. He saw a shirtfront soaked in blood and looked away, looked at the policemen again. One of them shouted, "Hey, you!"

Joe knew he should run—but wondered whether he should try and pull the lance out of Windsor. Would it be good for him, or do him more harm?

"Chyo!"

Joe turned his head so fast he hurt his neck. Per was riding toward him, was coming back to him.

"Go!" Joe said. "Get away!"

Per reined in beside Joe and, looking at the policemen, offered Joe his hand. *"Opp!"*

"I can't get up there! I can't ride! Go!"

"Chyo! Opp!" Per took his foot from the nearer stirrup, so Joe could use it.

Per obviously wasn't going to go without him. The policemen were still yelling at them from the other side of the parking lot. No time, no choice. He set his foot in the stirrup, grasped Per's hand in one of his and the back of the saddle in the other. He tried to heave himself up, and Per pulled, but Joe's already tired leg ached under his weight; he gasped for breath and dropped back to the ground. The horse shifted, and he hopped after it, still clinging to the saddle and Per's hand. Sweat ran into his eyes, and he felt as foolish as he did scared.

"Stand still or we'll fire!"

"Hoppa, Chyo. Opp, opp! Hoppa!"

He was hopping. The horse kept moving and he had

to hop, with fresh sweat breaking out under his arms and across his back.

"Hoppa, Chyo!" Sense broke through. He had to listen like his grandad. Per was urging him not to hop, but to jump, as the older Sterkarms did when mounting, giving three little jumps before hauling themselves up. Joe gritted his teeth, took a fiercer hold on Per's hand and saddle-bow, gave three little jumps and then pushed with his leg and heaved with his shoulder, gritting his teeth harder still. Just when he thought the muscles of his thigh would crack, and his arm come out of his shoulder, he found himself lifting up on a level with Per. Desperately, he swung his right leg over, and had no time to enjoy his triumph before the horse was moving, terrifyingly fast, and he was clinging to Per, his backside jolting against iron-hard bones, his inner thighs and bits being bruised against the high back of the saddle.

From behind them came the deafeningly loud crack of a firearm—but higher pitched than the sound Windsor's gun had made. The policemen were firing at them. Joe held his breath, thinking either he or Per, or the horse must have been hit. But Per laughed—he actually laughed, when Joe had never felt less like laughing—and the horse went on pounding along, the grass and red-brick going by in a blur. How much did it hurt, to fall off a horse? Joe wondered. As he was jolted again and again on the horse's hard bones, and the hard saddle, he thought it couldn't possibly hurt more than riding one.

Ingram had turned his horse back to look for them, and he fell in behind them, guarding their backs. They turned the corner of the Hall, and there was the Elf-

Gate, with a knot of Sterkarms, on horse and on foot, gathered before it.

"Entraya!" Per called out, and kissed his hand, and there was Andrea, on foot alongside them, trying to stay with them as they joined the other horses.

Per, still breathlessly laughing, reined in. Wat turned his horse toward them.

"*T'Erlf-Yett air lukket.*"

Joe thankfully slid down over the horse's backside— and then had to hop and jump away as it kicked out at him. But he was glad to feel his feet smack the ground. Then, belatedly, he understood Wat—or thought he did, while hoping he was wrong. The Elf-Gate was locked?

28

21st Side: "I Have No Wings"

GOBBY WRAPPED THE fingers of his big right hand about Andrea's arm and wouldn't let go. He dragged her about with him as he posted guards about the Tube's control room, and even if she could have thought of something to say, she didn't think she would have dared speak to him.

From the other side of the building, drifting over the rooftop, they heard the thumping hooves, the whoops and cries of the ride. There were other cries too, with a harsher edge—cries of fear. As Andrea listened, her hands clenched and she bit her lip, her imagination showing her atrocities and slaughters—showing her Per killing and being killed. It was miserable, not knowing for certain what was happening.

Small bands of Sterkarms returned on foot, bringing with them curtains, cushions, framed pictures, small coffee tables, coats and umbrellas. One pushed along a large, wheeled office chair. All the booty was carried up the ramp to the mouth of the Tube. Some men, despite being told that the Gate was closed, ventured inside and found that the road led only to another platform above the lawn at the rear of the control room.

"Tell them to stay out of it," Andrea begged Gobby. No one had been in the control room when the Tube had suddenly come home, so she suspected that it was running on a preset program. It might have been set to go traveling again in thirty minutes' time, or an hour—and what would happen if the Tube traveled while curious Sterkarms were poking about inside it? She had no idea. Would their very molecules be scrambled, reassembling them as parts of the cushions and coffeepots they carried? Or would they just vanish into the cracks between dimensions? She wouldn't have risked the life of a laboratory rat to find out.

Gobby said, "Quiet, woman!"

From the other side of the Hall came a wailing, a screaming. Gobby, alarmed, and with no idea of what the noise was, squeezed her arm painfully hard. Andrea, who did know what it was, was probably more alarmed. Police sirens. And blows and bangs, resounding on metal, and smashing glass. The Sterkarms recognized the explosions as gunfire before Andrea did. While she was still gaping in shock, they were jerking to attention, hefting their pikes, sickles, axes, even running a few steps toward the noise.

"Stand!" Gobby bellowed, his yell numbing Andrea's ears. The Sterkarms fell back into their places, their hands gripping their weapons, glowering at Gobby or staring in the direction of the gunfire.

And then the ride returned, a hurly-burly of racing horses and stamping hooves, of lances and yells and running men. There was Toorkild, clutching at his own ribs, and leaning far forward in his saddle, with Sweet Milk riding close beside him on one side, and his nephew Wat

547

on the other. Gobby let go of Andrea's arm to go forward and help his brother from the saddle.

Andrea, clutching at her bruised arm, looked for Per and couldn't see him. She tried to make her way through the gathering Sterkarms, now being shoulder charged and nearly knocked down by a man on foot—"Watch thysen, Honey!"—and now almost stumbling under the hooves of a horse.

She reached the edge of the crowd and saw, just at the corner of the Hall, a horse being turned in the center of the broad gravel path, its rider looking back. For a moment she thought the rider was Per—it looked like him—and then she saw that it was the youngest of Per's cousins, Ingram.

Another horse and rider appeared, pelting for the Gate, and Ingram fell in with it. Per was the rider of the second horse, and someone was clinging to his waist and jolting about on the horse behind him. As the horses came nearer, she saw it was Joe.

Waving, she turned and ran alongside the horse, though they soon overtook her. Per saw her, laughed, and kissed his hand. Then they were past her, and Per was reining in beside Wat, and Joe was awkwardly sliding down over the horse's tail.

She saw Per drop down from his horse, but instead of looking for her, he pushed into the crowd of Sterkarms, his reins looped over his arm and his horse following him. When she found him, he had his arms around his father. "Winded," Toorkild was saying, patting Per's chest. "Take more than a fall off hoss to finish me!"

"Per!" Andrea said, and was glad to see him turn to her, though for a moment she was shocked by his bruises, his closed eye and swollen nose and mouth. No one, seeing him then, would think of calling him "May." She put her arms around him, and felt his arms tighten across her back. "Oh, thank— I thought tha'd been shot!"

Per laughed. "So thought we!"

Joe was behind Per. "Police," he said to Andrea. "Fast-response units. Marksmen."

"Oh God!" she said, and Per, still holding her, said, "*Vah?*"

Joe said, "The Elf-Gate's *locked*?"

Andrea was looking toward the corners of the Hall, but couldn't see any sign of armed policemen. Perhaps they'd gone inside the building, to aim their high-powered rifles from windows overlooking the Sterkarms. Absently, she said, "It closed down."

"Oh, great!" Joe said. "Just—" A whirring rapidly rose to a whine, grew shriller, rising to a scream. Everyone turned to look at the Gate.

Andrea leaned close to Per's ear and yelled against the noise, "When that light turns green . . ." She pointed to the warning lights near the Tube's entrance. The scream abruptly stopped as it passed beyond hearing, leaving her shouting in silence. "That light, there. When it turns green, go! Go through!" The lights changed. "Go on! Quick! It's open now—go!"

Gobby lifted his lance above his head, pointed and bellowed. The Sterkarms moved. Footmen scrambled up the ramp and into the Tube, shouldering pikes and lugging curtains between them. One man carried a coffee table over his helmet, clutching a table leg and a sickle in one hand. Horses were led up the ramp and into the Tube, and across the horses' backs were slung curtains and rugs and coats.

Toorkild trudged up the ramp slowly, one hand on his ribs. Joe was close behind him. Per, holding his horse's reins in one hand and Andrea's hand in the other, started up the ramp. "Wait!" Andrea said, and pulled back against his hand.

Per looked around and stopped. Other people, on foot or mounted, some leading horses, passed them by. "Entraya, we must go."

Looking over her shoulder, Andrea saw a policeman look around the corner of the Hall and then quickly withdraw. The sight made her want to shove Per ahead of her up the ramp and hurry after him—but her heart seemed to be a weight of iron inside her, holding her back. "Nay. Nay. Wait."

Ingram was standing beside Per, waiting for him, and holding the reins of his own horse. Per handed him his reins too. "Go on. Grammie, go. *Go!*" Ingram led both horses up the ramp, and Per turned to face Andrea, taking both her hands, and trying to pull her along.

"Per, nay. I don't . . . I can't. . ."

"Tha must!" Only a few Sterkarms were left at the foot of the ramp, and they were climbing it fast, passing them. From the top of the ramp, Gobby shouted, "Per!"

Andrea's mind was in a panic. She had so much to decide, and she had to decide immediately. She couldn't think in words, only in a whirl of images. The warmth and darkness of her bower, with Per in the bed beside her, his smell and touch and laugh, and the rain dripping from the thatch outside the shutters, was replaced by the picture of her mother and father sitting together in their little house, with the radiator keeping them warm and the television crooning to them, and if she went with Per, she might never see them again. . . . But if she went with Per, she'd be the lady of the tower, and an Elf-May, with more power over the people around her, and more respect from them, than she could ever have 21st side, and she'd have Per. . . . And, after all, if she went to work at the other end of the country, or in America, she wouldn't see her parents either. . . .

Per dragged her a few steps farther up the ramp. They were nearly at the top, and there stood Gobby, glowering. Joining the Sterkarms again wouldn't be easy: Most of them must believe her a traitor, and not all of them would be willing to believe her account. Could she live among them, all alone? If they chose, when Per was absent, or when she and Per fell out, they could make her life miserable. . . .

"Per! Kom!"

"Entraya! Be kind, be so kind—"

An explosion—a shot fired from a rifle—set their hearts banging, and they ran, hand in hand, up the ramp and into the Tube. But once inside, Andrea stopped and dragged Per to a halt too. "I can't. I can't!"

Gobby gripped Per's upper arm and dragged at him. "Kom!"

Andrea tried, in the seconds that she had, to imagine living in her own twenty-first century again, without Per and without any hope of reaching him. She saw, in her mind, a bland, neat landscape, all pastel painted walls and smooth carpets. Warm, safe little boxes of brick and glass. All comfort and convenience, at least for her. Prepackaged food, and buses and trains and telephones.

And how lonely and drab and dull it was going to be without Per, without his foxy smell and loud voice, without the comfort of his hugs and self-assurance and readiness to defend her. She ached as if her heart were being dragged out of her. If she took her hands from Per's and went back down the ramp to the 21st, it felt as if she would leave her heart with him. It was no poetic turn of speech: That was exactly how it felt.

She let him pull her another step or two into the Tube, and a flock of terrors flew from it into her face. Sickness without medicine, accidents without hospitals—Per killed in some skirmish and she left alone and five hundred years from home. "I can't! I can't!" She twisted her wrists, trying to break his hold, but his grip was strong. "Per, let go!"

"Ssh! All's right. Little bird, it will be all right." He leaned back, pulling her on.

"Per—Per, come thou and live with me!"

Per's face was aghast, and Gobby said, "Nay!" and clasped one arm around Per, as if he thought Andrea had the strength or power to drag Per away against his will. And from the farther end of the Tube came Toorkild's voice, shouting Per's name in alarm.

"Per," Andrea said, "go!" The Tube had shut down once, and it might do so again. They shouldn't be lingering here inside it. But once they parted— But if she went with him— Oh, she hadn't time to start considering it all over again. Instead of pulling back against his hands, she went toward him suddenly, stretching her neck as she lifted her head to kiss him. He let go of her hands, and she put them around his neck. His arms clasped crushingly tight around her.

"Entraya, Entraya—" She felt his tears on her face.

"Per, we haven't time. I can't, I can't. I'd only end by hating thee—" She pushed him away, and he let her go. She turned to go but looked back over her shoulder. "Go! Run!" Gobby was already dragging Per farther into the Tube. Good. Gobby would see that he went. "Fare well!" she called.

Per called after her, but the ramp was before her, and she pelted down it, hardly keeping her feet, with a great, swelling pain in her chest that was relief and grief. She'd reached the gravel path at the bottom of the ramp before she remembered the police marksmen and raised her hands, feeling foolish, and called out, "Don't shoot!"

Someone shouted back, "Stand still!"

She stood still and heard, behind her, the screaming that meant the Tube was closing down. Was closing down and might never be opened again. Even if it was, she doubted she'd be going through it. The pain in her chest swelled into her throat, threatening to burst her. She sat down in the gravel, bowed over her knees and sobbed.

As if she were just hearing it, she suddenly heard what Per had called after her as she'd run away from him, back to the 21st. He'd shouted, "I have no wings."

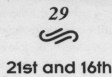
21st and 16th

THE DAY WAS BRIGHT and sunny, and Andrea was glad of the strong breeze that blew her hair behind her and kept her face cool as she climbed the steep hillside. The turf under her feet was thick and a rich dark green. Her boots sank into it, and it sprang back, making it a little like walking on a trampoline.

She reached the ridge of the hill, and the wind freshened, feeling colder and damper on her skin, making a lonely moaning past her ears. Below her the land fell away in a long steep slope into the valley that was still marked on her map as Bedesdale. The little river was still called Bedes Water, but it didn't run the course she knew. And, now, a narrow gray road ran beside the river, and a small metal sign pointed the way to the tower. It was "a place of historical interest," a "heritage site." Americans and Australians, named Stackam and Starkarm and Stairkarm, came to it looking for their ancestral home.

From the ridge she looked out into a wide sky, blue as harebells, and below it the green hills, all running their long spurs down into the valley. Cloud shadows moved over the slopes, which were still green and brown, but there weren't as many greens, nor were they as vibrant as she remembered. Though the nearest factories and towns were many miles away, still they'd dulled the air.

She said hello to an elderly couple out walking their Yorkshire terrier, and went on remembering two big, loping dogs, like giant, shaggy greyhounds. . . .

The tower stood just below the hill's ridge, built on a craggy rock pile left behind by a glacier. As she walked, the top of the tower came into view, poking over the ridge, and more and more of it could be seen as she drew nearer. It was in better repair than she'd expected, but the night before, she'd read in her guidebook that the owner of the land in the early nineteenth century had repaired and partly rebuilt the tower, to improve the view from his house.

There was no sign of the wall that had once surrounded the tower, or its gatehouse. All the outbuildings that had crowded the yard were gone. There was nothing but the crag, thickly overgrown. Not even a path led up the crag. To reach the tower, she had to scramble over boulders, and through thornbushes and briers and thickets of nettles.

Once on top of the crag, she was shy of approaching the tower. It never had looked welcoming; now there hung about it a forbidding chill of desolation. Instead, she wandered about the top of the crag, kicking amid the undergrowth, trying to find any trace, just one stone, of the wall or gatehouse or outhouses.

There was nothing. Probably, if she searched the countryside around, she'd find field walls and barns and houses built with stones taken from the tower's walls.

She went over to the tower. It seemed smaller and

more pinched than she remembered. The great door of wood and nails had gone, and so had the iron grids that had once guarded the door and stairs. There was nothing but a dark, square hole in the stonework. The lintel was so low that she had to duck to enter.

Inside, the windowless ground floor was dark. A twisted rectangle of light was thrown onto the floor by the doorway, with her shadow at its center. The light fell on a rubble of broken stone. It was damp in there, and chill, and she felt afraid of going in, but she made herself.

The stairs opened to the right of the doorway, corkscrewing counterclockwise—it was a Sterkarm tower. The plaster had gone from the stone walls, leaving them cold and damp, the gray gritstone streaked with rusty red.

She climbed the narrow staircase, where dampness hung in the air. The chill and darkness made her look quickly over her shoulder, fearing that someone was behind her. No one was. Her heart beat fast, and she was sad.

At the first turn of the stair, she found her way blocked by a wall of modern concrete blocks and had to turn back. There would be no visiting the hall, or the family's private rooms, or the roof where the watchman had stood guard.

Outside the tower, back in the sunshine, she looked up at the lintel. The keystone over it was carved. Wind and rain had worn the carving almost away, but she knew what it was. Emblazoned on a shield, an upraised arm, a left arm, brandishing a dagger. The Sterkarm handshake.

She sat on a boulder at the edge of the crag and

watched a kestrel as it hung over the valley. Below her, out of sight, a car purred by on the road, followed by a noisier truck.

Among the Sterkarms she'd heard many stories of mortals who'd found their way into Elf-Land. Some had been taken there by the Elves, as willing or unwilling captives. Some blundered unknowingly through the barriers that divide Man's-Home from Elf-Land. Others, with unwise curiosity, found their way there by exploring some cave in the hillside, by following the sound of ravishingly beautiful music or chasing down a snow-white, red-eared deer.

Most of the stories had ended with the wanderers being forever lost, nothing of them ever seen or heard again. But a few had told of visitors to Elf-Land who returned. They came home thinking they'd been away for no more than three days or three hours, and found that it had been seven years. They came back to a home still familiar, to a welcoming family who still knew them—but they were as lost as those who never returned.

No mortal food could ease their hunger, no drink their thirst. No company could please them, or music soothe them. They could not sleep or rest, and wandered the hills, searching for the door that opened into Elf-Land. These stories often ended with their vanishing again. Let's hope, the storyteller would say, that they found their way back to the Elf-Land they longed for. But maybe the truth was they'd lain down somewhere in the lonely hills and let the cold take them.

None of the Sterkarms' stories had told the other side; none told of what happened to Elves who ventured into Man's-Home and then returned to Elf-Land. If only she could have reached them again, Andrea could have told the Sterkarms that story.

No company pleased her. In a neat, clean flat, with central heating and electric lights to snap on instantly, she longed for the smoke and soot and stink and squalor of Toorkild's hall, for the dim flickering of candlelight and the reek of burning tallow, for all the difficulty of lighting fires, the throat-catching smoke and the smell of burning peat.

She missed the noise and jostle and chatter, but when she went to a pub in search of it, she couldn't find it. The music was loud and persistent, but not the same. Her friends talked of boyfriends and television, lectures, essays, films, books—and it wasn't at all the same.

Whenever she wanted clean water, she turned on a tap. She had oranges and bananas, and soft, fresh whole-wheat bread in a plastic wrapper. Everything she ate was tasty and hygienically prepared, but she missed the Sterkarm porridge, heavy bread and small beer.

Her bed was too soft, her room too warm. She didn't sleep well. Awake, she thought of Per and missed him to the point of tears. Every man she met made her think of him, and miss him more.

Asleep, she often dreamed she was in her bower again, laughing with Per in the warm dark under the scratchy blankets, Per's own musk mingling with the thick, sweet smell of old hay that rose from the mattress with their every move—and then she'd wake, snap on her electric lamp and lie, alone, between smooth cotton sheets that smelled of soap powder, on her inner-spring mattress. And she missed Per so much, so much . . .

. . . That she'd come here, to Bedesdale, to this ruin.

She knew she shouldn't be there, mooning, with James Windsor still seriously ill in the hospital, with Bryce dead, but . . .

The sun shone down on the boulders, warming them, drawing the scent from grass and leaves. Silence lay heavy over the hills and seemed to throb gently against the ear, but was underlain by a persistent drone from the distant main road and the occasional closer passing of a car in the valley below. It wasn't the deep, deep silence of the 16th. Per seemed even farther from her than he did in her dreams.

On Christmas Eve, the Sterkarms said, and on May Day, on Midsummer's Eve and Halloween, the barriers between the worlds grew frail as mist and people foolish enough to leave their firesides in the darkling hours, when it was neither day nor night, might pass through the mist between one step and another and, without knowing, leave the mortal world for Elf-Land.

Perhaps if she came back here on Christmas Eve, or May Day, on Midsummer's Eve or Halloween, in the darkling hours, she could stretch her hand out into the dusk, and Per's hand would meet it.

* * *

In the same valley, on the other side of the air . . .

"Here!" Per called. He came back to Joe from among the bawling black sheep, hauling another sheep along by its horns. Swart followed behind him, occasionally sniffing at the sheep, but too well used to them to bite or chase.

"This be my best ewe," Per said, though how he could pick her out from among all the others was more than Joe knew. Nor how Per had known that he'd find her on this particular hillside. Joe had a lot—well, everything—to learn about sheep. It was frightening how much he had to learn, but exhilarating too. He would learn. He'd be a mug not to put all his energy into learning whatever was needful. Here was his chance for all he'd ever wanted: his own home, a family. And more than he'd ever wanted: property, respect.

Per, still holding the ewe by one horn, rubbed his hand through the thick, greasy fleece. "She be a good mother, this one. Every year for the last three years she's had twins and both have lived. Whatever lambs she has this year are thine."

He'd already promised Joe a young ram and a breeding ewe. Adding the as-yet-unborn lambs made a generous gift, and Per was silent for an eye's blink as he considered the loss to his own flock. But better to be known for generosity than meanness. Every impulse toward meanness should be resisted. Per let the ewe go, looked up and said, "And I'll give thee another breeding ewe besides."

Per's bruises had faded. His nose was its right shape again, and both eyes were open, though one was still surrounded by yellow and brown marks, and the white bloodshot, but he was recognizable again as Per May. He gave Joe his big, bright smile.

"Thanks," Joe said. "It's good of you. Thee. You." He was never sure how he should address Per. Being a friend, and the younger, made Per "thou." But being the master to whom Joe had sworn faith made him "you."

"We be 'thou' to each other," Per said. Letting go of the ewe, he came over to Joe and hugged him in the affectionate way of the Sterkarms, which Joe still hoped he'd get used to one day. "But for thee, I'd never have won out of Elf-Land."

Hugging him back, Joe shook him. "But for thee, *I'd* never have won out of Elf-Land."

They laughed and sat down, side by side on the hillside. In the valley below, the river ran fast over rocks, and on the farther slope was the black, burned place where the Elf-Gate had stood. The fallen fences had all been cut up and dragged away, but some of the rubble of the broken Tube remained. Joe watched a couple of shepherds on black horses, carrying long lances, ride at a gallop by the riverside, just for the hell of it. I'll never be able to ride like that, Joe thought, but my son will. The idea both thrilled him and filled him with dread.

Per, beside him, stared and stared at the burned place.

Swart came over to them, sniffing, knocked Per flat on the slope and stood astride him, slapping his face with a long red tongue. Fending Swart off, Per said, "Chyo?"

"Joe. J-J-J. Joe."

Per, struggling up, hugged Swart, who licked his ear. Nodding, concentrating, Per said, "Cho. What was it like in Elf-Land?"

Joe was dumbstruck by the vastness of the question. It was like being asked what it was like to be alive. "Tha knows what it was like. Tha was there."

Per stared down the valley, toward where the Elf-Gate had been. "Tha lived there years, Chyo. Cho. Didst hate it?"

Joe considered, raised his brows, considered some more. "Some of it. I loved some of it. Most of it wasn't too bad. Wasn't too good. But . . . There was no place for me, tha knowst?" Per stared at him attentively, but Joe doubted that he understood. "It was like the music stopped and I hadn't got a chair." Per frowned, never having played that game. "But I reckon . . . Yeah, I still reckon I'm better off here."

Swart wandered off, and Per clasped his knees, rested his chin on them and withdrew from the bleating sheep, the damp hillside wind, the cloud shadows and the man beside him, as he gazed toward the hill of the Gate. A Gate he could never find, though he searched behind every blade of grass and every stone . . .

Staring, his eyes grew wide and unfocused, his mind drifted—and at his ear, so real he felt the puff of air against his skin, Andrea's voice said, "Per . . ." The very note and timbre of her voice was in it. His head jerked up and he turned—and there was Swart, ears pricking and tail beating on the grass. No Andrea, but— Per turned his head, looking all about.

"What's up?" Joe asked.

"Nowt," Per said, uncertainly, still looking around. "Nowt."

Joe watched tears gather in Per's eyes, sparkle, brim over his lashes and fall down his cheek, and he shook his head. If he lived with the Sterkarms for the rest of his life, he thought, he never was going to feel at home among them.

Maybe, Per was thinking, if he came here in the darkling hours, between night and day . . . If he came here in the darkling hours of Christmas Eve, when the year turned, and the borders between the worlds grew soft and weak as mist . . . could he touch her then, as well as hear her? Would the Gate stand open?

"Oh Chyo!"

"What?" Joe said.

"If I had the wings of a swan,

Over these stony hills I would fly,

I would fly to the arms of my true love,

And there I'd be happy to die."

THE END

GLOSSARY

a, to

air, are, is

at, that

av, through, of

ayn, a

bairt, brought

barn, child

braw, it's all right

brekker, break

brenna, burn

bror, brother

dag, day

dahla, dale

day, that, it

dem, them

der, there

dey, they

deyn, this

dick, ten

Erlf (plural: *Erlven*), Elf

erpent, opened

far, father

fars-bror, uncle (on father's side)

fen, friend

finner, find

foor, for

foorlet, stop, leave it

forby, finished, over, ended

forstaw, understand

fra, from

gaw, go

giffer, give

gigot, twenty

glayder, gladden

god dag, good day

halv, half

han, he

hander, hands

har, have, has

hayer, here

hite, called, named

hodda, head

hold, stay

honning, honey

hoppa, jump

hura, heard

hus, house

hyemma, home

i, in
inyen, no one

jakke, sleeveless, quilted
    jerkin

kaller, shout
karl, man, guy
kaster, throw
kenna, know
kews, kiss
klahr, clear
kneefa, knife
kom, come! (command)
kommer, come
kvenna, women

ladda, lad, boy
lam, lamb
lant, land
lerfta, promise
lilla, little
lukket, locked, closed
lutta, listen

maht, food
maun, must
may, girl

melk, milk
meth, with
migh, me
min, mine

nakka, neck
namma, name
naw, now
neath, down
nesh, soft
nie ting, nothing
nigh, no, not
nor, when

oh, and
olla, all
opp, up
oss, us

pa, by
penya, money

ridder, ride
rikti, right

sa, so
sawrer, hurt
seet, said;

sye, say;
    sayer, says
sertha, sweet
shoota, shoot
sikka, safe
sitta, sit
skal, shall
skyera, cut
slerssa, fight
snakka, speak
sootha, truly
spak, speak
staw, stands
sterk, strong
stilla, quiet!
stoor , big
sverer, swear

t', the
takh, thanks
tala, talk
tar, take
thine, your
thu, you
til, to, toward
tur, tower
tyan, two

urd, word
urst, cheese
ut, out

vah, what
vegg, wall
vem, who
venda tilbacka, return
vi, we
vilken, which
vill, will
vit, white
vor, where
vordan staw day, how stands it? (i.e. how are you?)
vorfar, why

wey, wee, small

ya, yes
yarl, lord (i.e. master)
yett, gate
yi, I
yunker, young